Song of the Axe

John R. Dann

TOR®
A TOM DOHERTY ASSOCIATES BOOK
NEW YORK

SONG OF THE AXE

Edited by David G. Hartwell

A Tor Book
Published by Tom Doherty Associates, LLC
175 Fifth Avenue
New York, NY 10010

www.tor.com

ISBN: 0-812-58950-5
Library of Congress Catalog Card Number: 00-048453

First edition: April 2001
First mass market edition: July 2002

Printed in the United States of America

0 9 8 7 6 5 4 3 2 1

Acknowledgments

THIS BOOK IS dedicated to the memory of our dear friend Marthe Commissaire, for introducing my wife, Barbara, and me to the ancient cliff shelters and caves of France, where our prehistoric ancestors lived and loved and left their beautiful cave paintings.

I also wish to thank the following people: my wife, and our children, John, Janet, and Catherine, for their love and encouragement; and, for their friendship and help, our good friend Ruth Beebe Hill; my agent, Bernard Shir-Cliff; and my editor, David Hartwell. London, 1890.

I offer my book as a contribution to that still youthful science which seeks to trace the growth of human thought and institutions in those dark ages which lie beyond the range of history.

—From *The Golden Bough*, by Sir James George Frazer

Contents

Prologue
The Storyteller

THE OLD MAN shoved the log farther into the fire. The arctic wind swept down from the ice fields, driving snow across the plain and over the cliffs that lined the river valley, and the cold seeped into the cave. A framework of branches covered with hides sealed the entrance, but still the cold grasped for the people. Without the fire they would die.

The old man hawked phlegm and spat into the fire. The gob bubbled and steamed, formed a baleful eye in the glowing embers, and disappeared. The old man spoke: "Once the cold drew back. Long ago."

The people stared at him.

He drew his reindeer-skin robe closer around his shoulders. "Green grass covered the plain."

The people murmured.

The wind shook the framework of hides, and snow drifted in around the frame. The old man gazed into the fire, looking into the past. "The river carried no ice, yet no one could cross it. Then someone came whose hair was like the sun."

Now he had the people's attention.

"He came first as a man, then as a woman, a spear woman, strong with magic, fit to be mate to the chieftain. But Axe Man took her from the chieftain. Axe Man and Spear Woman brought death to the people and wounded the chieftain. They were punished. The most terrible punishment."

The people drew closer to him.

The old man nudged the log deeper into the fire and settled back. When given a choice portion of meat, he would tell the whole story.

The woman sitting across the fire from the old man, an old woman, her face hidden within the cowl of her deerskin hood, spoke: "Spear Woman and Axe Man did not bring death to the people." She pushed a half-gnawed shinbone of horse toward the old man. "Eat this and listen. This is what happened. It began with the snake. . . ."

Part I

Axe Man and Spear Woman

The Black Raven

1

The Serpent

THE VIPER LAY in the bed of cress at the water's edge. The woman and girl came down the riverbank hand in hand, talking happily, the sun gleaming on their bare shoulders, on the dark glossy hair of the woman, the golden hair of the girl. They laid down their baskets of tubers and berries and poked in the grass with their digging sticks before they knelt to drink, bringing the water to their mouths in cupped hands, their eyes watchful.

The cress grew an arm's length away, and they smelled its crisp and pungent scent. The woman reached for her stick to probe the herb bed, then hesitated as a raven croaked and flew above them, its wings whishing. The woman watched the raven, then reached again for the stick that lay at the edge of the cress. The viper struck, driving its fangs into the woman's wrist.

The girl broke the snake's back with the first blow of her stick. She struck the writhing body until it lay broken and dead in the cress. The woman sucked at the wound, two punctures in the under skin of her wrist. She spat on the ground, then jerked a flint knife from her belt and cut twice into the punctures. She sucked the cuts and spat blood, again and again. The girl pulled the belt from her waist and tied it around the woman's forearm, working fiercely, silently. The only sound had been the thud of the girl's stick, the woman's spitting of blood. Now the girl cried out, a high keening.

The man and boy ran from the cliff shelter.

The woman lived until sunset. She clenched her teeth against the pain and dizziness, pale and sweating on the pallet of furs. Blood seeped from her mouth, and she thirsted. They brought her water and sat helplessly around her, touching her gently, reassuring her, watching her, hoping the evil would leave her. The man threw the dead snake far out into the river and cursed it, calling on the magic of his people to destroy the snake's spirit. As the last rays of the sun slid up the cliff wall, the woman tried to speak. They bent close to her.

She held the girl's hand, her voice barely audible: "Keep the dried meat from the foxes."

They watched her die. She became delirious and writhed on the pallet, speaking incoherently, staring beyond them at things unseen and terrifying. Then she weakened and grew silent. But as her spirit slipped away, she spoke for the final time.

"Beware of the dark serpent."

In the morning they carried the woman up through the hills to the grave site. She lay faceup on a litter made from two spears and laced deer hides. The man walked ahead holding the point ends of the spears, the boy and the girl behind, each struggling to support a spear with their thin arms. The man said nothing but plodded grimly up the slopes, not looking back, not stopping to let the girl and boy rest. Two extra spears lay beside the body.

The girl stared at her mother. The woman's arm lay swollen and black on the deerskin, but the glossy hair, the slender body, the gentle mother face seemed unchanged. Soon, they would bury her beneath dirt and stones. Tears came. The girl stumbled, caught her balance, looked fearfully at the man's back. Her mother's swollen arm had fallen from the litter, the fingers dragging on the rocks of the trail.

Something moved in the bushes on either side of the corpse carriers. The man plodded on. The moving things drew closer. Sloped backs. Hulking shoulders. A stink of carrion.

The boy said quietly, "Hyenas." The man did not seem to hear. The boy looked through tear-filled eyes at the girl. Although two winters younger than she, he dared speak where she did not.

The girl held the litter spear with one hand and used the other hand to pull one of the spears from its place beside her mother. The hyenas whined hungrily, moving closer. With all his strength the boy transferred his litter spear to one hand and reached for the loose spear. The litter spear pulled through his fingers and dropped to the ground.

The man kept on plodding forward, dragging the sagging, scraping litter. The hyenas sensed his incapacity for action and leaped toward the body of the woman.

The spear was in the girl's hands. She thrust, driving the flint point into the gaping jaws, felt it scrape on teeth, on bone, penetrate the slavering mouth into flesh, tongue, throat.

The boy cried hoarsely, victoriously, his spear in the red-spouting eye of the second hyena.

The man did not look back, continuing to drag the litter along the trail.

The girl and the boy watched the wounded hyenas slink into the bush, then they followed their mother's body up the hill to the burial place.

Three years pass.

2

Avalanche

THE IBEX LEAPED effortlessly across the almost vertical face of the wall to a tiny ledge four body-lengths away. A young male in its prime, the ibex's large three-sided and cross-ridged horns rose high from its forehead and curved back like two spears over its muscular shoulders and agile body. It balanced on the ledge, hesitating, sensing danger.

The ledge hung above the thundering falls that fed water from the lake into the river valley. Melting glaciers on the surrounding mountains sent milky torrents cascading down the slopes into the lake, a lake so large that the ibex looked across it as a plains animal might look across a sea of grass.

Now the ibex felt a soundless roaring, not the falls but a convulsive shuddering of the mountains. The animal leaped up the wall, instinctively knowing that safety lay in the heights.

The earth heaved. Above the ibex a mass of ice and rock broke from the mountain and fell toward the lake. The ibex turned and fled across the wall, springing from one foothold to another as the avalanche, gaining in strength and speed, plummeted down the mountainside. The ibex made one last desperate effort, a prodigious leap from a point of rock out across empty space toward a tiny platform on an adjoining wall. The ibex was in midjump as the roaring mass hurtled past and slammed into the lake.

Water shot up and out in a gigantic plume that crashed

upward, half the height of the wall. The water caught the ibex, smashed the creature from the platform, and carried the struggling body with it as the plume fell back into the lake.

The mass of ice and rock lodged at the top of the waterfall, partially blocking the egress of the lake. As the flow of water into the river slowed, the level of the lake slowly rose. The water gathered its strength, crouching high above the river valley, waiting. Waiting until it could burst through the melting ice.

3

Grae

LAST NIGHT THE earth moved. Grae, chieftain and sorcerer of the bison hunters, crawls deep into the cave to find meaning.

Fire	Stone	Water
Animal	Sun	Dance
Hunt	Bird	Dream

Grae makes the secret marks for the spirits of the Onstean on the limestone wall of the cave:

1.	1. .	1 . . .
11.	11. .	11 . . .
111.	111. .	111 . . .

Three and three and three and two. Three kinds. Three across. Three down. Two diagonal. Three is the magic number.

Why two?

Grae moves the torch closer, studying the marks. Why does two always come?

The symbols represent the invisible male stone spirits, the Onstean. *On:* invisible. *Ste:* Stone spirit. *An:* male.

Stone spirits because of the hardness of the male: the hardness of granite, flint, obsidian.

Earth spirits belong to the Onerana, the invisible female earth spirits. *On:* invisible. *Er:* earth spirit. *Ana:* female.

Female spirits because the earth is female, fecund, fruitful.

Grae knows the names of the female spirits, but never must he say them, or let Erida or the other women know that he knows them. Just as the women must never know the secrets of the men's society, so the men must not know those of the women's society.

But why two? What eludes him? Are there two unknown spirits? Or is one more needed to make three?

The flame of the smoky torch flickers, then steadies. Deep in the winding passages of the cave something moves. Grae waits, not breathing.

The flame wavers again.

He waits. Two.

The flame burns steadily, its light illuminating the animals on the cave walls and ceiling, totems of the hunters.

The stag, his own totem, the totem passed on to each Grae, each chieftan, each sorcerer. Symbol of masculine fertility, paramour of goddesses, the swirled antlers depicting latent power. Horses. Cattle. Bison. Ibex. Reindeer. Mammoth. Bear. Cat. Rhino. Each with its power, its magic.

Male: antlered stags, rearing stallions, earth-pawing bulls.

And female: belly-swollen mares, cows, deer and bison.

Each animal male and female.

Something moved twice. What?

Grae places the handle of the torch in a crack in the rock wall. He wraps his deerskin robe around him and lies down on the stone floor of the chamber. He lets his spirit wander.

Grae's body lies on the cave floor, but his spirit leaves his body and flies like thought out of the cave and through time and space back toward the beginning: beyond the Black Stone, beyond the river, before the cliffs. . . .

Sunlight flickering down through rustling greenness. Swaying gently, content.

The females forage on the riverbank, plucking ripe berries, lifting eggs from grassy nests, pouncing on frogs, grubbing for roots with sharp sticks.

A sinuous figure erupts from the water. Blood. Screaming. The females thrust with their sticks. The sticks search and find the life spirit.

Grae's spirit comes back to him. The torch flickers low, dying, and Grae rises, hurries through the passageways toward the light. He knows part of the mystery.

Snake.

Woman.

Ka

KA AND HIS tribe wound in a sinuous column through the forest. They advanced toward the cliffs and the river that lay between them and the plain to the north, the plain where herds of bison and horses grazed.

Ka had questioned the captive, hanging him over a slow fire. When the man finally died, still screaming that when the earth moved the river god became weak, that the river could be crossed, Ka believed.

Now he brought half the tribe with him—warriors and hunters along with enough women to satisfy these men. Also his wives, and his god, Kaan. Four men carried Kaan on a litter of poles, enclosed within a canopy of human skins. Skulls and bones and heads adorned the litter. Skulls of wolf, bear, lion, and snake. Bones of men's legs and arms. Heads of men, hung by their long hair, flesh rotting and putrid, eyeballs liquid and clustered with fat black flies. The men who carried the litter dared not look at it, and the power of Kaan emanated from the canopy like the stench and foulness of the rotting heads. Kaan, the god, the thing hidden within the canopy, was terrible and alive. Because of Kaan none could stand against the tribe of Ka.

They came to the edge of the cliff and looked out across the river valley. Steep cliffs and a black mountain loomed on the opposite side; beyond the cliffs, plains, covered with herds of game, stretched to distant hills on the horizon.

Ka pointed to a hole in the face of the cliff below the mountain. The column moved forward and oozed over the edge of the cliff like a flow of poisonous venom.

The men used vines to lower the being on the litter down the steepest parts of the trail. They were full of motion as ants, irresistible as flowing lava. They reached the bottom of the cliffs and, malevolent and monstrous, advanced across the narrow floodplain to the water's edge.

Rocks showed above the water. Ka motioned, and four warriors joined arms abreast and trailed long vines behind them, the vines to be grasped by the next four men, and the next, and the next. One man held back, and Ka drove his spear into the man's back with such force that the point came out through his chest. Ka hurled the quivering body onto the bank and motioned to another man with the bloody spear.

They crossed the river, some stepping on the rocks,

some in the water, some drowning and dying, but others always moving forward, like a huge serpent forcing its way across the rocks and through the water. They reached the opposite bank of the river and raced toward the base of the cliff, where the spearlike mountain rose. As they writhed snakelike up the slanting ledge and disappeared into the dark hole that gaped in the face of the cliff, a raven flew over the river valley.

5

Eena

EENA PICKED SUMMER flowers in the high meadow above the river: pink willow herb, lavender cranesbill, yellow buttercups, purple foxglove and vetch, yellow-bird's foot trefoil, and white daisies with their sunlike centers, all bright in the sunshine. Holding the flowers lightly in her arms, she carried them up the gentle slope to the hilltop where her mother's grave lay.

She knelt and spread the flowers on the grave, arranging them as her mother had done in the shelter, alternating their color and texture so that the flowers seemed to grow again.

Three years ago the viper, hiding by the water's edge, drove its fangs into her mother's wrist. That night her mother died without complaint, holding Eena's hand, telling her to keep the dried meat from the foxes. Her mother, dark eyed and slender, with glossy black hair that had glistened in the sunshine, now lay under the earth, never to smile at Eena again, never to laugh with joy again.

Eena placed her hand on the grassy mound. The sun-warmed earth and the perfume of the flowers brought memories so strong that she felt her mother nearby.

This had been her mother's favorite spot, and mother and daughter had spent happy summer afternoons here, sitting in the sunshine, the woman telling stories as she combed the girl's hair. Here Eena learned to weave baskets from the sweet-smelling meadow grass and to give names to the flowers and plants that grew on the green hills. Here she also learned about spirits, good and evil.

She gazed out over the river valley. To the east, white-topped mountains gleamed against the blue sky. Giants lived there, tall as trees with hair like snow. Only a moon ago the giants' voices had thundered in the mountains and shaken the earth. Fearsome, but not evil, the giants must be treated with respect; if people went to the mountains, they must ask the giants' permission before climbing the cold and snowy heights.

To the south, across the river, grew the forest. Here strange beings lurked: unknown creatures that lived under the roots of trees and ran through the undergrowth in the night. Evil spirits ruled the forest. Good spirits had lived there when the people came in ancient times, but evil spirits followed the people and overpowered the good spirits. The people fled the forest, crossing the river to the safety of the plains. The river protected the people, for after they crossed it the river spirit made the water rise, and ever after the river flowed too high and swift for the evil spirits of the forest to cross.

The river valley stretched to the west, where the peak of Spear Mountain thrust up like a black flint point. Beyond, almost lost in the distance, lay the massive cliffs where lived the powerful bison hunters, the people of Grae, the sorcerer. Dark-haired, strong, and fierce, the bison hunters lived by magic, a magic so strong that the game came to their spears and no enemy dared approach their hunting grounds.

Eena's mother had come from the bison hunters. She told Eena how it happened: Stig, Eena's father, left his father's tribe of golden-haired people when he was young and came to this part of the river valley, a lone hunter seeking a place to start his own family and tribe. He settled in a cliff shelter by the river, and after two years traveled down the valley to find a wife. Stig followed the river downstream for many days, past Spear Mountain and beyond. At the base of the cliffs he came to the camp of the bison hunters. Stig's sun-colored hair so fascinated the bison hunters that they did not kill him, but allowed him to live among them.

Old Grae, chieftain and sorcerer of the bison hunters, had many children from a succession of wives. Among these, Young Grae, his oldest son, and Reva, his youngest daughter, took the greatest interest in Stig.

Young Grae was older than Stig, but they became friends and hunted together, and Young Grae saw that Stig and Reva were drawn to one another. Old Grae died soon afterwards, and when Young Grae laid Old Grae's spirit to rest, he became chieftain.

When Stig asked that Reva come with him to his camp, Grae at first refused to let his sister leave, but finally he agreed on the condition that Stig help the tribe in time of trouble. He also made Stig and Reva agree that when their children were of age they would be brought to the tribe to learn the ancient rites and find mates.

Stig and Reva lived happily in Stig's lonely camp. Stig was a good hunter and provider. Reva, trained by her mother to perform the skilled duties of a wife, swept the rubbish and bones from Stig's shelter, gathered the tubers and nuts of the river valley, and dried fruit and the meat that Stig brought. Food filled their storage pits, even in the cold and rainy winters. Reva tanned hides and furs and made warm clothing for those times when a chilling wind howled around the shelter, and she made medicines from herbs and roots. But most important, her magic kept the evil spirits from the shelter.

She bore two children, Eena and Eran, both golden haired like their father. Stig taught them to hunt, and Reva taught Eena as her own mother had taught her. She also taught Eena how to keep herself clean and attractive, for females not desirable as mates might starve or be killed.

Then Reva's magic failed, and the snake killed her.

"Why?" Eena had cried to Stig. "Why did her magic let the snake kill her?"

Stig stared at her through his grief and made no answer. Later, when Eena cried in the night, he came to her. "I took her from her tribe. Her magic came from the bison hunters, and they are far away. . . ."

The bison hunters roamed the broad plain that lay north of the river, and Eena looked out over the plain, wondering whether the hunters were there now, remembering the time Stig had taken his family to the camp. She had been terrified and fascinated; terrified by the awesome appearance of Grae and the power of his magic, fascinated by the godlike bearing of Grae and his family—his wife, Erida, powerful sorceress in her own right; Zur, his oldest son and heir; and Agon, his second son, a hunt leader.

She remembered Agon best. Fierce-looking and stern, he moved with the strength of a young lion, his magic so strong she felt it radiate from him like heat from a fire. She feared him, yet during the hunt dancing she had hoped that he might look at her. . . .

Beyond the plain to the north lay another range of mountains, a place of mystery and strange spirits. Stig called these mountains the Blue Hills. The distant peaks and ranges showed every shade of blue and purple, and Eena marveled at their beauty. Her mother had told her that the most powerful spirits lived there, spirits who would help the people if worshipped properly, but wrathful if offended.

These spirits seemed feminine in nature: once her mother had uttered a word, *Onerana.* Eena said it to herself now, "Onerana," and the skin on the back of her neck prickled with the mystery.

The position of the sun indicated that she must go back to the shelter, for Stig and Eran would soon return from the hunt. She had not gone with them today, deciding instead to bring flowers to her mother's grave.

The breeze, like a caressing hand, gently touched her hair, and she heard her mother's voice in the song of the wind. The grass was soft under her feet, and she felt the beauty and warmth of the earth as if her mother's arms enfolded her.

She lifted her spear from the grass and left the hilltop, walking lightly down the grassy slope toward the oak tree where she had placed a basket of berries. She picked another armful of flowers for the shelter, and when she came to the oak tree, she thanked the tree spirit for guarding and watching the basket. Carrying the flowers, basket, and spear, she followed the game trail through the trees and down into the river valley.

6

Stig

STIG'S CAMP LAY at the base of a small cliff under a sheltering overhang, facing the river and the warm rays of the sun. During rainy or snowy winter days a protective wall of hides on a branch framework closed the entrance, but on clear winter days and all summer long the sun shone into the shelter, keeping it warm and dry.

Eena placed the flowers around the walls of the shelter, arranging them to look as if they grew from the smooth rock floor. She gathered wood for the fire and cut meat from the deer carcass hanging from the ash tree by the entrance. She sang as she worked, an old song her mother had taught her, a woman's song, not to be heard by men:

"Earth and Moon
Death gives Life
Tree and Air

Blood and Love
Magic circle."

Her father and brother came down from the hills as she tended the meat over the fire. Stig carried a gutted buck deer over his shoulder, and Eran held up three dead rabbits.

"The meat smells good." Stig hung the deer from the tree and leaned his spear against the cliff wall.

Eena admired the deer. "Young and fat. And Eran has rabbits. I will make rabbit stew."

Stig noticed the flowers in the shelter and studied them silently. "Just as she used to do." Sadness lingered in his eyes, but not the terrible grief when Reva died.

"Her spirit is happy," Eena said. "I heard her voice in the wind, and her hand touched my hair."

Lines marked Stig's face, his hair now more gray than gold. "Eran and I saw the flowers on her grave. You are good, Eena, just as she was." His arm circled her waist. "And you look like her, too."

Eran came to stand beside the fire. "You should have come with us today, Eena. We had a long run." He pointed to the rabbits. "As soon as you give us food, you can gut and clean them."

"You are a good hunter, my brother."

Eran gazed down the river valley. "Soon I will hunt bison on the plains." He asked Stig, "We are going to Grae's camp?"

Stig slapped him lightly on the shoulder. "We are. You have only asked me five times today." He winked at Eena. "I think Eran has picked out a girl in Grae's tribe."

Eran kicked at the fire log. "I have not! I just want to hunt bison."

Stig laughed. "We will see." He said to Eena, "We have not heard much from you about the hunt festival."

A faint voice called to Eena, the voice of her spirit mother.

"Why do you turn pale?" Stig asked. "The hunt festival should not frighten you."

"Three times she has called me," Eena replied. "Three times she has asked us not to go."

Stig frowned, looking first at Eena, then Eran, then at the fire, finally back at Eena. Eran, wide-eyed, watched Stig, waiting for his decision.

Stig spoke: "I have told Grae we will come. A hunter keeps his word. We will go with the new moon."

Eran shouted and waved his spear. "You can dance around the fire and sing with the girls," he told Eena. "And maybe one of Grae's hunters will look at you."

"Grae's hunters?" Stig frowned at Eena. "You were not thinking of one of them?"

"No." Eena lowered her eyes.

"We need you here. Who would keep our camp?"

"I will keep the camp."

"There is nothing between you and any hunter?"

"No."

"Maybe you don't like it here with us. Maybe you want your own camp."

She felt tears coming. "I want to stay with you. I want to stay here. . . ."

Stig shook his head. "You can hunt almost as well as a man, and can run faster than most, but you need to learn other things. Erida will teach you the women's secrets, and Eran will learn the hunters' magic from old Unser, keeper of the animal spirits. We will stay with Grae's people for a year. When you both have gone through the rites, we will come back here."

Gone from their home for a year. Gone from the rolling hills and flowering meadows. Gone from the warm and beloved cliff shelter where she had been born. Gone from her mother, whose spirit hand caressed her on the hilltop in the sunshine and gentle breeze. Tears filled Eena's eyes, and she looked down to hide them from Stig.

Stig lifted her chin. "Without the rites, the hunter's spirit can never reach its full magic power; without the rites, a woman cannot keep the evil spirits from her fire and family. We live too far from her people. We will go back."

She blinked the tears away. "I will get our things ready."

During the next three days they prepared for their journey to Grae's camp. They selected gifts for Grae's people: a robe of mink skins for Grae, nesting baskets for Erida, matched flint points for Unser. Eena cut up the deer meat and hung thin strips to dry in the sun, their travel food. She made new clothing for everyone; they would not be ashamed of their appearance when they came from the wilderness to the bustling camp of the bison hunters. For Stig and Eran she made buckskin hunting shirts, fringed and tasseled, cut and sewn as her mother had taught her, every seam a thing of decoration and beauty. For herself she made a white doeskin tunic, short-sleeved and above her knees for freedom in running. She made new sandals for all of them, and for Stig and Eran, new belts of heavy tanned horsehide with loops for attaching their knife sheaths and pouches.

She opened the wooden box Stig had made, the box holding her greatest treasure—the maiden's belt her mother had given her. Dyed and painted buckskin, a line of leaping female red deer circled the belt, their bodies graceful and delicate yet strong and tireless. They resembled the ivory totem that hung at Eena's neck, a young doe whose spirit and magic protected her.

"We will wear our new things when we go to the hilltop," Stig announced. "Then she can see that we will not shame her when we go to her people, and she will wait happily until we return."

They all bathed in the river, Eena in her place, Stig and Eran in theirs; then they dressed in the new clothing and went uphill to the burial place. Eena picked more flowers and spread them over Reva's grave.

Stig looked down at the flower-covered mound. "We go to your people now, where Eran and Eena will learn their ways and pass through their rites. Then, when their magic is strong, we will return and tell you about the things we saw, and maybe we will bring back some of your people."

Eena placed a clay bowl containing live coals from the hearth fire in the soft earth of the grave. "Keep the fire magic for us," she whispered as she covered the bowl with a flat stone. "We will sit around this fire again."

Eran stood silent, his eyes downcast.

Eena felt his sorrow, and she put her arm around him. "When you are a bison hunter, she will become even more proud of you."

Eran did not look up from the grave. "I will bring the horns from the first bison to her when we come back."

Stig put his arms around both of them. "She will wait for us, her spirit strong within us." He pointed to the evening sky, to the slender crescent of the new moon. "See the moon spirit. She has come again; tomorrow morning we go."

They slept in the shelter that night, and in the first light of morning they covered the fire and placed the framework of hides before the entrance. Then, with spears and packs, they began their journey to Grae's camp, following the game trail that led along the river to the west, leaving the cliff shelter where they had known happiness and sorrow, leaving the home where Eena and Eran had been born, leaving the sunny meadows and rolling hills; and leaving the flower-strewn mound.

7

The Journey

THEY MADE GOOD progress each day, following the trail down the river valley, stopping each night in a place remembered from previous trips. Stig and Eran traveled in high spirits, and because her father seemed so happy, Eena said no more of her apprehension about the journey. But Stig remembered her concern and so spoke one night when they sat around their fire:

"Eena, you have traveled well and fast with us, but I see in your eyes that your spirit is troubled. Has her spirit warned you again?"

"No."

"What, then?"

The cliffs, higher each day, now towered over them, and an ominous gloom filled the canyon. And while still two days' travel away, the peak of Spear Mountain loomed dark and sinister. But these things were not the sole cause of Eena's concern. She pointed to the river. "Rocks show. And the water flows more slowly."

Stig nodded. "The channel is deeper at our camp, and we could not see the change. But here the river has lost its strength."

They studied the river. Rocks protruded above the wide expanse of water from bank to bank, and the river, while flowing swiftly, no longer hurtled between the canyon walls like a mad beast.

"How can the river lose its strength?" Eran asked.

Stig considered Eran's question. "Maybe something happened to the river when the earth moved this spring." He gestured toward the distant mountaintops glowing pink in the setting sun. "I traveled through the mountains when I came here, and I learned their power. I left my father's tribe in the summer, for no man could cross the peaks in the winter, but even then, I almost died. The mountains rise steep into the clouds, walls of rock and ice blocking the way, higher than the cliffs here. The river flows from a lake in the mountains, a lake so wide and long that it is as the plain of the bison hunters, but the mountains are larger, stronger than the lake. They could weaken the river."

"How?" asked Eran.

"You heard the giants. They shook the earth. The giants rule the mountains, and the mountains rule the river." Stig rolled up in his sleeping robe. "Our spears are ready. The fire will keep the night creatures away. Now sleep."

Eena watched the stars as they appeared—campfires of the sky spirits, tiny spirit flames flickering in the night. As she neared sleep, a distant voice spoke to her, warning about the change in the river. But the water spirit sang strong and reassuring, and the familiar forms of her father and brother lay near her. She slept.

In the night, dream spirits invaded her sleep. Not the peaceful, happy spirits she loved, but strange spirits, foreboding and threatening, swirling around her, swooping like demons, eyes glaring. She dreamed of sorrow and loss, fighting and death, and she moaned in her sleep.

In the morning Eena hurried her preparations for the day's journey. She brought life back to the fire, hung pieces of rabbit over the coals, washed herself, and combed her hair. The night's dream remained vivid in her mind, and she wished to leave this canyon of evil spirits.

Eran crawled from his robe and stood by the fire. "Four more days! Then we will eat bison!"

Stig came from the river. "We might see the bison herds if we go up on the plain now." He smacked his lips. "I can almost taste hump meat or a piece of liver."

"Why not travel across the plain?" Eran asked. "We can kill bison!"

Eena knew Stig's answer before he spoke:

"Because of one more travel day, no water on the plain. We can eat rabbit and deer a few more days, and we will not go thirsty by the river." Stig looked closely at Eena. "You are not anxious again?"

"The dream spirits came to me in the night. I was afraid."

"Why afraid?"

"Evil spirits. They frightened me. I ran, but they followed me, always closer. . . ." She shuddered. "We should leave the canyon."

"Why?"

"I dreamnt of a snake. When mother died, she warned us. . . ."

Stig's eyes revealed his lingering grief. "It was an evil day when the snake bit her. I dream, too." He put his arm around her, awkwardly, stiffly, but she felt his love. "The dream spirits are a mystery. Erida will help you understand them."

"When we hunt," Eran reminded Stig, "Eena can see deer behind a hill. . . ."

Stig considered this. "Where do you see danger?" he asked Eena.

"I fear the black mountain."

Stig studied the river gorge. "We either go below the mountain or around it. Only three trails lead up the cliffs between here and Grae's camp. One is here. The other two are past the mountain. We have to decide now."

A raven came flying down the river valley, following their course. Stig watched the bird's flight. "We will let the raven choose."

The raven flew steadily toward them, wings whishing in the air. A shadow flashed over the travelers, then the bird flew on down the river valley toward Spear Mountain.

"He has told us." Stig lifted his pack and spear.

Eena watched the raven, a speck now, moving up and down on flapping wings. She still envisioned the bird's face, eyes cold and shining. But something else came to her mind—slit eyes and a row of black spots on a sinuous body.

Stig beckoned. "We go."

The raven was the wisest of birds, and she only a young female who trembled at her own dreams, sensed evil in harmless gusts of wind, and imagined danger from bare rocks in the river. Eena followed her father.

8

Agon

Son of Grae
Zur
First

Axe Man
Orm
Faster
Faster
Faster

Hunt Leader
Seeking
Circling
Running
Killing
Blood
Magic

Seeker
Dreamer
Warrior

9

The Hunt

AGON AND HIS hunters ran abreast in a line that forced the bull bison into the trap of the box canyon. Agon watched the bull, judging when it would turn and fight. At the same time he observed the hunters, deciding which one to send in for the first spear thrust.

The hunters ran easily as wolves, agile and strong, faces expressionless—except for the eyes: wolflike, unemotional, almost contemplative, but filled with a strange light, knowledge of impending violence and death. The men's long hair streamed behind them, and except for loin covers and sandals, their hard-muscled bodies were naked.

The bull grunted as he ran, sweat streaking his body, strings of ropy saliva dripping from his mouth. He ran heavily, head down, tiring, but his muscles still bunched and rippled with power, and his ability to kill was undiminished. Shoulders higher than a man's head, the bull could not be killed by men a tenth its strength and size without the help of magic. And the hunters possessed magic. Magic carried in their totems, the carved figures that hung on thongs around their necks. Agon's totem was the ibex, the strong and agile denizen of the cliffs and mountains.

The bull turned to face the hunters, sharp horns shining in the sunlight.

Agon motioned to Yan. Yan touched his totem, a red bird, then ran in, spear raised. Fearless and experienced, one of the best of the hunters, he had often made similar kills.

Yan drove his spear into the bison's side, the flint point

deep between the ribs, searching for the heart. The bull's horns hooked back, and the tip of one caught the thong that held Yan's totem and spun the bird spirit off through the air, leaving Yan unprotected and helpless.

Agon instantly rushed in ahead of the other hunters, but Yan's magic had failed, and he died before Agon could reach him. The bison hooked upward, the horns slashed into Yan's chest, lifted him, and threw his body back over the bison's shoulders.

Agon's spear went in hard, driving toward the heart, and the bison swung its head in a quick and deadly arc, one bloody horn swishing just under Agon's arm. The bison still lived, now in a killing fury.

Spears of the other hunters thudded into the bison, but it fought on, head swinging viciously, black body whirling, sharp hooves carrying it in short, bellowing charges. Finally the bull stopped and stood motionless, looking back at its spilling intestines. Then it fell slowly, heavily, kicked once, and died. The killing smell of hot blood permeated the air, the smell of violent death.

But an evil omen frightened the hunters: Yan's totem had left him, letting the bison kill Yan. And the bison had refused to die, fighting until its entrails dragged on the ground and its blood soaked into the earth.

Yan's body lay in the trampled and bloody grass, looking strangely naked without the totem. His eyes showed the terror of the thing he had seen. The other hunters fingered their own totems and looked from Yan's body to Agon.

Agon picked Yan's totem from the ground. The bird was a strong totem, but this evil proved stronger. Agon went to a rock by the dead bison. He knelt and placed his left hand on the flat surface of the rock while his other hand slid the flint knife from his belt. Cutting hard and quickly, he severed the end joint of his fourth finger.

Blood welled out of the stump, and Agon sucked in his breath and swayed above the stone. Then, he let the blood drip on Yan's totem so that the red bird became more red, wet and shiny, the blood renewing its strength.

Agon held his own totem, the ibex, below his finger, and the magic of the ibex grew even stronger as the red drops splashed over its body. Then the other hunters held their totems under the dripping blood. First came Orf with his bison, then Az with his elk, Emo with his hairy mammoth, Ord with his horse, Ean with his antelope, Uz with his wide-horned bull, and, finally, Orm with his red deer.

Orm was Agon's rite brother. Only he and Agon carried light axes, the blades of hard greenstone, the handles of carved antler, Agon's with an ibex, Orm's with a deer at the end of the shaft. Orm caught the blood from Agon's finger in the cup of his hand and rubbed it on his chest and arms. Then he knelt and placed his own hand on the rock as he drew his knife. Agon touched the knife with his foot.

"No."

Ord knelt by another rock, his knife already against his finger. Agon kicked Ord hard in the side, and Ord fell sideways in the grass. He rolled and crouched with the knife coming up toward Agon.

Agon looked into Ord's eyes. "Cut up the meat."

Ord rose slowly, watching Agon, but Agon turned his back on him and went to Yan's body. He tied the red bird back around Yan's neck and looked into the staring eyes.

Yan had seen the black thing that waited for men's magic to fail—the thing that howled in the darkness, watching them with its red eyes—the ancient evil spirit that tore at the flapping hides of the shelter in the storm and lightning—the bony thing that waited in famine and thirst and sickness to drag men into its cold grip. Yan had seen it, and his eyes still held the horror. Agon closed Yan's eyes. But something evil still lingered, watching the hunters.

When they opened the bison, the men drew back. They held their totems and stared into the steaming body. Agon came to the carcass and looked where Orf pointed: the huge heart of the bison lay out of place, far forward and to one side of the heart place.

Something rustled faintly in the grass, almost unheard, gliding unseen through the stalks.

A raven flew toward them from the north. It circled above, three times around, black knowing eyes shining down at them, wings swishing; then the bird flew off across the plain toward the river and the distant peak of Spear Mountain.

The wind grew colder on Agon's back. Emo said, "Three and three."

Agon scowled at Emo. He looked at the bulging intestines of the bison, and it seemed that some other creature lay open before them. The ibex vibrated against his chest, tensing, ready to leap.

Agon turned away from the animal. "The herd is close. Leave this thing. We will take another bull." He pointed to Yan's body. "Ord and Orf. Bring him. Grae will call his spirit back."

10

Camp of the Bison Hunters

AGON'S HUNTERS RETURNED to Grae's camp in the late afternoon. They left Yan's body at the cliff top on the ancient black stone of the tribe, then carried the meat from the second bison down the cliff face on the zigzagging trail that led to the shelter at the base of the cliff.

Zur, Grae's first son, leaned haughtily on his spear before the cliff shelter. The rest of the people had gathered in the open space between cliff and river where the tribal fire burned.

Alar, Agon's younger brother, raised his hand in greeting from the boys' hunting band that trained under old Unser, while his dark-eyed sister, Ara, watched from the group of maidens.

Grae and Erida came from the cliff shelter.

Grae carried his staff and wore the chieftain's bison horns on his head. He towered over the people, his craggy face and long gray beard giving him the appearance of an avenging god.

Erida wore a white doeskin robe, and on her breast hung the mysterious moonstone. Grae's second wife, Agon's mother, Erida possessed magic as powerful as Grae's. When Grae's first wife, Zur's mother, disappeared a year after Zur's birth, Grae brought Erida from a tribe in the mountains. A chieftain's daughter, she was still beautiful, standing slender and straight as a young woman before the people.

Grae's face was stern, his deep voice solemn: "Yan does not carry his spear with you."

Agon stepped in front of the hunters. Grae's second son, he could expect no mercy. He looked straight into Grae's eyes. "He is dead. We left his body on the Stone."

Yan's mate cried out. Erida went to her, holding her while the other women gathered around, comforting her.

Grae's eyes pierced Agon like two spears. "Tell us."

"His magic failed."

The people sucked in their breaths. They clutched their totems and glanced up at the cliff, then over their shoulders.

"Why?"

"Something evil came."

"What evil?"

"We saw bad signs."

Zur spoke, hot eyed and proud, future chieftain when Grae died. Disbelief and scorn filled his voice.

"What signs?"

Agon did not look at Zur. He spoke to Grae. "Yan's totem left him. The bison's heart had moved. A raven circled three times."

The people held their totems, watching Grae, looking quickly at Agon and the hunters, then back at Grae.

Grae's face did not lose its composure, but Agon saw a change in the chieftain's eyes: a look of challenge—like a stallion that watches hyenas circle the horse herd. But also a look of sorrow.

Erida came to stand beside Grae again.

Grae said to Agon, "Show us your hand."

Agon held up his hand. Blood still oozed from the mutilated finger, and his hand and arm were red. The people exclaimed, sucking in their breaths. They stared at the finger, then at Grae, waiting for his decision.

"Is your magic strong again?"

Agon pointed to the meat. "One thrust and the second bull died."

Erida nodded. "See their totems. The blood magic has made them stronger than before."

Grae looked at Agon's hand, then the totems. If he said the magic words, Agon would live. If not. . . .

Grae's eyes bored again into Agon, then he turned to face the people. "Blood flows. Blood flows. The game will come to our spears."

The people murmured in relief. The tribe's magic remained strong. Grae had said the magic words.

Grae raised his staff. "Darkness comes. We will call the hunter's spirit back now."

They went up the cliff path to the rock, the Stone, where Yan's body lay, his chest gaping and torn from the horn wound. Yan's spirit had gone out through that wound and would wander outside the camp, moaning in the darkness until Grae brought it back to him.

Erida rubbed red powder on Yan's body, then Agon and the hunters faced the dead hunter toward the spot on the plain where the bison had made the kill. They laid Yan's spear beside him.

Grae came forward in his bison horns and robe. He shook a rattle to attract the spirit's attention, calling it to come and reenter Yan so that Yan could become one of the ancestors, guiding and protecting the people. Grae raised his arms to the sky and stood silent. No sound, not even the sighing of the wind, could be heard.

A bird called. Something moved through the air, a sound of wind in feathers.

The people saw the red body on the rock change. They felt Yan's spirit return. His body became Yan again, dead, but whole.

Erida quickly sewed shut the wound in Yan's chest, and the women bent him with his knees against his chest, then wrapped him with thongs so his spirit would remain in him. The hunters carried Yan to the grave they had dug in the tribal burial place west of the Stone. They placed Yan's spear and knife beside him, along with a piece of liver from the second bison.

Yan's mate cut her arms and let the blood drip on Yan so he would forgive her if she mated with another hunter. Then the hunters covered him with earth and laid large stones over the grave to keep the carrion eaters out.

Grae stood over the grave and spoke once more to Yan, asking him to remember and protect the tribe, and he asked Yan's spirit to remain quietly in him and not howl in the darkness.

When Grae finished speaking, the people went back down to the camp at the base of the cliff, where the women silently prepared the evening meal. A feeling of loss hung over the tribe, also a sense of foreboding. Many of the people still looked apprehensively over their shoulders into the approaching darkness. Evil had come. Evil might still be watching . . . waiting. . . .

11

The Axe

AGON AND HIS hunters sat around their own fire, speaking little, feeling the eyes of the people on them. They worked at their spears, tightening the thongs that bound the points to the long wooden shafts, retouching the edges of the flint. Agon tightened the thongs on his axe, then slipped it back into his belt.

Zur and his hunting band sat nearby at their fire. Zur's voice was mocking. "What is the thing I smell? Is it fear?"

One of Zur's hunters, a big man known as Horn, replied, "It smells like an old woman running from shadows." He paused, looking at Agon's hunters. "It smells like fear."

Agon said in a clear voice, "The fear you smell is from your own fire."

"We do not fear. We kill the bull with the first spear thrust." Horn's voice carried through the camp. "A hunt leader who is afraid brings fear to his men."

Agon replied, "Come between the fires. Any one of my hunters will show you who fears."

Horn stood up. "Are you afraid to lose another finger yourself, Agon?" He walked into the space between the hunters' fires, eyes gleaming, muscles rippling.

Agon laid his axe and knife on the ground beside his spear. He came to his feet and hurled himself at Horn in a single motion. His shoulder struck Horn in the stomach, driving him back half a spear's length. They rolled on the ground, fighting silently and ferociously as was the way of their people. Then Agon threw Horn on his back and knelt with his knee on Horn's throat, his hands holding Horn's arms to the ground. But Horn was a strong and clever fighter, and he brought his legs up, grasping Agon between them. The blood from Agon's finger was slippery under his hand, and Horn's arm came free.

They twisted and tumbled again, fast and hard like wolves fighting, their bodies slamming into the ground, each seeking a final hold. Then Horn jerked a knife from his belt and slashed at Agon's throat, but before the knife struck, Agon seized Horn's wrist with his bloody hand. Agon's good hand had never left Horn's other wrist, and now he brought Horn's arm behind his back and forced it up, wrestling Horn onto his face and stomach. The arm joints creaked, and Horn stuggled fiercely as Agon forced the arm higher and brought his knee down on the elbow of Horn's other arm, pressing it flat to the ground.

Then Agon pulled Horn's knife from his hand and cut off Horn's middle finger at the second joint. The weak-man cut, not the cut of the hunt leader.

Agon tossed Horn's finger and knife into the center of Zur's group of hunters; then he released his grip on Horn and leaped up, his eyes on Zur.

His face pale, Horn staggered to his feet, his dripping hand held against his chest. He stared at Zur.

Zur spat on the ground and moved closer to his spear.

Horn turned toward Agon. "You need a hunter."

"You were Zur's hunter. Go and sit at the women's fire with him." Agon turned his back on Horn and walked to where his weapons lay. He slipped the axe and knife into his belt.

Zur reached for his spear. Agon ripped his axe from his belt and up in one quick motion, ready for the throw. Zur would die before his hand touched the spear; Agon saw the spot on his forehead where the axe blade would strike.

The earth moved. A grinding, rumbling roar came from deep beneath the river valley. The cliff swayed. Rocks crashed at the base of the cliff as the terrified people stared wildly at one another. Then all was still.

Agon lowered the axe. The earth spirits had spoken in anger.

Grae appeared at the entrance to the cliff shelter. His eyes penetrated Agon's spirit as he spoke: "The ancient spirits move in the earth. They warn us."

Agon felt the eyes of the people on him. Long ago, the tribe had learned that hunters must not kill one another.

Zur spoke: "Yan is dead. Agon sent him in to the bull. Agon would kill a hunter. The ancient spirits shake the cliffs. Agon has brought evil to the tribe. Agon should die."

Agon stood proudly before the people; a chieftain's son could not do otherwise. He threw his axe and knife on the ground and said the judgment words: "I am without weapons. Kill me if I have brought evil to the tribe." Only the line of chieftains could say the words, and the one who said them must be prepared to die.

"Let the people decide." Zur held his spear high, point toward Agon.

"No!" Grae pointed his staff at Zur. "Lower your spear. I see no cause."

Erida appeared beside Grae at the shelter entrance, her dark eyes fierce. "The bull was touched by evil before the hunters killed. Yan died because his totem left him. Horn fought with a knife. Agon brings no evil to the tribe."

Ara stared at Agon from the maidens' fire, her eyes fearful.

Grae raised his staff. "Agon lives. He has brought no evil to the tribe. But evil watches us. Let no one weaken our magic." He turned toward the entrance of the cliff shelter.

Agon bent down, lifting the axe from the grass, and Horn's spear flashed in the firelight. The axe spun out from Agon's hand as he leaped sideways. Horn fell with the axe blade in his forehead, his body dropping loosely like a skin bag of meat, the spear still in his hand. In that same moment Grae turned back, seeing the axe go to Horn's head.

Agon saw Grae's eyes, and Erida's eyes, and he knew that he was dead, even as Horn was dead.

Zur pointed his spear triumphantly at Agon. "Now he dies!"

Ara stood as though turned to stone, her hands over her mouth.

Grae spoke: "Will you die by water or stone?"

Grae had given him the choice. His spirit and pride were not to be taken from him. Not to be sent into the dark rushing water. He could die the chieftain's way, by the stone point of his spear. Die with honor, his spirit strong and protecting the tribe.

"Stone."

Erida stood straight and motionless as he replied.

Grae raised his staff. "Go to the Stone with your weapons. Wait there." He stared at Zur. "No others will come. I go alone."

Erida and Ara came to Agon as he approached the cliff trail. Although no tears showed, he saw that they wept. Ara clung to him.

He touched her hair. "I will be with the hunters. The ibex will guide them."

Erida spoke proudly, as when he came to her with his first game. "You are a good hunter, Agon." She tied a soft skin bandage on his finger, then gripped his arms, the strength of her spirit flowing from her fingers into his spirit. "Keep your magic strong. Always go forward."

Ara looked back sadly at Agon as Erida led her away. "Come back, Agon!"

Orm and the hunters appeared from the shadows, Alar with them. Their eyes showed their sorrow, their faces their anger.

"If you will lead us," Orm said, "we will go north, past the mountains, to a new land."

Agon put his hand on Orm's arm. "You will lead now."

Orm looked silently into Agon's eyes, then he touched Agon's axe. "I will sing the axe song for you as we did together."

Agon smiled at Orm and Alar. "Teach the song to Alar. Then I will sing it with you both."

He turned from them and started up the steep path to the cliff top, to the Stone where death waited.

12

The Onstean

GRAE CAME FROM the darkness as the crescent of the waxing moon sank below the western horizon. He circled the Stone to where Agon waited. His voice bore no anger, only sorrow and mystery. "Come. Leave no tracks."

They followed the cliff top to the west until they came to the wooded hills that bordered a small tributary of the river. Grae led the way, turning, reversing direction, clambering over and under fallen trees, climbing up gullies and rock faces in the starlight. Finally he halted in the brush at the base of a hill.

A feeling of ancient and awesome spirits filled the night air. Grae parted the brush to expose a hole in the cliff face. "The Onstean meet here."

The Onstean. The Invisible Rock Spirit Men. Agon felt the icy hands of death. He waited for Grae to speak again, the ibex cold against his chest.

Grae motioned toward the hole. "Go in. Leave your weapons inside the opening. Follow the main passage. Do not speak."

Agon knelt and pushed his body into the hole, into a corridor barely wide enough for his shoulders. He laid his spear, axe, and knife against the inner wall and crawled forward into the blackness.

The memory of his initiation rites returned—starved and

exhausted, crawling through tortuous and terrifying black passages, losing all sense of place and direction, then the shock of exploding light and sound—galloping hoofs, trumpeting mammoths, roaring bulls, gigantic beasts looming. And finally the combined rituals of singing, dancing, drumming, all performed below the great walls of colored animals, ending with the bloody and painful circumcision rites.

But now Agon knew that something yet more terrible lay ahead. The Onstean. Only whispered about by the hunters. Invisible beings, half men, half spirits, acting in secrecy, watching and protecting the tribe but merciless when angered.

The ceiling became so low that he was forced to crouch as he moved forward. He sensed passages on either side, but he followed the main corridor, penetrating deeper into the hill as the earth closed ever tighter around him.

A wall blocked his way. His searching fingers groped upward into space. He forced his body to follow, arching in a backbreaking angle, squeezing into a vertical chimney in the rock. He detected smoke, and strange and ancient scents: of unknown animals, of rock and water, of birds, of fire and shadows, of mystery, of death.

Something above him—a horned figure silhouetted against a faint glow of light, a massive club raised. He waited for the blow.

A muffled sound came from behind the figure, as though an animal had spoken. The club lowered, touched his head, lifted; the horned figure drew back.

"Come," said the animal voice.

Agon forced himself upward until his back was through the angle of the rock and he stood upright in the chimney, his eyes slightly above floor level of a red-lit chamber.

Grotesque manlike shapes sat in the circle around a fire, elemental beings brooding in the depth of the earth. Three and three and three—the magic number. Agon knew terror beyond terror. He stood in the presence of the Onstean.

One of the forms rose; a stiff hide resembling a slab of

granite covered the man or spirit beneath. Ancient power, primitive strength emanated from the being. Eyes like flint stared from two round holes in the hide. The being held its arms up, stiff like the stalagmites that rose from the chamber floor. Touching its right thumb it said, "Stone," in a voice hard and cold as obsidian. It touched each finger in turn, and the other figures spoke, their voices muffled and hollow:

"Fire. Water. Sun. Animal. Bird. Dance. Hunt. Dream." No name for the last finger.

Stone Man moved to the side of the chamber, where he held both hands against the wall as Animal Man approached. Animal Man had the antlers of a reindeer, the tail of a horse, the eyes of an owl, the body of a bear, and the paws of a wolf. Animal Man blew over Stone Man's hands from a tube. When Stone Man took his hands away, the wall showed the impression of his fingers and thumbs, each outlined in red.

Animal Man's paws held magic, for as he moved them over the wall a bull bison appeared. Spears bristled from the bull's body, and it stared back at its spilling intestines as its horns gored a sticklike man. In front of the bison stood a bird—Yan's totem.

Animal Man beckoned, and Agon pulled himself out of the chimney and went to the place where Animal Man stood. Agon's nose recognized reindeer, bear, horse, owl, wolf, but also the scent of animals unknown.

Animal Man's paw pointed to Agon's hands, then to the wall, and Agon held his hands against the wall as Stone Man had done. Animal Man's paws plucked the bandage from Agon's finger, and blood ran down the wall and over the bird. Animal Man blew through the tube, and Agon's hands and the wall around his hands turned red. Animal Man motioned, and when Agon removed his hands from the wall, the hands showed in the outline with the stream of blood going from the shortened finger down and over the bird.

Stone Man pointed to one side of the chamber, and

Agon went there, feeling the eyes of the Onstean on him. He knew that he would soon die; he smelled death in the chamber.

Stone Man's voice grated like grinding rocks: "The bird left Yan. The bison's heart moved. The raven circled three times."

Agon heard Emo saying *Three and three,* and he saw again the horror in Yan's dead eyes.

Stone Man spoke to one of the figures in the circle, and Agon felt the eyes leave him. He sucked in a breath of air and realized that his legs were trembling. The ibex hung motionless on his chest, and Agon felt its frozen terror.

"Tell us." Stone Man looked at Dream Man.

Dream Man wore a white robe, his hair hung down over the robe, and his face was a pale death mask with staring white eyes. Dream Man's voice whispered like trees before a storm:

"Something comes."

A cold wind filled the chamber. The torch flickered and almost went out, and something moaned in the dark recesses of the cave.

"What?" Stone Man asked.

Dream Man's white eyes shone like dead bones. "The game runs from it—deer, bison, horses—all running." Agon heard the distant drumming of hooves.

"What comes?"

Dream Man struggled silently with something unseen. Finally he spoke, his voice barely a whisper. "A dark thing and a shining thing."

Dream Man said no more.

Dance Man rose and started to move around the fire, inside the circle of figures. Deer antlers grew from his head, deerskin covered him, his face was a deer face. He stepped softly at first, like a young male deer entering an unknown woods, his feet delicately touching the earth, moving slowly forward, his head raised, alert.

Bird Man hopped up onto a flat-topped stalagmite. Feathers covered Bird Man, colored plumage gleaming in the torchlight. The red crest of feathers on his head swayed and danced as he moved. A long beak protruded below the crest, and Bird Man held his fingers on it. A bird voice came from the beak, a giant bird calling. The sound rose and fell in rhythm with Dance Man's feet.

Dance Man danced faster. He pranced like a deer in rut. He went step-leap, step-leap, his body bending forward, then backward with each step, and Bird Man's sound became high-pitched and trilling, ever faster. Dance Man now pranced like a great stag, his steps higher and higher, his hooves powerful against the earth.

Then the other figures began to dance, circling and whirling in the torchlight.

Stone Man carried a long staff, and as he danced, he repeatedly raised it high above his head and brought it down toward the rock floor like striking lightning. He danced heavily, treading deep into the earth.

Animal Man was all animals dancing—the prancing reindeer, the circling bison, the galloping horse, the pawing cave bear, the running wolf. His round, owl-like eyes glared. He danced from one wall of the chamber to another, and as he left each wall, a new thing appeared on the surface—quick small shapes of animals: bison, horses, deer, ibex, rhino, elk, bulls, and mammoth.

Fire Man's hands and arms flickered like flames, and his body leaped like fire in a lightning-blasted forest. He seized a blazing branch and leaped over and through the main fire, back and forth over it, faster and faster. His robe of red skin flared like flame, and he seemed part of the fire.

Water Man danced like rain falling, then a small rivulet, a stream, a river, a wild torrent surging between steep cliffs, leaping over rocks and falls, deep and powerful. Then he shuddered and slowed, his movements sluggish and weak, yet he slowly raised his arms as he danced, his fists clenched. Suddenly he brought his arms down and forward in a powerful movement like a wall of water crashing through a canyon.

Sun Man danced in his yellow robe as the sun crossing the sky, crouched low in the morning, reaching higher and higher, then sinking down in the evening. He danced to the south, then back to the north, using his magic to call the sun back.

Hunt Man became a shaggy bison dancing on hind legs. Black horns rose from his massive head, and he held in his mouth one end of a curved stick, a leather thong tied across it. As he danced, Hunt Man held the far end of the stick in one bison hoof and plucked the thong with the other. The thong produced a sound in rhythm with Bird Man's sound. Bird Man's sound was continuous, but Hunt Man made sound only with each of Dance Man's footsteps.

Now Dream Man danced in a circle that grew smaller and smaller until he spun around in one spot, his hair swirling straight out from his head. He spun so fast that his body blurred in the firelight, and the other dancers whirled around him, faster and faster. The flames of Fire Man's torch streamed out behind him in a glowing arc, and the figures spun like a whirlwind in the red chamber. All the while, Bird Man and Hunt Man's sounds grew louder and faster. Suddenly Dream Man called out and fell to the ground, his body twitching under his robe.

Bird Man and Hunt Man stopped the bird calling, the drumming sound, and the other dancers ceased their whirling and stomping. All stood motionless around Dream Man.

Dream Man's body stiffened and became motionless. Agon sensed that Dream Man's spirit was gone, yet Dream Man was not dead.

Stone Man raised his staff: "The mountain flew into the sky."

Fire Man dropped his blazing branch onto the fire: "Fire came from the earth."

Animal Man stamped on the ground, his feet striking like hooves: "We ran!"

Sun Man spread his arms: "The sky was red, and the spirit lights were lost."

Hunt Man raised his bison head and horns, the bison face menacing: "Spears in men!"

Water Man motioned: "A cliff of water came."

Bird Man said an even stranger thing: "Two great birds that take only one mate. One waits."

Dance Man spoke last: "Spear Woman waits."

Agon felt his body quiver with a premonition.

Then Dream Man stirred. He moved weakly and opened his white eyes. He pushed himself slowly to his knees, swaying as if his spirit had not yet completely returned.

Stone Man raised his staff above Dream Man. Dream Man looked at something behind Stone Man, his eyes filled with terror. He spoke, the words the most terrible known: "The Snake Demon!"

The Onstean drew back from Dream Man.

Agon heard his heart pounding, and the chamber held no air. He touched his totem, seeking strength and magic, but he felt only the terror of the ibex.

The thing in the darkness moaned again, then Agon heard the faint sound of something slithering through grass. Their magic was useless. The Snake Demon encircled them, slit eyes glaring.

Stone Man raised his staff, fighting, straining, struggling with something unseen.

"There is one way." Dream Man spoke.

Agon felt death reaching for him. Dream Man stared at him with his white eyes. "Agon goes to the Earth Mother."

Agon stood straight and still as the stalagmite on which Bird Man perched. The Being whose name could not be spoken by men—the ancient and primeval Earth Mother—so terrible that even Grae could not approach her—he, Agon, would go to her.

Sun Man looked into the darkness behind them. "The Onerana must agree."

The Onerana. The Invisible Earth Spirit Women. More secret and frightening than the Onstean. Agon fought for air, calling upon the ibex to give him strength and courage.

Stone Man's voice was cold as the ice fields. "They have agreed." He spoke to Agon: "Go to the Blue Hills. Wait at the waterfall below the breasts of the woman of the mountains. Give this to the Earth Mother." He placed a small object wrapped in white skin in Agon's hand. The thing felt heavier than stone, and its magic radiated into Agon's hand like heat from a live coal.

"If you fail," Stone Man said, "the tribe will die, and our spirits will wander lost forever."

Agon placed the object in the pouch that hung from his belt. "I will not fail."

A hide was thrown over his head from behind, and the light was gone. Hoofs and paws grasped his arms, and he was led through a long and winding passage. Then he smelled fresh air and felt grass under his feet. Suddenly the hoofs and paws were gone.

He pulled the clinging hide from his head. He stood on the dark plain, and in the starlight he saw his weapons at his feet. When he lifted the weapons, he found a small bag of traveling food tied to the spear. From its weight, he judged the bag to contain five days' food. He looked across the plain to the northeast. The Blue Hills lay four days away. One more day to find the waterfall. Then he would need food no longer.

The stars told him the night was half-gone. He moved forward across the plain, his axe and knife in his belt, his spear ready for use against the great cats who hunted at night. He directed his course toward Spear Mountain, the conical peak that lay two days' travel upriver from Grae's camp. From Spear Mountain he would cross the plain to the Blue Hills, to the Earth Mother. And to his death.

13

The Stranger

EENA SHIVERED WITH an almost forgotten fear. Spear Mountain loomed ahead, and she remembered the ominous hole in the cliff face below the mountain. The opening gaped like the mouth of a monstrous and evil beast crouching above the trail. Remembering it now, she felt the sunshine lose its warmth, and the premonition of death and sorrow came upon her once more.

A strange-looking man approached along the trail, a man taller than Stig, his head misshapen and huge. He held out a robe of black fur toward them. As he came closer, Eena saw that he was old, arms and legs stringy muscle and knobby bone under leathery skin, body twisted, face wrinkled. And what had looked like part of his head was a great knob of twisted coarse hair on top of his head. His face was so cruel-looking, and his eyes were so evil, that she held her hand in front of her face to ward off his gaze.

The man smiled, revealing long, sharp teeth, his mouth resembling that of a snake. He held up the robe to Stig and pointed at Eena.

Stig shook his head: No.

The man pulled a string of bright shells from his pouch and offered these along with the robe. He pointed at Eena again, then thrust the robe and shells at Stig.

Stig brought his spear up across his chest, point to the side. He gestured with the handle: *Go.*

The man's eyes burned with anger. He snarled something, his voice hissing like a snake, then he thrust the robe and shells once more at Stig.

Stig brought his spear around, point forward. He made the final sign with the point: *Go or I kill.* Eran raised his spear and came to stand alongside Stig.

The stranger looked directly at Eena. He made a fist with his right hand and rammed it upward with his stiff forearm, then he turned and ran back along the river trail toward Spear Mountain, the robe flapping on each side of him like bat wings.

As the man's figure grew smaller and disappeared around a curve in the trail, Stig turned to face Eran and Eena. "I have never seen his kind before . . . hair all lumped up . . ." He smiled at Eena. "Did you think we would trade you for his fur and shells?"

"He was terrible!" Eena shivered.

Stig laughed. "Just ugly. Like a mangy old wolf."

"He had snake teeth. His spirit was evil."

Stig patted her shoulder. "Don't be afraid of him." He looked down the trail. "I wonder where he came from? He can't be one of Grae's people; not with that face."

"If he comes again," Eran said, "I'll drive my spear right through him."

Stig laughed again. "Good. The pup is turning into a wolf."

"We must go back," Eena said.

Stig stared at her. "Go back because of a dried-up old jackal?" He shook his head. "Never."

"I beg you to go back."

"Our people fear no man," Stig said. "Our spirits are strong, our totems protect us. If trouble appears, better to face that trouble and die fighting. You know how to use your spears. Keep them ready. We will take whatever comes. We go forward."

14

Ambush

IN MIDMORNING AGON approached the first path that led down the cliffs into the gorge of Spear Canyon. Needing water, he went down the path, intending to follow the river trail until he came to the next cliff path that led up onto the plain.

He reached the river and drank, then proceeded along the trail through the gorge. The cliff walls closed in above him, the light grew dim, and the air became heavy with the smells of wet rock and the moss, mold, and fungus that lived in the shadows of the canyon walls. A feeling of evil grew stronger as he approached Spear Mountain, and when, in late afternoon, he came to the next trail up the cliff face, he drank again and left the gorge and its gloom.

He gained the top of the cliff and followed the game trail that led along the edge of the gorge, intending to strike off across the plain toward the Blue Hills before he reached Spear Mountain. But as he trotted toward his turn-off point, he felt a sudden urge to look down into the gorge again. He pushed through the brush and trees that grew along the cliff top, moving cautiously as he approached the cliff edge.

The river wound through the gorge below, the roar of the water muffled by the depth of the canyon. The face of the cliff dropped vertically beneath the rock lip on which he knelt, while to his left the cone of Spear Mountain rose above the river.

Movement in the gorge caught his eye. Three people came down the river trail, tiny figures at that distance, but he recognized them by their golden hair—Stig, the hunter, with his son and daughter—coming to the spring hunt festival.

The girl walked behind Stig, moving easily and gracefully as a young doe. He remembered her from the previous year's festival; her name was Eena, and she kept Stig's camp after his mate had been killed by the snake. It was said that she hunted with Stig and his son, not as strong as a hunter, but possessed of powerful hunting magic. Her eyes held mystery and sunshine and laughter.

Agon thought of the moon dance as he watched Eena. She had stood shyly at the edge of the firelight while the dancers leaped and circled. Some of the hunters had danced toward her, but Stig had moved forward to stand in front of her, and the hunters had danced back into the circle. Agon had only watched her from a distance, but it had seemed that she smiled at him whenever she looked in his direction.

He knelt on the edge for a moment more, knowing he must go. And where he must go . . .

Movement in the bushes around the three figures! He shouted, but his voice went unheard over the roar of the river. He saw a spear flash, and Stig's arms fly up. Men with immense heads leaped from the bushes, and a violent, whirling, fighting mass formed. At its center he saw the golden hair of Eena.

Blood sprayed in a red haze as spears plunged in and ripped out. Stig and his children fought fiercely as wolves, Eena driving her spear at the attackers, while Stig and the boy held the ground around her.

Foremost among the attackers was a giant of a man who fought with such powerful, reptilian motions that he seemed a huge snake. He wore a white bone in his great knot of hair, and he wielded his spear with such ferocity that Stig and the boy were ripped open like gutted deer. As they fell, the snake man seized Eena's spear and with a single blow struck her to the ground. He bent over the bodies of Stig and the boy, then lifted their dripping heads high in the air above their mutilated bodies. His mouth snarled open like a roaring lion. From the arrogance of his gestures Agon knew that he was the leader of the attacking group.

Snake Man tossed the heads to the other men, then bent over Eena, binding her ankles, tying her wrists behind her back. He lifted her limp body to his shoulder, hanging facedown, her golden hair like a waterfall. He waved his spear, and the men ran back along the trail toward Spear Mountain, leaving the headless bodies of Stig and his son on the ground along with the bodies of three of their own men. Two men carried the dripping heads of Stig and the boy, while three wounded staggered behind, limping.

Agon ran fast along the cliff trail, a terrible anger burning in him. Twice he slowed, going to the cliff edge, looking down into the gorge. His first look revealed the attackers still ahead of him, but on the second he was directly above them. Eena still lay across Snake Man's shoulder, her body swinging limply as he ran. The man moved with sinuous strength, carrying Eena as a lion carries a fawn in its bloody jaws.

Farther ahead the gorge curved abruptly, the mountain rising sheer above the canyon. Agon drew back from the cliff edge and ran along the trail again until he reached the place where the mountain forced the trail out onto the plain. Again he looked over the cliff edge.

The men passed below him, then disappeared around the curve of the wall. He could follow the attackers no further. He lay facedown, hanging partway over the edge of the cliff, contemplating the wall below. The black hole in the cliff face had to be around the curve of the wall.

The ledge was there. Not as wide as his hand, a spear-length below him, it led down and around the curve of the cliff, exactly as he remembered from when he climbed it with Orm a year ago. Agon shifted his axe to the back of his belt, left his spear on the cliff top, and slid over the edge. He hung by his fingertips, his face against the wall. Holding his breath, he released his grip on the lip of the cliff.

His feet struck the ledge, and his body slammed against the cliff face. He teetered, clawing at the rock as his body swayed out over the abyss. His fingers found a tiny protuberance on the wall, and he pulled himself back against the rock. He sucked in air and moved sideways along the ledge, his heels over the empty space below.

As he came around the curve of the wall, he saw the men again. They climbed the steep path that ran diagonally up the lower part of the cliff to the out-of-sight black hole. The man carrying Eena shouted, his lionlike roar answered by a shout from the cliff. People appeared on the stone platform at the top of the path, their voices harsh and strange. Their heads displayed the same grotesque knobs of hair as the men on the path.

Cautiously, Agon moved forward on the ledge. The platform was crowded with people who seemed to come out of the cliff, but the curvature of the rock wall prevented a view of the back of the platform.

Snake Man brought Eena up onto the platform, the two men holding the severed heads close behind him. The people crowded around, but Snake Man gestured, and everyone fell back. He carried Eena toward the rear of the platform and disappeared from Agon's view. The people followed, and in a few moments the platform was empty except for two sentinels.

Agon worked his way along the ledge and around the bulge until suddenly the ledge ended—only empty space lay beyond and below him. The smooth cliff wall leaned inward from the top, impossible to climb up or down. He sidestepped to the extreme end of the ledge; then, clinging to the wall, stretched forward around the curving cliff face.

A hole! A shoulder-sized entrance two arms' length beyond the end of the ledge! He drew back and slowly knelt, sliding his left hand downward until he gripped the narrow ledge. He swung down, hanging on to the ledge by his left hand, reaching for the hole with his right. His fingertips scraped the wall, an axe-handle length from the hole. He swung his body back, then forward toward the hole, and his fingers felt only smooth rock.

With his free hand he pulled the axe from his belt. A cracking noise came from the ledge. Once more he swung his body, reaching out with the axe as he came forward. The ledge cracked and broke, falling away under his fingers just as the blade of the axe caught the edge of the hole. The rawhide thongs binding the antler handle to the axe head creaked as the axe took his weight, but the thongs held as his body swung beneath the hole. He pulled himself upward and into the opening.

The next instant the form of a man loomed above him, and a spear drove toward his chest.

15

Inside Spear Mountain

EENA HAD SLOWLY regained consciousness as the man carried her along the river trail. Jolted head down, something hard pressed into her stomach. She became aware of her deer totem swinging and jerking below her face, a pair of black-haired, powerful legs thrusting below the totem. Someone was carrying her, running along the river trail. She tried to move, and thongs bit into her wrists and ankles, holding her arms behind her back, her feet together.

Something grunted animal-like behind her head. She closed her eyes as a hand grabbed her hair and jerked her head up. The grunt came again, and someone laughed. The hand released her hair, and she let her head fall limply. She felt dizzy and nauseated but made no movement, letting her head swing with the motion of the man who carried her.

The man slowed, climbing. Through half-open eyes she

saw a rocky path falling away steeply below her, emptiness on one side, a rock wall on the other. The man bellowed, and voices above replied.

The path leveled; she was taken onto a place where harsh voices, grasping hands, poking fingers, and animal sounds surrounded her. The man growled, and the probing hands left her as he moved forward.

A stench filled her nostrils—rotting meat, human excrement, sour sweat, filthy bodies. The man dropped her on a pile of furs, then spoke sharply. People moved toward her, and the man spoke again, his voice harsh and authoritative. Hands seized her wrists and ankles, and the thongs binding them loosened. Hands pulled her arms and legs, stretching them out against something rough. She opened her eyes.

In the firelight of a smoky chamber, four ugly women held her spread-eagled, lashing her hands and feet with straps to a frame of branches.

Rage born of overwhelming anger at the death of her father and brother erupted. She became a violent, twisting, kicking thing that tore the straps from the women's hands and hurled the women back, one into the fire, one against the rock wall. The woman in the fire screeched and leaped from the coals, while the others crouched, glaring at Eena.

A coarse laugh came from the other side of the fire. A giant of a man strode toward her, the man who had led the attack. She shrank back, his face so fierce, his presence so snakelike, his body so powerful, that her body trembled. It was as if the old man with the robe had been changed to a full-muscled, awful demon in its prime. Black eyes glared above a beaklike nose; half-covering the low, slanting forehead lay a great coil of coarse black hair, and from the coil protruded a human arm bone. The man's mouth contorted, exposing large canine teeth. His face was awful in its fierceness and savagery.

The man seized her wrist, his hand like the jaws of a hyena on her bones. Baring his teeth in a hideous grin, he touched his chest. "Ka." He pointed to her. "Kala."

She shook her head, defying him.

His eyes blazed. "Ka!" He slapped his chest. He poked her breastbone, his finger like a rock. "Kala."

She shook her head again.

The man spoke sharply to someone behind him, at the same time tightening his grip on her wrist.

Another man appeared from behind the fire—the old man who had offered the robe, his snake teeth yellow in the firelight. Seizing a burning brand, he waved it in Eena's face, lunging at her, thrusting his fist and arm upward, shrieking and slobbering. Ka growled at him, gesturing, and the man drew back from Eena and lurched into the gloom at the rear of the chamber, the blaze of the burning branch briefly lighting the walls and ceiling.

The people, like so many brutes, gathered around Ka and Eena. The women, slovenly and dirty, scowling, grouped behind the largest men. The four women with whom Eena had fought crouched behind Ka, hissing and glaring murderously at her, the burned one licking her scorched hand.

Suddenly the people drew back from the rear of the chamber. The old man with the torch came out of the darkness, and something came behind him, coming toward Eena.

Agon's axe came up, deflecting the spear as the man drove it toward his throat. Agon clawed at his knife and threw his body forward, low under the spear and against the legs of the man. They rolled and spun to face each other with the man's back to the opening and his spear raised again.

Agon moved the axe in the short motions of the little axe song—no space in the chamber for the long, sweeping strokes of the big axe song. He sang silently with the axe as he moved forward, his axe arm jolting, thrusting with the knife in the other hand.

The axe flickered like a star in the passageway, and the man staggered back with axe and knife cuts appearing like open red mouths on his face, arms, body. Then, Agon's knife in his chest, the man fell backward out of the opening.

Agon ceased the axe song; the axe became motionless, its magic litany of death ending.

Out the entry hole he saw only the river, far below in the dusk.

He ran into the passageway behind him. The corridor narrowed and twisted; in moments he was in complete darkness. Rushing back to the opening, he searched for a torch, for anything with which to make and light one. He found only bare rock and blood. The man who guarded the opening must have known the passageway so well that he needed no light.

Agon entered the corridor again, feeling his way. The ceiling lowered; the walls squeezed closer. He stooped lower and lower, finally crawling through the winding passage that led downward into the mountain. Crawling endlessly, helplessly struggling in the grip of the mountain, he moved forward.

He sensed evil in the twisting passageway, evil growing stronger. He crawled on. Now the evil lay just ahead of him, so strong, so close, that his body refused to move.

It seemed that Eena called to him. He touched the ibex and crawled forward. He rounded a sharp bend in the passage, entered a small chamber, and the evil closed around him.

In the dim red light from an opening in the far wall of the chamber, Agon saw a bed of branches and hides surrounded by a canopy of animal skulls and rotting human heads. On the bed lay a grotesque being—a horror of crooked horns and clawed hands, white skull head and shapeless body under a pale skin. The thing slept, but demons rose from it, filling the chamber.

Things darker than the darkness swirled around Agon. Icy hands tore at him, and the foulness of things long dead stank in his nose. The howling demons of disease and famine, cold and thirst, wounds and corruption, shrieked and whirled.

Agon knew them. Knew them from the ancient past. Knew them in the terror of black storm and howling wind, in the white fury of the blizzard, in the burning heat of the desert, in the cold hands of ice.

Death beckoned him forward. "Come!"

Agon moved past the clawed hands and horns while the demons circled him, tearing at his spirit with their bony fingers. He pushed through them, through the chamber, Death ahead and beckoning.

Silently, axe ready, Agon went down the passage toward the red glow, seeking the killers who took human heads and held Eena in their bloody hands.

Coals of a fire faintly illuminating a cavernous chamber! Figures slept around the fire, bestial human forms, male and female, sprawled open-mouthed, snoring, grunting, stinking. In the far wall a faintly lighted opening admitted the muffled roar of the river, and Agon knew from the dimness of the light that night had come.

He crept around and over the sleeping forms, searching for Eena.

There! She lay on a pile of furs beside Snake Man, the man with the bone in his hair. Her eyes were open, watching him as he approached. Blood stained her face, her throat, her body, her tunic. A leather strap circled her neck, the other end looped around Snake Man's wrist. As Agon bent over her, her eyes widened in recognition, but she made no sound. Blood covered her thighs, and a rank smell like that of an ejaculating lion lay over her. Snake Man had mated with her, brutally, cruelly.

Women taken forcibly by others must die. Agon raised the axe. One stroke to crush Eena's skull, the second blow for Snake Man. Eena looked up at him, her eyes thanking him as she waited for the axe stroke.

Agon's arm tensed for the blow. Then he lowered the axe.

He knelt on the furs by Eena. The strap around her neck

was double-knotted chokingly tight, both ends held by Snake Man, impossible to untie. Agon placed the axe head between his knees and carefully rubbed one of the straps against the blade.

Snake Man stirred and turned, one huge arm thrusting out toward Eena, and she drew her legs back as the arm came down on the furs. Agon raised the axe, ready to strike. Snake Man pulled on the straps in his sleep, dragging Eena toward him. Agon seized the straps and held them, the axe poised.

Snake Man gave a snoring grunt and relaxed his hand.

Eena leaned forward to give more slack to the strap, and Agon sawed it over the axe blade, watching Snake Man, listening for any movement among the sleeping forms.

The strap parted. Agon forced the cut end through the knot, feeling the tightness of the leather, the pulsing of Eena's throat. He lifted the strap from her neck.

Eena rose quickly to her feet. They moved away from Snake Man and around the fire toward the river opening, stepping around the bodies, over the outflung arms and legs of the sleeping people. When figures on the floor moved, Agon drew Eena down, waiting until the forms settled into their changed positions.

They reached the entrance, and Agon felt Eena stiffen, heard her small gasp of horror. Impaled on poles outside the entrance, pale hair swaying under the gibbous moon that shone through broken clouds, hung the heads of Eran and Stig.

Agon drew Eena back into the cave entrance. A guard stood on the edge of the platform, leaning on his spear, looking out over the gorge.

Agon motioned to Eena to follow and silently moved behind the guard. The axe cracked into the man's skull, and Eena caught the man's spear while Agon grasped the body under the arms to keep it from falling.

Then Snake Man roared inside the cave, a wild scream of fury.

Agon hurled the sentry's body into the entrance and

seized the spear Eena held out to him. They ran down the steep path toward the river, their feet searching the way while shouts, the hammering of running feet, and the rattle of spears echoed from above. They reached the bottom of the cliff and ran down the river trail as the noise of pursuit grew louder. They rounded the curve in the gorge, and in the dim light they saw the headless bodies of Eena's father and brother. Eena cried out and would have stopped, but Agon dragged her past the bodies, and they ran again.

They came to the cliff path and scrambled up the wall. Eena, ahead of Agon, ran strongly, swift and surefooted in the light of the moon. As they reached the cliff top, they heard their pursuers coming fast up the path.

Agon pointed to the plain. "Run!"

"If you fight, I fight."

"Go!" He pushed her toward the plain.

She turned back toward him.

Feet pounded on the trail below. Men appeared, running up the path.

Agon crouched just back from the cliff edge. As the first man burst over the edge, Agon thrust the spear into his neck then jerked the spear out as the body fell back. He sent three more men tumbling down the wall, and the spear handle cracked in his hands.

Snake Man shrieked a command below, then Agon heard the scrambling of many men climbing, all at about the same distance. He looked over the edge of the cliff. Men were spread out below, climbing upward in a line, some on the path, others on the wall.

Eena touched Agon's arm. "Men run along the cliff top toward us."

He heard them—still distant but coming fast. He quickly felt the cracked spear handle. "Now we run."

"If you are with me." She said it simply, quietly.

They ran out onto the plain. And as they ran, the moon hid behind the clouds, and Agon and Eena disappeared in the darkness.

16

On the Plain

THEY RAN UNTIL they were far from Spear Mountain, and still they ran, the cool night air in their faces, the grass brushing against their thighs. Finally they stopped to listen for any indication of pursuit. Nothing. They ran on.

The moon broke through the clouds, and they crouched in the shelter of the grass. Eena spoke, her voice filled with sorrow: "Why do they kill us?"

Agon understood her grief, her despair, her horror. He wanted to comfort her, but the smell of Snake Man's semen was foreign, challenging, insulting. His hand gripped the axe handle. "They are demons."

She stared back toward Spear Mountain. "Where did they come from?"

He touched the ibex. "From Hell."

She shuddered. "Can they find us?"

Agon looked at her bowed head, her hair pale golden under the moon. "They are many."

She was silent. Then she said, "You should have killed me."

"No."

"I asked my deer spirit to let me die."

He said nothing.

"Where can we go?" she asked.

"I go to the Blue Hills." He felt the weight of the object that Stone Man had given him. The white eyes of Dream Man seemed looking at him from the darkness. "I go alone."

She bowed her head and wrapped her arms around her knees in the death position.

"Try to reach Grae's camp." He pointed back toward the river. "Travel at night, hide in the grass during the day."

They heard a faint pattering in the distance—the running feet of men—men searching the plain. He saw the sudden tensing of her body. She stared toward the mountain, then lowered her head again.

"Run west," he told her, "then toward the river."

She did not look up or move.

He gathered his weapons and turned toward the Blue Hills. Then he turned back. "Come with me. We will go together."

She looked at him unbelievingly.

"Come." He held out his hand to her.

They ran again, their feet light in the grass, racing across the plain, away from the running men.

They ran through the rest of the night, and when the first gray light appeared, they saw a marsh in a low area of the plain. Tall grass swayed above them as they entered the marsh, shielding them from the view of any pursuers.

Shallow pools of water surrounded them, and Agon drank deeply from the nearest one. But Eena went to another pool.

Hidden from Agon behind a thick clump of grass, she rinsed her mouth again and again, then she bathed fiercely, her deerskin tunic and sandals laid on the bank. She washed her face, her body, her hair, then washed them again in another pool.

When she reappeared, Agon observed that the bloodstains were gone, but the bruises on her face and arms and the chafed circles at her wrists and ankles remained. Her eyes and face still showed her horror, her revulsion, but in spite of this, in spite of the bruises, he saw that she was beautiful: Her body was slender but fully formed, her arms and legs long muscled and graceful, her hands and feet small but strong and perfectly shaped. Her face, with its luminous eyes, high cheekbones, delicate nose and mouth, and white, even teeth, was lovely. And the alien smell, the stench of Ka's semen, was gone.

He noticed a cut on her upper arm. Not a jagged spear wound, but narrow, as though a knife had been drawn across the skin. "You fought hard," he said.

Her voice revealed her sorrow. "They were too many."

"I was on the cliff top. I saw them attack."

"Why did they take my father's and brother's heads?"

"Because they are evil."

"How can my father's spirit rest? My brother's spirit?"

"Grae will call their spirits back. Then they can rest." He touched her arm, near the cut. "Why?"

Eena trembled. "Ka."

Ka. Snake Man. An ancient hatred welled up in Agon's spirit memory. Ka, the enemy, the destroyer, the evil one. Agon knew him from an age before the tribes, before the river, before the cliffs, before the ice. . . .

She bowed her head. "Kill me."

"No." He wanted to touch her hair.

"They made me drink . . ." She stopped.

He stared at her.

"They made me drink blood."

"Your blood?"

"My blood . . . and Ka's blood. . . ." She looked up at him, then down at the ground. "They held my mouth. . . ."

Ka had lain before him as he cut the strap. One blow from the axe . . .

"They brought it from the darkness . . . it had claws and horns. . . ."

Agon saw again the thing that slept in the chamber. He remembered the terror of the demons that whirled around it and marveled that Eena still lived. He touched her hair at last, gently. "They are gone now. I will not let them hurt you again."

She cried then, silently, with her face against his shoulder, and Agon held her until her body ceased trembling.

He stroked her hair. "Sleep. I will watch."

He held her until she slept. Then he saw that the dream spirits came to her, for she moved her hands as though pushing something away and made small cries of sorrow.

He stroked her hair until she became still. Then he laid her down in the soft grass, moving her gently lest she waken.

Bending low, he went to the edge of the marsh and looked back over the plain. The cone of Spear Mountain seemed to rise out of the plain only a little way off, yet he saw from the distance to the line of the river gorge that they had run far during the night. He detected no sign of pursuit, but he knew from the rage in Ka's cry that he would come.

He examined the cracked shaft of the spear. It had broken partly through and split upward about a hand's length, almost useless unless he could wrap it. He had no knife to cut leather thongs from their clothing, and they needed their sandal straps for more running. The marsh grass growing around them was long and tough stemmed, and he wrapped strands of the grass around the split shaft and tied the ends. He balanced the spear in his hand, a weapon too weak to use for a direct thrust, but still deadly if thrown.

The blood-caked flint point was of a different design and workmanship than that of his tribe, cruder in some ways, yet expertly designed for killing. It had withdrawn more easily from the bodies of the men at the cliff top than did his own spears from the bodies of bison and horses. He thought, these are the first men I have killed with a spear. Maybe the point comes out of men more easily than from a bison or horse.

He inspected the thongs, blade, and handle of his axe. The blade and handle were intact, but the thongs had loosened, and he retied them around the antler handle. As he held the axe, he sensed the strength of the ibex carved in the handle flowing up his arm and into his body.

When the sun was halfway up the sky, he came back to where Eena slept. Her hair, almost dry in the sunshine, gleamed soft and golden. He sat quietly by her, shading her eyes from the sun with his hand so she might continue her sleep.

The blood on her tunic—her blood and Ka's blood. She had been made to drink it—her lips were bruised, and the marks on her face and neck and arms had been made by powerful hands. Ka had mated with her, forcibly, cruelly. Yet she had survived, and she had run through the night, never faltering.

She stirred and awakened. Her eyes were startled at first, then he saw her sorrow return with remembrance. But as she looked at him, the sorrow lessened. "You came for me," she said.

He had always known her. She had been with him in the past and would be in the future. He knew, without knowing how, that he had always loved her. But now he could not love her.

"You came in my dream." Her eyes glowed as she looked at him. But then she looked away. "It was only a dream. You could not want me." She unfastened the leather belt that circled her waist. "I cannot wear this now."

The belt was beautifully carved and dyed, but stained with dried blood.

He touched the belt. "The blood will come off."

"It is not the blood." Her eyes filled with tears. "My mother gave me the belt. It is the maiden's belt." Her hands clenched around the belt. "I tried to kill him. But they held me and he . . ."

"I will kill him." He touched her shoulder. "Put on the belt. You are the same."

"No . . . he did things . . ." She hid her face in her hands. "I am not the same. . . ."

"You are to me."

"You don't know . . . what he did. . . ."

"No. But I saw you fight Ka."

"I tried to fight all of them . . . there were too many. . . ."

"Erida will help you. Tell her what happened."

"I can tell no one. . . ."

"Erida is wise. She will help you."

"Would she? Will you take me to her? After you have been to the Blue Hills? Could we go home to your tribe? Could Grae bring my father and brother peace?"

"Grae and Erida will help you." He fastened the belt

around her waist again. "Wear this." Her eyes were blue and green with little golden suns in their centers. He saw them change, some of the sorrow fading.

He thought, I have made her happy by lying to her. I will never come home to the tribe with her. But she must keep on believing that I will; I will not let her have more sorrow now.

He said gently to her, "Grae will bring their spirits back."

"If Grae can do that, I will give my life to him. I will ask my spirit mother to find my father's and brother's spirits and tell them why they must wait." She looked at the sun. "You have let me sleep while you kept watch. Now let me watch while you sleep."

He thought, I will bring her home, to our home, sometime. He said, "Wake me if you hear or see men, no matter how far-off. We will leave here when night comes." He gave her the food pouch. "Eat some of this. We will travel far." He stretched out in the tall grass, the axe and spear in his hands.

Eena looked at Agon as he slept. His straight black hair was cut in short bangs above his eyes, but was long in back, coming to his shoulders. His face was hawklike, fierce, even in sleep, and his high cheekbones and strong nose and chin gave him a look of strength and leadership. His chin was scraped clean of beard, but the hunter's moustache drooped on either side of his mouth. His body was plated and ridged with hard muscles, and his bronzed skin carried several long scars, while one finger was shortened with a half-healed stump.

She thought, he looks so fierce, yet when he looks at me, his eyes are gentle, and when he smiles at me, I want him to take me in his arms. He touched my hair and held me.

She took a handful of the dried food from the pouch, and her fingers touched something wrapped in soft leather. Her hand drew back as from fire, for the object held magic, magic leaping toward her fingers. A thing of ancient mystery lay wrapped in the leather. She closed the pouch hurriedly, placing it next to Agon. She whispered, "Spirit, forgive me, I meant no offense," as her mother had taught her.

Agon had asked her to watch. She crept through the marsh grass and looked anxiously over the plain. Her heart seemed to stop. Distant black specks were on the grassland. Then she breathed again; the specks were bison and horses, grazing.

She made a wad of grass, dipped it in water, and scrubbed at the dried blood on her tunic and belt. She worked furiously, for while the blood remained, she imagined that Ka still held her in the cave, forcing his will and body upon her. She watched the plain as she scrubbed at the stains. Yesterday her father and brother had been strong, alive, laughing, longing for the hunt, protecting her. Now they were dead, and their heads hung on poles while their blood-covered bodies lay on the river trail. And she who had known the evil ahead had spoken only weakly of her fears. What had happened to her in the cave she could not think about, could not visualize, could not believe. . . .

The bison and horse herds were moving apart. Eena stared at them, not breathing, her hands frozen on the belt.

Five tiny sticklike figures appeared between the herds, running across the plain toward the marsh.

Agon woke instantly as Eena touched his shoulder, and he saw from her face that Ka had come. They crouched at the edge of the marsh, watching the figures, still faraway but moving toward the marsh.

"He has found us." Eena spoke flatly, the knowledge of approaching death in her voice.

"Yes."

They looked at the sun. Not yet noon. No escape in the darkness now.

The figures turned toward another part of the marsh, to the right of where Agon and Eena knelt.

"They followed our trail in the darkness," Eena said. "They could not have lost it now."

"They had not lost it." They are demons, Agon thought. Only demons could follow us in the dark. Only demons could hold us in place while they move toward us. They make us think we are safe, that they have lost our trail, yet they come closer. But if we run, they will see us. He touched the ibex on his chest. Help us, Ibex.

"Run," he said to Eena. "Keep running and do not look back. Go to the Blue Hills. Hide in the trees."

"I will not leave you to fight them alone."

"Run! Now!"

"No!"

The men were closer. Agon took the wrapped object from the pouch. "This must be given to the One who can save the tribe. You must take it. Find the waterfall below the twin peaks. Give this to the Earth Mother."

The Earth Mother! Eena placed her hands over her mouth. "I dare not. . . ."

"You must." He held the object out to her. "Take it. Run."

"Not without you."

He willed her to believe. "I will be with you. Run!"

Suddenly Ka turned and headed directly at them, not tracking, not seeing them, but guided by some demonic power.

He thrust the object into her hand. "Run! Now!"

The object burned like fire in her hand. "Not unless we go together."

She must believe this part, he thought. If I can make her believe me and she will run, she may live.

"We will go together. I will come behind you."

"You stay to fight. I stay with you."

He commanded her as he would a hunter. "Run!"

"No. Not without you."

Ka was closer, coming fast.

"Then we both run!" He seized her hand. "Now!"

They ran fast and low through the marsh, keeping in the tall grass, but Ka shouted behind them, and they knew that they were seen. They leaped from hummock to hummock, splashing through the shallow water, pushing through the thick grass until they came to the solid earth of the plain on the other side.

Agon had run through the night with Eena and knew

that she ran fast and tirelessly. Now, seeing her run in the daylight, he felt a surge of hope, for she ran like a hunter, so easily and strongly that it seemed possible they might outrun Ka.

Then he looked back at the men and knew that they could not: Ka had spaced the hunters into the rundown formation with one man already ahead of the others. Agon knew the technique; each hunter in turn running at full speed, then, as his strength failed, dropping back to be replaced by another, the quarry finally exhausted by the continuing and killing pace.

The white bone in Ka's hair gleamed in the sunshine. He ran arrogantly, confidently, waiting to make the kill.

Agon dropped behind Eena, but she looked back and slowed to run beside him. "I stay with you."

"They follow like hyenas."

"Then we will run like wolves." She held the wrapped object out to him. "You should have this."

"If there is fighting, I might lose it. Take it to the waterfall," he commanded.

She slipped the object back into her belt pouch. "I will, but when you fight, I fight."

Feet pounded, the first man almost upon them.

Agon and Eena leaped forward, running with all their strength. Agon gave one quick look back and saw the first pursuer, his teeth bared in the supreme effort of his running, his arm raised in the act of throwing his spear.

"Dodge!" Agon shouted, and he and Eena separated like wolves around a rock as the spear hissed between them.

Then slowly, step by pounding step, Agon and Eena drew away from their pursuer.

Twice more fresh hunters surged forward, and twice more Agon and Eena sped away, but they felt themselves tiring. Now the fourth man charged after them, and Ka had not yet made his run.

"Kill me," Eena gasped. "Before they take us."

"No! Keep on running!"

The man was almost upon them, the thud of his feet

loud and triumphant. A spear whirred by Agon's head as he turned, and he threw the broken spear in the same motion as his turning, hard at the man. But the enemy was too quick, leaping to one side as the spear flashed by him.

In the instant that the spear missed, Agon saw that the man had carried two spears. Now he ran at Agon with the second spear.

Agon ripped the axe from his belt and parried the first thrust, but the man moved the spear point like flickering lightning and drew back, laughing.

Ka raced toward them, his spear held high.

Eena seized the man's spear from the ground. She ran at the man and with both hands thrust the spear into his neck, below the skull. He fell, clawing at the spear.

Now Ka was upon them. His wild cry rang out as his first spear hissed toward Agon. Agon spun low under the spear, his axe spinning with him, singing with him in the big axe song. Ka held his second spear low and rushed at Agon, his face a demonic mask of rage. Agon whirled, spinning as the axe whirled up in the killing arc to Ka's head.

But Agon fought a demon, quicker and stronger than any man; Ka's arm deflected the singing axe, and the blade smashed into the great knot of hair on his head.

As Ka dropped, his last three men lunged toward Agon and Eena. No time for a second stroke of the axe. Agon and Eena ran once again.

Agon knew from the way Ka had fallen that he was not dead. And he knew from the hatred and ferocity in Ka's eyes that there would be no end to their battle until one of them killed the other.

They ran toward the Blue Hills with their last strength, gasping for breath after the terrible pace of the rundown and the violence of the fighting. They heard no pounding feet behind them and looked back, unbelieving. The chase was over. Ka's men stood over the two forms on the ground.

They slowed to a walk. Eena's breast rose and fell with

the depth of her breathing. Gripping the bloody spear, she stared back at the men. "Is he dead?"

"It was like hitting a lion—he may live." Agon touched the spear she held. "You killed like a hunter." He looked into her eyes. "My life is yours now."

"And mine is yours. I will remember."

"As will I."

They went toward the Blue Hills, keeping up a steady pace of walking and running until night came. They detected no sign of further pursuit, but after resting briefly they traveled throughout the moonlit night in case Ka's men followed. They hid in a wooded ravine the next day, alternately keeping watch and sleeping.

Needing another spear for defense, but unable to find any flint or obsidian for making a spearhead, Agon fashioned a makeshift weapon from a long, tough branch by rubbing one end of the branch against a granite boulder until he formed a sharp point.

They traveled again the next night, keeping in the shadows of the trees, and at dawn they entered the heavily wooded foothills of the mountains known as the Blue Hills.

They climbed high into the foothills before they slept, then the next day they climbed higher, and around noon they entered an open glade where a stream descending from the mountains formed a sunlit pool. They rested on the mossy bank, a place of such serenity and beauty that for the first time since their flight from the cave they felt released from a world of horror and violence.

But Agon knew that horror and violence waited to grasp them again. Soon he would go to his death in the arms of the Earth Mother. And Eena would never be safe while Ka lived.

Spirits

17

The Glade

WHILE AGON KEPT watch on their trail, Eena bathed in a corner of the pond that was hidden behind a low rock face. She washed her hair again and even her tunic and sandals, a symbolic act to remove the defilement of Ka.

Dressed in her wet tunic, her eyes excited, she led Agon to the face of the cliff.

"I saw it when I was in the water."

A slab of rock stood at one side of an opening in the wall. Sunlight streamed into a small cave that led back into the hill. The walls and ceiling and floor of the cave were a smooth light-colored stone, and the air was fresh-smelling and dry.

Agon contemplated the slab and the opening. "The slab fell long ago and sealed the entrance. Yet you knew the cave was here?"

"Yes."

He lifted the slab. "You are strong to have moved it."

"I have carried deer."

Agon peered into the darkness at the rear of the cave. The passageway appeared to extend into something larger than itself. "This will be your cave."

"Our cave."

"Yes, our cave." He thought, I will not be here, but it will be our cave.

Eena watched their trail while Agon dove into the pond to wash away the sweat and dust of the running and fighting. Afterward, they lay side by side on the mossy bank, the afternoon sun flickering down through the leaves. Although her eyes still revealed the horror of her ordeal, Eena's face had taken on the beauty of the glade. Leaves rustled drowsily above them, bees droned, and the little stream gurgled quietly.

"The spirits of the trees and the water are happy here," Eena said softly.

Agon nodded. "A good place."

"I wish that we could stay here forever."

He lifted her hand. Half the size of his, her fingers slender and tapered, it had driven the spear into the man's neck with the power of a hunter. "You have found the cave. The forest is full of deer; fish and crayfish are in the pond, blackberries grow thick at the edge of the forest. You could stay here and never hunger."

Sunshine illuminated her golden hair, touched the curves of her face. "I could stay here? You go to the waterfall, but you will come back."

"I may not."

A shadow of sorrow crossed her face. "I would not ask to be your mate. I would gather food, make clothing for you. You would not have to be near me. . . ."

"It is not that. . . ."

"It is. I am unclean. . . ."

"No. You were ready to die under my axe. You are not unclean." He touched her belt. "As long as you wear this, you are my sister."

"I cannot be your sister. You cannot accept my shame. If we return to your tribe, they will kill me."

"I will not let anyone kill you."

"I would let them kill me. Kill me and bring the spirits of my father and brother back." She bowed her head. "It is better that I die."

Agon touched the ibex. Let Ka come now. I will kill him and take away her shame. But even if I kill him, I can never live here with her. Tomorrow, Ibex, we go to the Earth Mother, you and I. He sat silently beside Eena, watching the forest, listening for any sound of approaching pursuers. He saw that Eena slept, and he moved her gently so that she lay on the soft moss.

When Eena awakened in midafternoon, she made Agon sleep while she watched. He was awakened by her light touch.

"A storm comes."

They heard a faint sighing, far in the distance. Tree leaves hung motionless in the still air, birds stopped their singing, and the forest grew silent, waiting. A green light filled the sky, ominous as the rumble of distant thunder.

Agon gathered up the axe and spears. From the plain he had often seen storms over the Blue Hills, fierce and spectacular even at a distance—black boiling clouds, thick streaks of lightning, deep and continuous thunder.

The wind moaned in the forest, and the leaves of the trees quivered. The green light darkened, then flashes of lightning streaked the sky, thunder boomed, and a black wall of clouds swept toward them.

Eena quickly gathered an armful of dry ferns, and as the wind came shrieking through the forest with the rain sweeping behind it, they entered the cave. As Agon pulled the slab across the entrance, the area outside flared with a brilliant flash of lightning, and a crackling blast shook the earth. Again and again the lightning struck, while the wind and the rain roared.

Eena said nothing while the thunder crashed, but in a quiet interval of the storm she spoke. "The storm spirits are angry. Is it because we have come to their mountains?"

He reassured her. "They are often angry here. Not because of us."

She arranged the ferns in two beds on the floor. "I should have picked blackberries, caught crayfish. . . ."

Agon held out the pouch of travel food. "We have enough for tonight." He sat down on the ferns near her, and she drew back. He smelled the sweetness of the ferns, but also the fragrance of her body and breath, like flowers and honey. He wanted to hold her as he had in the marsh when she slept. "I will kill a deer in the morning, before I go to the waterfall."

"Let me come with you to the waterfall."

"I must go alone."

She said no more. In the next flash of lightning he saw that she sat with her head bowed, her face turned from him. The intensity of the storm was increasing, and the wind howled outside the entrance. After a long while, she spoke. "My father and brother . . . where will their spirits go in the storm?"

He pulled her gently toward him now, holding her close. The ferns were soft around them, and in a little while she slept.

In the morning sunshine streamed in through the cracks around the slab. They slid the rock aside and stepped into a newly washed world. Each leaf, each blade of grass held sparkling droplets of water, the air was clear and light, and the pond reflected the clear blue of the sky. The stream, now a small river, dove into the pond, leaped out the other side, and rushed down through the hills. Eena seemed strangely happy, as if the rain had washed away her sorrow of the night.

Agon went into the forest with the good spear, and when he returned with a young deer, he found that Eena had built a small smokeless fire just inside the entrance of the cave. She was chipping the edge of a flint knife, and a woven grass basket filled with blackberries sat by the entrance.

Eena cut venison steaks and hung them over the coals. While the meat cooked, she sliced long strips of haunch, which she hung to dry.

Agon said, "I must go to the Earth Mother now."

"Eat first. You must be strong."

"I am strong enough. Give me the thing I gave you."

She took the wrapped thing from her belt pouch. "When you have given this to her, I will be here waiting for you." She smiled at him. "The dream spirits came to me last night, as they did before. You came for me, and we were happy."

He heard Bird Man speaking: "Two great birds that take only one mate. One waits." But the dream spirits had come to him, too, part of the storm. No man could see the Earth Mother and live.

He placed the wrapped object in his belt pouch. He could not leave her to wait for him after he died. "One thing more."

She looked at him, her eyes questioning.

"I cannot return from the Earth Mother."

Her eyes widened with sudden realization. She gazed at him with such sadness that he could not look at her. He stood up, reaching for the axe.

"Why must you die?"

"I killed a hunter in our tribe."

"No!" She opened her hands, her arms to him, offering her body. "Let me go in your place!"

"No."

"I want to die."

"I go alone. But I believe your dream. I will come for you sometime. Do you believe that?"

Her eyes were like Erida's, and he saw that she wept inside. "I know that you will come."

He gave her the good spear. "Keep this. It has strong magic."

She did not reply.

He turned away from her, moving quickly up the slope toward the peaks that loomed above. At the crest of the first hill he looked back. He saw her, a small, slim figure, standing by the pond.

18

The Earth Mother

AGON FOLLOWED THE stream up through the foothills, and at midday he came to the source of the water—a spring that gushed from the base of a vertical overhang. He circled the overhang and climbed higher, up the slopes of the mountains known as the Blue Hills. As he topped the first crest, he saw the entire range spread before him.

The mountains were massive, but in spite of their size no ice or snow covered their peaks. He knew then why they were called the Blue Hills: pine and spruce and fir covered their slopes. Gazing at the peaks, he sensed ancient and mystical power, a power not of stone and ice but of air and trees and light. He felt as he did when he stared into the face of the full moon as it rose above the horizon, floating mysterious and luminous in the shimmering night air.

Ahead two peaks of almost identical size and shape stood profiled against the sky, peaks resembling the upright breasts of a woman. He was to go to the waterfall at the base of the peaks. A valley and ridge lay between him and the twin peaks, between him and death.

He looked back the way he had come. The hills dropped away in a descending series of wooded slopes, and he tried to identify the place where he had left Eena. He thought, We could have been happy there together, but now I go to the Earth Mother.

He descended into the valley, then climbed to the crest of the ridge. The setting sun lay close to the horizon, and the tops of the twin peaks glowed in the last light. The valley below him lay hidden in shadows, dark and mysterious. He went down the slope and into a valley where trees grew so thick he could no longer see the peaks. Night came, and he lay down on the forest floor, the axe in his hand. He slept.

Agon awoke at first light and knew that Eena had come in the night. Her delicate scent still clung to the vegetation, and the imprints of her small sandals showed in the leaf mold beside him. Then he saw that the spear he had left with her lay on the trail he had come by, the spear pointing back toward their pond and cave. He called softly but heard no reply, and he searched quickly through the trees. Her trail showed how she had come to him and gone, and even before he felt of the pouch, he knew that the wrapped thing was gone.

Then he was running through the trees, toward the twin peaks, leaping over fallen branches and decaying logs, swerving around massive tree trunks, following her almost invisible trail. The sound of falling water reached him, and he ran toward the sound.

The waterfall sparkled in the morning sunshine, water tumbling through the air in a white cascade, the sound of its falling like women's voices—women quietly talking, laughing, singing.

Eena was not there.

Something watched him. Somewhere in the thick greenness of the surrounding trees unknown beings waited. He placed the spear and his axe on the ground.

Movement to his left. A figure came slowly out of the trees toward him, wrapped and hooded in a mantle of fur, the face invisible. Yet he felt its gaze from under the hood. The figure stopped a spear's length away, watching him, waiting. Power radiated from the figure like the warmth from a bed of glowing coals. He spoke:

"I come to the Earth Mother."

The figure remained silent, watching him.

"The girl was not sent. The Onstean gave me the wrapped thing."

Still the figure did not speak, but he sensed a strengthening of its power, as when coals flare up when the night wind sweeps over the tribal fire.

"Bring her back. I will go in her place."

The fur mantle moved, an arm motioning from side to side signalling *no.* The figure turned away from him.

"Ka raped her!"

The figure stopped, half-turning back toward him.

"Ka killed her people and then took her," Agon said. "She was a maiden, untouched."

The figure changed, a sudden strengthening of energy as when a branch bursts into flames. The figure faced him now. An arm moved under the fur, beckoning him. The figure turned and moved toward the forest, and Agon followed.

They went through the trees, moving fast, the hooded figure not looking back, turning to one side, then the other, following an invisible trail, going ever deeper into the woods while the light grew dim and dusky green, and a strange and ominous silence closed around them.

Finally the figure stopped. Dimly through the branches Agon saw the twin peaks rising above them.

The figure beckoned, and Agon moved forward.

A huge red eye glowed for a moment, and something roared, deep in the earth.

Terror melted his bones.

The hooded figure beckoned him closer. A wall of smooth stone rose before him, and in the face of the wall was an opening. The red eye glowed again, filling the opening, and the roaring issued from the opening.

"She is with the Mother." The voice was a woman's, a

voice filled with mystery, wisdom, sensuality, with things unknown to men.

Eena had entered here, into the terror, knowing she would die. Agon thought, She is stronger than any hunter, for we go in to the bull thinking we will live, but Eena went in here knowing she could not come back.

"She cannot come back this way. Find her. Go forward." The power of the woman's spirit enveloped him, strengthened him, willed him to enter the presence of the Earth Mother. "Sometimes She is merciful. Go now. Go quickly."

Agon slid through the opening. He stood in a wide passageway, and ahead of him the red light flared and darkened like distant lightning, and with the flaring came the terrible roaring. He approached a presence so awful and powerful that it was beyond his experience and understanding. He moved forward, and terror grew with each step, his body fighting to go back while his spirit fought to go forward. His magic was as nothing as he approached the Earth Mother.

He groped around a curve in the passage and entered an immense chamber, so huge, so limitless, that it seemed the hollowed center of a mountain. Then in the roaring, blinding redness, he saw Eena, a slender figure far below him, silhouetted against fire that billowed up beyond her. Her arms were raised to the flames, the gesture of a child coming to its mother.

He shouted her name, and Eena turned toward him.

He ran toward her. Abruptly the rock floor ended, and he understood why the hooded figure had said that Eena could not return; he stood on the lip of a vertical wall that dropped down into an abyss. Far below, the red flames reflected from black water.

Eena ran to the opposite edge of the water, her arms now stretched upward toward Agon. But the Earth Mother rose up behind her, grasping for her with arms of fire, calling Eena to her, a supreme being, goddess of primeval power who demanded the life and spirit of any who dared look at Her.

"Go forward." Erida and the hooded figure seemed to command him. And now Agon, stepping out over the edge, dropped down through the empty space below him. His feet struck liquid, and he sank deep into water, going down, down into the cold grasp of the water spirits.

He struggled upward, upward toward Eena and the Earth Mother.

His face emerged from the water. Eena knelt above him. He pulled himself out of the water, and she fell into his arms sobbing, crying, "Now you will die."

The Earth Mother roared up again, then sank back, the heat enveloping them.

"I will go to Her," Eena sobbed. "I will give Her the thing . . . not you. . . ." She held the wrapped thing tightly in one hand.

Agon pressed open her fingers and took the object from her hand. "I was sent by the Onstean. You must go back."

"We cannot go back." Eena clung to his hand. "We will die together."

Agon shouted at the Earth Mother. "Let her go! I come in her place!"

The Earth Mother roared, louder and fiercer than before, and they shrank back before her fury.

"Give this to Her." Stone Man's words commanded Agon.

The roaring died down, and the flame sank into the crack in the rock.

"Wait here. None said we should die." Agon ran to the edge of the crevasse where the Earth Mother lived. For a moment he looked into the depths, and he saw the swirling flame of the Earth Mother roaring up toward him. He threw the wrapped object into her grasping arms. "Save our people!"

He hurled himself backward as the flames billowed up and out, searing toward him as he and Eena dove into the water. He turned in the crimson water and came up beside Eena, holding her beneath the surface until the Earth Mother drew back and sank into the crevasse.

Erida's voice said, "Three."

They brought their heads above the water. Agon shouted to Eena above the roaring, "We are going to jump!"

"The Mother will take us together!"

"No. We are going across!" Agon grasped Eena's arms. "We wait until She appears three more times. Twice She is weak, then She is strong. Then we go!"

They hung by their fingers to the rock edge, only their faces above the surface. Twice more the flames leaped up, weaker, subsiding back into the crevasse. Then once again, the flames so violent this time that they hissed out over the water, forcing Agon and Eena to dive. They surfaced as the wall of fire drew back. The flames sank into the crevasse.

"Now!" They scrambled over the edge and with hands joined ran across the smoking stone toward the Earth Mother. They leaped up and out, over the abyss.

Their feet struck beyond the far edge of the chasm, and they ran forward as the flames exploded behind them, hurling them into the darkness of the mountain. Agon felt Eena's hand go limp, and he lifted her in his arms and staggered forward into the cool air of the passage as the Earth Mother roared behind them.

19

The Moon Spirit

AGON AND EENA came out of the mountain into twilight. Cool air bathed their faces, and they drew it gratefully into their lungs. The last rays of the sun shone on a cluster of white clouds in the east, turning them a brilliant pink against the deepening blue of oncoming night. The cool colors of evening were in soothing contrast to the red fire

... Earth Mother and the blackness of the passage they had followed after leaping over the chasm of flame.

They had seen the Earth Mother. They had given the wrapped object to Her. And they lived.

They stood on a flat shelf of rock, high on the side of the mountain. A wall of smooth stone dropped away below them.

"The Earth Mother has spared you."

They turned. The hooded figure stood in the opening from which they had come.

"You have done well. Now, there is one last thing. You will spend this night with us, thanking the Earth Mother."

The power of the hooded woman was like that of the flames in the mountain. They looked at each other, agreeing. Agon said, "We will do whatever you ask."

"Come with me, Eena." The woman turned to Agon. "Wait here."

Agon watched Eena and the hooded one as they entered the passageway. Eena looked quickly back at him, then they were gone, the touch of Eena's hand still warm in his, the fragrance of her body still in the air around him.

He looked out over the valley, the trees bathed in a faint mist that spread below the mountain peak. As he watched, the edge of the moon appeared on the eastern horizon, rising full and huge, its strange force growing stronger as the great orange disc loomed over the sharp peaks.

"Here is food and drink." A woman's voice came from the passageway. He turned. A wooden cup stood on a flat stone.

The cup contained a clear liquid, its aroma spicy and slightly pungent. He tasted it, and it was like the smell of springtime, filled with swelling buds, opening flowers, new grass. He drank, and it was like summer: ripe fruit, sweet hazelnuts, juicy berries. Its warmth spread through his body like the warmth of cooking fires in autumn with smoke spiraling up into the dusky golden air and the aroma of roasting meat enticing the hungry hunter.

The moon shone full upon him now, and he felt a renewing of strength as though he were a plant responding to the sun. A feeling of desire for Eena grew within him, passionate and unsatisfied, full of mystery and longing.

A voice echoed from the passageway. "Come."

He followed a dim figure down an unlighted passage, not the same way that he and Eena had come, and he realized that the mountain must be honeycombed with tunnels. They emerged into the night air where the moon glowed upon a glade surrounded by trees. A small stream flowed silver in the moonlight, and the air was heavy with the fragrance of flowers.

"Wait here." The shadowy figure disappeared, leaving him alone by the stream's edge.

On a flat rock by the water stood another cup of liquid. Agon tasted it, and it was like the first, but even more pleasant. He drank slowly, breathing its fragrance of sunshine and flowers. As he drained the cup, the moon slowly filled the sky, its power growing until a fierce yet tender longing flooded his heart.

A woman appeared, shimmering like moonlight on rippled water. She floated, swaying gently, coming to him.

Agon sensed the female spirit in her, the spirit of all things female calling to the male spirit, beguiling, seducing, loving, filled with desire and passion, ancient and unchanging.

The radiant face of the moon poured its light upon them, a shower of sparkling rays that entered his spirit, filling him with a passion that matched the female spirit. He saw eyes luminous as stars, skin lily white, shadows mysterious and enticing, all things calling him, calling his spirit to caress, to join, to enter.

Her voice was soft, sensuous: "Come, Agon, come, favored of the Mother. Come to me and join your spirit with Hers in the golden light of Her daughter. Learn from Her the happiness of love; learn what She desires; learn what

She can give; learn what you desire; learn what you can give. Come to me now."

He floated in the moonlight; closer, pressing, seeking, joining, finding, caressing, entering, floating together, weightless, tireless, formless; one with each other, pulsing, throbbing, surging, leaping, rising, soaring, flying into the light burst, high in the sparkling light, forever upward.

He lay motionless, alone by the stream in the moonlight. Had he slept or dreamed? All sense of time had left him so that he knew not whether a moment or a night and day had passed. He was filled with longing for Eena, longing more tender, more fierce than that of his dream.

Three figures approached, two robed in white, the center one clothed only in the sweep of her long hair, which shimmered golden in the moonlight. Eena. Her body slender and lovely, breasts firm and full, hips swelling gracefully above the curves of her legs. She smiled at Agon, her eyes telling her fear had ended.

One of the white-robed figures spoke: "The blood and seed of Ka have been washed away. Eena comes to you a virgin bride."

The other figure spoke: "The Mother knows no greater happiness than to have Her children love one another."

The first woman spoke again: "Will you take each other here in the place of the Mother while Her daughter the moon shines on you?"

"I will take her." Agon came to his feet.

Eena's voice was clear and unafraid. "I am his, now and forever."

"We give you three things," the second woman said. "Agon, leave yours in the place that you have found together, but let it be guarded by each of your spirits." She held out a small ivory figurine of a woman. Agon saw that the figurine was Eena.

Eena's eyes filled with wonder. "It is my mother."

"It is your mother, it is you, it is the you that could be."

The first woman fastened a leather belt around Eena's waist. "Eena, this belt is more powerful than you know. It is your mating belt, but much more. Keep it always with you."

The second woman gave a small wrapped object to Eena. "Give this to the Onerana of your new tribe." Sadness entered her voice. "Now we leave you. The Onstean have seen what comes. Love one another." The two robed figures turned and moved slowly toward the shadowy trees.

Eena held Agon's hand as they watched the white shapes disappear. The night was silent; no leaf moved, no bird called.

The moon power flowed over and into them, and Agon drew Eena into his arms. Her body against his, her breasts warm on his chest, the curve of her thighs enticing him. He kissed her eyes, her mouth, her throat, holding her to him as if never to let her go. Her body and lips were eager as she pressed against him, her breathing quickened as her arms tightened around him, and her scent of honey and flowers enveloped him. Agon caressed her, his hands telling her that the force and pain and violence she had known were no more.

They sank into the soft grass, joining in a throbbing, ecstatic union, and Agon knew that Eena was his forever.

They awoke in the night to discover a soft robe over them, and they joined again under its warmth. Eena's desire, her love, her passion, matched Agon's in their every movement, and Agon learned that his soaring into the sky with the moon woman had been only a preparation for his love with Eena.

They slept again in each other's arms under the moon as the water spirits called softly from the stream and the twin peaks of the Onerana stood guard over them.

20

The Figurine

WHEN THEY AWAKENED at sunrise, they found that Agon's weapons and Eena's tunic and sandals lay nearby along with a full food pouch. Eena glowed with joy, and she said softly to Agon, "I am yours now. You have given me such happiness that even if the death spirit takes me now I would only know sorrow because I had to leave you."

He stroked her hair. "You have given me that same happiness."

"The Earth Mother has mated us." She smiled, her face radiant. "Her helpers made me ready for you. They are wise, and they taught me much. They taught me that I could love you, how I could love you."

Agon saw in Eena's eyes that the moon women had indeed taught her much. She had been a terrified girl, ridden with shame and revulsion at the things Ka had done to her; now she was a woman, mature, unashamed, her eyes filled with wisdom and understanding.

She took the belt from her waist, giving it to Agon while she put on her tunic. Made of soft leather, the belt was braided in an intricate pattern that he did not recognize, but as he held the belt, the ibex seemed to leap on his chest.

Eena fastened the belt around her waist, turning so that Agon could admire it. "They have given me so much. . . ."

"They have given us both much, but best of all, they have given me you."

Eena lowered her head, tying her sandals. She stood and faced him. "You saved me from Ka. You took me safely through the fire of the Earth Mother. And you have brought me love such as I have never known. I will keep those things in my heart and love you, even when I am old."

"As I will love you." But as Agon picked up the axe and spear, he thought, we will not grow old. Ka is not dead, and the Onstean see evil coming. The hooded women know. We have been happy here, but Grae said the tribe may die. He spoke abruptly. "Grae does not know of Ka's tribe."

Eena's face showed her concern. "We must go to warn Grae." She picked up the wrapped object. "I am ready."

They left the robe behind and hurried through the trees toward the waterfall. They drank at the pool, then started back through the mountains toward the plain. They followed the stream down to their pool and cave, arriving in the late afternoon.

Eena exclaimed with joy at the sight of their secret place. She inspected the dried strips of deer meat hanging high above the ground. "These are cured. Now we have food for our journey back to your people."

They needed a second spear, and they searched the streambed until they found a suitable piece of flint. While Eena picked blackberries and caught crayfish, Agon set about making a spear point, using a hammer stone and a piece of deer antler to shape the flint. Eena came to watch his work.

"You bring magic from the stone."

"It is for you." He smiled at her. "It will be smaller than a man's spear, but it will be a magic spear. It will call the game to the spears of the hunters, and it will give strength to our arms when we fight with the enemies of our people."

In the morning, after they had eaten, they lit pine faggot torches and went into the cave with the figurine.

A winding passage led back into the hill, and they followed it easily, walking erect under the high ceiling. The air smelled dry and fresh, and the smooth walls exuded a feeling of good spirits. The passageway opened out, and they entered a large, high-ceilinged chamber. They raised their torches.

The walls and ceiling sparkled with light—shiny surfaces dancing in the flickering flames of the torches.

It seemed that the shapes and spirits of all the animals lived in the rock walls, waiting to show themselves, waiting to be called by the magic of a spirit strong enough to bring them into the vision of men.

"I can feel them," Eena whispered. She stood with her face raised to the lofty ceiling, her arms out as though reaching to embrace the glittering chamber.

Agon said, "They wait."

He took the figurine from his pouch, and the ivory was warm, alive.

Leave yours in the place you have found together. The white-robed figure was speaking to him from the twin mountains. He carefully placed the figurine in a niche in the wall so that the ivory woman looked out into the chamber, her face serene and beautiful.

The ibex leaped on his chest and vibrated in the axe handle. *Let it be guarded by your spirits.* The white-robed figure's second command.

The stone lay on the floor of the chamber. Soft and red, it fit Agon's hand, its spirit willing him to perform the magic. He saw the ibex above the figurine before the stone touched the wall. He moved the stone, and the ibex was coming out of the wall—curved horns, alert head, strong body, and quick legs appearing under his hand, the creature's form and detail growing more distinct with each movement of the red stone.

He stepped back. "Ibex! Be with her. Watch over her and guard her."

The ibex leaped in the torchlight, its eyes thanking him for bringing it out of the rock.

Eena took the red stone and touched it to the wall by the ibex, and the slender form of a doe came from the stone, standing close beside the ibex, facing in the same direction, the ibex and the doe joined in form and spirit.

She said softly, "Deer, be with the ibex!" and the doe leaped in the torchlight.

The face of the figurine contained a new magic now, a magic that would live forever in the darkness of the cave with the good spirits of the animals encircling her, the ibex and the deer guarding her.

Eena pressed close against Agon's side, and his arm encircled her.

Then Agon and Eena knew that their spirits would be united in life and death, even though the whole horde of Ka's demons might fight against them.

When Ka regained consciousness, he killed his three men who had let Agon and Eena escape into the Blue Hills. He left their spear-ripped bodies on the plain and ran raging back to Spear Mountain, carrying the severed head of one of the men.

He entered the foul chamber in the heart of the mountain where Kaan crouched, wrapped in his robe of human skin.

Ka held the head out, and Kaan grasped it greedily in his clawlike hands and ripped a great chunk of muscle from the face with his teeth.

Ka spoke: "Kill him who fights with the axe! Bring the woman to me!"

Kaan gnawed at the head. Blood dribbled from his mouth as he snarled like a gorging lion. He spoke: "Heads! Bring more heads!"

"You will have more heads. I will bring you the axe man's head. Tell me how to find him and the woman."

"Kill his people. Kill his men. Kill his women. Kill his children. They will come to your spear. Bring me their heads."

"Where are his people?"

"Bring me heads!"

"I will bring you a head when I find Axe Man!"

"Now!"

Ka growled savagely. "You are father of my father. But

you will not command me! I am chieftain! I will bring you heads when you tell me how to find the Axe Man and the woman!"

Kaan's red eyes glared beneath his headdress of curved black horns. "Bring me heads now, or I will bring my curse upon you!"

Ka raised his spear. "You will die before you can speak!"

The mountain moved. The rock floor of the cavern shuddered, and from deep in the earth came the sound of grinding rock.

Kaan raised his arms and clawlike hands. He spoke in an ancient unknown tongue, and Ka fell back in terror. "I will bring you heads. . . ."

"Now!"

Ka rushed into the huge, dank chamber where his tribe members cowered in terror among the filth and debris as the mountain shook. He seized a shrieking woman and threw her facedown on the shuddering floor; then, kneeling on her back, he cut off her head with his flint knife. Grasping the long hair, he ran back into Kaan's chamber and flung the dripping head before the bloodthirsty god of his people. Kaan snatched up the head, and the convulsion of the mountain ceased.

Ka wiped his knife on his breech clout. "Now tell me how to find the people of the axe man!"

Kaan fondled the woman's head. "Send for more warriors. Axe Man and the spear woman will come to the place of his people. Those who watch will tell me where they are. Bring me the heads of Axe Man and his people."

"The woman."

"Kill her."

"She is mine. Kala, Mate of Ka, Chieftain."

"No more. Axe Man has had her. Kill her."

"I want her alive. She must be Kala."

"Then take her again in the fire ceremony. Only then can she be Kala." Kaan held the severed heads of the man and the woman in his arms. "Fire will burn Axe Man from her."

21

The Old Ones

AGON AND EENA came out of the hills on the second day after leaving the cave. The deer meat had renewed their strength, and with two good spears Agon felt more confident about any future encounters with Ka's men. But as they approached the open plain, he had a premonition of evil.

"Ka will be watching the plain."

"We can run at night," Eena said.

"Ka wants you. He will watch at night." Agon pointed along the line of foothills. "A friendly tribe lives in the hills. If some of their hunters would cross the plains with us, you would be safer."

"I am safe with you."

"Not against all of Ka's men. Not against the evil one with crooked horns. Its power is too great."

Eena shuddered and moved closer to Agon. "Grae's power is greater."

"I hope so. We will go to Grae. But first we will find the Red People."

"The Red People! My father told us of them. He said they were good hunters, but quick to anger. We should never go near their hunting grounds."

"Not to hunt. But Grae knows their chieftain. We will ask for their help."

They kept in the shelter of the foothills, searching for the Red People, constantly on watch for Ka. They stopped that night in a small valley, low hills on either side.

They built no fire, but ate the dried deer meat and berries, then lay in their bed of ferns and leaves, watching the bright disc of the moon as it rose above the hills. Suddenly, Eena pointed to the summit of the closest hill.

Two motionless figures stood silhouetted in the moonlight. Human, but not human, strange and mysterious.

A moaning sound came from the hill, a sound so ancient and primeval, so filled with sorrow and longing, that it seemed a cry of despair from the earth itself.

The figures were silent now, standing motionless on the hilltop in the moonlight. Then suddenly they were gone.

Agon and Eena lay silent, listening, hardly breathing, their weapons ready.

The cry came again, from a distance, faint and bloodchilling. Then even farther away. Then silence.

Eeena shivered. "What were they?" she whispered.

"The Old Ones."

The Old Ones. The Old Ones who had been on the earth since its beginning, who lived unseen in places where hunters never go, who ran in the darkness, avoiding any contact with the People. The Old Ones who wailed in the night, in the storm, in the blizzard. The Old Ones who cried at the moon.

"My mother told me of them. I have never seen them before."

"I saw them once," Agon said. "Orm and I were alone in the hills."

"Will they hunt us?"

"I think they have gone, but keep your spear ready." Agon still gripped his axe. "Grae says we should never take game where they hunt. They will not fight unless someone hunts them, but they are strong. They keep hidden from us and move away when we come."

"When they cry," Eena said, "it is as if I cried with them."

"They carry an ancient sorrow."

"What sorrow?"

"No one knows. But they cry at the moon. Grae told us that they came from the moon. Maybe they wish to return to the moon."

Eena stretched her arms toward the huge lighted face of the moon. "They cannot be evil."

"No."

"Did we come from the moon? I feel it call me when it is full."

"Grae said that we came from a place behind the moon. We can feel but not see that place. The moon makes us remember."

"It must be a beautiful place, for we remember when we see beautiful things here." She rested her head on Agon's chest. "It seems I knew you there, for when you hold me and we love, it is as if we return to that place."

Agon held her close in the moonlight.

"Let us go there now."

22

The Red People

THE NEXT DAY Agon and Eena came upon a shallow river that flowed out of the hills. They waded across, and as they climbed the opposite bank, four large redheaded men suddenly emerged from the underbrush, their spears pointed forward, their faces unfriendly.

Agon held his spear point up and raised his left hand in the friendship sign. Eena held her spear as did Agon and stood by his side as the men approached.

The largest of the men, his blue eyes hard and challenging, spoke: "Why do you come here?"

"We ask your help. Men from a strange tribe hunt us."

"What is your tribe?"

"Grae's. On the big river."

The man stared at Eena, then back at Agon, something different in his eyes now. "She is not of Grae's tribe."

"Her mother was Grae's half sister."

The man considered this. "Rok wants to see you. Give us your spears."

Agon and Eena walked forward with the men's spears at their backs. Rounding the river bend, they approached a cliff shelter where a group of armed men stared belligerently at them.

A bulky red-bearded man sat on a slab of stone in front of the men. He studied Agon and Eena for a moment, then gestured them forward.

The man held a spear half again as large as Agon's. He wore a cave-bear skin draped around his shoulders, the bear's head and open mouth protruding over the top of his head. The man's broad red face held a look of puzzled amusement. His voice was a deep rumble. "What have you found, Ror?"

"They say they came from Grae's tribe. For help. Someone hunts them." Ror laid the captives' spears in front of the bearded man.

The man glanced at the spears, then spoke to Agon and Eena.

"I am Rok. Chieftain. This one who brought you in is Ror. My son." He indicated Agon's finger. "Hunt leader?"

"Yes."

"What happened?"

"Evil came."

Rok held his own hands out. The tips of two of the fingers were missing. "Your name."

"Agon."

"Son of Grae?"

"Yes."

"Your mother?"

"Erida."

Rok's eyes grew more friendly. "A strong woman." He spoke to Eena. "You carried a spear."

"My father taught me to hunt." She spoke proudly, standing erect before Rok.

"His name?"

"He was Stig."

"Hunts alone. Hair like yours. Why say 'was'?"

"Ka killed him and my brother."

"Ka?"

Eena's voice trembled. "Chieftain of demons."

Agon added, "He takes heads."

Rok leaped to his feet, his eyes suddenly fierce. "Does he wear an arm bone in his hair? Hair in a big lump?"

"Yes."

"Where is he?"

"Agon struck him with his axe," Eena said. "They chased us on the plain after Agon took me from Ka's cave."

Rok turned to Agon, eyes burning. "You killed him?"

"He went down, but I think he still lives."

"That lump of hair! He's hard to kill. How many with him?"

"Four then, but Eena killed one as we fought."

Rok stared at Eena. "You killed?"

"Agon's spear broke during the fighting at the cliff top."

Rok sat down on his stone. "The cave. The cliff top. The plain." He looked quizzically at Agon. "Grae's people have few words. How many did you kill on the cliff top?"

"Four."

"And in the cave?"

"Two. One going in, one coming out."

Rok suddenly roared with delight. He rose to his feet and put one hand on Agon's shoulder, the other on Eena's, almost crushing her. He bellowed to his men, "Bring the people here! We'll drink and eat, and these two will tell us their story. I foresee a good night for feasting!"

They celebrated far into the night. Hunks of meat roasted over the fires, and the women brought out leather containers of fermented fruit juices into which the people dipped their wooden cups again and again. Rok had Agon and Eena sit next to him in the place of honor as he gulped the fermented juice from a giant cup and gnawed at huge chunks of meat. His laughter rang between the cliffs, and he called for the guests' cups to be refilled each time they drank.

Rok's people accepted Agon and Eena as their own when they heard the story of Eena's abduction and rescue. When Rok held up Eena's spear and shouted, "She killed one of them with this!" the people screamed their approval.

Ror lifted Eena onto a boulder by the fire and gravely presented her with her spear. Then the hunters raised their own spears to her, crying, "Spear Woman! Spear Woman!" They gave Agon's spear back, chanting, "Spear Man! Spear Man!"

But then Rok spoke directly to Eena, his voice grim. "Did you see any of our women when you were in Ka's cave?"

Agon saw the remembered terror in Eena's eyes. Her voice was low. "No women with red hair."

"Good. They're better off dead."

Agon's hand touched his axe. His voice was harsh. "Where did Ka come from?"

"No one knows," Rok replied. "We saw the first of them half a moon ago when an old man came to our camp. Ugly as a vulture."

Rok heard Eena's gasp and questioned her. "You saw him?"

"An old man came down the river trail toward us before Ka . . ." Eena shuddered. "He wanted to trade a black fur and some shells."

"For what?"

She looked at the ground. "For me. My father told him no."

"What next?"

"He ran back along the trail."

"He lived in the cave?"

"Yes. . . ."

Rok's voice grew savage. "We should have killed him! He brings death. He came here, to our camp, alone. We pitied him, welcomed him, for it is our way with strangers, as you see. We gave him food and drink. He smiled while he counted our women and our hunters, and he smiled when he left. Smiled like a skunk eating eggs out of tall grass." Rok shook his spear. "But he made one mistake. He thought we were all here, but Ror had gone out with a hunting party. When Ka attacked our camp next night, Ror and his men had returned. We drove Ka off, but he killed many of us and stole some of our women." Fury choked Rok's voice. "My youngest son was sentry. He warned us, then fought them as they came out of the night." He stared into his cup. "They took his head. Now they have gone to Demon Mountain, and you tell us they keep their shaman there."

"Can anything kill their shaman?" Agon asked. "I saw him asleep and felt his power. Ghosts and evil spirits danced around him. I wanted to sink my axe into his head, but he was too powerful. How can we kill him?"

"We'll ask Arvenios."

"Arvenios?"

"Our wizard." Rok pointed upriver, seemingly into the sky. "He lives up there. He'll want to talk with each of you."

"Does he have horns?" Eena asked.

Rok laughed. "Sometimes."

"Like Ka's shaman? I see him at night, and I cannot run. Is Arvenios like that?"

"Arvenios won't hurt you. Come with me tomorrow, both of you. You'll see."

"We must warn Grae of Ka and the old man," Agon said. "We should leave tomorrow."

Rok waved his cup in a half-circle toward his people. "Some of us will go with you, but we must kill game for the people who stay here. We'll visit Arvenios at sunrise, before the hunt. The next day we leave."

"We will not forget that you have helped us," Agon responded.

"Well-spoken." Rok nodded approval of Agon's words. "Soon the dancing will begin! Drain your cups and be ready!"

Eena sipped her drink, but Agon saw that she drank little of it. To him it tasted somewhat like the liquid he had been given at the Earth Mother's glade, but its effect seemed different; he experienced only a warming in his insides and a feeling of comradeship with Rok and his people.

The hunters gathered around their guests, shouting, rejoicing over Agon and Eena's battle with Ka. Ror suddenly lifted Eena to his shoulder and danced around the fire with her. "Spear Woman! Spear Woman!" he chanted in rhythm to his steps.

The other hunters raised the young women of the tribe to their own shoulders and danced while the women laughed, struggling with the men, kicking and screaming in mock alarm.

Rok thrust his elbow into Agon's ribs. "Grab a young one before they're gone."

Agon shifted his feet uneasily. He saw that Eena was wide-eyed in the firelight as Ror carried her.

"What if two men want the same woman?" he asked Rok.

Rok guffawed. "They fight for her."

"How?"

"Any way they choose."

Agon loosened the axe in his belt. He stood up and moved through the dancers to where Ror carried Eena, one huge hand around her ankles, the other over her knees.

"I will carry her now." Agon's voice was not loud, but suddenly every dancer stopped, the couples silent, watching.

Ror, heavier than Agon, regarded him with the same unfriendly look in his eyes as when they first met. "I carry her."

"I will fight you to see who carries her. Rok says it is the way of your people."

Ror carefully placed Eena on her feet, then he faced Agon. "It is our way. How will you fight?"

Agon shrugged. "Your custom. You decide."

Rok looked around at the other dancers.

The dancers shouted, "Bear wrestling!" "Ram butting!" "Horse kicking!" "Hitting!" "Wolf fighting!"

"Choose. You are our guest."

Agon regarded Ror's bulk. "What is wolf fighting?"

"Fight any way until one stays on his back." Ror's face was expectant.

Agon smiled. "I like that better than butting heads."

Ror laughed. "That may happen." He glanced at Eena. "One thing. This fight is not just for tonight. I want her."

Agon stepped closer to Ror. "Then I choose axes."

Ror looked into Agon's eyes, and he saw death. "I am not an axe fighter."

"I am."

The only sound was the crackling fire, the sighing wind. Eena's hand reached Agon's, her clasp firm and strong as she stood beside him.

Ror laughed and clapped Agon's shoulder. "She is yours. I would like to have her, but not with my head split." He glared at the other dancers. "If anyone tries to take the spear woman, he will have to fight me first. Our way." He waited, staring at each man in turn, then he turned back to Agon. "I should have known you were an axe fighter. Who taught you?"

"I never knew his name."

"I hear there is an axe song."

"Yes."

"Show me."

"It takes two men."

"Why two?"

"It is a ceremony."

"Teach me."

"When you come to our camp, Orm and I will perform it for you. Then decide if you want to learn the song."

Rok came forward from his seat by the fire. "I saw the axe song once. The axes moved so fast they could not be seen." He glared at Ror. "You were stupid to try to take her." Then he chuckled. "But wise enough to recognize an axe fighter."

He said to Agon, "Not all who carry an axe know how to fight with it. When I heard how you came in under Ka's spear with the axe, I knew you were an axe fighter. I was told that if an axe fighter uses the axe song in fighting, his strength and magic grow with every stroke of the axe."

Agon said nothing.

"I should have warned Ror," Rok said. "He is the only son I have left, and I am trying to teach him how to stay alive." He winked at Eena. "Agon may have to kill many over you. If you wish a more peaceful life, come to us."

Eena smiled shyly. "I will remember that." Then her face became grave. "I am only the daughter of a hunter, and could have been left to die as many females are. When men lift me onto their shoulders or put me on top of boulders like a goddess, the spirits may become jealous and punish us."

Rok frowned in thought. "We must not offend the spirits. But Ka took you and you lived. Ka's shaman has laid his claws on you and you lived. You saw the Earth Mother and lived. And you, a woman, have killed an enemy with your spear. The spirits can only be helping you."

Agon, seeing that Eena remained troubled, spoke then: "Grae and Erida will know what to do. Until we return to them, we will make offerings to the spirits. When we hunt tomorrow, I will offer the liver of any game I kill."

"Good. Now we celebrate!" Rok bellowed to the hunters and women who stood watching, "Eat and drink and dance! We have an axe man with us! Show him and the spear woman that the tribe of Rok is alive!"

A redheaded girl ran to Rok, and he lifted her above his head. "Where have you been hiding, my fox? The moon is still bright, and the cups are full. Dance with me awhile, and then we will perform the moon leaping in the shadows, and you will call the game to our spears!"

Later that evening, as Agon and Eena lay in the sleeping place given to them, Eena spoke her thoughts.

"I do not want to be a spear woman or any kind of a spirit thing; I want only to be your mate."

Agon replied, "We will return to our place in the hills after we warn Grae and help fight Ka's people. You will not need to be a spirit thing there."

Eena whispered, "Do you know the great birds that live in the river marsh? They take only one mate until they die. Will you take me like that, Agon, until I die?"

Agon took her in his arms. "I will take you like that."

Eena pressed close to him, and he sensed that she cried—so quietly that he could barely hear it.

"Why do you cry?" he asked gently.

Eena raised her face to his. "I cry because I am so happy."

Agon kissed her. "You must always be happy, and I will love and care for you like the great birds until we both shall die."

23

Arvenios

AT SUNRISE ROK led Agon and Eena up the river trail beyond the cliff shelter. Oak and beech of great height grew along the river, and Rok took a faint path into the midst of them. He stopped at the base of an ancient oak. "Arvenios lives up there." He pointed into the leaves above them.

High in the branches they saw a platform of slender logs and branches, carefully and cleverly fitted to look like part of the tree. Rok called like a bird, and in a moment another birdcall answered from above. Then an opening appeared in the platform, and a device of leather straps descended from the opening, slowly stringing out into a long double line with short wooden pieces tied between the lines at equal intervals.

Rok saw his friends' amazement and chuckled. "This is how we go to Arvenios! Come up after me, but only one at a time." He climbed up the lines, his hands and feet on the wooden crosspieces, climbing quickly and easily for all his bulk. "Come up," he called down from the platform, his red hair and beard like some great gaudy bird.

Agon ascended the hide ladder, surprised at the ease of the climb. Eena followed, hesitant at first, then nimbly and lightly. As she climbed, a feeling of returning to an ancient homeland came to her, and when she stepped onto the slightly swaying surface of the platform among the green leaves, she felt a sense of peace and tranquillity.

A man stood on the platform at the doorway of a small hut of branches and hides. He was not old as Eena had expected, but young and beardless with long red hair. His eyes were blue as Rok's, but serene, without Rok's fierceness. His voice had a peculiar depth. "I am Arvenios. The son of Grae and the daughter of Stig honor me." He smiled at them. "Let us talk."

They sat on the platform, and Arvenios began by addressing Agon. "Rok told me you killed six of Ka's men, rescued this woman from Ka's cave, and brought her back from the hands of the Earth Mother. People will tell of such feats through all the coming generations, and I honor you for your bravery. But now I would learn of Ka's shaman, for he threatens both our tribes." He asked Eena, "Will telling me about him bring too much sorrow to your spirit?"

"This is such a peaceful place," she answered, "I would not bring his spirit here."

"He is powerful in his mountain, but has little strength here. I need not know what he demanded of you. But tell me what he looked like, what he wore, what he said, what he carried."

"He had crooked horns."

"Of what creature?"

"None that I know. Black and twisted horns."

"What more?" Arvenios asked, his voice intense.

"He had claws."

"Not hands?"

"Like hands . . . but more like claws . . . sharp and cold . . . when he . . ."

"His robe?"

"Skins . . ." She hesitated. ". . . but not from an animal. . . ."

Agon spoke. "I saw. His robe was from the skin of men."

"What did he carry?"

"A bowl." Eena bit her lower lip.

"What kind of a bowl?"

"Bone."

Rok growled one low word. "Skull."

Arvenios looked at Rok, then back at Eena. "What was in the bowl?"

Eena seemed unable to speak.

Agon answered for her. "Blood." He pointed at the scar on Eena's arm. "Eena's blood and Ka's blood. They made her drink that blood."

Arvenios did not look at Eena. "What more was in the bowl?"

The tree swayed, and the ground below moved slowly back and forth. Eena, trembling, took Agon's hand.

"What happened next?" Arvenios spoke softly.

"They held me . . ."

Arvenios's forehead beaded with sweat. "Enough. Tell me of the shaman. Did he speak?"

"He made sounds."

"What kind?"

"Hissing. Like a great snake hissing."

Arvenios's face grew pale as death. "Did you hear his name?"

"They called a name . . . when he entered from the darkness. . . ."

Arvenios's voice was barely audible. "What was his name?"

"Kaan."

Grasping the small bag that hung at his neck, Arvenios spoke, but in a strange language. Then he seemed to die, slumping down limply on the platform.

"His spirit leaves him," Rok said.

"Will his spirit return?" Agon asked. Arvenios looked the way Dream Man looked after the spinning dance.

"Maybe." Rok nudged Arvenios's limp form. "Always before, it has come back. But who can tell about shamans?" He spoke now to Eena. "Do you know what Arvenios said? He jabbered in a language that could have been bird talk for all I knew."

Eena stared at Arvenios. "I understood a little . . . the women who served the Earth Mother taught me. . . ."

"What did he say?"

"He said, 'He is the most powerful.' "

But Eena did not tell Rok or Agon what else Arvenios had said in the strange language. She told herself that she must have been mistaken. It seemed that Arvenios had said, "Only a goddess could live."

24

The Journey

EARLY THE NEXT day, after the hunt, those going to Grae's camp gathered at Rok's shelter; along with Rok and Ror, ten hunters. Agon looked at the surrounding hills. "Do you leave enough hunters to protect your women?"

Rok pointed upstream. "In that canyon two men can hold off a tribe. The women will be safe."

As Rok spoke, Arvenios approached carrying the green branch of an oak tree. Rok greeted him good-naturedly. "You have come back."

Arvenios's face showed weariness, but he spoke lightly. "I would meet with Grae."

"The trip will be hard," Rok said. "Likely some fighting."

Arvenios studied his tree branch. "I foresee other things." He spoke to Eena. "The hunters tell that you brought good luck in the hunt."

"I did nothing."

Arvenios shook his head. "They tell how game threw themselves on the spears." He spoke aside to Agon. "She has more power than she knows. We must get her to Grae's camp. The danger is great, and there is little time."

Rok gestured to his hunters, kissed the redheaded girl, and gave a final order to those who remained behind: "Keep a guard day and night. We will be back when we have killed Ka and all his miserable stinking tribe."

They began the journey across the plain.

Arvenios grew more and more agitated as they traveled toward Spear Mountain. He carried his tree branch before him and muttered in his strange language, and Agon sensed his uneasiness and apprehension. When they camped by a tree-circled pond that night, Arvenios disappeared among the trees.

After they had eaten, Rok and the hunters settled down for the night by the pond's edge. Agon and Eena sought a place by themselves, a little distance away under the trees. Arvenios had not reappeared.

In the night Agon awoke. Movement in the darkness. As his hands tightened on his axe and spear, he felt Eena move beside him, grasping her spear. Something large and deadly moved silently toward them.

The night wind shifted, bringing the scent to their nostrils.

Cat! White fangs and yellow eyes, tawny body pressed to the ground, moving soundlessly, muscles rippling under the sleek hide, long tail flat in the grass, twitching. Talons extending from the great paws, sharp and curved, ready to tear and hold while the long, spearlike teeth drove into the neck. Shadows in the bushes, moving silently.

A stallion cried out, a challenging call reverberating in the night air. Then a stamping of hooves and again the wild cry. Then whinnying, the sound of a horse herd running, hooves beating the earth, racing away across the plain.

The cat smell lessened, only faint traces clinging to leaves and grass.

Rok spoke from the hunters' place. "They were close."

Another voice: "Knife teeth."

Arvenios's words seemed to come from above them. "One finds it difficult to sleep. Why do hunters shout in the darkness?"

"Go to sleep, Arvenios," Rok said. "I'll explain it to you in the morning."

The hunters talked among themselves, but in a little while they quieted and slept again.

Eena, pressing close to Agon, whispered, "The moon shines on the plain. I heard horses, but I could not see them."

"I did not see them either," Agon replied. "Strange things move in the darkness."

In the morning Arvenios seemed amazed at the hunter's description of the night's happenings. He wondered aloud: "The night wind rustled the trees. Perhaps two branches scraped together, sounding like a stalking cat?"

Rok watched Arvenios from the sides of his eyes. "You would have made a juicy meal for the branches."

Arvenios laughed, then asked Eena, "Did those loud ones let you sleep?"

Eena looked at Agon before she spoke. "My father said

that the great cats do not like human smell. Those cats last night were stalking us until the horse chieftain called."

Rok gestured toward the hunters. "My hunters smell like horses."

Arvenios sniffed the air. "Worse." He winked at Agon. "Now you know why I sleep in the trees."

Agon noticed that the hunters laughed, not angry at Rok or Arvenios. "We should have all slept in the trees," he said. "The cats were ready to leap on us."

Arvenios's face became serious. "Worse things may happen," he told the hunters. "We come nearer the mountain. When I tell you 'Do this,' or 'Don't do that,' you must listen."

The hunters guffawed. "Arvenios commands us."

Rok shouted at his men, "You juice-soaked, knuckle-walking apes will obey, or I'll bash your skulls! Do you hear?"

Ror yawned. "We hear. Our spears are ready. Let Ka come. We have fought him before."

A stallion whinnied, then the sound of galloping horses came from the plain beyond the water hole. The men stared. No horses were on the plain.

Arvenios raised his oak branch. "When Ka came before, he was far away from the mountain where comes his strength, far away from Kaan, his shaman. Now we approach that mountain, approach Kaan. Our magic must be strong. Believe me. Do as I say, or you may die."

Ror picked at his teeth with a fingernail. "There was no horse herd. It was a trick."

Rok clubbed Ror with a massive fist and sent him reeling back into the arms of the hunters. "It was magic, you ignorant lout! Now shut up and get ready to travel!"

Arvenios drew Agon and Eena aside. He spoke to Eena. "You carry something from the Earth Mother."

Eena stared at him in surprise. "In my pouch. How did you know?"

Arvenios continued without a direct reply. "And you wear the belt She gave you."

"My wife belt."

"It is more than that." Arvenios's blue eyes were piercing. "The Onerana will know." He responded to her perplexed look. "You are chosen."

Eena drew closer to Agon. "I only want to live with Agon in the hills."

Arvenios's eyes did not relent. "Our tribes will die unless we overcome Kaan. Grae is powerful, and I have certain strengths, but even together, we are not strong enough. If you help us, we may have the power to survive."

"I have no power. . . . I could not move . . . when Kaan . . ."

"But you lived! Others would have died, their spirits leaving them in terror." Arvenios touched Eena's belt. "The Earth Mother knew what you are." He held up his oak branch. "Certain things increase our power. Mine is the tree. Agon's, the axe. Yours, the spear and the belt."

"No. I feel no power. I will offend the gods."

"Believe me! You have power!" Arvenios grasped her arm. "Keep the belt and spear with you always."

"Always?" Eena's face reddened. "The women of Agon's tribe will laugh if I wear a belt in the bathing place."

"They will not laugh. Erida will know and help you."

"I pray that she will."

"Good." Arvenios turned to Agon, "You have a friend who knows the axe song?"

"Yes. Orm."

"The axe magic may be stronger than any of us. Will you show us the axe song?"

"We will," Agon repied. "But Ka has demons helping him."

"He does. But demons can be defeated if our magic is stronger." Arvenios raised his branch. "Come now. Rok is pawing at the ground."

As they rejoined the group and continued across the plain, Rok's voice assumed its good-natured roar. "I saw Agon fingering his axe. What magic are you planning?"

Arvenios answered lightly. "We spoke of simple things. Trees and spears and axes."

By evening they reached the marsh where Agon and Eena had hidden. The cone of Spear Mountain seemed to tower over them now. Arvenios, pale and tense, refused to sleep in the grass, but stood watching the mountain as daylight faded and darkness swept over the plain.

Then they heard something running, coming fast toward them from the direction of the mountain.

"A horse galloping." "No, a bison." "A great stag." "A bull." The hunters crouched in the grass, faces perplexed, spears ready as the running thing neared them.

The running sound grew louder, pounding across the hard ground of the plain, splashing through the marsh, springing toward them. There! A huge, unearthly creature loomed over them in the dim light.

Arvenios shouted, waving his tree branch. "A Hell Beast! Let it go through! Don't use your spears!" His voice was lost in the roaring of the black form that came bounding over the hummocks, feet throwing up a spray of water, eyes white and wild. Then the form was upon them and among them and in them, and the roaring and splashing and pounding exploded around them. Then it was gone.

Arvenios stared after the running, splashing thing; then, at the dark cone of Spear Mountain, and he began speaking in his strange tongue.

Rok's voice was almost a whisper. "A Hell Beast . . ."

Arvenios swayed, as though about to fall. "He is too powerful . . ." He recovered himself and spoke to the hunters. "None threw a spear?"

Silence. Then Rem answered, "I did." He looked at Rok, then at Arvenios, his eyes pleading. "I missed. It still ran." Now Rem's hands went to his throat, he swayed forward, and he fell on his face in the marsh grass.

Arvenios knelt over Rem and looked into his eyes.

"He is dead."

Eena made a sound of sorrow, her hand tightening in Agon's.

Rok bent over Rem, then he shouted at his hunters, "Now you know! Now you believe!"

Ror wiped his hand across his eyes. "We believe."

"Never throw your spear at a Hell Beast!"

"Never."

Arvenios closed Rem's eyes. "Now they know."

"Call his spirit back so we can bury him," Ror demanded.

"There is no way," Arvenios told him. "His spirit will be a ghost." The hunters drew back from Rem. Arvenios looked across the plain toward Spear Mountain. "Kaan has called Rem's spirit to him." He rose to his feet. "Kaan has used his power twice. We should travel now before his strength comes again."

"How far to Grae's camp?" Rok asked Agon.

"Two days' running."

Rok raised his spear. "We keep on. The moon will soon rise. Show us the way, Agon."

They ran through the night while the waning moon crossed the sky and dropped toward the western horizon. At dawn they stopped at a water hole to drink and rest.

While the hunters noisily splashed in the water, Arvenios said to Eena, "If you go into the water, remember to take your belt and magic spear."

Rok rose from the water, snorting like a horse. "Magic spear?"

Eena blushed. "Arvenios says my spear is magic."

"We all need magic spears," Rok growled, "to kill Ka."

Arvenios looked thoughtfully at Rok, then said to Eena, "Will you touch their spears? Give them your magic?"

Eena's eyes sought Agon's.

Agon shook his head. "Kaan will see her. . . ."

Rok pointed to the mountain, now even closer. "He sees all of us. Let him see the magic come to our spears!"

Arvenios nodded. "We need her magic. Kaan is growing stronger again. I feel it."

Agon looked toward the mountain. For an instant he imagined a giant horned thing standing on its peak. He touched the ibex on his chest, felt the ibex quivering in the axe handle. He held out his spear to Eena.

"My spear asks for your magic."

Eena stretched one hand slowly and hesitantly toward Agon's spear, and when her fingers touched the flint point, her eyes closed and she swayed as if she would fall. Then, as Agon watched her, he saw the power of the Earth Mother come to her: her body straightened and strengthened, her eyes opened, and in them he saw the ancient strength of the female spirit. As her hand closed on his spear point, he felt the magic flowing from her to him as though her hand and the spear led a stream of cold fire into his spirit.

Arvenios shouted, his voice triumphant, and he leaped into the air, shaking his tree branch. "Now horned one, see and tremble, for the spear woman has received her power!"

Then, while Eena stood by the water hole, the hunters came to her, first Rok and Ror, then the others, each holding out his spear. And Eena grasped each point, letting her magic flow into the spear and the hunter.

When she had touched each spear, Arvenios spoke to the hunters. "See her belt! The belt of a goddess. The Mother Herself gave the belt to the spear woman. You need no longer fear Ka and his tribe; the Spear Goddess has given you such power that nothing can stand against you."

Rok's hunters roared in excitement and shook their spears at the mountain, challenging and taunting Ka and his shaman while they leaped and circled around Eena, splashing in and out of the water hole as they danced.

Eena stood beside Agon as the hunters circled, and he felt her sway against him; she had given much of her strength to him and the hunters. He took her cold hand, willing his own strength to her, and he felt warmth return to her fingers.

"The axe man has more magic than the spear woman,"

she said. Her head touched his shoulder, lightly resting on it.

The ground trembled—only a little—the dancing hunters unaware. But Agon felt Eena's hand tense in his, and he saw that Arvenios, too, had felt the earth move. As they stared at one another, Agon knew that the power they fought was only waiting, and that all of their magic could not prevail.

Demons

25

Blood on the Stone

ROK'S HUNTERS KILLED two young aurochs bulls as they crossed the plain, wanting to bring meat to Grae's camp. As they approached the river gorge, Agon's hunters ran to meet them, leaping and waving their spears in welcome. Agon saw that his young brother, Alar, was with them.

Alar was the first to reach them, his eyes expressing his joy as he embraced Agon. "I knew you would come back!"

He had barely spoken before the hunters surrounded them, laughing and shouting, mauling Agon. Orm clasped Agon's arms, his voice strangely husky. "You have returned, axe brother." Then Orf lifted Agon high in welcome while Ord pranced like a horse, and the others danced around them.

Agon observed that Alar now carried a light axe, patterned after his own and Orm's. Orm smiled. "We took this one into our band to keep him out of trouble. Someday he may learn to use the axe." He spoke to Rok and his men, raising his hand in welcome. "Grae welcomes you! We are to bring you to our camp."

Rok raised his own hand in the peace gesture. "I am Rok." He swept his arm around toward his men. "These are my hunters. This big one is my son, and this one that looks like a red bird is my wizard." He winked at Orm. "Somehow they stumbled across some scrawny bulls, too old to run, too tough to eat. The meat is worthless, but maybe you can use the hides."

"The game is young and fat. The magic of your spears is strong." Orm said the hunter's praise words, and Agon's hunters agreed, nodding their heads in admiration, speaking highly of the meat and the skill that must have been shown in obtaining it.

Eena had been standing behind the hunters. Now Rok drew her forward. "The spear woman has given her magic to our spears."

Stig's daughter. Spear Woman? The hunters gazed at her in wonder, remembering a shy girl. Now a beautiful woman stood before them. Az slapped his spear handle. "I was going to ask Stig for her." He looked around. "Where is he?"

"He is dead." Agon felt Eena's hand slip into his as he spoke. Something seemed to move silently in the grass.

"Dead?" Az backed away, aware of the joined hands.

Arvenios spoke for the first time since the two groups had met. "Evil has come."

The hunters stared at Arvenios, their hands going to their totems. Arvenios pointed toward Spear Mountain with his tree branch. "Even now the evil watches us."

Orf spoke. "The game runs from the mountain."

"Ka," Rok growled.

Agon asked Orm, "He has not attacked yet?"

Orm's face showed his puzzlement. "Attacked? And who is Ka?"

"Their leader." Agon grasped Orm's arm. "Have you seen strange hunters?"

"None." Orm replied. "Only an old man. An old man with his hair in a knot."

"Krak!" Rok's voice boomed above the angry shouts of his hunters. "Where did you see him?"

"He came to our camp. We gave him food."

"When?"

"Yesterday."

"Now they come!" Rok lifted his spear. "Quick! Warn Grae!"

They ran toward the river and the cliff shelter, the hunters looking over their shoulders at the dark mountain as they ran. The evening shadows were creeping across the plain, and Agon felt the power of the horned and clawed thing strengthening with the coming darkness.

They approached the cliff top and the ancient black stone of Grae's people. The Stone, flat on top and almost square, was as long on each side as two men, and it rose out of the surrounding softer rock as high as a man's chest.

Arvenios stopped, staring at the Stone as Rok and the hunters ran down the cliff path. Agon, Eena, and Alar waited for Arvenios.

"The Stone." Arvenios's voice was filled with awe. "The Stone of Beginning."

Agon nodded. "Our people have lived by it almost since the beginning. Once we left it."

"But you came back." Arvenios cautiously reached his hand toward the Stone, as to a bed of coals. He touched the surface, then drew his hand back as if burned. He began speaking in his strange language, then walked slowly around the Stone, sunwise, and at each side he bowed down, as though to a chieftain. When he completed the circle, he seemed increased in strength, and his eyes burned with a strange blue fire.

He spoke to Agon. "Now we must see Grae."

They went down the path, Agon leading, to the fire in front of the cliff shelter where Grae and the people waited. Erida and Ara ran to Agon with their arms outstretched and embraced him, then Eena, their faces wet with tears of happiness.

Erida said to Eena, "You are as beautiful as your mother." She touched Eena's head. "Your hair shines like the sun." She hugged Eena again, then gazed into her face. "Will you come into our tribe and let me take you as my daughter? You have suffered much, but now you have come home."

Eena came into Erida's arms as she had come into her mother's, and Erida held Eena to her breast, stroking her hair, comforting her as they both cried.

The women gathered around, touching Eena gently, stroking her hair, their own eyes wet.

Grae said to Agon, "You live. Has the thing been done?"

"Yes."

Grae clasped Agon's arms, love and pride in his eyes, and for a moment he appeared to smile at Agon. Then his face took on its usual stern appearance, impassive and strong as a mountain crag. "Rok has told me of the invaders. We have sent hunters to guard all sides of the camp." He turned to Arvenios. "I have waited long to meet you."

Arvenios made the same motion to Grae as he had to the tribal stone. "And I have waited long to meet you. My father told me of you." Grae held his staff as Arvenios held his tree branch, and as they faced each other, something flashed between the branch and the staff, as a ray of sunshine flickers through the leaves of the forest.

"We will talk soon." Grae moved toward Erida and Eena, his voice kind as he welcomed Eena: "We are your people now. Rok has told me of your father and brother. If we can, we will give their spirits rest."

Eena did not speak, but knelt before Grae with her head bowed and her hands clasped before her. Grae gently touched her head, but as he did so, Agon saw a look of wonder flash in his eyes. Grae and Eena seemed to change for an instant, as though their bodies had suddenly been illuminated by some unseen light, strengthened by some unknown power.

Arvenios spoke softly in his strange language. Power and magic radiated among Grae, Eena, Erida, and Arvenios in an invisible shimmering circle, so strong that Agon felt the ibex leaping on his chest as if the creature lived. He touched the handle of his axe, and a shock of magic leaped up his arm and raced into his body, spreading power through every muscle.

Grae drew back from Eena, staring at her belt and spear, then at Arvenios, and Arvenios nodded in a tiny motion unnoticed by the people. Erida also nodded, a look in her eyes that Agon had never seen before—an expression of wonder, but also of secret triumph, fulfillment, ancient mystery.

Grae spoke to Eena again, a new tone in his voice. "Do you have anything that belonged to your father or brother?"

Tears filled Eena's eyes. "Nothing. Ka's people . . ."

Grae raised his hand. "I see another way. Your father's totem is the stag. What is your brother's?"

"The horse."

"Strong spirits." Grae was watching Eena's face.

Eena spoke sadly, yet proudly. "They fought Ka's men with spears in their bodies, their blood spurting out."

Grae nodded. "Will you help us call their spirits back?"

"I will do anything."

"Others will help, too. We must act now, before darkness."

Eena stretched her arms toward Grae. "My mother's spirit cries for my father and brother. Take my spirit if you will. . . ."

Grae touched her arm, gently. "No. Not now. Your spirit is needed here."

He spoke to Agon. "Bring the spirit heads to the Stone." Then he called to the people, "Bring torches, many torches, up to the Stone, quickly! We will hold the darkness back!"

Agon ran through the milling people to the fire. He seized a burning faggot and ran into the cliff shelter. The opening was in shadow, and as he ran back beneath the great stone slab of the overhang, the torch flame illuminated the tribe's ancient dwelling place with its limestone ceiling, smoke-stained by the winter fires of uncounted generations of bison hunters.

The spirit heads lived in the farthest recess of the overhang, the sacred place of the animals. As Agon entered the area, he felt the power of the creatures that waited there. They stared at him in the torchlight, their hollow eye sockets filled with the mystery of their spirits, the white bones of their skulls clean and shining, their teeth longer and stronger than when they had cropped at the grass of the plain, the horns on the split-toed ones rising in branches and sharp-tipped curves. The combined power of their spirits pulsated around him, the skulls alive, their eyes watching him as he came into their sanctuary.

Agon lifted the stag skull with its branching antlers, and he sensed the creature leaping in his hand. The horse spirit was already galloping when he touched it, a stallion with raised head and flaring nostrils, racing over the plain with its herd.

He uttered the hunter's words of reconciliation to the animals: "Thank you for your lives." Carrying the skulls, he ran back toward the entrance and into the dimming light of the gorge.

The people were still climbing the cliff path, their torches strung like giant fireflies above him. He ran up the trail, swerving around the people on the narrow track until he reached the cliff top, where the front climbers, their torches held high, were gathering in a large circle around the Stone. He brought the skulls through the circle to the Stone, where Grae waited with Arvenios, Erida, Rok, Eena, Zur, Ara, and old Unser. Three and three and two. He, Agon, would make the magic number.

Agon placed the two skulls in Grae's hands, and Grae carefully laid them on the Stone, their hollow eyes looking down the river gorge toward the distant peak of Spear Mountain. Grae then took Eena's spear and laid it beside the skulls, pointed toward the mountain.

Eena spoke to Erida in a low voice. "Rok's hunter died on the plain. Can Grae call his spirit?"

Grae heard. He explained to Eena, "Those taken by the Hell Beast must be called back in a different way. And your father and brother have wandered long and far; we must not wait."

Grae had those persons at the Stone join their hands in a circle around the black bulk: Eena between Grae and Arvenios, Ara between Zur and Agon, and Erida between Rok and Unser. Zur had only stared at Agon upon seeing him, and now he ignored the hunter, watching Grae, Arvenios, and Eena instead.

They circled around the Stone three times, slowly, sunwise. When Grae was on the side of the Stone opposite Spear Mountain, he stopped. "Hunt leaders open the circle. Let the spirits enter."

Ara swung in between Agon and Arvenios, leaving Zur and Agon at the two ends of the broken circle. The opening faced the mountain and the place where Stig and Eran had been killed.

Grae shook his rattle and called to the homeless spirits of Stig and Eran, reminding them that Stig's mate came from the tribe and that the people welcomed them. He invited the spirits to come to their totems that lay on the Stone. Then he waited.

No sound. Grae's craggy face grew bleak and stern under the bison horn headdress, his gaunt but powerful frame like an ancient lightning-blasted tree. Agon felt the magic strength of the broken circle, a huge heart pulsing, its power increasing as each member sent his or her strength into it.

Nothing. No sound. No flight of spirits into the circle.

"He is too strong," Arvenios whispered. Grae looked at him, and their eyes met, agreeing.

Grae motioned to Erida. She went to the skulls and rubbed red powder on them, the white bone becoming blood-colored in the last rays of the sun. She placed the skulls back on the Stone, and again they waited.

Again, no sound, no sign of the spirits. The stag skull and horse skull sent long, grotesque shadows across the surface of the Stone as the sun sank lower.

Grae and Arvenios climbed onto the Stone and held the skulls skyward, Grae with the stag, Arvenios with the horse. The others closed the line so that Eena was between Ara and Unser, while Zur and Agon were still at the open ends. Grae raised his staff in his free hand, Arvenios raised the oak branch in his, and they faced the distant mountain, chanting together, calling Stig and Eran. They ceased the chanting and waited. Nothing.

The people began to stir, looking over their shoulders into the approaching darkness, touching their totems. The edge of the sun was barely visible above the horizon.

Grae's tall figure was rigid, his arms with the skull and staff raised to the sky, his bison horns shining in the last light. He looked down at Eena. "They call for you."

Eena gazed upward at the skulls. Then she stepped up onto the Stone, next to Grae. "I am ready."

Grae placed the stag head at her feet, and Arvenios did the same with the horse head. Grae held out a knife. "Blood will give the power."

Eena took the knife and slowly raised it.

Suddenly, Zur leaped onto the Stone and took the knife from Eena. He drew the knife down his arm, forming a red line. Blood welled from the cut, dripping on the two skulls while Zur stood motionless and proud, looking into Eena's eyes as the blood ran.

The stag skull and horse skull shone wet and red, and the Stone and Eena's feet were spattered with the blood. The bleeding slowed, and still Zur stared at Eena. Then he handed the knife back to Grae. "A hunter's blood calls the hunters."

Grae lifted the skulls and gave them to Eena. She held the bloody spirit heads out toward the distant spot where her father and brother had died.

Silence.

Then, far down the river valley, a stag called, and a young stallion answered.

Eena stretched upward, lifting the skulls toward the sound, and the calls came again, louder and closer. Something moved in the air, rushing toward the rock from the river valley, and the sound of running filled the air. Then Eena cried out, and the two skulls glowed alive in her hands as she fell forward. Grae and Arvenios supported her, lowering the spirits of Stig and Eran to the Stone while something howled soundlessly in rage in the shadows.

26

The Onerana

After Stig and Eran's spirits were laid to rest in the burial ground, the people returned to the cliff shelter, jubilant and secure after the demonstration of the power of their shamans. The women cooked the meat that Rok had brought, and the feasting that followed, coupled with the excitement of having visitors, kept the camp awake long into the night.

Erida led Eena and Agon to a secluded bower, a traditional sleeping place for newly mated couples. Eena exclaimed with delight as she looked into the bower. The light of the distant tribal fire flickered softly through the branches, while the leafy walls and the sweet grass and ferns on the floor filled the place with a woodsy fragrance.

Erida hugged Eena before she left them, and she whispered something to her. To Agon she said, "I will come for Eena after midnight."

He protested. "She has not slept for two days."

Erida's eyes reflected the firelight. "We will not keep her long." Then she smiled at Agon. "Sleep all day tomorrow if you choose." She touched his arm. "You have done well."

After Erida left them, Eena took Agon's hand. "Erida is my mother now. I must do as she asks."

"I want you here."

"I am here now." She drew him to her. "It is still long until midnight. . . ."

When the moon passed the curve of the cliff wall, Erida came to the bower and gently awakened Eena. Agon woke with his axe in hand, but Erida whispered to him, "We will bring her back soon," and he lay back in the grass and ferns.

Erida led Eena along the river to a thick grove of oak. In the near-darkness they went deep into the wood, and they entered an open glade where shadowy forms stood in a circle, hooded and motionless in the moonlight. The circle opened, and Erida brought Eena into the center, the circle closing around them. Eena felt the waves of magic around her like a pulsing sun.

Erida faced her. "You have brought the sacred object?"

Eena took the wrapped thing from her belt pouch, silently holding it out to Erida.

"Tell us who sent it."

"One who serves Her."

Erida accepted the object. She held it a moment, then raised it toward the moon. "Daughter of the Earth, see the sign of the Mother. Help us guard and keep it. Strengthen our spirits and our magic. Protect our people. Our circle is not yet full. Guide us in the filling."

She lowered the object. "Name your spirits."

Womens' voices, one by one, called from the circle of figures. "Earth." "Moon." "Life." "Tree." "Air." "Love." "Blood." And finally, "Death."

Erida spoke again. "The circle is not full. Will she fill the circle?"

A voice replied. "She has been given power by the Mother."

Another voice said, "She has not passed through the tribal rites."

Erida turned to Eena. "You went to the Mother?"

"Yes."

"Did she receive the sacred object?"

"Yes. But Agon, not I, gave it to her."

"Did you help Agon bring the sacred object?"

"Yes."

"Why?"

"I wanted to die in his place."

"Did Her helpers teach you?"

"Yes."

"And they gave you the belt?"

"Yes."

Erida looked around at the hooded figures. "Is this enough?"

The voices answered in unison, "It is enough."

"Name the signs."

The voices spoke as one:

"The Onstean saw her before she came."

"She has been taken into the underworld and has escaped."

"She has killed a demon."

"The Mother has spared her."

"She wears the belt."

"She brings the sacred object."

"She has shown her power on the Stone."

Erida spoke again. "Seven signs. She is favored by the Mother."

A voice said, "We wait."

Another: "We die."

Erida faced Eena. "Will you come into our circle?"

"Whatever you ask, I will do."

"Then join hands with us."

Eena felt hands take hers, drawing her into the circle of dark figures. As the hands touched hers, a strange force permeated her body, a power flowing in through her hands and arms, ancient and mysterious, filling her with magic.

Erida spoke: "We are the Onerana, the Invisible Earth Spirit Women. Through our joined hands, learn the wisdom of the Onerana."

Then Eena felt the spirit of the Earth, the greatest of all the spirits: the Earth spirit flowing from the hills and mountains, the cliffs and valleys, the plains and woodlands. Strong, fertile, enduring forever.

The spirit of the air engulfed her, light and invisible, caressing her. Saying, "I am in your breath, the summer breeze, the night wind, the racing clouds, the black storm, the howling whirlwind, the shrieking blizzard."

The life spirit entered her, flowing strong, the spirit that formed in the womb of every female thing, living, growing, struggling, surviving, forcing itself into the world, seeking, changing, dying but never dying, renewing itself forever.

The moon spirit swam above her, waning now, but dying only to live again, swelling into full power, calling, drawing, floating in the darkness, throwing its mysterious light upon the earth, its rhythm surging in all things.

The spirits of the trees sang around her, leaves quivering, boughs murmuring, trunks swaying, rising up from the Earth's breast, telling of an ancient home, sheltering, nurturing through the ages. And now giving their life in the fire's glow to warm, protect, hold back the dark spirits.

Blood. Red mystery spirit, sign of life and birth, of woman's moon cycle, of wounds and death and magic. Spirit of the animals, flowing, spurting, living force of life, soaking back into the earth, renewing all things.

Love, the spirit that called to her under the moon, that stirred in her body when Agon touched her, embraced her, entered her spirit; the gift from the world behind the moon, not only for her, but for all people.

She saw the Death spirit, hovering over the people; hollow eyed, howling in the night, coming with bony arms outstretched, coming with blood and violence. In storm and blizzard. In earthquake, fire, and flood. In blazing rock and mountains bursting. Grasping and rending the people, leaving despair and desolation.

The people called her: babies, children, boys, girls, women, hunters, the old. Saying, *Help us, Spear Woman, help us live.* She felt the spear thrusting in the frenzy of battle, and she was fighting beside Agon against the hordes that poured out of a dark mouth where a thing with crooked horns and claws shrieked in hellish rage. Then she was alone, running, running, the horror behind her, closing on her in the wind and storm while lightning flashed and thunder exploded. She cried in her anguish, but only the wind answered, moaning as it swept around the black rock. She heard Arvenios calling, *Wait for him,* and she cried, "I will!" Then the moon swayed above her and grew dim, and she fell forward into blackness.

Someone held her, stroking her hair, rocking her, comforting her. Erida's voice was kind. "You have come back."

Eena pressed her face against Erida's breast, secure in the love of Erida's spirit, and she seemed in her mother's arms again.

Erida smiled down at her. "Do you remember?"

"The spirits came to me."

"Also a new spirit."

"The people called. . . ." She looked up at Erida in wonder. "My spirit."

"Spear Woman. You have completed the circle. Now we are nine."

Eena sat up, a new strength within her, the magic of the Onerana, the Invisible Earth Spirit Women. "I feel the power of the spirit circle, even now."

Erida nodded. "The spirit circle will strengthen you in all things, all times, all places. But you have given the circle strength, too, greater power than the circle has ever known." She looked deep into Eena's eyes. "I know now that the tribe will live." She smiled at Eena. "Now we will go back. Agon waits for you, and soon the day will come."

But Eena saw a sadness in Erida's smile, as though for a moment the Death spirit had touched her.

27

Festival and Dance

AGON AWAKENED PAST midday to find himself alone on the bed of ferns. Then Eena entered the bower, her face radiant.

"Look! New sandals for each of us! And a new loin cover for you, a new tunic for me! Ara brought them!" She knelt beside him. "See how beautifully they are made!"

He fingered a sandal, then touched the bare skin of her shoulder. "I like the way you are made. You do not need these."

"I cannot go naked among your people."

He pulled her down beside him. "Here you can."

She snuggled close to him. "Perhaps." Her voice was teasing, yet he sensed a new maturity in her, as if overnight she had attained greater wisdom and power.

He unfastened her tunic. "We will throw this old one away."

She raised a bare leg. "When I have bathed, you can see the new tunic and sandals on me."

Agon stared at her leg and foot. Splattered dried blood covered the skin; Zur's blood, splashed on her as Zur postured on the Stone, looking into her eyes. Zur's blood—*Ka's blood*—on the body of the woman he loved.

Eena saw the change in Agon's eyes. "I should have

washed the blood off. I will go to the women's bathing place now."

"Zur will be chieftain when Grae dies. He marked you as his."

"I am not his. I am yours."

"I should have given my blood, not Zur."

"You have given me more than blood." Eena turned to face him. "You saved me from Ka. You brought me back from the Earth Mother. We were mated by her women. You would have killed Ror for me. I am yours. I will be yours forever."

Agon felt such love for her that neither the blood of Ka nor that of Zur mattered—red stains no more important than the dust of the plain. He drew her to him, and she came into his arms, eagerly and passionately.

When Agon went to bathe in the river, he found Rok and his men already splashing in the men's place below a sandbar. Arvenios was not present.

"Our wizard disappeared before we woke up," Rok explained after he came snorting to the surface. "I think he went somewhere with Grae."

"And your hunters are gone, too," Ror added. "Zur and his men are guarding the camp." He spoke solemnly, watching Agon's eyes.

Agon dove under the water and stroked along the river bottom. He came to the surface and scrubbed himself vigorously, removing the sweat-caked dust of their run across the plain.

Ror said to Agon, his face innocent as a child's, "Zur bleeds well."

Agon felt Rok's men watching. "Zur is a hunt leader," he said indifferently.

Rok's hand smacked the surface of the water. "Agon, come to our tribe. I need men who talk little."

The other hunters smacked the water with their hands,

slapping Agon on the back, throwing themselves playfully into the water guffawing.

Ror gasped for air between bellowing laughter and words. "I was watching—your eyes—when—he—scratched himself—with the—knife." He collapsed into the water, howling gleefully. But, looking at Agon, he ceased his joking. "You will have to kill Zur, Agon."

Agon gazed upriver toward Spear Mountain. "Not yet. Something else first."

"Ka." Rok corrected Ror. "Zur is nothing." He put his hand on Agon's shoulder. "I have sworn to kill Ka. But I see you and Ka. You will fight him. I know that as surely as I know that night follows day."

When the men came back to the cliff shelter, Ara called to Agon. "Erida combs Eena's hair dry in the sunshine. Soon they will come."

Agon indicated his new breech clout and sandals. "You worked all night to make these."

"I made them when you left. I knew you would come back."

Erida could see into the future. Did Ara possess that same power? "You made a tunic and sandals for Eena, too," Agon said. "How did you know she would come?"

"Erida said you would not come alone. We knew it would be Eena; we remembered how you looked at her at the last hunt festival." Ara laughed joyfully. "Eena was so happy when she put her new things on. Wait until you see her."

Rok had been gazing at Ara. "Agon, has anyone spoken for your sister?"

"Every unmated hunter wants her. Grae and Erida guard her like two lions. Grae waits for a man who can make strong magic."

"Magic?" Rok smacked one hand into the other. "Arvenios! I should have left him in his tree!"

"Arvenios? In a tree?" Ara stared at Rok.

Rok touched her arm. "He lives in a tree. Like a bird. You wouldn't like it."

"I wouldn't?"

"Wind howling, rain dripping through the leaves, birds crapping on you . . ."

Ara began to giggle, but Agon scowled at her.

Rok nudged her with an elbow. "What you want is a chieftain. One with experience . . ."

Ror interrupted. "Experience? Old age, you mean." He flexed his muscles. "Now, a younger man, a hunter . . ."

"Old age?" Rok glared at Ror, his face reddening, his blue eyes burning. "I can satisfy more women in one night than you can in three! Now move back while I bargain with Agon." He asked Agon, "How old is your sister?"

Agon held up the fingers on one hand three times. "She had the rites a year ago."

"And not yet mated?" Rok was incredulous. "In my tribe they mate as soon as the rites are completed."

As Rok spoke, Erida and Eena came from the river. Every hunter sucked in his breath and stared. Eena truly looked a goddess. Her hair, washed and combed, had been partially braided in the married woman's style with two braids wrapped around her head, the rest flowing over her shoulders. The new tunic blended with her golden skin, her belt circled her waist like a band of light, and her sandals were designed to emphasize her graceful legs and feet. The dark bruises on her face and body had faded, and her eyes and skin shone with inner beauty.

Erida led her to Agon. "She is beautiful."

Eena looked shyly at Agon, aware that the hunters stared at her. Agon thought, She is beautiful now, but she was as beautiful to me when I first held her on the plain. As beautiful when she drove the spear into Ka's hunter. As beautiful when she stood ready for sacrifice before the Earth Mother. As beautiful when she stood on the Stone, dusty and blood-splattered, holding two red skulls to the sky.

He said only: "She is beautiful." He looked into Eena's

eyes, telling her silently of his love, and he watched her eyes respond to that assurance. Her shyness disappeared, replaced by happiness and love.

Ara threw her arms around Eena. "She is my sister! We will make beautiful things while Agon hunts, and when she has children, I will help her care for them."

Erida hugged the two girls. "And you are both my children, my daughters."

Rok cleared his throat. "And I would like to be your son."

"My son?"

Rok shifted his feet uneasily under Erida's gaze, but he pressed on. "In our tribe, when a man takes a mate, her mother . . ."

"You want Ara?"

Rok dug at the ground with his toe. "I had thought about it. . . ." He grinned expectantly.

For an instant Erida looked at Rok the way a lioness might regard a vulture approaching her kill. Then her dark eyes lightened. "You honor our tribe." She placed her hand on Rok's arm. "I would have proudly claimed you as my son."

Rok's grin faded. "Would have?"

"Too late." Erida sighed, glancing at Ara. "Your wizard has already asked Grae."

"I knew it!" Rok slapped his spear. "I'll wrap his tree branch around his neck!"

Erida drew back. "You would fight for her?"

"Fight? It would be no fight! I would make sandal straps of him!"

Erida sighed again. "I am sad for each of you."

"Each of us? Why? Once I have put Arvenios back in his tree . . ."

"Oh, no. It is a law of our tribe." Erida touched Rok's arm once more. "If two men fight over a woman, one may be killed." She looked sadly at Rok. "Then the tribe loses a man. No. Instead of that, the woman has one moon to decide who is braver in the hunt. But your wizard does not hunt." She paused. "It is sad. There is no way to decide."

Rok stared at Erida, then at Ara, then back to Erida. He started to speak, but said nothing while he thought again. Finally, he shook his head and sat down on a boulder. "No way to decide. . . ." he mumbled.

Erida comforted him. "Only a chieftain such as you could understand my sadness." She gestured toward the other women who worked in the camp area. "Many of our other young women would be honored to become your wife."

Rok looked at the women, his expression brightening. "Do you dance in your tribe?" He stood up to see better. "I have found that good dancers make good wives."

"Tonight, we dance." Ara's eyes flashed. "Grae has said so."

As Ara spoke, Grae and Arvenios came down the cliff trail from the Stone, Grae with his staff and Arvenios with his branch. They walked as if exhausted.

As the two shamans approached, Rok exclaimed, "Arvenios, I was going to make thongs out of you for asking for this girl, but you look half-dead already."

"You might as well finish me." Arvenios smiled ruefully.

"Why?"

"We failed. We could not bring Rem's spirit back from Kaan."

Erida spoke to Grae. "You tried everything?"

"Everything." Agon had never seen such weariness on Grae's face, never heard his voice so weak.

Erida's eyes shone with a strange light. She took Ara's and Eena's hands. "The women go to gather berries for the dance feast. Come. We will join them."

Eena looked longingly at Agon, and Erida, observing, reassured him. "I will bring her back before sunset."

Agon felt the ibex quivering on his chest. "Ka looks for her. Her hair . . ."

Ara held up a dark fur hood worn by the women for

head cover in rain and snow. "We made this for Eena, but we will all wear them." She hugged Eena. "We will truly look like sisters."

Rok's voice was troubled. "Send hunters with the women."

Erida seemed different to Agon now, not his mother, but a powerful female spirit who neither wanted nor needed the protection of men.

"No harm will come to us where we go." She looked at the hunters. "If anyone follows us, his spirit will not even be a ghost." No threat in her words, only a statement of fact. For a moment Agon envisioned an ancient and terrible ceremony, a circling in dark woods with female spirits leaping, and a red feast with a torn and quivering male body.

Arvenios staggered, wiping his hand across the eyes as if to remove something from his vision. He spoke in his strange language.

Erida looked sharply at him, then answered in the same language, and Arvenios's face paled. Then Erida turned with Ara and Eena, and with six other women they entered the thick brush that led along the cliff base to the west.

Ror scratched his head. "They go to pick berries, yet I sense something different about this berry gathering."

Rok had been watching Erida with a growing look of wonder. He spoke to Grae: "And you are chieftain of such a woman."

Orm, Alar, and the others of Agon's hunters returned to the camp shortly after the women left. The hunters were excited and laughing, for they had made many kills. Also, as Ord shouted, they were "ready for the dancing." But they again reported the strange behavior of the game.

"The herds continue to move away from Spear Mountain." Orf pointed north. "Toward the pass. They will have left the plain in another moon if they keep on."

Arvenios glanced toward Spear Mountain. "They flee from evil. There is little time."

Rok agreed. "Let us go and kill Ka now."

Grae stood listening, his face haggard. "We do not kill another tribe without reason."

"We have reason. You have reason." Rok's tone showed his impatience. "Ka has killed our people, taken our women. He has killed the Spear Woman's father and brother, taken her."

Grae shook his head. "That is not enough for war." He raised his staff. "We might have made them decide to leave. If they go back where they came from, we can all live peacefully."

"If." Rok slapped his spear. "This is the way to make them go back."

"We will wait one more day." Grae put his hand on Rok's shoulder. "You have crossed the plain to help us, and we shall remember. But give us one more day. If the herds still move from the plain, we will go together to kill Ka."

Rok was stubborn. "I see no way to defend your camp. Ka could strike from three sides at once."

Agon pointed to the northwest. "Alar and I found a place in the hills. We can take the people there."

"Does this place have water?" Rok asked.

"A spring."

"How many men to hold it?"

Agon considered. "Six men. The entrance is a narrow gorge."

"How far to this place?"

"Half a day, running."

Rok spoke earnestly to Grae. "We should take your people there now."

Grae looked at the sun, now halfway down the sky. He shook his head. "Not now. Night approaches." He pointed with his staff. "We have guards on every side. Tomorrow we will take the women and children to the hills."

"Then, we go to kill Ka!" Rok shook his spear in the

air, his men joining him, shouting their approval. "And this night we dance!"

When Rok's men quieted, Agon's hunters went to the river to wash off the dust and blood of the hunt, while Agon climbed the cliff path to the Black Stone. He felt strangely apprehensive, not only about the women, but for the whole tribe.

The sun was nearing the horizon as he reached the Stone. Shadows lengthened across the plain, and the peak of Spear Mountain loomed ominously on the eastern horizon. A feeling of impending violence permeated the air, the same feeling he had experienced when the great cats stalked their sleeping place.

He climbed a tall oak at the top of the cliff and looked across the plain toward Spear Mountain, searching for any sign of Ka. The herds were far out on the plain, the masses of animals indeed moving away from the mountain; horses, cattle, bison, all following the herd leaders toward the distant pass that led to winter grazing grounds. Yet it was midsummer.

He saw no men on the plain. But the river valley, filled with brush and trees, could hide a tribe of invaders. Even now, Ka and his men could be preparing for an attack, moving unseen through the underbrush. Zur and his hunters guarded the camp, yet Agon sensed an approaching evil, an evil growing stronger as the sun neared the horizon. He stared anxiously toward the west, searching for sight of the women.

South across the river valley and cliffs lay the forest. Grae said that the tribe had come from the south long ago when the world was new, coming from the place where there was no winter, the people searching until they found the Stone. But now the south was a place of demons, of evil spirits that howled in the forest, of ghost drums that boomed from the cliffs when the people danced, a place of mystery.

Mysterious, because it was unknown. The river rushed between steep cliffs, the current so strong that none could cross. As far as men had traveled up or down the river, it was always the same, the powerful river spirit separating forest from plain. Yet lately the river seemed lower, the churning water less violent.

A sudden vision of men crossing the river came to Agon, a vision so vivid that for a moment he saw a line of dark forms in the water far to the east. He cupped his hands before his eyes, gazing through the opening. The line was only a floating tree trunk swinging crosswise in the water.

Agon looked north across the plain toward the Blue Hills. Somewhere in the foothills lay the secret place he and Eena had found, their pond with shimmering water and gurgling stream, their sunny cave with a bed of ferns, their chamber deep in the hill where the figurine waited with the ibex and deer guarding her. There with Eena he had known happiness and contentment, a joy in living from discovering, loving, joining the magic spirit in her golden body.

Magic. He thought of the Earth Mother and Her terrible strength, Her ancient fiery power that demanded human sacrifice, yet was capable of mercy. The hooded women who served Her were part of Her mystery. And now another vision, a fleeting image of Ara, hooded and silent, before the Mother.

Grae had brought Erida from the Blue Hills. Were they saving Ara, keeping her from mating so that she could serve the Earth Mother? And why had Erida come for Eena in the night?

His eyes searched the wooded area to the west again. Still no sign of the women, of Eena. Arvenios had seen something in Eena that caused his spirit to leave him; Rok and his hunters called her a spear goddess; Grae had looked at her in wonder when he touched her head. Now Erida had taken her and Ara to the woods. The Onerana, the Invisible Earth Spirit Women, met in the dark woods. A feeling of foreboding and separation came to him. When the Onstean or the Onerana asked for obedience and sacrifice, they could not be denied.

Then he saw the women coming along the riverbank, and he left the tree and hurried down the cliff trail toward them.

The women carried baskets of berries and tubers on their heads, walking easily and gracefully. Eena and Ara were hand in hand beside Erida, and they waved at Agon, smiling as he waited for them at the cliff shelter.

Erida placed her basket on the ledge by the shelter opening. "You came fast down the trail." She reassured him: "I have brought them back safely."

The two girls approached, taking off their head coverings.

"See the berries we picked. They are sweet as honey." Ara showed her basket to Agon. "But take Eena's. She picked every berry just for you."

Agon took berries from each of their baskets, blackberries, purple and plump, their juice sweet in his mouth. Eena smiled at him, watching his face as he ate. But Agon, while glorying in her beauty, sensed in her the same exhaustion of spiritual energy as when she gave her strength to the spears of Rok's hunters.

"You have picked many." He glanced at Erida. "The berry patches are far down the river."

Erida laughed. "Women can move fast when they desire."

"Tomorrow we move to a safe place, one that we can defend," Agon said. "Here we are like a herd of deer with lions on all sides. Ka could attack from any direction."

"I know, Agon," Erida said. "I will not leave the camp again." Her face revealed for a moment a look of sorrow, and Agon had a premonition of death.

Then Erida smiled. "But now I see hungry men coming from all directions. We shall feast and dance."

Smoke from the cooking fires rose in fragrant curls up through the evening air, carrying the scent of roasting meat throughout the camp. The people crowded around the fires, eager for the feasting and dancing. The hunters came from the river, the old men and the boys appeared from the woods, and Zur's guards moved in, leaving sentries on either side of the camp. The children were everywhere, all watching the women as they turned the meat and laid wooden platters of roasted tubers, baked ferns, berries, nuts, and dried fruit on the eating hides.

The women sliced the meat, the choice portions going to Rok and his people, then to Agon and Zur's hunting bands. After that they served the older men, the boys, the girls, and finally, themselves.

Rok and his men received places of honor at Grae's fire, and Zur and Agon also were invited for this special occasion. Erida, Ara, and Eena served, at the chieftains' fire, bringing the food in intricately carved wooden bowls and platters.

Rok belched appreciatively after each course and used his fingers to wipe the grease from his red beard, politely licking the fingers clean. "This food makes me want to eat until I split a gut," he said graciously to Erida. "Some women's cooking would choke a vulture, but not yours."

"You honor our poor food," Erida replied.

"No, no. You deserve my praise." Rok belched again. "I remember once we visited a tribe down the river. They laid out a dead horse that was so ripe the flies wouldn't get near. When the chieftain's wife started to slice up that horse, it burst. Green slime and gas spewed out."

Arvenios stopped eating. "Agon, you agreed to show us the axe song." He pushed aside his plate of meat.

Agon felt Zur's eyes. "It is only a game that Orm and I play."

Erida moved to stand beside Agon. "They played the axe song as a game when they were little boys, but it is more than a game now. Agon and Orm were always together. A hunter journeying down the river stopped at our camp. He showed Agon and Orm how to make axes, how to swing and throw an axe." She shook her head. "Look at their scars. I had to patch up their cuts for many years, but they never stopped their axe game."

Arvenios nodded. "My father told us of that hunter. He would teach the song only to those in whom he saw the axe power."

Grae spoke: "I saw no use for the axe song then. Yet now I believe the song has great power. Agon has fought Ka's spearmen with the axe."

"And killed our own hunters," Zur mocked. "Axes are toys for little boys. A man who knows how to use a spear has no need of an axe."

Agon responded quietly. "Ka's men carry two spears each. They have fought men before, they can dodge a thrown spear, and their magic is strong. When I fought Ka's spearman, he would have killed me if Eena had not driven her spear into him. And when I fought Ka, his magic kept the axe from killing him."

"As I said." Zur scorned Agon. "Axes are toys."

"Blue balls of the great bull bison!" Rok roared. "Agon killed at least six of Ka's men!" He glared at Zur. "How many have you killed?"

"My day will come." Zur's eyes were cold. "When I fight Ka, he will not live."

Grae held up his hand. "We may not have to fight Ka." He stood up, holding his staff. "Rok's hunter has his spirit back."

At this, Rok and his hunters leaped to their feet, shouting. Arvenios added, "Something has weakened their shaman." He looked at Erida, Eena, and Ara. "Or strengthened us."

Erida's face showed no change in expression, but Agon recalled his vision of the dark woods.

Rok put his hand on Grae's shoulder. "Arvenios's father told me that your tribe possessed the strongest magic of any people this side of the mountains. Now I see this is true."

Grae pointed his staff toward Spear Mountain. The moon had not yet risen, yet a faint reddish light glowed in the east. "Something evil lurks in the darkness. We have been warned of its coming."

The people sucked in their breaths, glancing over their shoulders.

Grae continued, his voice carrying through the camp. "Our tribe is an ancient one. Our people have lived by the Stone almost since the beginning. The Stone is our strength. Now something evil comes." He raised his staff. "But we will fight that evil with our magic. We will conquer it. Yesterday we fought it. And we won. Today we fought it. And we won. Tomorrow we will fight it. We will win!"

The people rose as one body, shouting and waving their arms.

Grae waited until they had quieted. "The tribe will live." For a moment his eyes fell on Erida. "No matter what happens, the tribe will live!" He held up his arms, his staff in one hand. "Tomorrow we move to a safe place, but tonight we welcome our guests. Now the axe song; then we will dance!"

"The people would rather dance than see the axe song," Agon said.

"First the axe song!" Rok shouted. "Agon, we ran across the plain to see the axe song! We want to see it now!"

Orm moved toward Agon from the hunter's fire. "Agon!"

The axe spun from Orm's hand toward Agon, its blade flashing in the firelight.

Agon's axe met Orm's, flashing by in an identical trajectory, spinning into Orm's hand as Orm's axe spun into Agon's hand. Then the axes whirled and spun back through the air, Agon and Orm each catching an axe by the handle and hurling it back, faster and faster. The axes hummed in the air like giant bees, flying between the hunters' hands in two identical arcs of spinning blades.

Suddenly, the axes were spinning with each hunter as

Agon and Orm whirled their bodies, throwing the axes ever faster. The axes whispered; then, as the speed of the whirling and throwing increased, the axes began to sing, the sound low, sighing like wind, then louder, higher pitched, an eerie whistling like the wailing of lost spirits. Now the axes spun even faster, and their singing changed. They became magic axes, almost invisible, spinning, whirling, growing in power around Agon and Orm even as a tornado increases in strength until everything falls before it.

Agon and Orm moved closer together, and there was a new sound, a rising and falling, a blending of sound, unearthly and terrifying as the hunters whirled around one another, spinning in and out like flickering lightning, men and axes one, whirling spirits of axes and axe men.

Slowly, the axe men backed away from each other, and slowly, the singing changed as they threw the axes ever faster, spinning invisibly, the magic pulsating in a terrifying song of death and destruction. The people held their totems, scarcely breathing.

Then the singing axes slowed, stopped, and Agon and Orm stood facing one another. Orm clasped Agon's arms silently, then turned to Rok and Arvenios. "That is the axe song."

Arvenios's eyes blazed. He rushed to Agon and Orm, holding out his hands. "Our people will tell of the axe song from this day on!"

"By the gods," Rok bellowed, "that made my prick stand up!"

Grae raised his staff. "Let the drums speak."

Old Unser and his assistants brought the three great tribal drums from the cliff shelter. Made of hollow logs and bison skin, the drums held the magic of the trees, of the bison. Unser struck the largest drum with a single blow, and the drum bellowed, deep and resonant, echoing between the cliffs. Unser struck again, then again, slowly, ponderously, and the people felt the hair on the backs of their necks rise. Now the other drummers began, and as

Agon and Orm's axes had pulsated together, so the drums joined, their voices rumbling in a mystic harmony, a harmony of bellowing bulls, of thundering hooves, of herds rushing over the plain.

As the drums rumbled, the people responded to the rhythm of the drumbeats. They rose from their fires and began to dance around the center fire. The drums beat slowly, in unison, and the people danced slowly, in rhythm with the drums, legs rising, bodies vibrating with each beat. Some bent low, while others arched their bodies as they felt the spirit of the bison enter their spirits. The drums beat faster, and others joined the circle. The firelight threw the people's shadows on the cliff, and a ghostly, undulating, flickering spirit circle danced on the great rock wall, rising up into the shadows of the night.

Rok and his men had not yet entered the ring. Then Una, one of the most attractive of the young women, broke from the weaving circle and danced toward Rok. Rok, with a rumbling laugh, leaped toward her, and together they joined the circle of dancers. Now other women joined Rok's men, and two by two they entered the dance.

Erida said to Grae, "I hope that our own hunters are not left by the fire."

Eena clasped Agon's hand and drew him toward the fire. "The hunter who saved me from Ka will not be left."

That night the hunters of Rok's tribe and the tribe of Grae danced as one people. The women of the bison hunters bestowed their favors on red-haired and dark-haired hunters alike, but Eena danced only with Agon. And when the moon's magic rays enveloped them, Agon lifted Eena in his arms and carried her to their bower.

28

The Snake Demon

THEY AWAKENED IN the night. Eena whispered, "The night birds are afraid."

Agon moved silently to the low entrance of the bower, his axe and spear ready. The ibex vibrated on his chest and in the axe handle, warning him. The moon had passed into the western sky, beyond the curve of the cliff, and the riverbank and camp were in deep shadow. The embers of the center fire still glowed, and he detected the sleeping forms of the people around the fire.

He looked toward the cliff shelter where Grae, Erida, and Ara slept. His hunters formed a half-circle before the opening, guarding it. He gazed up and down the river, alert to any movement. Rok and his men were on the eastern approach, the place they had insisted upon, the most likely point of attack. Zur's hunters on the west also guarded the cliff trail.

Now Eena was at his shoulder, holding her spear. Her hand found his, and again he felt the strength of her spirit. He drew her back into the bower.

"Stay here while I go to talk with Orm."

Her hand tensed, but she did not speak. He touched her hair. "If Ka attacks, he will look for you." He found the head covering that Ara had given Eena. "Wear this." He placed it over her hair.

Eena's hands touched his as she tied the thongs beneath her chin. "Let me come with you."

"No. . . ." He hesitated. The feeling of danger grew stronger. A vision of Eena alone in the bower, with Ka crashing through the entrance, changed his mind. "Come.

Stay close to me," he told her. "They could attack from any direction."

They went silently through the near-darkness to where Orm and the hunters stood. Orm, raising his axe to Agon, spoke quietly. "Something watches us."

Movement. Something sliding through the grass. The same silent movement Agon had felt by the dead bison, the same sinister movement he had felt in the cave of the Onstean. Now coming closer, moving toward the people.

"Where are Alar and Ean?" Agon spoke almost soundlessly in the hunters' way, his lips close to Orm's ear.

Orm shifted uneasily. "I sent them to guard Grae."

"Grae? He is not in the shelter?"

"He went with Arvenios." Orm pointed up the cliff trail.

"When?"

"After the dancing. We tried to stop them." Orm shook his head. "It was like talking to the cliff."

Agon nodded. "I know. You were wise to send hunters after him."

Zur had two men at the top of the cliff, and Alar and Ean would defend Grae with their lives. But Agon's feeling of apprehension grew ever stronger. Too many women and children, too many places for the hunters to guard. And somewhere Ka was watching.

Agon and Eena went to where the old men and boys slept. Unser was awake, his white hair and beard a tangle around his face.

Agon knelt by him. "We need you."

Unser nodded. "Something comes." Agon could feel the old man's pride at being called. Unser sat up, holding his spear.

Agon pointed at the cliff top. "Grae has gone to the Stone. Help Orm guard the people while I go to find him. We need every spear."

Unser's eyes gleamed. "We are ready." He made a small sound, the call of a night bird, and around him boys and old men rose from their sleeping places, spears in hand.

Agon clasped Unser's arm. "Stay by the shelter, even if Orm and the hunters are drawn away."

"We will stay." Unser stood straight as his spear.

Agon went to Orm again, Eena at his side. "We go to find Grae."

For an instant Agon saw in Orm's face the expression he had seen in Erida's: a look of death.

Orm laid his hand lightly on Agon's arm. "When Ka comes, you and I will sing the axe song together."

Agon clasped Orm's arm, then turned toward the cliff trail, Eena alongside him.

Zur's men stood at the top of the cliff near the Black Stone, their forms dim in the light of the half-moon. Agon recognized Van and Xo. He came close before speaking. "I look for Grae."

The men stared insolently at Agon, then at Eena. Xo spoke: "The golden one covers her hair."

Agon stepped closer. "Where is Grae?"

Van spat on the ground near Agon's feet. "We are not your men."

The side of Agon's hand struck Van just below the ear, dropping him as if he had been axed. Before Xo could move, the point of Agon's spear was under his chin, lifting him so that Xo stretched upward on his toes to keep the point from penetrating farther.

Agon spoke over his shoulder, keeping his eyes on Xo's face. "Your men do not remember well."

Zur came out of the darkness. "My men do as I tell them."

"Then tell them to learn how to answer. We look for Grae."

Agon lowered the spear, letting Xo come down off his toes. Van came slowly to his feet, watching Agon.

Zur stepped between Agon and Eena. "Why do you bring her here?" He turned to face Eena. "When you are mine, I will keep you in a safe place." He moved closer to her. "You know the way of our tribe with brothers. If one dies, his mate becomes the brother's woman."

Eena moved around Zur to stand beside Agon, placing her hand in his. "Agon and I will live together or die together. If one is lost, the other one will wait until the lost one comes."

Zur sneered. "Not when I am chieftain. You will wait long for a lost spirit who howls in the night wind."

"If you even look at Eena again," Agon said, "I will send you howling into Hell. Now tell me where Grae is before I spread your intestines over the cliff top."

Zur glared at Agon, his spear trembling as he slowly raised the weapon.

Shouts and screams tore the night—from the trees, from the plain, from the river valley below them. A spear flashed from the trees, striking Zur in the side. He fell, clawing at the spear. Agon's spear sliced through the darkness, and a man screamed. The sounds of fighting rose from where Rok and Zur's hunters guarded the river approaches.

Agon grasped Zur's spear and leaped to the edge of the cliff. Something black and writhing moved at a frightening speed from the river toward the cliff shelter, a dark mass of running men that smashed through the line of old men and boys, struck Agon's hunters, recoiled, and then fell upon them—a demon serpent of death with Ka shrieking at its head.

Men rushed out from the trees behind them, and Agon and Eena turned to face the enemy. Two were interlocked with Xo and Van, but three came on, screaming, their spears raised above the knots of their hair, running at full speed, their feet pounding the cliff top.

Agon drove Zur's spear into the belly of the lead man, lifting him in one motion up and over the edge of the cliff as the spear handle snapped. Then the axe was in his hand, whirling, spinning in the fury of battle as Eena fought beside him, thrusting fiercely with her spear.

The demon men fought savagely, shrieking their hatred even as Agon's axe whirled and tore through their bodies, jaws shattering, ribs bursting, blood and flesh spattering with each stroke. They fell in red quivering heaps of gashed and bloody flesh, of shattered bone.

Agon and Eena ran down the cliff trail, but Ka had run shrieking and slaughtering through the camp and disappeared in the darkness before they reached the bottom.

Grae and Alar ran down the trail just as Agon met the last of Ka's men—an old man with sharp teeth and bloody spear who leaped toward Eena, snarling. Agon chopped his axe below the knob of hair, and the man sprawled forward, grasping for Eena as he died, his brains spilling upon the ground.

A woman threw branches on the fire, and as they blazed up, Agon saw that the ground was littered with the dead and wounded. He seized a burning branch and ran past the bodies of his hunters into the cliff shelter. Eena cried out in horror as she glimpsed what lay inside.

Grae knelt, his face bowed over Erida and Ara; mother and daughter were dead, their throats torn open.

Agon's spirit turned cold, cold as a frozen river, cold and empty as an ice cavern in the long sunless night, cold and hard as an ice wall that grinds out of the frigid north.

He knew what he must do. He knew what Grae would do.

All that night and through the next morning Grae sat by the bodies of Erida and Ara, sat like stone, neither seeing nor hearing the people as they, the living, counted their dead and bandaged the wounded, trying to keep their spirits alive in the midst of the slaughter Ka had brought upon the camp.

Ka had attacked from all sides at once, but the main thrust had come from the river, where the serpentine mass of killers had emerged from the water to strike the heart of the camp. Agon's hunters had taken that blow. Outnumbered, they had fought until their blood soaked the ground, until their spears lay broken, until their spirits left them. Now the six hunters lay where they had fallen, their line still intact in death, with the bodies of fifteen of Ka's men scattered among them.

Agon went to each of his hunters, touching each face, closing each man's eyes. Orm's hand still grasped his axe, four of Ka's men dead before him. The red deer on Orm's chest still held its magic, for it was covered with his blood. Orm smiled in death as in life.

"You died with honor, Rite Brother," Agon said. "We will sing the axe song together soon."

Each of the hunters' totems was strong with blood. Orf's bison, Az's elk, Emo's mammoth, Uz's bull, and Ord's horse. Ord had died with his hands driving an enemy spear into the third man he had killed.

Old Unser was dead, as were six boys and nine old men who had first taken Ka's charge. Along with Erida and Ara, four women, five girls, and three babies had been killed, all by spear thrusts in their throats.

Of Rok's hunters, three had died; the rest were wounded. Rok had deep spear wounds in his thigh and shoulder, and he limped badly. But he had brought his men in after killing the attackers on his side of the camp, and they had helped drive Ka and his surviving men away.

Zur's men had fought courageously for all their insolence, and three had died. Zur lay with a spear wound in his side, his face white with pain. He appeared near death, yet he glared at Agon with burning eyes.

They found Arvenios's body in the trees at the cliff top. Ean and the bodies of three Ka men lay nearby. Agon saw that Grae's staff had been driven through the neck of one of these men.

Alar knelt through the night with Grae by the bodies of Erida and Ara, but in the morning he came to Agon to tell what happened. His face was streaked with tears and blood, and he had a spear wound in one arm. He stood straight before Agon, refusing to let Eena bandage his wound until he had told his story.

"We followed Grae and Arvenios to the Stone as Orm told us. We kept out of sight, and we could hear them chanting. Then the men with big heads attacked. . . ."

"Which direction?"

"Everywhere."

Agon nodded. "We heard them."

"Ean and I ran toward the Stone to get closer to Grae. We fought the men, but then . . ." Alar's eyes viewed something that had been terrifying. "Something came out of the dark. . . ."

Agon felt the coldness on his back. "What?"

Alar swallowed. "It crashed through the trees . . . big and black . . . claws and horns . . . screaming like a great cat . . . it leaped onto Arvenios. . . ."

Eena stepped closer to Agon.

Agon waited, his spirit growing even colder.

"Then Grae drove his staff into it . . . and . . ." Alar's eyes reflected his horror.

Agon gripped his axe. "Tell us."

Alar stared up at the cliff top, then back at Agon. "It screeched at Grae. Then something even worse spewed out of it, red and shrieking, flying toward Spear Mountain. And there was a man with Grae's staff through his neck, and Arvenios was dead. . . ."

Grae and Arvenios had called Kaan, challenging him, and the shaman had come. Come from the dark mountain through the night to fall screaming on Arvenios, killing him, shrieking his triumph as Ka killed Grae's people.

Agon spoke slowly, calmly to Alar. "The fight is over now. You have seen great evil, but you saw Grae's strength prove greater than the evil one. Our magic is strong. Our tribe will live."

The fear receded from Alar's eyes. Agon touched his arm. "Let Eena bandage your wound. Then we will bury our people."

Ka's men were dragged to the river and their bloody bodies hurled into the rushing water. Old Asom used a stick to scratch in the dirt as each body splashed in. Rok and his men had killed six, Agon's hunters fifteen, Zur's hunters five, Agon and Eena five. Grae, Ean, and Alar had killed three. But the number of women and children killed in the bison hunters' camp made Grae's losses far greater than Ka's.

Rok shook his head. "Ka had twice as many men as when he attacked our tribe. Where did they come from?"

"From the river." Old Ulam pointed with his spear. "They came from the water."

The people gasped. Van, Zur's hunter, sneered at Ulam. "Fish men."

"Ulam is right," Agon said. "We saw them from the cliff top. They came from the river. They must have crossed it."

Rok glared at the cliffs on the other side of the river. "If they come again, all your people will die."

Agon looked toward Spear Mountain. "As soon as we bury our dead, the rest will go to the safe place in the hills." He said to Rok, "You have fought alongside our people. They will always remember."

"And we will remember," Rok replied. "We will help take your people to the safe place."

Then Agon went to where Grae knelt beside Erida and Ara. "We will dig the grave now. Then I will come for Ara."

Grae did not respond. His face was like stone, his eyes without spirit.

The people went to the place west of the Black Stone where their ancestors lay. With digging sticks, clam shells, and flat pieces of rock, they worked all that morning digging a large grave. They laid the bodies carefully in the earth, side by side, mothers and children together, hunters, old men, boys, girls. But they did not take Erida or Ara, for Grae still remained by their bodies, and none would disturb him.

When they could wait no longer, Agon came for Ara. Then Grae's spirit returned to him. He slowly rose to his feet, lifting Erida in his arms as easily as a young hunter. He carried her up the cliff trail and laid her in the grave.

Then Grae went to the bodies in the grave and touched each face, for they were his people. But still he had not spoken, and the people stood silently in his presence.

Finally, Grae stood at the edge of the grave and faced the setting sun. His voice was strong and clear.

"The spirits of our people now go from us as the sun goes from us. But as we know that the sun will return, so we know that their spirits will return and live among us again. For in us live the spirits of our ancestors, and we are the same people who long ago came here from the home of the sun.

"And now we bid the spirits of these, our people, to rest until they shall be called again. For they shall live again to play as children on the riverbank, to dance with us under the moon, to hunt the bison, to sit around our fires at night, to bear children, and to love them even as we did these."

Grae held a spear as he had held his staff, raising it to the sky. But now he lowered the spear and placed the end of the handle on the ground, the point against his chest. He fell forward onto the point, falling as a tree falls in the forest, slowly and with gathering force, his body strong and straight, his eyes calm. There was a dignity in his dying, a greatness filled with magic and strength.

Grae spoke his last words. "Blood flows. Blood flows. Let this blood strengthen our spirits and save our people."

Agon, looking into Grae's eyes as he died, answered, "The people will live."

Grae smiled at Agon, the chieftain's face that of a young hunter; so he must have looked when he brought Erida back to the tribe as his mate.

Agon closed Grae's eyes, then laid his body between Erida's and Ara's. He placed Grae's staff beside him and set the bison horns on his head so that he would remain a chieftain. Grae's totem lay on his chest, the antlered stag, symbol of the sorcerer, the chieftain.

The women spread grass and flowers over the bodies; then the men replaced the earth and covered the grave with flat stones to protect the bodies from the beasts of the night.

Agon went to Eena and led her to Alar. "You and Eena will take the people to the safe place. The place you and I know."

"You lead us, Agon," Alar told him. "You will be chieftain."

"No. I go to another place."

Then Alar knew, as Eena knew, and Agon saw the sorrow in Alar's eyes, as in Eena's eyes.

Agon touched Alar's axe. "An axe man must guard the people. Ka still lives." Then Agon took Eena's hand. "When I saw you in the river valley, I journeyed to the place of death. Now I finish that journey. But I have known your spirit in the days between, and my spirit will find yours again."

Eena laid her head against his chest—her love, the beauty of her spirit entering him. "Twice," she said now, "you have brought me back from death. My spirit will wait for yours: I know that you will find me."

Agon turned toward the east, toward Spear Mountain. He did not look back, but began to run into the approaching dusk, running at a hunter's pace, axe and spear his companions. The ibex on his chest and the ibex in the axe handle felt cold and hard, as cold and hard as the Black Stone that watched over the grave of his people, as cold and hard as Agon's spirit.

29

Alar

ALAR AND EENA watched Agon as he ran along the cliff edge, their eyes following him until he disappeared in the twilight.

Rok limped toward them, old Ulam alongside. Ulam had survived Ka's attack, but not without a spear wound in one shoulder. Rok was using his spear as a crutch for his wounded leg.

"Agon goes to kill Ka," Rok growled. "If he finds him, I would not want to be Ka."

Alar's eyes were filled with sorrow, but he spoke proudly. "Agon will find him."

Ulam nodded. "He will."

No longer a boy, Alar stood straight as he spoke to Rok and Ulam. "Agon told me to lead the people to the safe place. We will start now."

Rok nodded agreement. "Good. Even when Agon kills Ka, Ka's men could still attack. We cannot defend this place."

"We will have to carry some of the wounded."

Rok glanced at the place where Zur lay. "Leave him here."

Alar shook his head. "If Zur lives, he will be chieftain."

"Maybe he will die soon," Rok said hopefully. "Then Agon becomes chieftain."

Alar asked Ulam, "Will Zur die?"

Ulam tugged at his beard. "I have seen hunters live with worse wounds than his. . . ."

Alar studied the sky and the approaching night. "We must go." To Eena he said, "Will you bandage Zur so we can lift him? We will carry him with two spears and a hide, the hunter's way."

Eena remembered Zur's hatred for Agon, his lust for her on the cliff top. But he was Agon's brother, and Alar asked for her help. "I will bind him."

Zur was barely conscious. Eena removed the bloody dressing that covered the spear hole in his side and strapped a leather pad tightly against the wound. As she worked, she felt his eyes upon her. He whispered, "Agon will die."

"Agon will live." She tied the last knot. "I will wait for him until he comes."

Zur showed his teeth. "You will be mine."

Eena turned silently away from Zur and went to where the surviving women and children huddled. Tears fell on her cheeks as she felt their sorrow and misery. She knelt and lifted one of the babies and took an orphaned child by the hand. "Now we will go to the safe place," she told the child. "We will go like the bison herd, and when Agon has killed Ka, you can come back here and live with the spirits of your people again."

Alar and Rok led the people down the river trail. They moved slowly, wounded and grieving, carrying the badly hurt on litters. Each able person—man, woman, or child—carried a spear, ready to fight if attacked. At nightfall they crouched beneath a cliff overhang with the men forming a line of spears in defense. They made no fires but ate the dried food they carried.

At dawn they found that one of the wounded hunters had died in the night. They piled rocks over his body, and Alar asked the man's spirit to remain with him. Then they moved along the river again, more slowly than before as their wounds stiffened.

Rok came to limp alongside Eena. "Agon will have a family when he comes back." He chucked the baby under the chin and patted the child's head. "This one will soon carry an axe."

Eena glanced behind them where Spear Mountain

loomed against the sunrise. "Dream spirits came to me in the night. Agon was in the dream, fighting." She shuddered. "Fire and stone fell around him . . . then a great wall of water. . . ."

Rok tried to comfort her. "He will come back. His magic is strong."

"But the one he goes to fight is powerful. Grae and Arvenios could not stand against him."

Rok stared at her. "He goes to fight their wizard? The thing with horns and claws? I thought he went to fight Ka."

"I saw in my dream . . . the horned thing was leaping at Agon. . . ."

Rok slapped one huge fist into his palm. "And not one hunter strong enough to help him!"

"Hunters could not help." Eena touched the deer on her breast. "A powerful spirit has decided."

"You know this?"

"Yes. But I will wait for him."

"At Alar's safe place?"

"No. In a different place, far from here."

Rok shook his head in wonderment. "I believe you, but . . ."

Eena said, "Agon will find me."

By nightfall they had reached the hills that led to the safe place. Alar spoke to the people: "We will travel all night and reach the safe place by morning."

Van and three other of Zur's hunters had been talking to Zur in low voices. Van said loudly, "Zur says we will camp here, in this valley. Zur is chieftain."

Ulam came to stand beside Alar. "I am old and will die soon, but I do not fear Zur. Zur raves like a body whose spirit is lost, and I hear no wisdom in his words. We cannot defend this place. Agon has told Alar to lead us to the safe place. We should go there now."

Van answered in a commanding voice, "Zur has decided. We stop here."

Rok spoke: "I am not of your tribe, but I have fought Ka twice. If he attacks here, you will all die. Let Alar lead you to the safe place now. He speaks for Agon."

"Agon is not chieftain." Van spat. "Agon has run away. He is afraid."

Alar stepped toward Van. "Agon has not run away. He has gone to do what you are afraid to do."

Zur beckoned from his litter. Van knelt by him, then arose and spoke to the people. "Zur is chieftain. We stop here. If Alar tries to act as chieftain, he will die. Any who do not obey Zur will die."

The people murmured their concern. Whom should they obey?

One of Zur's hunters said, "Zur is oldest son of Grae. Now Zur is Grae."

Van raised his spear. "Obey Grae or die!"

The tired people laid their burdens down. Zur was Grae. Grae was chieftain.

30

The Axe

AGON RAN ALL night along the cliff top toward Spear Mountain, and as he ran, the evil that festered within the mountain pressed against him more and more strongly.

In the first dim light of morning he searched the river valley for signs of Ka and his men. Seeing none, he came down the cliff trail to drink from the river, then climbed back up and ran on toward the mountain, keeping hidden in the trees and undergrowth that lined the cliff top. The evil from the mountain became almost unbearable, and he fought against it, forcing his body toward the source, the center, of the evil.

He reached Spear Mountain in late afternoon and cautiously circled its base, searching the plains side for the opening he knew must exist, the opening from which Ka's men had run out upon the plain in their pursuit of Eena. He saw no sign of bird or animal. The mountain was bare of any vegetation, and the brush at its base was twisted and stunted, all thorns and prickers, seemingly as evil as the mountain's inhabitants.

Then he saw them, seven men with grotesque heads bringing meat in from the plain. They approached within three spear-lengths of where he lay, the knobs of their hair bobbing above the undergrowth. They came to the base of the mountain, then suddenly disappeared.

Agon slipped down into the brush to wait for the night. He had found the entrance.

The sentry stood outside the opening, leaning on his spear. Agon crawled through the brush, circling behind the man. A rough bandage covered the man's shoulder, and he muttered angrily as he fingered the covered wound. Agon's spear struck between the man's shoulder blades, a hand's length down from the base of the skull. The man's arms flew up, but the only sound was the soft thud of the spear.

A second man ran forward from the cave entrance, and Agon's axe smashed into his skull below the thick knob of hair. Agon whirled, the axe singing, and the blade caught a third man full in the face, smashing into his teeth and jaws. Agon jerked his spear from the first man's body and ran into the passageway. Another man rushed toward him. The spear ripped into the man's throat. Agon shook the body off the spear and stalked forward through the passageway, feeling his way in the darkness like a cat, every sense guiding him.

A red glow appeared ahead, and Agon moved silently

toward it. He stopped at the entrance to a large chamber, the same chamber where Eena had been held. Ka's men sat around a fire, tearing at chunks of meat, growling as they ate, their voices harsh and guttural.

Agon studied the figures. Ka was not among them.

Something shrieked behind him—a howl from Hell.

Agon whirled. Clawed hands reached for him, crooked horns swayed above him, red eyes in a skull face glared at him. And below that face a white monstrous form crouched like a giant bloated spirit. Instantly the thing leaped upon him.

Agon struck with the axe. Struck through the demons, through the evil, through the clawed hands, straight into the awful face.

Lightning cracked through the axe handle, up Agon's arm, and into his spirit. But the axe blade penetrated deep between the red eyes. The head exploded, brains splattering out, eyes bursting, skull fragmenting, crooked horns collapsing.

The earth shook. A grinding roar filled the world, and the mountain shuddered and began to crumble.

"Ka!" Agon shouted his challenge, dodging through the falling rock, calling for Ka, his axe slashing, bodies crumpling before him. But the axe could not find Ka.

Then Agon knew where Ka had gone. Eena!

He rushed from the cave and down the path to the river trail, the cliffs swaying, lurching, masses of rock crumbling from the walls and crashing into the canyon. He raced along the trail, leaping over the fallen stones, his feet barely touching the heaving ground as he came to the bend in the gorge.

Then the red core deep within the earth convulsed and burst, and a great blast of primal energy hurtled upward. The earth rolled in one final tearing wave, and the mountain exploded in violence beyond sound, beyond feeling, beyond knowing.

31

Goddess of the Spear

EENA HELD THE two motherless children, looking toward Spear Mountain, her spirit searching for Agon, when the mountain exploded.

The earth shuddered under her, then the peak of Spear Mountain glowed for an instant and burst in a great expanding ball of flame that rose into the night sky, a red demon leaping up through the earth, shattering the mountain, hurling the fragments upward in fiery trails. Eena and the people stared in disbelief as the blast drove upward toward the stars. Then, as the light faded and sank back, a red glow appeared at the base of the shattered mountain, a river of fire that crawled over cliffs like a crimson serpent.

Eena felt her spirit shaken by the blast, and she cried out for Agon. Then a blast of sound, a roaring thunderclap, struck. Eena cried out again, her voice lost in the booming concussion, and the children, their eyes closed in terror, clung to her as the blast roared by.

Then a shrieking wind came from the mountain, crashing through the wooded hills, striking the people like a club, hurling them back against the earth as branches snapped and trees crashed down. Eena held the children to her, shielding them with her body as the clawing air tore at them.

A wall of water and mud struck them, a deluge of rain and ash powerful as a waterfall, and with it cracking lightning, booming thunder. Eena clasped the children even more tightly, willing them to live and endure.

Water rose around them; she lifted the children and

forced her way against the wind and water to a high flat rock. Slowly, weakly, the people rose from the water and mud and struggled toward the same rock. Eena, Alar, Rok, and the hunters guided the old and the wounded, lifted children, and carried babies to the rock, a place where the people could see and touch and comfort one another. All through the night they clung together while the rain beat down and the wind howled.

In the dim morning they found that Zur was unconscious. Then Alar and Rok led the people toward the safe place. Cold and wet, the people still lived, still belonged to the tribe.

The valleys and ravines ran with water. The litter bearers slipped and staggered with their burdens, the injured weakened, and the children grew hollow eyed. A pall of darkness hung over the earth, and the gray rain, filled with mud and ash, beat down upon the people. A sense of desolation pervaded the air, a bleakness that led to despair.

The sun was not visible, but at what seemed midday Alar stopped briefly on a hilltop to let the stragglers catch up. The people sank wearily to the ground as they halted.

Alar spoke: "The safe place is over the next hill. We must keep on moving. One more hill, then we will come to our stopping place." His eyes were unnaturally bright, and his wound was red and swollen.

Eena came to him. "You have lost your bandage."

He tried to smile. "Your knots stayed tied. I took the bandage off." He felt near the wound. "The rain cools the cut."

"You should rest." Eena touched his skin, feeling his body heat. "I will look for plants to draw the evil from the wound."

"Ara and my mother would have said the same thing." Alar looked toward Spear Mountain, where a faint red glow shone. "Agon was at the mountain."

"Yes."

"He lives?"

Eena bowed her head. All through the night and the long

day she had told herself that Agon was alive. Now as they neared the place of safety, she felt a coldness and weariness in her spirit like an omen of death. "I will wait for him."

Alar touched her hand. "He will come. He will be chieftain, and we will hunt together on the plain."

Eena raised her head. "And I will make hunting shirts for you and Agon, and when Agon and I have a son, we will make you the child's other father."

"Agon was lucky to find you." Alar looked around at the people. "They are too weak to travel, but I promised Agon." He spoke to Rok, who came limping toward them. "We should go on."

"Yes, if they can." Rok shook his head. "If Ka remains alive and has any men left, he could slaughter us. There aren't more than five men here who can lift a spear."

"Enough to guard the safe place." Alar asked Eena, "Can you get the women to cross one more valley, climb one more hill?"

"They will come." Eena lifted the two children in her arms and went to the other women. "Now we go to the safe place."

Lightning cracked in a jagged line across the sky, lighting up the dark hills surrounding them. Tall forms with obscene bulging heads loomed on the nearest hilltop, and a white bone gleamed for an instant in the lightning glare.

Eena pushed the children into a woman's arms, and then she was running, pulling the cover from her hair, running back toward the river in the light of the flickering lightning.

Ka's harsh voice screamed behind her. Her hand found the deer at her throat, and she felt the strength of the deer flow into her. She ran as the deer runs, lightly, enduring, leading Ka away from the people.

32

The Offering

THE BULGE IN the cliff wall had saved Agon by a handbreadth. Impelled by the the blast of the exploding mountain, a great mass of rock hurtled down the gorge to smash against the opposite wall of the canyon, but in the moment between explosion and impact Agon was thrown forward past the curve of the wall, just beyond the trajectory of the rock mass. In that moment it seemed that the whole world had been destroyed.

Jagged pieces of the mountain rained down, and Agon pressed against the gorge wall as huge chunks of rock crashed around him. The mass of flame that shot up from the mountain illuminated the canyon momentarily, but now a cloud of ash and powdered rock filled the sky, and the canyon was lighted only by fiery lava, which spewed from the shattered mountain and poured over the broken cliff into the river. A great cloud of steam boiled up, and in the fire and steam the canyon became Hell.

Agon staggered over the fallen rock and around the glowing lava through the steam, the heat, the ash. Kaan was dead, but Ka lived. Ka, who would find the fleeing tribe and destroy it. Ka, who would never rest until he took Eena.

Agon emerged from the narrow canyon into the storm unleashed by the exploding mountain, a storm of such fury that the howling wind, the crackling blasts of lightning, the crashing thunder, the torrent of rain all seemed a continuation of the explosion.

He ran through the night, through the storm. Morning came as only a dim light, the storm worsening, the sky black, the wind and rain increasing. Yet Agon saw that the river scarcely flowed, so low that the rocks on the bottom lay exposed.

He reached Grae's deserted camp and found food within the cliff shelter. He rested briefly and then ran west along the river toward the safe place, fearing that Ka ran ahead of him.

He came to the trail that led up the cliff and into the hills. Two bodies lay on the trail at the top of the cliff. One body was knob-headed. The other was Alar.

Agon knelt by Alar. Blood seeped from a spear wound in Alar's chest, but he still lived. Alar stared up into Agon's face, then tried to speak, but blood filled his mouth. Agon gently lifted Alar's head, cradling him in his arms. Alar coughed blood, then whispered, "Ka came back. . . . I tried . . ."

"Eena? The people?"

"People . . . safe . . ." Alar coughed more blood. "Eena . . ."

Agon's spirit grew cold. "Is she safe?"

"Eena . . . led . . . Ka . . . away. . . ."

"Which way?" Agon gripped Alar's arms, sending his strength into Alar's spirit, willing him to live another moment.

"I . . . tried . . . to . . . save . . . her. . . ."

"Where is she?"

Alar was dying. His hand still gripped the handle of his axe, and Agon placed his hand over Alar's. "We will sing the axe song together."

Blood poured from Alar's mouth, but with his last strength he spoke: "The Stone." Then Alar died.

The Stone! Eena led Ka toward the Stone! Agon closed his brother's eyes and placed the hand holding the axe on the boy's chest. Then he ran back along the cliff top toward the ancient stone of his people.

High in the snow-covered mountains to the east, the ice dam that had choked the river outlet collapsed. The water in the vast lake had risen over a period of months, gathering its strength. Now it burst free and exploded out over the falls and into the river valley. A wall of water high as the cliffs raced to the west, sweeping everything before it.

Uprooted trees clogged the game trail, and Agon ran out upon the plain. In the lightning flashes he saw Eena's footprints in the wet earth, and the large prints of three men, all running in the same direction, the men behind Eena.

He neared the Stone, and in the lightning glare he saw them—Ka and two other men struggling with Eena, dragging her from the black surface of the Stone.

Agon shouted and raced forward. In one powerful motion Ka threw Eena over his shoulder and plunged toward the cliff trail as the other men turned to face Agon, their spears coming up.

Agon sang the axe song as he closed the distance between them. He hurled himself upon the men, the axe whirling in its song of death. The axe smashed into the face of one man. Whirled again. Crunched the arm bone of the second man. Struck again, squarely in the man's forehead.

Lightning flashed again, illuminating the river valley, and Agon saw that Ka had triumphed. Ka carried Eena across the river, springing from rock to rock through the shallow water. And pouring across the river from the opposite side, the side of the demons, came a mass of men, spears held high above the knobs of their hair.

Instantly, Agon knew where Ka had come from, and that the visions of the Onstean had proved true. Truly, the undulating line of Ka's men was a giant snake, come hissing across the river to destroy Agon's people even as Ka carried away the beautiful golden spirit that Agon loved.

Agon met the line of men in the river. He stood among the rocks, blocking their way with his axe, singing in unison with the blade as the axe whirled in a song of death.

Bodies fell before him, but more men came on, their spears thrusting at him, an endless line, a serpent of men and spears, each section that he killed replaced by another. A spear drove into Agon's shoulder, another into his leg, and still he fought, the axe smashing bodies and faces that rushed toward him. He heard the cracking bones, splitting skulls. He saw the growing pile of dead. But still the men came.

Ka roared from the far bank, and the men spread out. They came at Agon from all sides, circling behind him as hyenas surround a fighting stag.

Then, above Ka's shrieks, above the battle noise, above the thunder, another sound shattered the air, terrible in intensity and unleashed power. And with the sound came a black wall of water hurtling down the river valley. Trees crashed, boulders were lifted and thrown, everything was swept away by its ferocity.

Agon's axe continued to whirl in the death song even as the water struck him, struck Ka's men. He knew then that the Earth Mother had accepted his offering and had replied. The tribe would live.

In that final moment he saw that Ka carried Eena up the opposite cliff. She looked back at Agon as the wall of water seized him, hurled him into the black awfulness. But he still saw her beautiful face, saw her outstretched arms reaching toward him.

Through the Shadows

33

The Search

BRIGHT GOLDNESS LAPPED softly around Agon, and he rose and sank back, lightly, borne up, weightless, caressed, cradled in the gentle arms of golden lightness. The goldness was around him and above him and in him. He lay in the womb of the Earth Mother.

His forehead pressed into the black mud of the riverbank. Below his mouth the water grasped at him, hissing snakelike, creeping up the wet earth of the riverbank, sliding down again. Beyond his feet the water demons grasped at him with cold hands. He lay without moving in the darkness.

Slowly, light came, and warmth. Warmth on his back, his body. He lived. He raised his head. He lay at the edge of the river in a bay of quiet water. Outside the bay the river foamed.

Now he remembered, and he saw again the face of Eena as Ka carried her up the bank on the opposite side of the river. His spirit, cold and black, stirred within him. He willed his spirit to leave him, to howl in the darkness while his body rotted in the mud of the riverbank. Rotted until his flesh was gone and his bones sank into the grasping claws of the river demons. His spirit obeyed, slowly leaving. He felt himself dying, and he welcomed death.

His hand grasped something. He held the axe.

He called his spirit, willed his spirit. Slowly, his spirit came back, called by the magic of the axe. Bright pain seared his wounds, and he willed the pain into nothing.

Agon crawled from the black water of the river, from the darkness of death. He crawled away from the grasping hands of the river demons, crawled onto the warm breast of the Earth Mother. He lay on the earth, and the strength of the earth and the strength of the axe flowed into him, and his spirit sucked in the strength of the earth and the axe as a newborn child sucks milk from its mother's breast.

Hunger twisted his stomach, and he waited with the axe.

A viper slid through the stones and grass, and Agon crushed the viper's head with the axe. He tore the skin from the writhing body with his teeth and ate the raw flesh. Strength slowly came to him, but he was still weak.

The white-peaked mountains were small in the east, and he knew he had been carried far by the river. The river that now flowed higher and faster than ever, that could not be crossed. He would have to cross the mountains to find Eena.

Brush and trees grew along the river, and he found flint on the riverbank. Working slowly and weakly, he chipped a blade from a piece of flint. He made a knife from the blade and a broken piece of ash limb, tying the stone into the wood with the skin of the viper.

He killed a rabbit with a rock, and opened and skinned the body with the knife. The meat gave him more strength, and he made a spear. He hid by a game trail, and after a long wait, killed a deer with the spear. He ate the raw organs and flesh and felt the strength and quickness of the deer flowing into him.

While strips of meat dried in the sun, he dug tubers from the earth with a digging stick. With a flint stone and a hard green rock, using dry grass, twigs, and dead branches, he made a fire with which he baked the tubers and roasted deer meat.

He softened the skin of the deer with its brains. He made a stone awl with which he punched holes in the skin, and he tried to sew as the women of the tribe did, using thin strips of deerskin, and saw that he could make rough seams.

He found that his strength had increased, so that he could run and throw his spear. He hid again by the game trail, and killed three more deer. With their softened hides and the first hide he made two long-sleeved cowled shirts, one to go over the other. He made wrappings for his legs, and mittens for his hands; for his feet, moccasins, fur side out. He stuffed the mittens and moccasins with dry grass for warmth, for he would go where the ice spirits snapped their jaws in the great cold.

He filled a skin bag with dried meat, fat, dried berries, and nuts, and he fastened the bag to his waist with a deerskin belt. Carrying the warm clothing, with axe and spear, Agon began his search for Eena. He had been on the riverbank for one moon.

He followed the river upstream, toward the white peaks of those mountains that rose in the east. He found the flood-scoured remains of the cliff shelter at Grae's camp and climbed up the cliff to the ancient Stone of his people. He laid his axe and spear and body on the smooth surface and prayed to the spirits of his ancestors while the strength of the Stone flowed into his body and weapons.

He stood by the mass grave of his people, and he said to their spirits, *Rest. I go to kill Ka.*

He continued on to the east, circling the smoking, shattered remains of Spear Mountain, picking his way through mammoth chunks of rock now littering the plain.

The season was summer, but as he climbed into the foothills of the mountains, the nights became colder, and as he climbed higher, up past the trees and mountain meadows, the wind howled over bare rock, and snow swept down from the ice fields.

Giants lived in the mountains, and Agon asked the giants to let him come onto their hunting grounds, a lone hunter who carried his own food and asked nothing but to cross the white peaks.

He came to a place where the river plunged down through space, and he climbed the almost vertical rock face. Finally he stood on the bare rock of a mountain peak from where he saw the source of the river: the River Mother.

She was overwhelming—a vast plain of water that lay within the giant cupped hands of the snow-covered mountains. She was so immense that the mountains on her far side loomed distant and mysterious, and the falls and the river below her seemed merely a trickle from the nipple of her breast.

The mountains rose one upon the other around the River Mother, higher and higher to the end of the world. White plumes streamed from their peaks, and the sky rang with the clanging of their awesome and silent immensity. Agon stood as a pebble, a mite, a mote, in the presence of the mountains. Their power was such that no human could long live in their presence. His spirit quailed and weakened.

He saw the ibex. The creature balanced on a point of rock high above an abyss, head and sweeping horns raised proudly to the sky, fearless and wild, a spirit strong and free. Agon's spirit strengthened as he gazed at the ibex. And now the animal bounded strongly and fearlessly up the perpendicular face of the cliff, and Agon accepted the sign given him, a signal by his totem to accept the challenge of the mountains.

He put on the cowled shirts, the leg wrappings, the furry moccasins, the mittens, and he climbed upward into the snow. He was like a hare in the snow, his moccasins supporting him, gripping the crusty white surface. Ice walls towered above, wind created a blizzard, blinding him, trying to push him off the peaks. But he kept on, upward into the thin air, one labored step after the other as he circled the River Mother.

The cold deepened, and at night he burrowed in the snow to live, while each day he struggled upward.

The food in the bag froze into hard lumps, and he gnawed at it, and ate snow, to live. He wore the cowls of his shirts around his head, and he saw his shadow on the snow like some monstrous man-beast with enlarged hands and feet and head, a thick furry body struggling up the snowy ridges.

Only the sky was above him. The mountains spread below, descending in an unending series of snow-covered peaks. He stood at the top of the world.

He looked back to the west and saw the River Mother below him, and beyond, the thread of the river winding between the lines of the cliffs only to disappear in the haze of distance. North of the river lay the plain and the Blue Hills. On the other side of the river crouched the dark mass of the forest. He need only come down through the mountains on that side to enter the forest and find Ka.

Snow whirled in a blinding dance of death. Demons closed cold hands around him; icy wind sucked life from his body. He could not breathe, could not live on the top of the world. He plunged down the south side of the ridge, moccasins and spear supporting him.

Halfway down the long slope, the giants saw him. A muffled thud came from above, a huge foot stomping. Then something hurtled down the mountainside, a white monster advancing at terrible speed, hurling itself upon him.

He leaped sideways as a hunter leaps from a charging bison, calling on the magic of his totem. A blast of air struck him, tumbling him like a pinecone in a whirlwind. But the roaring thing rushed by, down the mountainside and out into space.

He lay in the snow, waiting for the giant's stamp of death. But the giant did not stamp again.

To one side of Agon the snow lay smooth, unmarked; on the other side was a wide tear in the white skin of the mountain, a wound made by the giant's spear. Agon drove his own spear deep into the snow and struggled to his feet.

Where the giant's spear had gone, the snow was scoured away to bare gleaming ice. He must cross the ice to come down the mountains. Must move laterally across the slippery path or be trapped forever between the ice and the edge of the slope that dropped away into empty space.

He pulled the spear from the snow and drove the point down upon the ice, like striking rock, but the point made a tiny indentation in the glassy surface. He placed the point of the spear in the indentation, and the point held.

Slowly, carefully, he edged out across the ice, driving the spear point in with every step, using the spear to hold him as he moved forward.

The deerskin moccasins slipped on the ice, and he dropped to all fours, crouching on the ice like a bear. Then he was sliding, the spear point not enough to stop him. He went down flat on the ice, arms and legs spread, spear point and mittened fingers clawing at the ice, sliding toward the edge where death waited.

He groped for his axe and drove the blade into the ice as his feet slid over the edge.

He stopped.

He sensed empty space below him. Not the space of the river cliffs, but space dropping down, through the swirling snow, down, down . . .

Slowly, he placed the spear point beside the axe blade and pushed the point into the indentation made by the axe. He lifted the blade of the axe.

The spear point held.

Delicately, carefully, he reached upward with the axe

and chopped a new hole in the ice. He hooked the axe blade in the hole, pulled his body upward, brought the spear point up beside the axe blade, chopped another hole, moved the spear point. Slowly, gradually, he moved away from death, chopping, pulling himself upward across the path of the giant's spear, leaving a track of holes in the ice surface until he reached the snow on the other side.

He crossed the snow field, probing with the spear, the axe ready. Then he worked his way down to the next ridge, and then another, descending the mountains while the giants watched.

Three days later, Agon reached bare patches of rock, the snow and ice disappearing. He walked between stunted trees, then down into the foothills, where the sun shone through tall trees. He looked unbelievingly at green grass and late summer flowers, heard the birds singing around him, felt the soft warm air caress his face.

He threw off his heavy hides and rested and soothed his body in the water of a sun-warmed pool, floating on his back in the tepid water, dozing in the sunshine. His wounds had healed during the journey, leaving only scars.

His food bag was empty, and he killed a young buck deer. He ate its raw liver hungrily, even before he made a fire. He broiled slices of the haunch on a stick, and the strength of the deer was in the meat. He rebound the axe head and the spearhead with rawhide; he made a flint knife with an antler handle.

He came down through the foothills and into the forest. The trees were the world here, giant beings that stretched their arms and heads into the sky, trees as numerous as the grasses of the plain. Tree spirits were strong, even in lone trees, but in the forest their spirits combined into one great forest spirit, ancient and powerful, alive since the Beginning, filled with mystery and power.

Other spirits were in the forest, strange spirits that watched from shadowy depths, moving silently and unseen, night creatures that saw in the darkness. Owls hooted and glided on noiseless wings in the night. Bats flickered in the dimness, their high-pitched voices like tiny, lost spirits, crying.

He circled back to the north until he reached the river valley, then followed the river downstream, past the shattered Spirit Mountain on the other side, to the place opposite Grae's camp where Ka and his men had crossed. The boulders were covered with tumbling, rushing water now, but he could see still see Ka as he jumped from rock to rock, Eena over his shoulder.

Agon turned and began to follow Ka's trail through the forest.

34

The Camp of Ka

EENA WORKED AGAINST the thongs that bound her wrists behind her back. She lay on her side on the dirt floor of the hut, rubbing the thongs against the rough edge of a rock near the fire hole. She felt the leather beginning to weaken, and she strained to keep the thongs pushed hard against the stone. Her ankles were tied, and to keep pressure on the wrist straps she bent her legs at the hips and knees, giving her body the stability it needed.

Through the openings in the branch walls of the hut, she saw the guards leaning on their spears, their knobbed heads menacing in the firelight. She had almost escaped earlier that evening, running from the camp after learning of Ka's return, but the guards had caught her, dragged her back to the hut, and bound her.

Tonight the moon would be full, and the ceremony was to take place at moonrise. The ceremony of her mating by fire with Ka, delayed for two moons while Ka hunted down an enemy.

But she would never submit. They would have to kill her, and if they did, her spirit would go free. Free to join Agon. Agon. She had seen the wall of water sweep over him, yet she had never given up hope that his spirit would find hers.

Feet scuffed the ground outside, and she rolled on her back, hiding her wrists under her.

Kara and three of the priest-women came through the opening with a torch. The flickering light illuminated their faces, showing their hatred, their loathing for her.

"Still you struggle." Kara kicked her. "Roll over."

Eena lay motionless, looking past the face of the woman, gazing at the ceiling of the hut.

Kara motioned to the priest-women. "Turn her. She tries to hide the straps."

They bent over her, strong hands grasping her body. She twisted and kicked out, her bound feet striking the stomach of one of the priest-women, sending the woman staggering back against the wall. The other women fell on Eena, tearing at her, striking her, kicking her. But she fought back, kicking and biting, her spirit stronger than all of theirs.

Kara shouted, and the guards burst into the hut. They stared, then laughed. The leader spoke. "She will be interesting for Ka."

Kara snarled at them from the floor, "Kill her!"

"Ka wants her alive."

Kara pulled herself up, clutching one of the poles that supported the roof. "She will not live long. Tie her to these poles. We are to get her ready."

The man looked at Eena and showed his teeth. "She is ready. I would take her now."

"She is Ka's. Tie her to the poles, or I will bring him. He will cut your limp organs off and stuff them in your mouth."

The man growled at Kara, but he signaled the others. They held Eena and cut the thongs that bound her wrists and ankles. Then they lifted her, their hands savage and cruel on her body as she struggled, and stood her between the two roof poles. They tied a wrist to each pole, then each ankle, so that she stood spread-eagled between them. They stared at her, their eyes gleaming.

"When Ka is finished with her," the leader said, "we will tie her again like this to poles on the ground. When we have finished with her, we will sell her to the hunters, one spear point for each man's turn."

"Get out!" Kara gestured obscenely. "Ka will not finish with her until she dies. You will spill your slime in each other's mouths before he gives her to hyenas such as you!"

The men backed out of the hut, laughing hoarsely. "Call us if she throws you to the floor again. Call us if she overpowers you."

Kara stood in front of Eena. She took a knife from her belt and pressed the point into Eena's arm. "If you even show your teeth, I will cut pieces of meat from you."

Eena gazed beyond Kara. The strength of her spirit was still greater than Kara's, than all their spirits.

Kara saw the pride in Eena's eyes, and she pressed the knifepoint in until the arm bled, but Eena made no sound. She was stronger than all of them—all except Ka.

Their hands tore at her, ripping off the belt given her by the Earth Mother, stripping away her short tunic. As the belt left her waist, Eena felt the strength of her spirit weaken, but she made no sign.

The women performed the mating preparation of the chieftain's bride. They anointed Eena with civet and musk, and wove bird bones and wings into her hair. They painted her face, her body, her hands and feet in the death signs of their tribe.

Kara held a wooden cup to Eena's mouth. "Drink."

The liquid smelled sickly sweet—overripe fruit and pungent herbs, and something else, a smell of fermentation and fungus. She held her mouth closed, but the women pulled her head back and stifled her, their hands over her nose until she gasped for air and the liquid entered her mouth and throat, choking her as hard hands forced the cup against her mouth. The liquid burned her bruised lips and throat, and spread like fire through her body. They forced her to swallow a second cupful, and a strange weakness overpowered her spirit and she could fight them no longer.

They saw her weakness, and cut the thongs holding her to the poles. They tied sandals on her feet and dressed her in a short skirt of white skin, her breasts bare. They placed a necklace of teeth around her throat, then stepped back to look at her.

"Now she is ready for Ka. She will become the bride of Ka."

Eena swayed, weak and helpless. Her hand went to her throat. They had not removed her totem, the ivory doe given to her by her father and mother. Her hand closed around the deer. "I will wear the belt." Her voice seemed to come from a great distance.

"That old thing!" Kara glared at her. "Not for the mate of my son!"

"I will wear the belt, or you will have to kill me."

Kara's loathing pressed against Eena like the knife blade, and the priest-women's hatred joined with Kara's, their spirits against Eena's spirit. Kara fingered her knife, and her eyes narrowed. "When Ka tires of you, he will give you to me. Then if you try to run, I will heat the knife in the fire and hold it against the smoking soles of your feet. You will obey me, or I will push the hot knife into your eyes, cut you everywhere, slowly. Before I finish, you will beg me to kill you."

A single ponderous beat of a drum sounded from the clearing.

Eena saw the women's faces change, fear entering their eyes. She went to the wall where they had thrown the belt, walking proudly, her head up. She knelt, picked up the belt, and fastened it around her waist. Instantly she felt the magic, the strength of the belt flow into her. She rose. She did not look at the women, would not let them see her eyes and know that tonight Ka would die.

They led her from the hut and toward the fire, Kara in front, a priest-woman on either side of her, one behind. They walked slowly, letting the people feel the women's magic as they brought Ka's bride, letting them see the sensuality of this woman as she came to the chieftain. Filled with lust, the people of Ka raised cups filled with liquid scooped from a wooden trough, and they screamed in brutish expectation as they saw Eena's breasts, her painted body, her hair adorned with dead birds.

The drums throbbed as Eena approached the fire where Ka waited. His cruel eyes shone in the firelight, his face triumphant, a leopard at the moment of kill.

Eena held herself erect, looking over the heads of the people, her face proud, her eyes unafraid. Her body trembled inwardly at what was about to happen, but her spirit stayed strong. *Wait,* her spirit whispered.

Ka's terrible eyes looked down at her. He took her wrist in one powerful hand and raised her arm, shaking his spear. He shouted, "Ka has returned!"

The wild-eyed people roared back: "Ka has returned!"

"See Kra who claimed to be chieftain while Ka found new hunting grounds!"

The people roared, "See Kra!"

Four men carried in a framework of branches. On the framework lay a bloody and mutilated man, lashed spread-eagled.

"For two moons, Ka has pursued this man through the forest. Now, while Ka takes his bride, Kra will die!"

The men carried the litter to the blazing fire, placing the frame above the flames on four short vertical poles. The flames rose up to meet the writhing body. The man was engulfed in fire, yet he made no sound.

"Kra dies!"

"Kra dies!" shouted the people.

Eena stared into the trees beyond the fire. Her body recoiled as if she were burning in the fire. Her eyes avoided the man's tortured body, her ears shut out the crackling of his skin, her nostrils denied the smell of his burning flesh. Yet she felt, saw, heard, smelled these things. Her spirit weakened and trembled within her.

Ka raised her arm higher. "This woman comes to Ka!"

The people shouted, "This woman comes to Ka!"

The drums beat louder, and Ka, seizing Eena, lifted her above his head, turning, showing her to the frenzied people. The drums changed to a faster rhythm, a savage pulsing like the beating of some monstrous and bestial heart. The people began to dance around the fire, around the burning body of Kra. And Ka shrieked in exultation while he danced, carrying Eena high above the dancers.

Eena made no struggle. She let her body hang as the fawn hangs from the lion's mouth. Her spirit weakened, but still it cried out: *Wait.*

35

The Mating Dance

AGON CIRCLED BEHIND the guard.

Firelight like spraying blood flickered from the clearing into the forest. Drums throbbed a demonic rhythm of lust and death. Hoarse shouts, yells, screams tore the night. The smell of burning flesh and hair stank in the air.

The axe crunched into the man's skull below the knob of hair. Agon caught the man's body and lowered it silently to the ground. He watched from the shadows as Ka held Eena's limp body above the dancing circle of people.

Agon wound his hair into a knob. Then he stepped into the guard's place at the edge of the clearing.

The first light of the rising moon appeared above the shadows of the trees. Ka shouted and threw Eena into the grasping arms of the man behind him. Ka tore off his breech clout, and his great male organ stood out like that of a stallion.

The dancers howled. They grasped Eena, lascivious hands demeaning her body. They passed her back over their heads to those behind them, moving her slowly, agonizingly, above the circle of dancers. Demon howls pierced the air, clawing hands grasped her, wild eyes glared up at her. Her body whirled in the red flame light, and the pounding of the drums crashed into her brain.

When she completed the circle, thrown from one pair of hands to the next, she would come to Ka. She closed her eyes. Her spirit said, *Wait.*

Agon lifted the dead guard and held him upright, one arm around the man's chest. As Eena was carried past, Agon danced drunkenly into the circle with the dead guard reeling beside him. Men in back of him snarled, and Agon snarled back. The man who carried Eena danced two places ahead of Agon.

The man pawed at Eena, slobbering as he held her, then the man ahead of Agon dragged her away, lifting her above his head.

Agon tore loose the knot of the dead guard's hair, lifted him, and threw his body back to the man behind. Almost in the same motion he drove his knife into the neck of the man who carried Eena. As the man dropped, Agon caught Eena and carried her into the shadows of the forest.

Eena danced in another time and place, under a cliff wall with one she loved. His hands held her, his arms encircled her.

Agon held her. The black mists of sorrow and waiting parted, and joy burst upon her spirit. She floated as in a dream, and as Agon carried her through the forest, she pressed her face against his chest and cried silently in her happiness.

Agon held Eena close to him as he ran, carrying her with such joy that she seemed weightless, her body one with his, running effortlessly and lightly, racing as the night wind through the forest.

Finally, he stopped and placed her gently on her feet, and they held each other close. Her face was beautiful beyond his remembrance. "You came for me." Her voice was soft as the evening song of the birds.

Agon touched her face gently, lovingly. "I will always come for you."

Harsh shouts came from the direction of Ka's camp. "They will run like hyenas," Agon said. "Can you run?"

"I can." She took his hand. "And we will run like wolves."

They pulled the bird wings and bones from Eena's hair and carefully buried them; then they ran together, lightly and fast, the sounds of pursuit fading behind them. Guided by stars they saw through openings in the trees, they circled north, toward the cliffs and the river valley. All that night they ran. When morning came, they stopped by a stream to drink and rest.

After they drank, Eena bathed, washing the painted death symbols, the filth of Ka's tribe from her body. When they had eaten from the bag of food Agon carried, they hid themselves in the thick undergrowth to sleep. Agon held Eena close in his arms, and she spoke with her lips touching his throat.

"I cannot live without you. If they find us, before they come to us, let your spear send our spirits together into the mists."

He stroked her hair. "If the time comes. Our spirits will always stay together."

She curled her body into the curve of his. "Then I will not be afraid."

They slept, but ominous sounds wakened them, foreboding as the hiss of a snake: the sound of running men.

Eena made no sound, but Agon felt her body stiffen.

He held her close. "They will not take you again."

"No."

"Now we run again. If we have to fight, stay near me."

"I will. But give me one of the spears. We will kill them as we did on the plain."

He gave her the spear. "The spear has magic in your hands. Touch my axe and spear, fill them with your magic."

She placed her hands on the weapons. "If I have any power, let it flow into this axe, this spear. Let them avenge our people."

They drank from the stream, then ran again, away from the sound of the running men. Eena ran strong and fast, carrying the spear, not looking back, touching Agon's hand only when they paused to rest and listen.

In midafternoon they came to the edge of the forest. The tops of the immense cliffs that hung over the river valley lay just beyond the undergrowth at the rim of the forest.

Agon told Eena, "A path goes down the cliffs near here. If Ka has not found our trail, we will go down the cliff, and you will be free."

She took his hand. "I am free now. I have been free since you carried me from Ka's fire."

They crept to the edge of the trees and lay flat on their stomachs, looking through ferns and bushes toward the cliff top. Scattered trees grew along the edge of the cliff, even on the stone lip; ancient, windswept giants with their roots deep in cracks in the rock. They saw no sign of Ka's men.

They went cautiously to the edge of the cliff. They had come from night into day, the green gloom of the forest giving way to the high blue vault of the open, sunlit sky. Hawks circled lazily above the bend of the river, fluffy white clouds floated in the sunshine, and below them the river curved in a sweeping arc through the valley. On each side of the river the vertical cliff walls glowed in the slanting sunlight, while in the shadowed areas blue and purple haze spread like soft mist.

Far to the north across the plain the Blue Hills rose, mysterious home of the Earth Mother and the good spirits.

Agon saw tears in Eena's eyes. She spoke softly: "If the world can be so beautiful, it cannot all be cruel. The spirit who made this world must be a good spirit. When we return to our cave in the Blue Hills, we will be with the good spirits, and we will be happy."

"We cannot return to the cave," Agon told her. "The river is impossible to cross, and even now the snow piles deeper in the mountains." He pointed. "The hunter who taught me to throw the axe told of a place in the west, a place of green plains thick with game, a place of friendly people. Will you go there with me?"

"I will go there with you, and we will be happy. We will have children. You can teach the boy to hunt, and I will teach the girl to gather food, and to keep our camp. . . ."

The sound came again, the drumming of running feet.

Agon said, "The trail is below a point of rock, around that curve in the cliff. We must go carefully."

They crept back into the forest and slipped quietly through the trees until they were around the curve of the cliff. Again they crawled through the underbrush and peered out.

Men waited at the point. Men with spears and knobbed heads.

36

Axe and Spear

THEY BACKED SILENTLY into the forest.

"Use your spear now," Eena said quietly. "We will go into the mists together."

"Not yet. I will not let them take you."

"I am not afraid. Hold me while you take my spirit."

He took her hand in his. "I will if they trap us, but I see one chance."

Hope returned to her eyes. "Another trail?"

"Farther along the cliff top. We will have to go out over the cliff edge, swing down to the trail on a vine." He looked at her intently. "Can you do that? We may die that way instead of by the spear."

"I will be with you," she answered, "and I will not be afraid."

He pointed to the west, past the point. "We will go between the men at the point and those coming through the forest. A great tree stands on the cliff top, and I have tied a vine to it. When we reach the tree, the sun will be almost down. If we can reach the trail at that place, they can never find us."

They ran through the forest. The sound of the pursuing men was closer now.

The tree, an ancient lightning-blasted oak, stood on the very edge of the cliff, defying the empty space below. Agon and Eena, holding onto the gnarled roots of the tree, leaned out over the cliff's edge. Far below they saw the base of the cliff, but the cliff face was not visible. They hung out over empty space.

A vine knotted around the tree trunk dangled below the bulge in the cliff top.

"I have seen this place from across the river," Agon said, pointing. "The ledge and trail are back under the bulge of the cliff. We will go down the vine, swing in, and drop onto the ledge. Can you do that?"

"Yes."

"I will go first."

Eena said, "If you fall, I will fall with you. They will not take me again."

Agon thrust the two spears into the back of his belt, then he grasped the vine. His face to the cliff edge, his feet against the stone wall, his body outward over the abyss, he went over the bulging edge of the cliff. Eena watched, hardly breathing.

Agon backed farther down the cliff, and the vine creaked as a strip of bark snapped. His feet reached the bottom of the bulge, and he let his legs drop until he hung by his hands. He dropped lower, one hand at a time, until he dangled below the overhanging bulge.

Eena spoke from the cliff edge. "Ka comes from the forest with three men. Many others come along the cliff top, not yet close."

"I am coming up." Eena heard death in Agon's voice.

"I will wait for you. Ka comes fast and will cut the vine."

Ka's harsh cry rang out as he ran toward Eena. He gestured to the first man behind him. "Take her and bind her while we find the woman stealer. Do not kill her. We will cut them and hang them over a slow fire." Ka and the other two men spread out along the cliff top, spears ready, searching behind rocks and trees.

The first man approached Eena, grinning evilly, his spear raised, a coil of thongs in his free hand. Then he pointed and shouted to Ka, "Look, he crawls in the rocks!"

Agon came up over the cliff edge, and in one motion he threw his axe into the man's skull.

Ka shrieked and turned back as Agon hurled a spear

into the chest of the second man. Now the third man was upon Agon. Agon hurled the second spear, and the man dodged to one side. Snarling, the man ran toward Agon with his spear low for a disabling gut thrust. Agon had no weapon.

They were on the plain in another time. The man was almost upon Agon, and Ka was running in fast with one spear raised and another ready.

Eena seized Agon's spear from the ground and drove it into the man's neck, just under the skull, and he fell from the cliff, clawing at the spear.

Now Ka attacked. He hurled his first spear, and it flashed beside Agon's chest as he sidestepped the weapon.

They faced each other—Ka with his second spear, Agon weaponless.

They had come to the place of death.

Agon's back was to the cliff edge. Ka moved forward, his spear held low in both hands, his eyes burning hatred, his face a mask of fury under his great knot of hair and the white arm bone. He moved with the sinuous power of a giant snake, hissing in his awful anger and demonic strength.

Eena picked the axe from the ground, called "Agon!" and threw the axe spinning into Agon's hand.

Agon began the axe song.

He sang with the axe as it whirled, the blade singing a litany of death, spinning ever faster, an invisible spirit of magic that gained in power as it advanced toward Ka, singing death as it whirled past the spear that drove into Agon's leg, whirling as it splintered the bones of Ka's shoulders, Ka's arms, Ka's legs.

Agon lifted Ka by his throat and one shattered leg. He raised him facedown, high above the cliff edge, and held him so that he could see what lay below.

Then Agon threw Ka out over the edge.

Eena ran to Agon, then drew back, for the terrible light of death and battle still shone in his eyes. He turned slowly toward her, and his face and eyes softened. He lifted the bloody axe from the ground. "He will kill no more."

Eena placed her hand in his. "He died as he would have killed you." She knelt before Agon. "The spear went deep. I will bind the wound."

Agon shook his head. "The others come. Will you follow me over the cliff?"

"I will follow you."

Agon went down the wall again, and his blood dripped on the stone and into the empty air. When he hung below the bulging wall, he pushed with his feet against the slope of the overhang and swung out away from the cliff—in, out, in. He released his grip on the vine.

Eena held her hands over her mouth, not breathing.

Agon's voice came from below the wall. "Come now, and I will guide you."

Eena came down the wall as in a dream, and as her body swung out over the gorge, she had no fear, only a fierce joy. As her feet pushed against the wall for the last time and she swung far out in the cool twilight air, it seemed that her mother's hand gently caressed her hair.

She paused for a moment, high above the earth, then soared back in a long, slow arc. Letting the vine slip through her fingers, she sank down through the shadows into Agon's arms.

They held each other for a moment. The sound of Ka's approaching men reached them from above—pounding feet, harsh voices. Agon and Eena drew back under the overhang as the men gathered on the cliff top. Agon drew the axe from his belt.

A man spoke, then others. Agon heard the name *Ka* repeated, but could understand nothing more. Eena listened intently to the voices, her hand on Agon's arm. They heard sounds of anger, then brutish laughter. The vine quivered and was drawn up out of sight. The men's voices became hushed, filled with awe. Then the sound of the men receded, grew faint, and was heard no more.

Agon stared up at the overhang, the axe ready. He whispered, "It is a trick. They have not gone."

Eena touched his axe hand. "They have gone. It is over."

"You understood them?"

"Yes. They saw Ka's body on the rocks below, and they shrieked with joy that he was dead. Then they saw the vine hanging empty below the cliff. They have gone back to their camp in the forest." She knelt and examined the spear wound in Agon's thigh. "It still bleeds. I will bind it."

"Not now. We must go down the cliff before night comes."

"I will bind the wound first."

"You have nothing to bind it with. Come."

"I will cut a strip from my skirt."

"We have no knife. Bind it later."

"I have a knife." Eena took the belt from her waist and removed a small flint knife from inside. "I would have killed Ka, then, myself."

She cut a leather strip and a pad from the bottom of her skirt. As she positioned the pad against Agon's wound, she said to him, "You are worshipped now."

"Worshipped?"

"They saw you kill Ka and throw him from the cliff. They saw us go over the edge of the cliff, yet they saw only two bodies at the base of the cliff—Ka and the man I killed." Eena wrapped the strap around Agon's leg and over the pad. "They think we are gods."

Agon stared at her.

Eena nodded. "They have given us names."

"What names?"

"They call you Axe God."

"And you?"

"They are ignorant people. They call me Goddess of the Spear." Eena knotted the bandage and rose to her feet. She smiled at Agon. "Now we will go to the land you have told me about."

On a sunny afternoon in late summer, a man and woman walked along a river that ran through a green plain thick with game. The man's body was laced with scars, but he walked easily, carrying a spear and an axe. The woman's hair shone golden in the sunlight, and she moved gracefully as a young doe. She carried a spear. She often looked up at the man, and when she did so, they smiled at each other and touched hands, as lovers might who have long been separated and have found each other.

Part II

Sons of Spear Woman

The New Land

1

The Strangers

EENA FIRST SENSED the child within her as she and Agon made their night camp near the base of a low cliff. For two moons they had traveled down the river valley, fleeing from the tribe of Ka, from the place where Agon had killed Ka, the place where Eena had fought beside Agon, killing Ka's men. Agon, called the axe man by those who had seen him kill his enemies in the mystic axe song. Eena, called Spear Woman by those who had seen her use her spear in battle, seen her bring magic to the spears of the hunters.

Eena studied the cliffs. "The hills rise behind the cliffs as they did where our family lived when my mother was alive." Her face grew sad for a moment, then she smiled. "When we have a daughter, I will take her into the hills as my mother took me. I will teach the child the names of the plants. We will make baskets together, and I will tell her stories and comb her hair as we sit in the sunshine."

"A daughter?" Agon looked up from inspecting his axe

and spears. "First we will have a son. I will teach him to hunt, and how to do the axe song. Then we can have a daughter."

Eena bowed her head in mock humility. "As you command."

Agon looked closely at her. "You know something."

"I am only a woman. What could I know?"

"Tell me."

She spoke shyly. "I am with young."

He stared at her. "You know this?"

"Yes."

"How?"

"I feel it inside me." She took Agon's hand and held it against her body.

"I feel nothing but your muscles. Your stomach is flat and hard as a hunter's."

"Soon you will feel him. It is a boy."

"How can you know this?"

"Women know. You will have a son!"

"A son. How soon?"

"Six, maybe seven moons."

"When we come to the place we seek in the west," Agon said, "we will start our own tribe!"

"The blood of Grae and Erida and the blood of Stig and Reva will combine to give strong hunters!"

"And wise women." Agon lifted Eena high in his arms. She placed her arms around his neck. "We were mated by the women of the Earth Mother. The child will be strong and wise."

The women of the Earth Mother. Agon remembered a shimmering figure in the moonlight, a female spirit joining with his spirit. . . .

"When you are too old to be chieftain, he will become chieftain, and his magic will be strong. Like yours. Like Grae's."

"My only magic is in the axe. Let the child's magic be like Grae's, magic that makes him a leader of men, a chieftain." Agon felt Eena's body suddenly stiffen. He said quietly, "What?"

Eena replied softly, "Someone watches from the cliff."

Agon continued to hold her. "By the oak tree?"

"Yes."

"Enemies?"

"Someone young. Someone afraid."

Agon placed her on her feet, and she knelt and turned the venison on the wooden spit over the small fire, not looking at the cliff.

Agon tightened the rawhide strap that bound the greenstone head of his axe to the antler handle. "Have your spear ready. Someone may have sent children to trick us."

"I think they are alone."

The roasting meat sizzled and sent its aroma wafting up into the darkness. Eena sliced a brown and juicy outside piece with her flint knife and held it out to Agon. She spoke in a normal voice: "We cannot eat all of this. We will have to give it to the foxes."

Something moved on the cliff edge—a small stone sliding.

They waited, Eena's hand near her spear, Agon's near his axe.

A thin figure stood at the edge of the firelight. Eena sliced two thick pieces from the roast and placed them on a flat rock. "Could hungry ones eat with us?"

The figure took two small steps toward the fire. A boy. Shaggy haired. His winters less than the fingers of three hands.

Eena held out the meat on the rock. The boy's eyes gleamed in the firelight. He pointed to the ground between himself and Eena.

Eena placed the rock where the boy pointed, then she walked back to the fire. Agon sat quietly eating, not looking at the boy.

The boy stepped cautiously toward the meat, watching Agon. In one quick motion he seized the pieces of meat and darted back into the darkness.

Eena sliced more meat and placed it on a rock near the fire. Agon said, "Hunters eat together by the fire."

Two figures stood at the light's edge.

Eena smiled at them. "Come. The meat tastes best when it is hot."

They inched slowly forward. The boy and a girl. Tangled dark hair. Starved-looking bodies. Scraps of hide covering their loins. The boy held a crude spear. The girl stood painfully bent, as if crippled or hurt, and her legs were strangely dark.

Eena held out the smoking meat, and they seized it greedily, gnawing at the pieces like wolf cubs. Eena gave them more, and their eyes showed their gratitude.

Eena touched her chest. "Eena." She touched Agon's shoulder. "Agon."

The boy pointed at Agon's axe and spoke, his voice half man, half boy: "What?"

"Axe." Agon slipped the weapon from his belt and held it up for the boy to see.

"What for?" The boy reached toward the axe, and Agon shook his head no.

"The axe song."

The boy drew back. "Can it kill?"

"Yes."

"Have you killed men with it?"

"Yes."

The boy stared at the axe. "Will it kill many men?"

"Only in the axe song."

"Kill Hornsa and his men."

"Who is Hornsa?"

"He killed our father and mother."

Eena made a small sound of sorrow. She held her arms out to them, and the girl leaped back, her eyes filled with terror. The boy raised his spear. "Don't touch her!"

Agon spoke quietly. "We will not harm her. Lower your spear. Why is she frightened?"

"They hurt her. Hurt her many times. All of them. A

stallion broke my father's leg. I was away hunting when they came. I will kill Hornsa."

Agon looked into the boy's eyes. "Wait until you are bigger and stronger. Come with us, and I will teach you the axe song. When you are a strong man, you can kill Hornsa."

"I will kill him now. When he sleeps. I will drive my spear through his throat."

Eena spoke to the girl: "Ka did to me what Hornsa did to you. Agon killed Ka with this axe. When your brother learns the axe song, he can kill Hornsa. Stay with us. We have left the land of Ka's people and will find a new home in the west. We will be father and mother to you and your brother."

The girl shook her head, staring at the ground. The darkness on her legs was dried blood.

The boy motioned toward the girl. "She cannot sleep. She will watch while I kill Hornsa. Then she can sleep."

Agon asked, "How many men has Hornsa?"

The boy silently held up the fingers and thumb of one hand.

"You cannot kill all of them."

"At night I can. First I will kill Hornsa, then each of his men."

"What does Hornsa look like?"

"Like a giant."

"And you will kill him."

"Yes."

"You will not stay with us?"

"No."

"Leave your sister with us."

"No. She must see me kill Hornsa."

The boy beckoned to the girl, and before Agon or Eena could stop them, they ran into the darkness.

That night Eena cried silently against Agon's shoulder. Cried for the girl who had suffered under the bodies of six men. Cried for the boy who would die so that his sister could sleep.

Agon and Eena tried to track the boy and girl in the morning, but there were no marks of their feet on the smooth rock of the canyon floor or on the cliff walls.

They traveled downriver that day, and the next day they saw vultures circling ahead. The spear-torn body of the boy lay in a dried pool of his blood, his spear still in his hand. The girl's body lay nearby, bloody and flattened as though she had been crushed under some great stone.

Hornsa and his men moved silently down the game trail that led through the brush along the river. Ahead of them the golden hair of the woman shone in the sunshine as she and the man emerged from a grove of willows, walking fast but not running. Hornsa saw that the man could kill him, and he waited to attack until night came and the man and the golden-haired woman slept.

Yount lay in the tall grass on the edge of the cliff, watching the man and woman come down the river valley. He had first seen the golden hair of the woman far up the valley when the sun was directly overhead, and now the sun hung halfway down the sky, and the two people were almost directly below him.

Never had Yount seen a woman such as this. Her hair, gleaming like the sun, hung down to her shoulders in back with two long braids circling her head. She was young and slender, but she carried a spear, holding it as a hunter does, ready for thrust or throw. She moved so easily and lightly that she seemed to Yount like a young doe, stepping gracefully and alertly along the riverbank.

The man frightened Yount. He walked with the supple ease of a great cat, strength and killing power evident in the ripple of his muscles, the posture of his body. Dark-haired and hawk-faced, his body laced with scars, he carried two spears and an axe. Yount backed cautiously away from the cliff edge, fearful that the man might see him. He would go back to the camp. Yurok would want to know about the woman with the golden hair.

The horror of the girl's death brought back to Eena the horror she had known when Ka had taken her as his bride.

The child she felt within her was Agon's child. Not Ka's. Not the child of cruelty, of pain, of death. Not the child of the man-demon Ka, who cut off the heads of her father and brother. Not the child of Ka, who carried her bound and helpless into his dark cave. . . .

It was Agon's child. Agon, who had rescued her from the cave, who had fought Ka's men to protect her, who had taken her with him across the plain in the darkness, who had gently held her while she cried for her dead, who had saved her from the fiery grasp of the Earth Mother, who had mated with her in love and ecstasy under the twin peaks of the Onerana. Agon, who had killed Ka.

Her fingers found the carved deer totem that hung from her neck. Let it be Agon's son. A son strong as Agon. Brave as Agon. Gentle as Agon. Loving as Agon. . . .

"Someone watched us from the cliff top." Agon loosened the axe in his belt. "Keep close to me if men come."

Eena gripped her spear with both hands. She should have been watching the cliffs, not dreaming about the child.

Agon looked back, studying the river valley behind them. "The men of Hornsa still follow us. The man on the cliff top could be one of them. We have to find a place where we can fight them. Soon the sun will go down. If the men behind begin to close on us, can you run carrying the child?"

"I can run."

They walked along the river, seeming unaware of Hornsa and his men, searching the cliff face for a hiding place or a trail up to the plain.

People had lived in the canyon sometime in the past. The ceilings and walls of the cliff overhangs were smoke-blackened above fire pits, and flint chips littered the rocky ground.

Agon gazed up and down the river. "We can be trapped here. Enemies can come from both sides as Ka did at Grae's camp. Only a large tribe would be safe here." He pointed. "The canyon opens out ahead."

They rounded a bend in the river and came out of the canyon. Eena made a sound of awe. Before them, thrusting up from the trees at its base, lay a massive hill. Its sides almost vertical, its rounded top covered with a thick growth of trees, it resembled a giant bear—a bear asleep on its stomach, head on its paws. The setting sun illuminated it from behind with a halo of golden light.

Agon studied the hill. "We could hold off a tribe if we were on top. . . ."

They looked at each other. Then they ran toward the hill.

They circled it. The smooth walls rose abruptly from the plain, impossible to climb. Impossible except at the head end of the bear, where a stream gurgled out from between the paws and down a steep escarpment.

They climbed the escarpment, following the only possible pathway, the course of the stream, a pathway so narrow it could only be traversed single file. They came to the bear's head and stopped, gazing in surprise at what they saw.

The escarpment led into a narrow porch, a platform with low rock walls on either side, open to the sky and sun. The river valley, plains, forests, and hills spread out below them—the herds of game, the cliffs, the river sharp and clear in the luminous glow of sunset.

At the rear of the porch, a graceful rock arch formed an entrance to a cave. The rock was light colored and smooth, and a pleasant feeling of safety and comfort filled the porch and entrance.

They looked into the cave, and there was no sign of

humans, or even of animals. Eena touched the wall. "This is a good place. We can defend it."

"Yes." Agon shifted one of the huge boulders that lay around them. "Hornsa and his men are cowards and will attack at night. I will set trip lines to tell us when they come."

Eena said, "If they come to the top, we will fight them here. If you die, I will kill myself. Our spirits will go together into the sky."

Agon touched her face, gently. "We will not die yet."

Hornsa and his men climbed stealthily and silently up the escarpment in the darkness, their spears ready, their male organs gorged with blood in anticipation of what they would do to the golden woman.

Hornsa's shin touched something so slender it seemed but a stem of grass across his path. From above came a little sound, like a cricket chirping. Hornsa stopped, listening. Only silence above him.

Hornsa crept cautiously upward again, motioning his men to follow.

Something heavy moved above him. A creaking sound like stone rubbing stone came to his ears. Then he knew.

Hornsa shrieked and ran up the slope, his spear raised. But death came to him and his men as a huge boulder hurtled down the streambed, smashing into them, crushing their chests and hip bones, hurling their broken bodies and their spears in a bloody mass from the top of the escarpment.

Then Agon and Eena came down the escarpment, and while Agon crushed each skull with his axe, Eena drove her spear into each throat, bringing vengeance to the men who had left the boy and the girl for the vultures.

2

Yurok

THAT SAME NIGHT Yount had returned to the summer camp of Yurok's aurochs hunters with news of the strangers. But Yurok was involved with one of the tribal maidens and could not see Yount until noon the next day.

The hide huts of the aurochs hunters stood hidden in the depths of a huge pine grove. White-and-red-spotted aurochs hides cured on wooden racks, aurochs carcasses hung from branches, and smoke from the evening fires curled up through the trees. The aroma of broiling meat, rank hides, raw meat, tanning pits, offal, and smoke was strong and pungent.

Yurok stood in front of the largest hut. A head taller than the hunters, he was broad in proportion, deep chested, and powerful. He wore the polished bull's horns of the chieftain on his head, the pure white bull's hide of the chieftain over his shoulders. His voice was strong and deep as that of a bull aurochs as he spoke to Yount.

"Two people?"

"Yes."

"And the woman had hair like the sun?"

"Yes." Yount pointed to the totem at Yurok's throat. "Like the sun discs."

Yurok lifted his disc and studied it. "That cannot be. The sun was in your eyes."

Yount shook his head.

"What else?"

"She carried a spear."

"A woman carried a spear?"

"Like a hunter."

Artron, the shaman, spoke. He wore deer's antlers on his head and was wrapped in a deerskin robe. "It is as I told you. A woman would come with hair like the sun disc, carrying a spear."

"Tell me now," Yurok said, "why she comes."

"To help the tribe. She has strong magic." Artron glanced toward Hura, the priest-woman. "Stronger than any other woman."

Hura glared at Artron. A dark, hard-faced woman, she stood strong as a hunter, and her eyes glinted like black ice. "I will test her magic. Her strength."

Yurok spoke to Yount: "Tell me of the man."

"He could kill me."

"You are safe here. Tell me what he looked like."

"He walked like a lion. Killing magic around him."

"His weapons?"

"Two spears. An axe in his belt."

"An axe? A wood-chopping axe?"

"No. Smaller."

Hura spoke: "An axe man."

They stared at her. Yurok said, "What do you mean, 'axe man'?"

"A man who fights with an axe. A man who knows the axe song."

"What do you know about axe men?" Artron's voice was scornful.

"I knew an axe man once," Hura replied. "He was all man. He was not afraid to die, and the magic in his axe was like a growing whirlwind, building in strength so that none could stand against him. There are only a few axe men, for they only teach the axe song to those in whom they see the magic."

"What is the axe song?" Yurok asked.

"The magic of the axe. Two axe men do it together, if two can be found. But one does it alone in battle. Spears cannot harm him when he sings the axe song. He can kill ten men in ten blows."

"How do we know this is an axe man?" Yurok said.

"Any boy with a stick and stone can make an axe. Even a woman can make one to break wood. They are of no use in fighting. A man who knows how to handle a spear can easily kill a man holding a clumsy axe."

Yurok spoke to a bearded hunter: "Emar, tomorrow morning take Yount and ten men. Follow the trail of the strangers and bring them here." He looked at Hura. "We will find out how strong their magic is."

3

The Streaming Star

EARLY THE NEXT morning after the attack, Agon and Eena went down the escarpment. They dragged the bodies of Hornsa and his men to the riverbank andrew them into the racing water along with the broken spears. Then they carefully brushed away the drag marks with tree branches.

Eena gathered wood and built a small fire at the cave entrance while Agon entered the nearby forest in search of game. When he returned with a gutted deer, they skinned it and cut strips of haunch, which they broiled over the fire. All day they watched for any men who might attack them, and they saw none.

That evening the firelight threw a warm glow over the walls of the porch and the arch of the cave entrance. The last colors of sunset still lit the western sky, and through the narrow entrance of the porch the two people could see below them the shadowed river valley, the pale curve of the river, and the darkening plain stretching to the horizon.

Eena snuggled close to Agon. "It is the most beautiful place in the world. I wanted to return to our cave and pond in the Blue Hills, but I will be just as happy here."

"This is better," Agon said. "Either one of us can hold

off a tribe here. We have water, wood, and game. The walls of the porch protect us from the wind, and in winter the sun will shine deep into the cave, warming it."

"I wonder why the cliff people have never come up here."

"It is too small for a large tribe."

"But big enough for us—for our family, our tribe . . ."

"Yes." Agon placed his hand on Eena's abdomen again. "Does the child move?"

"You must wait. One more moon. Then you will feel him move."

"How do you know these things? When he will move, when he will come?"

She took his hand. "All women know these things."

As they spoke, the evening stars appeared above them. The air seemed clearer here, as though they were closer to the stars, for never had they appeared so brilliant, so large, so near.

Eena gazed at the heavens in delight. "The sky spirits are happy. They come with the new moon, and their campfires burn bright."

The slender crescent of the moon floated low in the dark blue southwest sky. Agon pointed. "Look!"

Above the moon a faint trail of fire streaked the sky, steady, unwavering.

"What is it?" Eena's voice was hushed.

"I don't know. . . ."

"It is not a falling star . . . it does not move. . . ."

"No."

They watched as the last light of the sun disappeared. The object was brighter now, its fiery tail fanning out behind it, its blunt head rounded and glowing. Eena shivered and moved close to Agon. "A powerful spirit comes."

"It comes as our son comes." He put his arm around her. "He will be strong and brave. A hunt leader, a chieftain. We will be proud of him."

Eena put Agon's hand over the place where the child

lay. "Then it is a good omen." She touched the deer at her throat. "Nothing bad will come from it."

Artron, shaman of the aurochs hunters, stared at the streaming star. Never in his lifetime had such a thing appeared. Nor in his father's lifetime. But Tron, his grandfather, had told of a burning star. A burning star that brought strange things to the earth.

Had the star been there and he had not seen it? How else to explain the shaking of the earth? How else to explain the great noise that had come from the east, a noise like the thunder of all the storms of all time? How else to explain the darkness of the sky that had made day seem like night? The darkness was gone now, but it had seemed of evil portent.

But the star was new. He had not seen it before tonight.

Artron brought the white bull skin from his hut. He unrolled the leather and laid it flat on the ground by the fire. With a piece of charcoal he drew the burning star on the bull skin, showing its fiery tail, the moon, the last tiny edge of light from the departed sun. Then he drew his totem, the deer. The star had come in the time of Artron. Whatever it might mean, whatever it might bring, it had come in his time.

Far to the east, in the tribe of bison hunters, Zur watched the star. What did it mean? Grae had never spoken of such a thing. Grae? He, Zur, was Grae. Sorcerer and chieftain.

The spear wound in his side burned like a hot coal. The skin had healed, but deep in his flesh the wound still flared. Agon had caused it. Agon, standing with Spear Woman on the cliff top. Agon, threatening him. Threatening Grae, the chieftain. Threatening him while Ka surrounded the camp in the darkness. Agon should die. But Agon was gone.

The star would tell him what to do. People hated him.

Grae's young sons hated him. They waited for him to die—waited as they had when he lay wounded with the spear, hoping he would die so that Agon would become chieftain. Zur ground his teeth. Agon should be punished for what he had done. Without Agon, Zur would have taken Spear Woman for his mate. Had not Zur brought back the spirits of Spear Woman's father and brother? Zur, giving his blood, standing on the Black Stone beside Spear Woman while Zur's blood dripped on the skulls of the stag and the horse? And what had Agon done? Nothing. Yet Spear Woman had gone into the bower with Agon. . . .

They were both gone . . . but they could come back . . . and Agon would try to kill Zur so that Agon could be chieftain. . . .

Zur stared up at the star. It was a sign. A sign to Zur that he would triumph over Agon. Would triumph over those who hated him. Triumph over those who lusted for his life, for his position as chieftain. . . .

4

The Test

SHORTLY BEFORE NOON, Emar and the hunters came to the paws of the bear.

"Their trail ends here," Emar said. "The man and the woman came first, then six men went up. Many came down dead. See the blood on the rocks."

One of the hunters spoke: "They are all dead. The spirits of Bear Hill have eaten them."

Another hunter said, "Let us go from this place."

Emar motioned with his spear. "We go up!"

The hunters drew back. "The spirits will tear us into pieces!"

Agon and Eena watched from the edge of the porch, their faces hidden by a juniper bush.

"Something frightens them," Eena whispered. "Maybe they will go away."

"One is the watcher I saw on the cliff top."

"They must have followed our tracks."

"And the tracks left by Hornsa as he followed us. They know we are here."

The leader of the men began to climb the escarpment.

Agon loosened the axe in his belt and laid one of his spears on the ground. "Have your spear ready. If he pretends he wants to talk and then throws his spear, I will kill him. If the others try to come up, we will roll another boulder down on them."

The man came slowly up the streambed. He was bearded, dark haired, as tall as Agon. He carried his spear point to the side. When the man was two spear-throws away, Agon stepped out onto the top of the trail. He held his spear point to the side.

The man stopped abruptly, staring up at Agon. "You are alive!"

Agon nodded.

"I am Emar, hunt leader. From the tribe of Yurok. He wants to see you and the woman."

"Let him come to us if he wants to see us."

"You are in our hunting grounds."

"We did not know this."

"Our summer camp is in the forest to the north. In the winter we live in the cliff shelters on the river."

"We saw them."

"We saw blood on the rocks below. The blood of many men."

"They tried to come upon us in the night. They were the men of Hornsa. We found a boy and a girl they had killed."

"I know of no Hornsa."

"He followed us to kill us."

"How many men?

"Hornsa and five."

"Did you kill all of them?"

"Yes."

Emar smiled. "Good."

Agon said, "We are not of your tribe. We will go. We have killed one deer. We will leave you the hide and the meat."

"I am to bring you to Yurok's camp. He wants to see the woman with the golden hair."

"She is my mate. If anyone tries to take her, I will kill him."

"We will not try to take her."

Agon looked back at Eena, and she came to stand beside him.

Emar gazed at her in wonderment. "What Yount said is true!" He turned and called to the men at the base of the escarpment. "See the woman's hair!"

A man called up, "Bring her down. We want to see her better!"

Emar spoke to Agon: "Will you come with us to our camp? We will not kill you or take the woman."

"Only if we keep our weapons. We come in friendship, but we will not give up our weapons."

"Keep them, but if you try to kill our chieftain, we will kill you."

"We will not harm your chieftain or any of you if you let us come as friends."

"Agreed." Emar looked at Agon's axe. "Hura told us of an axe song. Do you know that song?"

"Yes."

"Do you fight with the axe?"

"Yes."

Emar pointed to Agon's hand where the tip of the little finger was gone. "What happened?"

"Evil came. A hunter lost his magic and died on the bison's horns. The hunt leader must bring back the magic of the hunters with his blood."

Emar touched his totem, a carved bear that hung at his neck. "Do you bring that evil with you?"

"No." Agon touched his ibex totem. "We destroyed the evil."

Emar studied Agon's face, then Eena's. "Yes. You have seen evil and lived. Now I see why you did not die here."

"Why should we have died?"

"Spirits. Ancient and fearsome."

"Why fearsome?"

"The storytellers say that long ago strange beings lived here. Their spirits remain."

"If they are not evil, we do not fear them."

"Did you go into the cave?"

"Not yet."

Emar touched his totem again. "Do not go."

"Why?"

"Years ago, boys from our tribe went into the cave. They told of a horrible face, huge beings." Emar pointed at his men. "See Yount, the strange one?"

"We saw him as we came here."

"He was one of the boys. He became strange after he came to this place. Now none of our people dare come here."

Eena, listening, felt a tiny wave of apprehension.

"We do not fear good spirits," Agon replied. "We will go with you to see your chieftain. If he decides that we can stay in your hunting territory, we will come back to this place."

"You would live here, knowing what I have told you?"

"We do not fear animals, or men."

Emar shrugged. "You have been warned."

They went down the escarpment. The men below stared up at Eena, exclaiming in wonder as she approached.

Yount held out his hand toward her. "Touch?"

Eena looked at Agon. Emar said, "He is like a child."

Agon nodded. Emar motioned to Yount. "Touch her hair only."

Yount slowly brought his fingers to Eena's hair. He

stroked it softly. "The spirits in the cave won't harm you. They wait for you."

"Enough of this!" Emar spoke to his men: "We go to Yurok. The strangers keep their weapons."

One of the men objected, a big, pugnacious-looking man with small, mean eyes and the build of a bull. "Keep their weapons? You talk like a woman, Emar. Take their weapons. Kill the man and take the woman."

Emar looked coldly at the man. "You coward, Buner. You lump of bullshit. You were afraid to go up Bear Hill. Now you say 'take their weapons and kill the man.' " Emar spat on the ground. "Will you take the man's weapons?"

Buner stared at Agon. "I could take his weapons. After I kill him."

"After you kill him." Emar spoke to Agon: "Will you fight him?"

"We come in friendship. But if this man wants to fight, I will fight him."

Emar smiled. "I would like to see that. But first we go to Yurok."

They went to the northwest across the plain, skirting the hills that lay south of the river. Thick forests of pine covered the hills and flowed down upon the plain.

Outside a grove Emar stopped and called, a yodeling cry strange to Agon and Eena. A similar cry issued from the depths of the grove, and Emar led Agon and Eena through the trees to a clearing where low hide huts stood in a circle.

In front of the largest hut they saw a tall man wearing aurochs horns and a white hide cape. He held a spear in one hand and a hide shield in the other. A woman and a man wearing deer antlers stood behind the tall man.

"So," the tall man said. "You found them."

"They were in the cave on Bear Hill," Emar replied. "They come in friendship."

Yurok stared at Agon, at his weapons, then at Eena.

"You enter our hunting grounds. You come carrying weapons. This is friendship?"

"We did not know we were in your hunting grounds," Agon said. "We carry weapons because we search for a place to live, and must protect ourselves in this new land."

"Why did you come here?"

"When I was a boy, a hunter told me of this land."

"A hunter from here?"

"He had been here."

"Why did you leave your own people?"

"A tribe from the south killed our people."

"What tribe from the south?"

"The tribe of Ka."

"Ka!" The man wearing deer antlers spoke. "Ancient tales tell of an evil tribe by that name. But there was another name, like Ka. . . ."

"Their shaman was Kaan."

"Yes!" The antlered man stared at Agon. "You saw Kaan?"

"I killed him."

"Kaan cannot be killed."

"My axe split his skull."

"He lives forever. He comes again and again. His body may die, but the demon within him finds a new body. . . ."

"This is my wizard, Artron," Yurok explained to Agon. "He sees demons in every shadow."

Artron touched the sun-colored disc on his chest. "Demons are clever. Not all men recognize them."

The woman who had been standing behind Yurok spoke now: "We welcome the warrior who slew Kaan." She held out her hand to him. "I am Hura. Touch my hand that I may feel the strength of your magic."

"I have no magic." Agon did not touch the woman's hand.

"You have. I feel it." Hura glanced at Eena. "I feel no magic from this woman. Why does an axe man travel with a woman of no magic, no power?"

"She has power. Her magic is stronger than mine."

"This I do not believe." Hura smiled at Agon. "Perhaps you are dazzled by her hair. But it is known that only dark-haired people possess true magic."

Agon made no reply.

"You did not know this?" Hura said. "You must learn of these things. No doubt you found this woman somewhere and took pity on her, but it is impossible for her to have magic like yours. . . ."

Agon felt Eena's hand slip into his. He squeezed her hand lightly. "This woman is my mate," he said. "If any man talked of her as you have, I would kill him."

"Of course. You should defend her." Hura looked into his eyes. "I respect you for doing so."

Yurok motioned Hura back. He asked Agon, "What tribe do you come from?"

"The tribe of Grae, chieftain of the bison hunters."

"I have heard of him. A strong leader. Does he still live?"

"After Ka killed Erida and Ara and many of our tribe, Grae fell on his spear."

"He died with honor."

"Yes."

"Who were Erida and Ara?"

"My mother. My sister. Erida was Grae's mate."

"Then you are son of Grae."

"Yes."

"Why are you not chieftain?"

"Zur was Grae's first son. He is chieftain."

Yurok glanced at Agon's hand. "You touch your axe. You are not friends with this Zur?"

"No."

"Ah!" Yurok looked at Eena. "Perhaps Zur would have this woman?" He winked at Agon. "How many times have you had to fight for her?"

Agon said nothing. Yurok spoke to Eena: "Will he fight for you?"

"He killed Ka for me."

"Killed Ka? And Kaan?"

"Yes."

"How many others?"

"I don't know. I have seen him kill ten."

Yurok looked at Agon. "What if I took this woman?"

"I would kill you."

"My men surround you. I only have to raise my spear, and they would have ten spears in you."

"I would still kill you."

"With your axe?"

"Axe. Spear. Knife. My hands."

Yurok studied Agon's face, his eyes.

"You would die, too. My men would take the woman. I can see that many want her."

"They would never take her."

"Why not?"

"Ask her."

Yurok spoke to Eena: "Why not?"

"I would kill them. Then I would kill myself."

Yurok studied Eena's face and eyes as he had Agon's. Agon's hand closed on the handle of his axe, and he felt the carved ibex in the handle vibrating with magic and death. The place in the center of Yurok's forehead where the axe would strike grew larger and larger, so large that Agon saw every pore in the skin.

Buner cried, "I challenge him! I will take the woman!"

The camp became silent. Every motion ceased, the people still as the boughs of the forest before a storm.

Yurok spoke: "You, Axe Man, will fight Buner. You will fight our way. If you win, you can remain in our hunting grounds. If you lose, you die. The woman will be given to Buner."

The people yelled in excitement. Yurok said, "Are you ready, Axe Man?"

Agon touched his axe. "I am ready."

"You will not have your axe. We have our own way. If you will not fight that way, we will call you a coward and chase you from our camp. The woman will be taken by the man who challenges you."

"No one takes this woman. I will fight with any weapon you choose."

"You will have no weapons."

Buner scowled at Agon. "Run now while you can, or I will kill you like a snared rabbit. Your woman will be under my robe tonight."

Agon said nothing, but his eyes grew cold as ice.

"Put all your weapons down, Axe Man," Yurok said. "Emar will tie Buner first so you can see how it will be."

Buner laid his weapons aside and lay facedown in the dirt of the clearing. Emar looped a strap around Buner's ankles, then pulled them up behind his back and tied the other end of the strap around his throat.

"This is how we fight," said Yurok. "Now show us how brave the axe man is."

Agon gave his weapons to Eena. He said quietly, "Kill their chieftain first."

He lay facedown on the ground and raised his feet. Emar looped a strap around Agon's ankles, pulled them up tight behind his back, and tied the strap around his throat. Emar spoke softly: "He will try to roll on your strap or seize it and break your neck. Go for his wrists and throat." He said loudly, "They are ready."

The strap held Agon's body in an arched position, his head pulled back, his legs bent. The strap around his throat was like a powerful pair of hands choking him.

Yurok raised his spear. "Fight!"

Buner threw himself toward Agon, grasping for Agon's strap. Agon spun on his stomach to face Buner and seized his wrist with one hand. Buner clawed with his free hand at Agon's strap, and Agon rolled on his side, the strap beyond Buner's fingers. Buner rolled away, his strength like a mad bull, then rolled back toward Agon, throwing his weight toward Agon's strap. Agon rolled on his side and threw Buner over him, then twisted fast around and faced Buner, his hand still gripping Buner's wrist. Then Buner, experienced and bull necked, rolled again, completely over, his heavy body striking Agon's strap, and

Agon felt his head snap back and the strap tighten on his throat. But in that moment Agon's other hand seized Buner's throat, sinking into the beefy, corded neck. Buner brought his free hand in a spearlike jab toward Agon's eyes, and Agon turned his head barely in time, Buner's nails slicing into his cheekbone. Agon twisted and threw himself on Buner, forcing Buner's free arm under his body. Agon's fingers tightened ever deeper into Buner's throat.

Then Buner's face began to turn blue. His eyes bulged, his tongue protruded from his mouth, and he grunted spasmodically, his body jerking and twitching.

Emar tapped Agon's shoulder. "You have won. You can kill him or let him go. If you let him go, he will be your slave."

"I want no slave."

"Then kill him."

"No." Agon released his grip on Buner's throat. "Cut our straps."

"I could kill you now," Emar said, "but I fear the vengeance of the spear woman." He smiled. "I will cut the straps."

Agon felt the tension on his neck and legs fall away. He tore the strap from his neck as he came to his feet. "This is no way for men to fight."

Yurok stood among the circle of men who had watched the fight. "Look at your pecker. Look at Buner's, even though he is half-dead. This kind of fighting shows who the real men are!"

Agon stared at Buner, then felt under his own loin covering. His penis was erect and hard as stone.

"It comes with the choking," Yurok winked. "You should go to Spear Woman now."

Agon looked around the circle of faces. "Where is she? If anyone has touched her . . ."

Yurok laughed. "Look behind me. Tell her she can take her spear away from my neck now."

Eena came around Yurok and silently gave Agon his

axe, spear, and knife. Yurok said to her, "Would you have killed me if Axe Man had lost?"

"Yes."

Yurok slapped his thigh and let out a bellow of laughter. "You two are the kind of fighters we need in this tribe." He nudged Buner with one foot. "He lives. You should have killed him. I doubt if he will be grateful to you." He raised his spear and shouted, "Build up the fires and roast the meat! We will celebrate having Axe Man and Spear Woman join our tribe!"

As they sat around the chieftain's fire with Yurok and Artron, Yurok spoke seriously to Agon and Eena.

"You should think carefully about living in Bear Hill cave."

"We have," Agon replied. "We want to live there."

"Did Emar tell you of the strange things there, of what has happened to those who entered the cave?"

"He did."

"And you aren't afraid?"

"No."

"To not be afraid is good. To be foolish is not good."

"We slept there last night. We are still alive."

"True. But did you go back into the cave?"

"No."

"Wait. Go into the cave. If you come out alive and not crazy like Yount, then decide." Yurok spoke to Eena: "Doesn't the cave frighten you?"

"No."

"Does anything frighten you?"

"Yes."

"What?"

"To offend the gods."

"How does one offend the gods?"

"By disobeying their commands. By acting as a god."

"So Artron tells me. But I think the commands are Artron's, not the gods'. And sometimes a chieftain must act like a god."

Artron protested: "Only the gods truly command us. And a chieftain who acts like a god will be punished by the gods."

Yurok grimaced. "All this from a man who was only supposed to be my wizard and bring good luck in the hunt." He said to Eena, "Would you have really tried to kill me if Axe Man had lost in the fight with Buner?"

"I would have killed you."

"Maybe. Have you killed men before?"

"Yes."

"How many?"

"Three."

"With the spear?"

"Yes."

"Is that why you are called Spear Woman?"

"No."

"Why, then?"

Eena glanced at Hura, who sat with six other women at a nearby fire. "Some thought I gave magic to their spears."

"Some? Who?"

"Hunters."

"Did you give their spears magic?"

"I don't know. . . ."

Yurok looked at Agon. "Did she?"

"When she touched my spear point, I felt magic. Grae felt the magic, as did Arvenios."

"Who's Arvenios?"

"Shaman of the Red People. The people of Rok."

"I never heard of the Red People."

"They live far away, beyond the Bison Hunters. At the edge of the Blue Hills."

"Blue Hills? What are they?"

"Only some mountains."

Artron spoke: "Home of the Earth Mother."

"Never say that name!" Hura spoke from behind them. "She is sacred to all women. In most tribes a man would have his heart ripped out for saying Her name!" She appealed to Agon: "Wasn't that so in your tribe of bison hunters?"

Agon looked quickly at Eena. "I know little of the women's goddesses."

"But men, true men, would never say Her name. Isn't that so?"

"In Grae's tribe the men had their own society, the women theirs. Each was secret from the other."

"There! Didn't I say so?" Hura smiled triumphantly at Artron. "You could learn much from Axe Man. . . ."

After they had eaten, Agon and Eena prepared to return to Bear Hill. Artron gave each of them a shiny golden disc hanging from a neck thong.

"Wear these. They will give you magic in the hunt and help protect you from evil spirits."

The discs were thin, but heavy, and they had a curious feel, soft yet hard and strong. As they placed the thongs around their necks, Agon and Eena felt the discs' magic, a warmth and power like tiny suns. Artron said quietly to Agon and Eena, "They are the color of Spear Woman's hair. Do not believe what Hura said. Spear Woman has magic and power, just as the discs have magic and power. I feel it. I know it."

Agon nodded. "I know it also."

"Good. But be careful."

"Why?"

Artron said to Eena, "You have not seen a woman like Hura before?"

Eena shook her head.

"Be careful. She senses your power and hates you." Artron added, "There is one more thing."

"What?" Eena asked.

Arton watched Agon's face as he replied.

"She wants your man. She wants Axe Man."

Eena smiled. "I know that."

Agon said, "Eena and I have promised that we will have no other mate as long as we live, and when we die, our spirits will be together."

Hura spoke loudly to the women around her.

"Axe Man speaks well. But I have heard that a spear woman is like a lioness in heat who mates with every male who desires her."

5

Hura

THE FULL MOON rose over the pine forest, enormous, luminescent, mysterious. Hura went silently and secretly into the wooded hills that lay south of the river. She climbed up the side of a hill where bare rock allowed her to gaze out across the river valley and the plains to the east. She let her robe drop from her shoulders and stood naked in the moonlight.

"O Great Kaan, come. Come from the dark earth. Come from the dank fens. Come from the cold depths of the sea. Come from the blue ice of the glaciers. Come from the darkness of the storm. You are not dead. Come across the plains, over the mountains, up the hills to where I wait for you."

She stood silent and motionless on the hilltop, her arms outstretched to the moon, her face lifted to the sky.

Sullen clouds scudded across the face of the moon, and the night wind stirred uneasily. Hura waited, her body trembling in anticipation, in longing, in desire.

She cried again, "Come, O Great Kaan! Come!"

Something called in the darkness. Something behind her, faint and far in the distance. She turned to face the west, her eyes searching the shadowy hills, her ears alert to the smallest sound.

The call came again, from the west.

The streak of fire hung in the western sky, soundless, alien, unnatural, just visible above the hills and trees.

Hura stared at the fiery star. She had seen it from the summer camp and watched it with awe and fear, but now it had called to her! Why? What was it? What did it mean?

She called out. "Great Kaan?" The streak of fire remained motionless, silent, baffling.

Yet Kaan had answered her! Somewhere beyond the hills Kaan was alive. Somewhere in the direction of the fiery star. But even now the star was sinking below the tree-covered hills to the west.

She seized her robe and ran toward the star in the moonlight, down the hillside, up hills and down, clambering through brush and undergrowth, around trees, through gullies, over fallen trees, splashing through streams, always with her eyes fixed on the star.

She came out of the hills onto the plain. The star seemed no closer. Where was it leading her? She ran out onto the grassy plain, hurrying toward the star.

Ahead of her dim shapes, bulky massed forms. Sounds of movement, stamping feet, breathing, rumbling stomachs. Pungent smells of dung, urine, milk, grassy breaths. The great aurochs herd was gathered for the night.

Hura stood motionless. She feared the aurochs beyond anything else. Huge brutish creatures, powerful, driven by unknown impulses, capable of trampling her into a red mush of meat and splintered bones, evil-tempered beasts who could rip the entrails from her body with one slashing hook of their great horns.

Something loomed high in the midst of the herd. A huge wide-horned bull. Hura crouched trembling in the grass, her dark robe pulled around her face, hoping she was unseen. A primeval terror overwhelmed her spirit. A creature of ancient power had joined the aurochs herd. A creature so terrifying that she prayed to her gods to save her:

"Kaan, come to me now. Kill the great bull. Kala, come to your daughter. Save her from the bull."

She peered from the fold of her robe. The thing had not seen her yet. She began to crawl slowly backward toward the shelter of the trees and the hills, her heart racing, her mouth dry. When she could no longer see the herd, she ran toward the safety of the trees, feeling the massive bull galloping toward her, its huge hooves pounding the earth, its horns swinging.

She reached the trees and climbed frantically into a tall pine tree that stood at the edge of the forest. When she could breathe again, she peered through the branches and found that she was safe. The herd and the great bull were invisible in the darkness.

Then in the western sky she saw the flaming star again, now near the horizon. Hura drew in her breath. Directly below the star a lone hill stood silhouetted against the faint afterglow of the sunset. The hill was Bear Hill! The flaming star was over Bear Hill!

Bear Hill, where Axe Man and the woman would live! Hura felt a great surge of joy. She had called upon Kaan, and he would come! He would come to Bear Hill. Axe Man would be hers, and the woman would be destroyed!

6

Return to Bear Hill

AGON AND EENA arrived back at Bear Hill at sunset, and they climbed the escarpment with a sense of coming home. They looked with fresh vision at the ease of defense of the narrow trail, the shelter of the porch, the security of the cave, and the availability of water and food and firewood. The beauty of the land below them—the river valley, the plain, the hills—added to their feeling of satisfaction and happiness.

And they had been accepted by Yurok and his tribe—they were no longer intruders. No longer need they flee for their lives. No longer need they fear every noise in the night, every shadow in the forest, every bend in the river.

But other things intruded upon Eena's happiness: Emar's tale of the ancient and fearsome spirits that inhabited the cave, the ancient people from another world, the huge animals the boys had seen, and the strangeness of Yount, which Emar attributed to his experience in the cave.

But she said nothing of her unease. She hugged Agon. "We are in our own home."

"When we were in the Blue Hills," he said, "I talked of bringing you to our home. I thought then it would never be possible. Now we have found a home. Our home. We can be happy here."

"I am happy now. You made Yurok's people accept us, but fighting while a strap tied your neck to your feet must have been terrible."

"It isn't a way I like to fight."

She shuddered. "It made me think of Ka . . . how he tied me with the straps around my throat. . . ."

"Ka is dead. No one will tie you ever again."

"No. Never again."

Agon placed his hand on her abdomen. "Does the child move yet?"

She smiled. "Will you ask me this every day?" She placed her hand over his. "But I like to have you ask. I like to feel your hand on me, on the child. He will know that his father waits for him."

"Can you have the child here, by yourself?"

"Why not? Does, mares, cow bison all have their young by themselves."

"But in our tribe Erida helped the women. . . ."

"My mother bore me by herself. Bore Eran by herself. I can do the same."

"Maybe a woman from Yurok's tribe could come . . .

one like Erida, who knows the women's magic, the magic of birth. . . ."

Eena moved away from Agon. "One like Hura? I would rather have my child alone in a blizzard on the plain than have her touch him."

"I didn't mean Hura."

"She's an evil woman who schemes and smiles and speaks like honey while her words drip with hidden poison."

"We won't have her."

"Even if I were dying, I wouldn't let her touch the child. Promise you will never bring her here."

"I have said we won't have her."

Eena bowed her head. "I've angered you. . . ."

"You haven't angered me." He touched her arm. "Hura is nothing. You are my wife, my mate, my friend. We have fought Ka together, seen the Earth Mother together and lived, been mated by Her women. You are everything to me—Hura is nothing."

She came into his arms. "I know that."

"I only fear for you, for the child, if something doesn't go right. . . ."

She kissed him. "Everything will go right." Suddenly she placed his hand on her abdomen. "Feel!"

"He moves!"

"Yes! He tells us everything is all right. He is strong and healthy."

Agon kept his hand on her body, feeling the tiny movements, his eyes fixed on Eena's face. "You said three moons. . . ."

"It has been three moons since the Earth Mother mated us."

"Then . . ."

"Then he'll come in six more moons."

"In the spring," Agon said. "The best time. He will come with the bison calves, the wolf pups, the bear cubs."

"And with the foals and fawns."

"He will be like a wolf pup. He will grow into a strong hunter, a fierce fighter."

"Like his father."

"Like a wolf."

"Yes. But he will be loving and kind, too." Eena held her hand over Agon's. "As you are."

"I will be satisfied if he is strong and brave."

Eena touched Agon's arm lightly with her lips. "I want him to be as you are. Then I will be satisfied. I will be happy."

Agon pointed to the southwest. "Look. The streaming star has come again. It is a good omen. The child will be all that we ask."

Eena gazed at the star. "It grows larger. Just as our child grows larger. The star will be his sign, his magic. I will pray to the gods that he will be as magical as the star."

"The star is magical, but we don't know what it will do, what it will mean. Don't ask the gods for too much."

"You are right. I might offend the gods. . . ." Eena bowed her head. "Maybe I have offended them already."

Agon lifted her chin. "You haven't offended them. All mothers hope for a child with magic."

"I have asked for too much. I will ask the gods to forgive me so that they won't look with anger on the child."

"They won't do that. The Earth Mother, the most powerful of all the gods, mated us."

Eena's eyes lost their look of apprehension. "Then the child will be favored by the gods. I will only ask that the gods have mercy on us."

"Have mercy? What does that mean?"

"That they will spare us if we offend them. As you did with Buner. You could have killed him, but you let him live."

Agon considered this. "If an animal is badly wounded and escapes the hunters, we follow and kill; the animal spirit thanks us for ending its suffering. If a hunter is shamed because he fears, he is better off dead. I let Buner live because he was not worth killing. Should the gods spare us to let us suffer more, like the wounded animal? Should they spare us if we wish to die because of our shame? Or do they spare us because we are not worth their notice?"

"The Earth Mother spared us," Eena replied. "I have thought about this many times. I think she spared us because she wanted us to live and help save our tribe. I believe that if the gods spare us it is because they have something they want us to do."

"Even if living is worse than death?"

"Even then. But the gods are not cruel. They also bring us great happiness." She gently touched Agon's face. "After Ka took my father and brother's heads and hurt me, I wanted to die. By the ways of our tribe you should have killed me. But you spared me and let me live. And you have brought me such happiness that I thank the gods every day for their kindness and mercy."

When the time came to sleep, Eena carried their bed of ferns and grass from the cave entrance into the porch. Agon looked questioningly at her.

"We can watch the star," she explained, "and hear better if anyone tries to come up the stream."

"The star is following the sun. Even now it sinks below the horizon." Agon pointed toward the top of the escarpment. "I have fastened long trip lines that come right into the cave. They will warn us of anyone coming up. We can sleep safely in the cave."

"I would rather sleep out here."

Agon touched her face. "You feel danger."

"Not danger . . ."

"What, then?"

"The things Emar told us . . . I fear for the child. . . ."

"Why?"

"The one called Yount . . . he is strange. . . ."

"Because he saw something in the cave? You think our son would become strange, like Yount?"

"I hope not. Our son will become a chieftain."

Agon gazed intently into the mouth of the cave. "I feel nothing evil in there. We slept in the entrance last night and are still alive. The cave has only good magic."

"Yes."

He smiled at her. "Tomorrow I'll make a torch and go into the cave. Tonight we'll sleep under the stars, and we can watch the flaming star that tells of our son."

Eena came to him. "I will fear nothing if we are together."

He lifted her and carried her toward the bed of ferns. "We will always be together."

7

The Cave

IN THE MORNING, after they had eaten, Agon gathered an armful of pitch-laden pine faggots. He said to Eena, "I will go into the cave while half the torches last, come out with the rest. If anyone tries to come up the stream, call into the cave, then hold them off until I come out."

"I am going with you."

He shook his head. "There may be powerful spirits in the cave. Yurok's hunters thought we would die if we went in."

"If you die," Eena said, "I want to die."

"But the child . . ."

"He will be with us. His father's magic will protect him."

Agon touched the ibex on his chest, then the one carved in the handle of his axe. "My magic is in fighting men. Not spirits."

Eena touched the deer on her breast, then her belt. "The deer was given to me by my mother, my belt by the Earth Mother. They will protect us. The belt encircles the child.

The spirit of my mother and the Earth Mother will protect him, too."

"Come with me then," Agon said. "I know that your magic is strong."

The floor of the cave was of hard limestone, covered with a layer of windblown sand at the entrance. They carried their bed of ferns back into the cave, lighted one of the torches, then covered the ashes of their fire with sand. They carefully brushed out their tracks as they crossed the sand at the entrance and entered the large bright entrance chamber. Another, smaller chamber opened at one side of the first chamber, but at the rear of the large chamber a dim passage led back into the hill.

They enter the passageway, and the magic of the cave grasps them like a great hand closing. They go forward through the dark twisting corridor, deep into Bear Hill, feeling ever more strongly the power of the ancient beings watching them.

Like animals of the subearth, they memorize each turn, every distance, floor, wall, slope, ceiling, space, echo, reflection, smell, feeling, touch, impression. As the first torch burns short, they light a second from the dying flame. Agon carries the ingoing torches, Eena the outgoing; seven each.

They squeeze through a small opening into a huge chamber, so large thay cannot see its end.

Two huge eyes glare from the darkness. The eyes of a giant. A massive and bestial humanoid face. Lowered eyebrows, heavy forehead, shadowy nose and mouth, pale jaw.

Eena presses close against Agon and touches the deer totem at her throat.

Agon raises the torch, and the face disappears. He lowers the torch, and the face reappears. They step cautiously further into the chamber, and Agon holds the torch high, feeling the ibex vibrating on his chest.

No face, but a giant stallion. Shadows on the rocks looked like a face.

A mare. Beside her a foal.

They look up. Huge animals cover the ceiling, moving, alive in the flickering torchlight.

Masses of animals: bison, aurochs, deer, horses.

Alive: standing, running, falling, plunging, rearing.

Colored: red, brown, yellow, black, violet.

Eena cries out in amazement. She has seen an ibex and a deer appear under their fingers on the wall of the cave in the Blue Hills, but never animals like this. She touches her totem again, and the doe is trembling, pulsing with energy. The chamber is magic—magic with the life force of massed animals, animals vibrant with motion, color, form, depth, life.

The child stirs within her, reaching toward the animals. A great surge of happiness and excitement sweeps through Eena's being, her spirit. She feels tears on her face and realizes that she is crying.

Agon turns, the torch high, gazing at the animals. Never has he seen animals such as these, never felt such massed magic, never experienced such a concentration of life force.

Eena speaks softly to the animals: "The gods of all animals have made you. . . ."

They continue into the depths of the cave, exploring while Agon's torches last, going through smaller chambers. Other animals appear: ibex, mammoths, reindeer. On the walls. On the ceilings. High up in chimneys, barely visible in the murky dimness.

The chambers end. A low and narrow tunnel leads from the last chamber. Agon lights the last torch of his ingoing bundle, and they crawl into the tunnel. They feel the earth closing around them as they progress on hands and knees. Then, deep in the farthest recesses, they find painted on the curved walls the fiercest animals: lions, bears, rhinoceroses.

Unexpectedly, the torch flickers, wavers. Before they

can bring the first of Eena's torches to it, the tiny flame disappears.

They are in absolute blackness.

Terror. Terror of lying trapped and helpless in the earth until they die. No water. No food. No light. Death.

Agon speaks calmly. "We can find our way out."

"Yes." Eena touches Agon's foot in the darkness. "I have fire stones and tinder in my belt pouch. We can light a new torch."

They feel a strange weakness. They force their breathing, and strength returns. But they know that they must get out of the tunnel quickly or die. Eena gasps for breath. Agon commands, "Back out, now!"

They cannot turn around in the constricting walls of the tunnel. Eena, behind Agon, leads as they crawl backward.

They pant. Bands of tight shrinking rawhide seem to circle their temples. They feel their strength leaving them. But they keep on. Crawling backward in the blackness, they move toward the end of the tunnel and the open chamber.

They are out! They gulp in huge lungfuls of air and feel their strength return.

Then, working carefully in the darkness, Eena brings the fire stones, tinder, and twigs from her pouch and strikes the stones together above the tinder. Sparks appear with each stroke, their fleeting lights like tiny shooting stars. The tinder shows a red glow, and Eena lifts it in her hands and blows gently on it, nursing the embryo fire magic until it is born in flame. She lowers the burning tinder to the cave floor and holds the twigs in the fire until they ignite. The small flame is as filled with comfort as cooking fires at the end of a hunt. They light the first of the remaining pine torches. The light is like the rising sun, brilliant, beautiful, filled with glory.

Then they retrace their path out of the cave, using their memory of every detail to bring them to the glow of daylight at the cave entrance.

They come out into the sunshine.

Moon of the Golden Days

8

Preparation

NOW CAME THAT time of early autumn when a drowsy, dreamy indolence crept over the plains and the river valley. The game put on their winter fat, ducks and geese gathered in the marshes, fish lay quietly in sunlit ponds, and the people lazed in the sunshine, feeding themselves almost without effort on ripe berries and fruit, on nuts and tubers, and on the fish and fowl that lay within easy reach.

In their home on Bear Hill, Agon and Eena made preparations for the coming winter and the birth of the child. Agon hunted deer, whose meat Eena dried in the sun and whose hides she tanned for winter garments. They fashioned a framework of branches and lashed rawhides to it for sealing the entrance to the cave in time of blizzard or cold winds, and Eena dried berries and fruit and collected nuts in baskets she wove from the long marsh grasses.

The small chamber to the left of the cave entry chamber was found to be ideal for storage of their food and clothing—dry and fresh aired with enough light from the entrance to give it a soft illumination, yet sheltered from the weather.

Eena kept a bed of ferns just inside the cave entrance for summer use, and for winter she planned a bed of furs, soft warm pelts of mink and marten that would be taken when the animals had their winter coats.

Agon discussed with Eena an idea that had come to him:

"When I traveled through the snow of the mountains, I made big moccasins stuffed with grass and moss for warmth. They supported me on the hard snow, but on soft snow they still broke through. What if I made even bigger moccasins, to use in winter hunting? I could go over the snow like the big-footed rabbits."

Eena smiled. "Watch out that the wolves don't think you are a rabbit."

"We'll have wolf soup if they do. But what do you think? Could you make moccasins like that?"

"I can make them, but they'll be soft and floppy. I think you would trip over them."

"Emar says the winters are not very cold here, but much snow can fall. I need something for winter hunting."

"What do Yurok's hunters wear on their feet?"

"High moccasins. But Emar's men follow the trail of the aurochs herds, and the snow is beaten down. The deer we hunt here leave only narrow trails."

"But we get better meat. Aurochs meat is soft and without flavor. I like venison and bison meat better." Eena studied their sandals. "If we could use sandal straps to hold something big and flat and stiff on our feet . . ."

"Pieces of rawhide?"

"Perhaps. I'll make sandals with big rawhide soles. When the snow comes, we can try them." She smiled again. "We will skim over the snow like water bugs on a pond."

"Or tumble like grouse struck by a hawk." Agon tied the last knot in binding a new flint point to a spear shaft. "When I hunted yesterday, I met Emar and his hunters. Yurok's people will soon be moving back to the cliff shelter for the winter."

"They will be closer to us."

"Yes. When you have the child, the women can help you."

"I want no help."

Agon looked at her uplifted chin. "I don't mean Hura."

"She must never come here. She would put an evil spell on the child."

"I won't let her come."

"She would like to have you try to stop her. She wants you. I have seen it in her eyes."

"I don't want her." Agon touched the ibex on his chest. "She looks like the women in Ka's tribe."

Eena stared at him. "Like Kala!"

"Kala?"

"Mother of Ka. She was more evil than Ka. . . ." Eena shuddered.

"How could she be more evil than Ka?"

"Because she planned evil things . . . she found pleasure in evil, in pain, in telling me the horrible things she would do to me. . . ." Eena touched her deer totem and then held her hands protectively over her abdomen. "I should never have mentioned her name . . . she might harm our child. . . ."

"She's far away. We need not speak of her again." Agon saw Eena's distress and spoke of other things. "I should have killed Buner when I fought with him. Emar told me that Buner has made Yount his slave."

"His slave? What is that?"

"Yount has to do anything that Buner demands."

"That is not right. How could Buner make Yount his slave?"

"Buner challenged Yount to fight, fight while the strap was tied to his neck and feet. Yount is not a fighter. He refused. By the law of their tribe he became Buner's slave."

"Poor Yount." Eena looked toward the cliffs that lined the river. "Maybe when the tribe moves to the cliffs, we can help him."

"If we can," Agon replied. "But we are strangers here. If we want to live in peace with Yurok's people, we can't go against their ways."

"Buner is a coward. People like Yount are touched by the gods. They should not be expected to fight." Eena gripped her spear. "Someone should kill Buner."

Agon smiled at her. "Having the child has made you fierce. You are like the lioness who protects her cub. Would you kill Buner?"

"If he tried to hurt our son. But I shame you. I shouldn't talk of killing as though I were a man, a warrior. I'm only a woman."

"You don't shame me. You are a warrior—you have killed Ka's men in battle. But if the time comes, I will kill Buner."

"And Hura."

"No."

"Why not?"

"Because she looks like Ka's women doesn't mean she should be killed. I would be shamed if I killed a woman without reason."

"Yes. I could not ask you to do that."

"Forget about Hura. She's nothing."

"Nothing to you?"

"Nothing to me. Nothing to us." Agon looked closely at Eena. "You're crying. Why?"

She came to him.

He held her awkwardly, stiffly, confused by her tears. "Are you sick?"

"No. . . ."

"Then what?"

"I don't know. . . ."

"Is it about Hura?"

"No . . . yes . . . I don't know. . . ." She drew back from him and wiped at her eyes with the back of her hand, like a little girl. "I'm sorry. I won't cry again."

He drew her to him and held her close. He stroked her hair. "It doesn't matter."

"It does. . . ."

"Maybe it's because of the child. Ara told me that the women in our tribe acted strangely when they were with young."

Her expression changed. "My mother told me that! Do you think that's why I cried?"

"It must be. Crying is strange for you." He smiled at her. "You don't need to be sorry."

"I won't cry again."

He studied her face. "I see that."

"I'll never forget the good things you've done for me. Now I have one more good thing to remember."

"What's that? I've done nothing."

"You could have been angry with me or beaten me when I acted strangely. But you were kind to me. I won't forget that."

"Being kind to you isn't hard." Agon picked up his spear. "We need more meat for drying. Will you come with me?"

Eena lifted her spear from its place against the wall. "I'll come with you. Come with you always."

9

The Moon of Turning Leaves

THE LEAVES ON the hardwood trees began to change color. Gradually the green of the maple, hickory, and walnut turned to yellow, then orange, then scarlet. The hills glowed with color, the bright hues of the hardwoods contrasting with the dark green of the conifers, some in discrete patches, others mixed, the trees and color mingling like colored shells.

The nights grew cool. Eena made a deerskin robe for the bed of ferns, and each night she and Agon lay snug under the robe as they watched the stars in the western sky. The flaming star was brighter now, an omen that the child, now showing as a bulge in Eena's abdomen, would be a powerful chieftain. The fetal movements became stronger and more frequent, and every day Agon placed his hand over the child and felt with wonder the motion of the tiny body.

Eena's face took on a new beauty, a look of contentment, of mystery and expectation. She was supremely happy, singing at her work as she made garments for the child, robes for his bed, a carrying sling, a backpack for carrying him when she hunted. She sewed winter garments for Agon and herself: hunting shirts, leggings, moccasins, hooded overshirts, mittens. She also fashioned the large, flat-soled rawhide sandals that they would strap over their moccasins in the hope of allowing them to travel in deep snow.

On the day of the full moon, Yurok's tribe moved back to the cliff shelters for the winter.

Yount, now Buner's slave, carried the heavy hides and poles that made up Buner's hut while Buner walked behind him, urging him on with a heavy stick, striking Yount's back, buttocks, and legs, laughing as Yount stumbled, cursing him if he went slowly up the hills. They were among the first to arrive at the line of cliffs along the river, and Buner forced his way through the other people to a prime spot far back under the overhang. He supervised Yount's erection of the hut with more blows and curses and then sent Yount to find food. When he had eaten, Buner sprawled on his furs in the hut and ordered Yount out.

Yount went happily to his secret place, a little niche in the cliff wall beyond the main camp. From his belt pouch he took a horn handle, leather thongs, and the almost-finished flint blade of a knife. The blade was beautifully formed—slender, slightly curved, symmetrical. It needed only the final retouching of the cutting edge, the removal of tiny chips of flint with firm pressure from a sharp piece of hard greenstone. Yount loved working with flint, loved seeing the little chips part cleanly and uniformly from the edge, loved the clean perfection of the finished blades.

When he had completed the blade, he bound it to the polished horn handle with the thong. He held the knife up, admiring it.

Buner loomed over him, heavy face threatening, scowling. He held his heavy stick.

"Give it to me."

Yount tried to push back deeper into the niche. "No."

"No?"

"It's for Axe Man."

Buner's mean pig eyes shone red, angry. "You made this for Axe Man?"

"Yes."

Buner brought the club down on Yount's legs. "Give it to me!"

"No."

Buner struck again, hard and viciously. Yount held the knife by the blade, and Buner seized the handle and jerked the blade through Yount's hands. Blood spurted, and Yount looked at the palm of his hand where the flesh lay sliced open in a deep gash.

The sight of the blood roused Buner. He dropped the knife on the ground at his feet. "Take it, Yount! Come get it!"

Yount bent forward, reaching for the knife, and Buner struck Yount on the head with the club. He struck again and again as Yount sprawled forward on the ground with his bloody hand stretched toward the knife.

That afternoon Agon and Eena saw smoke spiraling up from the tribe's cooking fires and heard the distant sound of voices, and after dark a row of tiny points of flame could be seen along the base of the cliffs. The sounds and fires gave a sense of security and companionship, yet to the two people on Bear Hill it seemed that some of their domain, some of their freedom, had been lost. As they lay in their bed at the cave entrance, Eena spoke to Agon of her feelings:

"My father left his father's tribe in order to be alone. We came here to escape from Ka's tribe. Yet it seems that wherever my father went, wherever we go, people are already there. Are people spread all over the earth?"

"I don't know," Agon replied. "Grae told how once our tribe went far to the south, to a place where winter never came. Other people, strange people, lived there."

"What kind of people?"

"Big people. But no one knows what they were like. It was so long ago that almost all has been forgotten."

"My father said that a kind of people live in the north, in the ice fields. Strange creatures—huge men with long hair."

"Did he see these people?"

"No. But a man in his father's tribe said that he had seen one." She shivered. "He said that the creature wore no hides, but ran naked in the snow and ice."

Agon put an arm around her. "Are you cold?"

"It makes me cold to think of the creature." She snuggled close to him under the deerskin robe. "I'm warm now."

The next day Emar came to Bear Hill. He called from the base of the escarpment, and when Agon waved a friendly spear, Emar climbed up to the porch entrance. He gave

Eena a rolled-up, tanned aurochs hide. "The women sent this. Maybe you can use it."

Eena admired the hide. "It's soft and warm. Tell the women I thank them."

"I will." Emar smiled. "You probably noticed; we've come back to the cliff shelter."

"We saw the cooking fires last night."

"And heard the noise." Emar gave Agon a flint knife with a horn handle. "This is the kind of skinning knife we use for aurochs. Maybe you can find some use for it."

Agon examined the knife. "It was made by a craftsman of great skill."

"Yount made it."

"Yount makes knives?"

Emar nodded. "He made this for you."

Agon handed the knife to Eena. "Look at this. I've never seen such perfect edging."

"It is beautiful."

"Does Buner still keep Yount as his slave?" Agon asked. "I would not think he would let Yount make a knife for me."

Emar's white teeth gleamed behind his short black beard. "Buner has gone."

They stared at him. "Gone?"

"Left the tribe. Yesterday."

Eena exclaimed in delight.

Agon touched his axe handle. "He could come back."

"Maybe. I don't think so, though." Emar spoke of another subject: "Yurok invites you to come feast with us tomorrow. We celebrate the autumn hunt festival."

Agon glanced at Eena before he replied. "We thank you. Tell Yurok we are honored that he has asked us."

"I will." Emar looked toward the entrance to the cave. "You've met no evil spirits yet?"

"No."

"You've been in the cave?"

"We went to the end."

"And you saw nothing strange or evil?"

"Strange. Not evil."

Emar studied Agon's face, then Eena's. "You both look the same; no evil spirit has harmed you. What was strange?"

"A part of the cave. Fire won't burn in it."

Emar touched his bear totem. "I would never enter such a place." He picked up his spear to leave, then glanced back at the cave entrance. "You should leave here. Live with us in the cliff shelters."

"This is our home."

Emar shook his head in wonderment. "You are brave. But don't be too brave. A place where fire won't burn will kill you." He turned toward the escarpment. "Come at noon tomorrow, if you're still alive."

As Emar neared the bottom of the escarpment, Eena said to Agon, "He is a good man. Do you think he killed Buner?"

"I hope so." Agon watched Emar as he turned and waved his spear at them, and he waved his spear in return.

Eena gave the knife back to him. "Yount was good to make this for you. I will make a deerskin hunting shirt for him."

Agon smiled at her. "He will like that."

Eena smiled back, then her face became serious. "Could you go alone to Yurok's camp tomorrow?"

"Why? Don't you feel well?"

"It's not that. . . ."

"You don't want to go because of Hura?"

"I don't want to bring our child near her."

"I have told Emar we will come."

Eena was silent.

"The women sent a gift to you."

Eena looked out over the river valley. "I'll go. But if Hura tries to harm the child, I will kill her."

They approached Yurok's winter camp at noon on the following day, carrying gifts: a deerskin robe for Yurok, a set of marsh grass baskets for the women, and a deerskin hunting shirt for Yount.

The bank of the river and the area under the protective wall of the cliff were filled with people in the same kind of bustling activity that Agon and Eena had observed in the camp in the pine forest: aurochs hides being pegged on the ground and stretched on wooden racks, women butchering, tending fires, cooking, men dragging aurochs carcasses toward the fires, children running and shrieking at their games.

Yurok stood before one of the hide huts that had been erected under the shelter of the overhanging bulge of the cliff. He wore his polished aurochs horns and the white robe of the chieftain. He raised his hand to the visitors. "You're still alive."

"Yes." Agon held out the deerskin robe. "We hope you can use this."

Yurok took the robe and studied it. "Who made this robe?" He looked at Eena. "Spear Woman?"

"She did."

"And who killed the deer?"

"We hunt together."

"I'll keep it for my bed." Yurok winked at them. "I'd rather have Spear Woman's robe over my loins than have her spear at my neck."

Eena silently handed the baskets to Agon. He presented them to Yurok. "These are for your women."

Yurok beckoned to a sturdy-looking woman who was directing the butchering. "Come over here, Yeta. Spear Woman has made something for you."

The woman approached, walking solidly, strongly. She had a broad, smiling face, blue eyes, and her dark hair was parted in the middle with a thick braid hanging down each side of her head. She inspected the baskets carefully, making little sounds of approval. She looked up at Eena.

"Who taught you to make these baskets?"

"My mother."

"From the tribe of Grae?"

"Yes."

Agon saw a look of mystery flash in Yeta's eyes. "Your mother taught you well," she said. "Our women could learn much from you."

"They're old designs. But I could show you how to weave them."

Yeta smiled. "Yes. That would be good. Teach us the designs of your baskets."

Yeta and Eena talked of baskets and designs, but Agon sensed that they spoke of a woman's mystery, unknown to men.

Hura spoke from behind them: "What nice little baskets. Our little girls make ones like these for play."

Eena said nothing, but turned to face Hura, her hand tightening on her spear.

Yeta looked quickly at Eena's face, then spoke to Hura: "These baskets could not be made by little girls. If you knew anything about baskets, you would know that."

"I have more important things to do than make little girls' baskets."

"Yes. Like casting evil spells." Yeta put her hands on her hips. "You are not of this tribe. Why don't you go back where you came from?"

Hura's face darkened. "Beware!" She pointed at Eena. "This woman is not of your tribe, either. Yet you fawn over her while you insult me. Beware! My magic is stronger than all of you. Watch what you say."

Artron, the shaman, came from one of the huts, wearing his deer antlers and robe. He spoke to Agon and Eena: "Do not listen to this woman and her threats. You have gone into the cave at Bear Hill, and you still live. You both have strong magic. Will you stay there?"

"We hope to." Agon touched the ibex on his chest.

Artron pointed toward the western sky. "Have you seen the fiery star that comes each evening?"

"We have watched it since the night we came here."

"Do you know what it portends?"

"No."

"It came the night that you came. Now it grows larger." Artron fixed his eyes on Eena. "You know what it means."

Eena made no reply.

"You carry a child."

"Yes. . . ."

"I knew it!" Hura said triumphantly. "I knew it the first time I saw her."

Artron pointed to the west. "The fiery star is an omen. You will be the mother of a special child."

Hura looked at Agon as she spoke. "The mother is not important. But the child will be like his father. Strong, brave, a warrior with the blood of chieftains."

Yeta took Eena's hand. "The mother is not important? Don't listen to this woman!"

Artron touched the golden sun disc on his chest. "The child's magic will come from the mother as much as from the father. You will bear this child and others. And one of your sons will be a great chieftain!"

Yurok raised his spear. "Now let's feast! Axe Man and Spear Woman honor us by bringing gifts. And when we've eaten, we'll dance and drink the magic liquid!" He shook the spear. "The tribe of Yurok has come home!"

As they sat down to feast, Eena looked around at the people. She said to Emar, "We have a gift for Yount, but we do not see him."

Emar replied, "Yount is dead."

10

The Red-Spotted Aurochs

DEAD?" EENA LOOKED unbelievingly at Emar. "Yount is dead?"

"Buner beat him to death."

Eena made a sound of horror.

Agon touched the handle of his axe. "When?"

"Two days ago."

"Why?"

"Yount made the knife for you, and Buner found out."

Agon's hand closed on the axe handle. "Which way did he go?"

Yurok spoke. "You need not track Buner."

"No?"

Yurok's eyes became as cold as Agon's. "We know where he is."

While the people ate and drank, four men dragged two huge aurochs-hide drums from the cliff shelter. Yeta said to Eena, "Here, both men and women dance. Will Agon let you dance?"

"I dance only with Agon."

Yurok winked at Agon. "I understand that. But you must wait. First, we have contests."

"What kind of contests?" Agon asked Yurok.

"Running. Jumping. Spear-throwing. Wrestling."

Eena raised her spear. "Wrestling with the straps?"

Yurok smiled at her. "No. The straps are only for serious fighting. Axe Man won't have to fight that way again unless he makes an enemy."

"I'm glad. Men should not fight in such a way."

Yurok agreed. "It's not a good way to fight." He got to his feet. "Try any of the contests you want to." He looked at Eena. "Both of you."

Yurok walked into the open space in front of the cliff shelter. His voice boomed out: "Running. From here, around that big oak at the end of the canyon, and back."

Hura said loudly, "We are told that the spear woman hunts like a boy. She looks like a boy. Does she run like a boy?"

Yeta patted Eena's knee. "Don't listen to her."

"Would it hurt the child if I ran?"

"I've helped many women at birthing. The ones who

have the most trouble are the ones who sit and do nothing."

Yeta looked questioningly at Eena. "How did you become a runner?"

"When my mother died, my father would not hunt. I had to run after game as the hunters do."

Yeta studied Eena's legs and felt of the muscles. "They don't bulge like a hunter's, but you're like a young lioness. I think you can beat these clumsy hunters of ours." She spoke to Agon: "I've seen her running with you in the hunt. You're like two wolves."

"She can run faster than most men."

"Never." Hura pushed through the people toward them. "She'll probably trip and fall and hurt the child."

Eena grasped her spear. "Don't come near me."

Hura stopped and glared at Eena. "You and your spear don't frighten me. I doubt if you know how to use it."

"I know how to use it."

"I don't think so. And you probably run like a wounded jackal bitch, limping and whining."

Eena replied softly, "A jackal bitch may limp, but she still can kill the yellow-toothed rat that spreads its foulness in its nest and the nest of others."

Yurok bellowed from the clearing where men and boys had collected for the race. "Get ready!"

Agon drew Eena back from Hura. "We have run together. Run with me now. Show this woman how you run." Eena nodded, and together they ran toward the clearing as Yurok cried, "Go!"

Agon and Eena started a spear-throw behind the other runners, and they carried their spears. But slowly they gained on those in front of them. They passed the stragglers, the boys, the heavier men. But two young hunters ran like deer ahead of them, their hair flying, their legs flashing in the sunlight.

Agon glanced at Eena, and she was running easily, lightly. She felt his gaze and smiled quickly at him. "We'll run like wolves."

They rounded the oak tree, and the young hunters still

led. But now, steadily, Agon and Eena began to gain. Agon spoke to Eena. "We shouldn't shame them. We'll come in together."

She nodded and smiled. They continued to gain, but slowly. And Yurok stood three spear-throws away. "Now!" Agon and Eena came abreast of the two hunters just as all four of them swept by Yurok.

As Agon and Eena watched the jumping and wrestling, many of Yurok's people gathered around to congratulate them on the race. The two young hunters won in the jumping, then came to stand beside their guests. Their names were Berg and Redon.

Berg smiled at them. "You could have beaten us. We thank you for not shaming us before the people."

"We never thought a woman could run as you do," Redon said to Eena.

Berg asked, "How old are you?"

Eena held up the fingers and thumbs of both hands, then one hand.

"Our age. And you're with young!"

"Yes."

"Why are you called Spear Woman?"

"Because I hunt with a spear."

"Yurok said you have killed three men in battle."

"Yes."

Berg studied her appreciatively. "If Axe Man ever tires of you . . ."

"I won't tire of her." Agon looked into Berg's eyes.

Berg stepped backward, and his face turned pale. "I meant nothing. . . ."

Redon explained: "It's the way we talk to the girls of our tribe . . . joking . . ." His voice trailed away as Agon looked at him.

Yurok bellowed from the contest area. "Spear-throwing!" He beckoned to Agon and Eena and the young hunters. "Show us how the people of Grae hurl the spear!"

Two hunters set up a target of an aurochs hide stretched on a wooden frame. Cut in the center of the hide was a small hole no wider than a man's hand. Yurok scraped a line in the dirt a short spear-throw back from the target.

"You each throw once. If your spear goes through the hole without tearing the hide, you throw again until one wins."

The hunters and boys crowded along the line. Yurok cuffed them back good-naturedly. "Chieftain first, and don't crowd me." He lifted his big spear, eyed the target, and threw. The spear whished through the hole without touching the hide.

Hunter after hunter threw, then Agon, then Eena. Yurok, Emar, Berg, Agon, and Eena had clean throws. They retrieved their spears, ready to throw again.

Yurok went to the target and cut a hole half the size of the first one. "This won't be so easy."

He came back to the line, raised his spear, and threw. The hide quivered, but the spear went through the hole without cutting the leather.

Emar threw cleanly, but the leather quivered. Berg's spear made a tiny cut. Agon threw cleanly, but the leather quivered. Eena's spear went through without sound or motion of the hide.

Yurok cut a smaller hole. He held his spearhead beside the hole. "It's bigger than the hole." He shrugged. "You with your little spears keep on."

Agon took a piece of charcoal from the fire pit and made four tiny black spots, each a forearm-length apart on the white auroch hide. "We could throw at these."

Yurok grinned. "Now watch this." His big spear flashed through the air and ripped through the hide. When they examined the tear, the black spot was on the very edge of the cut.

Emar threw. His spear took a tiny edge off his black spot.

Agon threw. His spear took a slightly larger edge off his black spot.

Eena smiled at the men. "I can't match your skill. I'll go and sit with the other women."

Yurok stared down at her. "You'll throw."

She bowed her head. "I will throw." She raised her spear and eyed the target. Agon said harshly, "Throw it right!" She looked quickly at him, then she smiled and threw her spear. The spear went cleanly through the center of the black mark.

Agon drew Eena aside. "You were going to miss the target on purpose."

"I didn't want to win."

"Why?"

"Men have pride."

Yurok beckoned to them. "Let's see if Spear Woman can throw the long spear as well as she does the short."

Eena shook her head. "I can't throw the spear as far as a man. This time I'll watch."

"I want a chance to win over you."

"Even if you command me, I can't throw the long spear."

Yurok seemed to grow a little taller. "We could let you throw from a shorter distance."

Eena's chin came up. "I want no favors because I'm a woman."

Yurok looked quizzically at Agon. "She's stubborn."

"Yes."

"You may have to beat her to make her understand certain things."

"Perhaps."

"Good." Yurok turned and bellowed to the hunters. "Bring out the spotted aurochs."

Four hunters dragged a grotesque-looking creature from the cliff shelter, the red-spotted white skin of an aurochs, not alive, but stuffed with something to give it the size of a live beast. The hunters propped its head and wide horns against a post and tied them in place. It seemed to Eena the creature moved slightly, and she drew in her breath.

Yurok painted a small black circle on the side of the creature, then made a line in the dirt two normal spear-throws back. "Run to the line and throw. If you cross the line before you throw, you lose. If you hit the circle, you throw again."

He backed away from the line and raised his spear. "Boys run first, hunters next." He motioned the boys forward. "Go!"

Boy after boy ran to the line and threw his spear. Not a single spear reached the creature. Now the hunters came. Each man ran at full speed to the line and threw his spear with all his strength. Spears thudded into the aurochs hide, but none into the black circle.

Yurok nodded to Agon. "Your turn."

Agon ran to the line and threw his spear. It swished over the creature and drove into the earth two spear-lengths beyond the spear-bristling hide.

Yurok looked strangely at Agon. "Too strong." He backed away from the throwing line, raised his big spear, and ran forward. He threw the spear into the center of the circle.

When Agon went to retrieve his spear, he stopped at the spear-pierced creature for a moment, then joined Eena in the circle of spectators.

She spoke quietly to him: "The aurochs hide moved when the hunter's spears struck. After Yurok's spear went into the circle, the hide became still."

"I saw that."

"Something alive was in the skin. Is that why you threw your spear high?"

"I want to see what I kill."

"You knew what was inside the hide?"

"Yes."

Eena's eyes held a look of horror. "It was . . ."

"Yes. I could not torture him by only wounding him."

"He deserved to die . . . but not that way. . . . Is he still alive?"

"Yurok's spear finally killed him. Buner is dead."

11

Moon of the Cold Rain

THE SKIES TURNED gray, and cold rain began to fall. It came down steadily, continuously, day and night.

The land ran with water. Rivulets streamed down from the hills, creeks overflowed, wide ponds formed on the plains, the marshes doubled in size, and the river rose above its banks and spread out onto the floodplain.

The hardwood trees stood bare and darkly wet in somber groves, while the pines and fir and spruce hung their sopping branches low and dripped great blobs of water onto the soggy floor of the forest.

But all was not gloomy. The grass of the plains and hills became emerald green, and the thick moss that lay over the rock outcrops turned overnight from gray, brittle deadness into lush, springy green carpets. And the cave at Bear Hill was warm and cozy, lit by the cheerful fire that burned just inside the entrance, sheltered and dry, a place of comfort and happiness.

Agon and Eena had collected a huge pile of logs and branches within the first chamber of the cave, enough to keep their fire burning all winter. In the side chamber were stored dried venison, blackberries, plums, and apples; also hickory nuts, hazelnuts, walnuts, tubers, stalks, and onions. In the space left lay a bed of hides and warm furs, the neatly folded piles of their winter clothing, and the tiny wrappers, shirts, hoods, moccasins, capes, and robes for the expected child.

Yeta had given Eena a leather bag filled with aurochs tallow for waterproofing their outdoor clothing. Eena warmed the tallow and rubbed it into their hunting shirts, leggings, moccasins, hoods, capes, and mittens. The leather darkened and smelled of aurochs, but it shed water and kept them dry and warm when they hunted.

Agon fashioned wooden traps in which to catch the fur-bearing mink, marten, sable, and fox when the weather grew colder. But they would need larger furs also. Wolves howled in the hills at night, and Agon discussed with Eena the possibility of obtaining wolf skins for their winter robes and clothing. Eena objected.

"Wolves are too much like people."

"But we need warm furs. I would have to trap many mink to make a robe. Five wolf skins would be enough."

"They have eyes like us."

"And they hunt like us. But they are not us."

"They call to each other in the night. I have heard the pups learn to call. They're like children."

"Your pup may be cold unless I get furs."

"He won't be born until spring is near."

Agon regarded Eena's face. The look of mystery, of magic, was growing stronger. Her belly was swelling now, and the child grew more active each day. Yet she had never seemed more desirable, more lovely. He touched her cheek. "I won't hunt the wolves."

While the rain poured down, the couple at Bear Hill seemed as isolated, as alone, as if they were the only people in the world. Gray mists hid the cliffs where Yurok's tribe wintered, and at night the cooking fires were no longer visible. But on a clear, cold day when the rains finally stopped, Emar came to visit. He carried a heavy fur robe as a gift.

"Bearskin. There's nothing warmer."

Eena stroked the brown fur. "It's so thick. It will be warm."

Agon studied the hide. "This was a big one. Where did you find it?"

"Way back in the hills."

"I've never killed a bear."

"They like wild country—hills, mountain slopes, canyons." Emar reached in his belt pouch. "These are his claws." The claws were fearsome: long, curved, strong, black. Eena touched one. "They're like knives."

Emar nodded. "He can rip a man wide open with one swipe." He indicated the cave opening and the low walls of the porch. "You know this is called Bear Hill. Some say that long ago, giant bears lived here."

Eena shuddered. "I'm glad it was long ago."

Agon closed his fingers around one of the claws. "It has strong magic."

Eena said to Emar, "Will you eat with us? I'm making venison stew with tubers and onions."

Emar contemplated the entrance. "Onions and venison! Can I eat out here?"

"Wherever you like. It's warmer inside by the fire."

"I'm not cold."

Eena entered the cave mouth and in a little while brought out two wooden bowls of hot stew. The aroma of venison, onions, and tubers was rich and strong. She gave one bowl to Emar, one to Agon. The men used their knives to stab the juicy pieces of venison, then drank the thick soup that remained.

Emar wiped his mouth and beard. "If I could find a woman who could cook like that . . ."

"You have no wife?" Eena asked.

"Wife? What's a wife?"

"I'm a wife. I'm Agon's wife. He's my husband. We'll live together until we die."

Emar considered this. "We don't have wives in our tribe."

"But you need someone to cook for you, make your clothing. . . ."

"The women of the tribe do that. I give them meat. They cook it. I give them skins. They tan them and make skirts and moccasins for me."

"But if you get sick, or hurt . . . who takes care of you?"

"Yeta."

"She takes care of everyone?"

"She has women who help her."

"Who takes care of the children?"

"Their mothers. Yeta helps with the birthing."

"But the fathers? My father hunted for his family, taught us, protected us. . . ."

"Fathers? No one knows who the fathers are. Yurok sleeps with the maidens first. But after that it's whomever the women choose."

"The women choose?"

"Of course. And they change their minds about once every moon." Emar looked into his empty bowl. "I don't suppose there's any more of this?"

As Eena took the bowl into the cave, Emar said to Agon. "She seemed surprised about our ways. Don't you do things the same way in your tribe?"

Agon lowered his voice. "We have a different way."

"What do you mean?"

"The men pick out the woman they want."

Emar stared at him. "I'd like to be a bison hunter!"

Eena came from the cave entrance with Emar's refilled bowl. She smiled at him as she gave him the bowl. "Tell your women that I would be happy to tell them how to make venison stew. Perhaps we could even talk of other things."

After Emar had gone, Eena went into the cave while Agon set his warning trip for the night. When he entered the cave, she took his hand and drew him into the sleeping and storage chamber.

"Look."

The great black bearskin robe had been spread over their bed of hides. She drew Agon down onto the robe.

"We are part of Yurok's tribe now, aren't we?"

"We are our own tribe."

"Yes. But tonight I will be a member of Yurok's tribe."

He eyed her, smiling. "So?"

"So I choose you as my mate." She pulled the corner of the bearskin back. "Come into our magic bear den."

Magic. Coming nearer. Trip lines silent.

In the dim glow of the embers they seize their weapons and move quickly, cautiously to the entrance. Nothing in the porch. Something on the escarpment. Moving upward toward them. A feeling of powerful animal magic, growing stronger.

Agon crouches at the porch entrance, spear poised.

The thing moves closer. Bloody white figure, broad, manlike but huge, ponderously moving four-legged up the slope. Great jaws open.

Eena runs back into the cave, then out with the bearskin.

She holds the robe out to the creature. It rises up on its hind legs, twice the height of a man, great curved arms reaching.

Eena throws the robe over it. "Forgive us!"

The creature roars. It turns and runs down the escarpment.

But now it is black.

It disappears. But the magic still hangs in the night air.

12

Moon of the Great Snow

THE SNOW BEGAN in the night, softly, secretly.

It coated the grass, the moss, the evergreen trees, the ponds, marshes, hills. It sifted down on the backs of the aurochs on the plain. It covered the deer trails, the sleeping deer, the grouse in their nests in the long grass. All through the night it fell, building a world of snow.

Agon and Eena felt it within the living chamber of the cave, a soft white heaviness weighing down on the earth and stone above them, a difference in the light, in the texture of the air, in its smell. They got up in the night and looked out the cave entrance.

Eena pressed close to Agon. "The snow goddess has awakened."

In the morning the snow was waist-high outside the entrance, and the air was so filled with the swirling flakes that they could not see the end of the porch. Agon squeezed a handful, and the snow was heavy and wet.

"If frost comes, this will turn to ice. The game will be hard to find."

"Now we can try out our snow sandals," Eena said. "Now we can skim over the snow."

They strapped the huge rawhide sandals over their high moccasins. Agon heaved himself up onto the snow that filled the porch. He stood for a moment on top of the snow, then took a step. One sandal slid backward, the other forward, and he wobbled precariously and collapsed as the sandals shot apart.

Eena giggled as he crawled back to the entrance. "You looked like a big frog on a slippery lily pad."

"You said we would skim over the snow. You didn't say anything about going in two directions!"

She unstrapped her sandals and examined the flat bottoms. "They're too smooth."

Agon unstrapped his and threw them against the wall of the cave. "They're no good."

Eena studied the arm of her deerskin parka. "When you crossed the mountains, you wore big deerskin moccasins. Were they smooth leather, or did they have the hair left on?"

"I left it on, with the hair slanting backward. That way I could climb up through the snow. . . ." They looked at each other.

"With the hair slanting backward!" They said it together.

Eena ran to their pile of hides and brought back a deerskin. "I'll cut deerskin the same size as the rawhide and sew them together." She knelt by her flat-topped wooden cutting block and, using the rawhide sandals as templates, neatly cut four ovals of deerskin. With a stone burin she made matching holes in the rawhide and deerskin, then stitched them together using a bone needle and deer sinew. She handed Agon his new, hairy sandals.

"Now try them."

They came up on the top of the snow together. They took little steps forward, then larger steps. Eena laughed with joy. "Now we can skim over the snow!" She danced around Agon, shrieking like a little girl.

Agon said, "Look at me."

She stopped and looked at him. He was slowly sinking into the snow. The big floppy soles of his sandals were crumpling, bending upward. Eena bit her lip.

"It doesn't matter." He struggled to pull the misshapen moccasins out of the snow. "I like them." He stared at her. "Are you laughing or crying?"

She looked helplessly at him. "Both."

They went back into the cave.

Eena unstrapped her snow sandals. "You sank. I didn't. You're heavier than I am."

"A leaf can float on water," Agon said. "A rock sinks."

"Something else . . . ?" Eena took one of Agon's crumpled sandals. "Yours should be bigger than mine." She looked up. "And stiffer! I'll put two or three layers of rawhide in yours."

"When rawhide gets wet, it softens. We need something better than rawhide." Agon reached for the basket of walnuts that stood by the fire. "You haven't fed me this morning." He took a handful of the nuts and gave the basket to Eena. "Maybe you could weave big, flat baskets to go on our feet."

She hugged him. "Big, flat baskets! I'll weave them out of willow. They'll be stiff and strong. I can sew the deerskin to the bottom of the baskets if we need it. All we need are some big armfuls of willow branches."

Agon looked out at the snow. "The nearest willow trees are far down the riverbank. It would take a day to go there and back, pushing through this snow."

"My snow moccasins held me above the snow. I could get the branches and be back before noon."

"No. You would die. No one can see in this snow."

"When the snow stops?"

"No. You will never go out alone in winter."

She bowed her head. "Never."

"Now get me some food before I eat these rawhide moccasins."

The snow continued all that day. Agon chafed and paced around the fire, periodically peering out at the storm. Eena worked by the fire, fashioning something from hides and branches.

Agon took little notice of her work until she came to him late in the afternoon. She held four wooden hoops to which deerskin was tightly laced.

"I had to use ash instead of willow for the hoops. I'll

stitch these to the bottoms of our snow moccasins. I think they'll be stiff enough to hold you up."

Agon flexed one. "They are strong. What made you think of these?"

"Dancing."

"Dancing? How?"

"Remember how I danced around you in the snow? When I dance, I hear drums. These are like drumheads. Listen." She struck one of the deerhides with a short stick. The hide boomed. She struck again—hard, soft, hard, soft. The booming sounds echoed in the cave.

She smiled at him. "Now we can dance. We can dance over the snow."

Agon lifted her in his arms. "As long as we dance together."

13

Bring Back the Sun

THE DRUMHEAD SNOW sandals worked so well that Eena was ecstatic. She danced on the snow, circling around Agon as he piled his traps at the top of the escarpment. The snow had stopped in the night, and now the whole world shone white under a clear blue sky. The evergreen trees bowed down under white mantles, and the plains and hills lay like a huge, rumpled white robe. Only the river and streams remained unchanged, their channels of water black against the snow.

Agon and Eena sidestepped down the escarpment with the traps, precariously balancing on the edge of snow that rose above the little stream. Their ability to walk on the surface of the snow was so exhilarating that when they reached the flat land below the hill they raced off toward the river like two children.

They had all the traps in place on the riverbank by mid-morning and were cutting willow withes when Emar appeared, coming along the riverbank toward them from Yurok's camp. He walked on the wet rocks at the river's edge to avoid the high bank of snow.

He stared at the drumhead sandals on their feet. "We saw you running over the snow. Many thought it was magic."

"It is magic." Eena demonstrated by dancing in a circle on the snow.

"Come to our camp. Show the women how you made these. Everyone will want them."

Agon glanced at the sun. "The days are getting short. We wanted to bring these branches back, then set more traps in the hills."

Eena showed Emar her sandals. "You can make them yourself. I used ash for the hoops, but I think willow would be better."

"And you have the hair on the bottoms slanting back." Emar studied the sandals. "I could never make any as perfect as these."

"I'll make you a pair."

"You will?" Emar glanced at Agon. "Axe Man won't mind?"

Agon looked up from the bundle of withes he was tying a strap around. "Not as long as you don't think she has chosen you."

"I won't think that." Emar moved a step back from Eena. "Maybe it would be better if you showed our women . . ."

Eena's face showed her concern. "Yes. That would be better."

"Could you come tomorrow? Artron will bring the sun back."

"Artron?" Agon stood up. "Grae brings the sun back."

"Your tribe does that, too?"

"Since ancient times."

"Ours the same." Emar pulled his beard. "How can that be?"

"Once our tribe went to the south, the home of the sun," Agon said. "Maybe yours did, too. Grae learned the secrets of the sun. Ever since, Grae brings the sun back from the south."

"Is that Grae still alive?"

"Every chieftain is Grae. Grae never dies." Agon shifted uneasily on his snow sandals. In his mind he saw Grae, his father, falling on his spear, dying. He, Agon, had closed Grae's eyes and placed his staff by his side in the grave. And now Zur was Grae . . . Zur, who had stood with Eena on the Black Stone as she raised two bloody skulls to the sky . . . Zur, whom Agon should have killed. . . .

Emar was watching Agon's face. "Maybe," he said, "every Grae is not as strong as the Grae who went to the south."

"Maybe."

"Someone has to bring the sun back."

"Yes."

Eena spoke: "Maybe every chieftain, every sorcerer, all together bring the sun back."

They stared at her. "All together?"

"Maybe it takes all the magic of every tribe together to bring the sun back."

Agon and Emar considered this. Agon shook his head. "Some chieftains, some sorcerers, are evil. Ka and Kaan would have driven the sun away. Grae would never have worked his magic with them."

"Maybe all the good chieftains, the good sorcerers, have to work their magic together," Eena said. "Work against the evil ones."

Emar nodded. "That could be."

"Maybe." Agon looked at the sun. It was noon, yet the fiery ball was low on the southern horizon. "We'll come tomorrow unless there's a storm."

Emar smiled. "Good. And Spear Woman can show our women how to make the magic snow sandals."

The following day was clear, but the sun hung even lower in the southern sky. Eena and Agon packed dried meat and plums in their belt pouches, and each carried a rolled-up deerskin robe strapped on their back in case they were caught in a storm. In addition to their weapons they carried willow withes and Eena's sewing pouch. They arrived at Yurok's camp in midmorning to find the usual bustle of activity taking place in the trampled snow in front of the cliff shelter. Emar met them and led them to the place where Yeta was supervising the roasting of a whole aurochs.

Yeta hugged Eena. "You look so happy and healthy!" She placed a big hand under Eena's hunting shirt. "He is growing fast. Two moons left."

"Yes." Eena held out the withes. "I brought these. Emar asked if I would show you how I make the snow sandals."

"We saw you yesterday. Running like two rabbits over the snow." Yeta looked down at Eena's feet. "Come over to this ledge under the cliff. I want to see how you did the sewing."

As the women walked toward the ledge, Emar pointed toward the cliff top on their side of the river. "See how the sun lies just touching the edge? And the two big rocks on the cliff top? I'll show you how we tell the first day of winter." He pointed to the cliff wall on the other side of the river.

"See the lines across the wall? And the straight up-and-down line that crosses them? The shadow of the other cliff creeps along the wall, and the shadow of the two rocks comes to the up-and-down line at noon. If at that time the shadow of the cliff goes higher than the top line, the sun will never return."

"We have the same marks on our cliff! We use the shadow of a rock pinnacle, because the other cliff is too far away." Agon gazed at the wall. "What do you call this day?"

"Sunstand. The day the sun stops."

"Ours is the same!"

Artron came from a nearby hut. "Welcome, Axe Man. You have come with your magic to help bring back the sun."

"I have no magic."

"You have more than you know." Artron studied the shadow on the cliff. "I heard you say that your tribe has the same marks."

"And the same name. How can that be?"

"No one knows. I know of two other tribes that have the same marks and name."

"Could all tribes have been one?"

"They could have."

"Even the evil tribes?"

Artron touched the golden disc on his chest. "Even the evil ones."

"And all people learned the same things?"

"Yes."

"But then why are we different? How can a tribe like Ka's have come from the same people that made your tribe, or Grae's tribe?"

Artron contemplated Agon's face, his eyes. "It's part of the mystery. The mystery you already know. The mystery you learned with certain spirits. The mystery you learned with the most powerful one. The one whose name may not be spoken by men."

"How do you know these things?"

"I knew them when I first saw you. Just as I knew when I saw Spear Woman."

Emar asked, "What mystery do you talk about?"

"The Great Mystery."

"I am only a hunter. How am I to know of any Great Mystery?"

"The hunter knows better than anyone. You will find the mystery in something you know well."

"What is that?"

Arton took a small flint knife from his robe. He pricked one finger and let a single drop fall into the palm of his hand. "Understand this one drop of blood, and you will understand why the sun stands still. Know the secrets hidden in this red drop, and you will know good from evil. Learn the magic of blood, and you will know the magic of the stars."

Yurok came from his hut with a blushing girl behind him. "All your talk has disturbed my magic. Bring the sun back now, Artron, so we can enjoy winter as we should."

The shadow of the two stones crept slowly toward the vertical line of noon. Artron assembled the people around a huge pile of brush and logs that had been built below the line.

Artron raised two pieces of wood to the sky—one like a short spear handle with a point at one end, the other flat. "Oak and Ash. Bring the sun fire!"

Hura led six women forward. Artron gave Hura the pieces of wood. "Bring the fire from the wood in the ancient way."

The women knelt in a circle. Hura placed the flat piece of wood on the ground, held the pointed piece against the center of the flat one, and began to rotate the pointed one rapidly between the palms of her hands. She worked furiously; then, with hardly a pause, another woman began to rotate the stick. Woman after woman knelt over the wood, their hands a blur of motion. Then a tiny wisp of smoke curled up from the point of contact. Hura sprinkled brown powder into the smoke, and the people shouted as a tiny flame leaped up.

The women fed tinder and twigs to the flame and then carefully placed the burning wood beneath the smaller branches of the great pile. The little fire flickered, then strengthened and caught, and with a crackling and snapping the great pile ignited.

The people yelled in excitement. Artron took the golden sun disc from his neck and held it in his right hand, high before the people. Slowly, he swung his right arm down, lowering the disc. With his left hand he pointed to the wall of the opposite cliff.

The shadow of the two rocks on the wall straddled the noon line. And the straight shadow of the cliff top fell exactly on the highest horizontal line on the wall. If the shadow moved above the line, the sun would never return.

Artron began to chant. He chanted in a strange language, his voice deep and sonorous. Beads of sweat appeared on his forehead as he struggled to raise the sun disc in his hand. The flames of the great fire roared up toward the sun.

Slowly, agonizingly, Arton raised the golden disc.

The sun stopped.

The shadow stopped.

The sun would come back.

14

The Moon of the Great Cold

THE WIND SWEPT down from the ice fields in the north. Tree branches cracked and split in the night, creeks and streams froze and vanished under fallen snow, and the river flowed almost unseen beneath blue ice.

Agon fastened the protective screen of hides and branches across the cave entrance, and following the example of Yurok's people, built a small sleeping hut of poles and hides inside the cave near the fire. The hut served two purposes: trapping the heat from the fire and keeping out the smoke.

Eena now had fur robes of mink, fox, and marten, and she made their bed within the hut. With their deerskin clothing and fur robes they were warm and comfortable. And they ate well: a large leather cooking bag near the fire held simmering rich stews heated by hot stones dropped into the liquid. Agon, unable to sit quietly by the fire, hunted every day except during blizzards.

The child grew larger. Eena bulged under her loose deerskin shirt, and she moved carefully now, no longer dancing around Agon on her snow sandals or racing up the escarpment. Her face became fuller, more serene, and her actions became more mysterious to Agon.

On a day when a blizzard howled outside, Eena made a nest. She shooed Agon from the hut and then brought their every hide, every fur, every spare piece of clothing into the tiny dwelling. She busily folded and stacked and arranged and rearranged all day long, humming to herself, smiling vaguely at Agon whenever she emerged from the hut. Finally, at dusk, she led Agon to the low entrance and pulled back the flap of hide.

The circular space was a huge furry nest. Built up waist-high at the walls, concave in the center, lined with furs, the nest looked as though some giant bird had built it for eggs and young.

"Do you like it?"

Agon gazed silently, careful not to change his expression or look at Eena. "It should be warm," he said.

"And see, the baby can't fall out."

"No."

"And I can keep him warm and safe by curling around him like a wolf mother. There's just enough room."

"Just enough room."

"You don't like my nest!"

"I do."

"Why don't you like it?"

"Um . . . just one thing."

"What?"

"I was just wondering . . ."

"Wondering what?"

"Where I'm supposed to sleep."

On another day Eena rearranged all of their supplies in the storeroom. She selected branches from their woodpile and made racks for all of their clothing—one rack for Agon, one for herself, one for the child. She made racks to hold all the baskets of nuts, dried fruits, and berries. She made racks to hold the racks that held the dried venison. She made racks to hold their extra furs and hides and robes. She made racks to hold their snow sandals and extra moccasins and sandals. She made racks to hold their extra spears.

She showed the room to Agon. They were barely able to squeeze in.

"Now we can find things when we need them."

"Yes."

"It looks better this way."

"Yes."

"Before, we could never find anything."

"No."

"You don't like it."

"I do."

"Why don't you like it?"

"Um . . . I was just thinking."

"Thinking what?"

"I'd better bring in more firewood."

Eena decided she did not have enough clothing for the baby. She had Agon bring in more furs. She wanted rabbit skins for swaddling clothes, mink skins for robes, and more deerskin for shirts and leggings and moccasins.

Agon set his traps again, hunted more deer. Curing and tanning the hides was difficult in the frigid weather so he was forced to do the work inside the cave, which soon began to smell like Yurok's summer camp. When the tanning was completed, they pulled back the framework of hides from the cave entrance for half a day to let the wind sweep out the smells.

As Eena sat by the fire sewing the garments, she spoke to Agon of things she had been wondering about.

"Why have you never hunted for bear?"

"Because I feel about bears as you do about wolves."

"Because they're like people?"

"Yes."

"When the white bear came up the trail that night, I thought at first it was a man. A huge man."

"If we had claws and long jaws and fur, we would look like bears."

"Bears must have strong magic. They can sleep all winter without food. And my father told me that the bear cubs are born while the mother sleeps."

"Would you like to do that?"

She pondered this. "I would rather see the baby when he is born. Hold him and nurse him. Watch him change and grow."

Agon nodded. "And keep him safe in the nest."

She looked quickly at him, then smiled. "Something told me I had to build a nest."

"And make racks for everything we have."

"And you had to bring in more wood."

"The racks can be used for firewood if we have a long blizzard. And you have made room for me in the hut."

"If I do any more strange things, you must stop me."

"Maybe."

She cut the end of a thread. "I wonder why we act the way we do. Do we have the same feelings as animals?"

"Sometimes."

"Why?"

"Because we are animals."

"Yes. But I think we are different from animals sometimes."

Agon held up the spear point he was working on. "We make tools and weapons." He indicated her sewing. "And clothing. I've never seen an animal do those things."

"Or look at the stars and wonder."

"Or put paintings on ceilings."

"Or make fire."

"Or stop the sun."

Eena's face became sad. "Or take heads. Or burn other animals over fires. Or put them in aurochs hides and throw spears into them. . . ."

Agon came to her and put his arm around her. "Don't think of those things."

"I can't help but think of them. I can never forget seeing my father and brother's heads on the poles outside Ka's cave. . . ."

He stroked her hair. "We killed Ka. We avenged the death of your people, of my people."

"Yes." She turned and held her face against his shoulder. "Your people too . . . Grae and Erida and Ara . . . I loved them . . . so much. . . ."

On a clear, cold day, Emar came to visit them. He wore snow sandals on his feet and carried a leather bag. Because of the cold, he finally entered the cave. He looked with surprise at the comfortable home Agon and Eena had made. "I thought I would feel evil spirits. This is a good place. I like it."

"We like it, too," Agon replied. "But we ask you a favor."

"What?"

"Don't tell others of this."

"Why not?"

"Because we like to live alone. If others knew that the cave is not evil, they might all decide to move up here."

"Ah! That would be something." Emar gazed around the chamber. "I can see it: Yurok's hut there. Artron's there. Hura's there . . ."

Eena grasped her spear in her agitation. "If that woman ever comes in here . . ."

Emar winked. "I was only joking."

"Don't say it, even in a joke."

"I won't."

Agon interceded. "Just don't tell anyone that this place is liveable."

"I won't." Emar gave the leather bag to Eena. "Yeta sent you this for when the child comes. I am also to tell you that Yeta will come night or day if you need her." He grinned. "She likes her snow sandals so well that she threatens to become a hunter. You should see her on the snow. All bundled in furs and walking wide as the sandals make her do, she looks like a bear."

Agon and Eena looked quickly at one another. "We thank her," Eena said. "I won't need help, but it's good to know that she would come." She pointed to a log by the fire. "Sit down, and I'll bring you a bowl of stew."

"I'll tell her." Emar sat down and looked around the chamber. "Have you found the bearskin robe warm?"

Agon glanced at Eena again. "The robe was warm. We thank you for it."

"You say 'was warm.' Don't you use it?"

"We are warm-blooded people. We found it too warm."

Emar nodded. "I can understand that. I myself find bearskin too warm. Maybe if the weather turns colder, you'll need it."

"Maybe."

Emar took the bowl of stew Eena brought him and inhaled the steam. "Onions and venison. My favorite." He speared a piece of meat with his knife. "You remember the bear claws I showed you when I brought the robe?"

"We do."

"A strange thing happened. I put them back in my pouch. When I got back to my hut that night, I laid the pouch on the floor, next to my bed." Emar speared another piece of venison and chewed thoughtfully on it. "In the morning the pouch was gone."

"Someone took it?"

Emar shook his head. "No one would steal from me. I've killed two men in thong wrestling." He speared another piece of venison. "It was strange, though."

They waited for him to finish chewing. Emar took a big sip from the bowl and wiped his beard. "I smelled bear in the hut."

The Sons of Spear Woman

15

The Birth of Eran

EENA SECRETLY COLLECTED the things she would need for the birth: a flint knife, two lengths of thong, a bundle of dry moss, three rabbit skins, and a small robe of mink skins. She kept the objects in a leather bag that she stored beside the baby clothes and the bag Yeta had sent.

Agon still felt a sense of unease. He spoke of it again to Eena: "You should ask Yeta to come and help you."

"I will need no help."

"But you have never had a child."

"The priestesses of the Earth Mother taught me."

"You have never seen a child born."

"I have seen animals give birth. Does, mares, bison."

"What if something goes wrong?"

"Then you can go for Yeta."

"What if a blizzard is blowing?"

"Spring is near."

Her confidence, her air of mystery, partially reassured him. But he also felt a sense of frustration, of alienation. He, the protector of his family, was not only not needed, but his advice was ignored. He hunted now only close to Bear Hill, and he appeared at the cave entrance so frequently, claiming hunger, that Eena accused him of becoming gluttonous.

"You're like a wolverine, hungry all the time." But she knew why he came, and secretly she was glad.

As the moon waxed and grew full, Eena knew that her time was near. She had made a small birthing hut behind the other hut, and here she placed the two leather bags and three deerskin robes. She closed the flap over the hut's entrance and spoke to Agon:

"The child will come today. Now I must do certain things. You must go out and stay until nightfall. When you come back, you must not go near the little hut until I call."

When Agon had gone, Eena laid wood for a small fire in the birthing hut. She spread one deerskin robe beside the wood, and upon it she carefully placed the knife, thongs, moss, rabbit skins, mink robe, and other deerskin robes. Then she opened Yeta's bag and withdrew three bunches of dried plants: one bunch tied with a single thong, one with two thongs, the last with three thongs.

She brought coals from the hearth fire, ignited the pile of wood, and reached out to close the entrance flap of the hut.

She removed all of her clothing and laid the garments on the deerskin. Then she spread the dried plants of the one-thong bundle over the flames.

A thick, pungent smoke arose. Eena held each article in the smoke, just above the flames: the knife, thongs, rabbit skins, moss, mink robe, deerskins, her own clothing. Then she placed the second bundle of plants on the fire and stood close over it, rubbing her body as the smoke enveloped her. She undid the braids of her hair and spread the long tresses so the smoke could penetrate them. Then she placed the third bundle of plants on the fire. The hut filled with smoke. Slowly, dreamily, Eena danced naked around the fire. Now the contractions began, but Eena danced until the fire died down and the smoke ceased and cleared.

The contractions were strong and regular now. She wrapped another deerskin robe around her body and squatted in the center of the semicircle. She grasped the deer totem at her neck and held it as the contractions grew stronger. . . .

Agon went as far as the river. He no longer trapped, but he inspected the lairs of the mink, the muskrats, foxes, rabbits. He circled back into the hills and followed deer trails, but took no deer. He returned to Bear Hill, and it was only noon.

He stood at the bottom of the escarpment. What if Eena called for him now? What if she had called earlier? He hurried up the escarpment and stood silently listening outside the hide closure. No sound came from the interior. His nose detected a new scent—a faint smell of aromatic smoke.

He peered through a crack beween the hide screen and the cave wall. The logs in the fire burned steadily. Beyond it, the family hut blocked the view of the birthing hut. There was no sound but the crackling of the fire. The aromatic scent was stronger than outside, a smell of mystery and magic.

He pulled back from the screen. Eena had told him to stay away until nightfall. He turned and went back down the escarpment.

The magic of birth is upon Eena. The contractions are stronger, yet she knows the child has not moved downward. But now something is happening. She places a rabbit skin beneath her. Blood suddenly flows from her vagina, staining the white rabbit skin. She feels an instant of fear, but the blood ceases. She covers the blood with a section of dry moss. Something is moving, stretching, opening within her. With each contraction the stretching, opening feeling becomes stronger.

A sudden gush of liquid onto the moss. No blood. Now she knows the time of birth is very near.

The contractions become powerful. She must push. With each contraction she pushes with the strong muscles of her abdomen.

She feels the child descend. Something presses hard against the very floor of her body—something pressing, turning, moving down.

The contraction again. She pushes.

Now! Now! Now!

He floats in soft darkness. Warm. Content. The mother heart beating.

Now he is squeezed. Again. Again. Again.

He moves downward, away from the mother heart.

His head presses, turns, enters, squeezes downward.

Turns.

His body follows.

Eena feels the head emerge. She supports it with her hands.

Push. Again. One shoulder out. The second shoulder.

Her hands support the head, the body, and lower them gently from her body, turning and lifting.

She sees him. Membrane over the face. She tears it gently off.

The baby stares up at her.

Light.

Something in the light.

He feels death.

Then he gasps, sucks in.

Air life. Air. In. Out.

He lives again.

She sees the first breath. The second. He lives.

Now she slowly sits, holding the baby. She places the tiny live child between her legs on a soft rabbit skin.

The cord leads, pulsating, from the child up into her, from her into the child. They are still one.

The cord becomes still. The bond of life between them is weakening, dying.

She ties one thong around the cord, close to the child. Ties the second thong one hand-width higher.

Now the knife. Blade between the two thongs.

She cuts, severing the bond forever.

He feels the life bond sever. He is alone.

Eena wiped the baby clean with the rabbit skin, gently wiping the face, the black hair, the body, the arms, the legs. He was male. Strongly, largely, male.

She wrapped him in the third rabbit skin, then she laid him in the mink robe, bundled warm with only the face exposed.

Something more was happening. She squatted again, placed her hands over her abdomen, now almost empty. She massaged gently, strongly.

The afterbirth slid out onto the moss.

She placed the afterbirth, the wet and bloody moss, and the bloody rabbit skin in the leather bag.

She was empty. Done.

The child cried, a strong deep bellow.

She lay beside the child, pulled the deerskin robe over them both, and brought the child to her breast. His searching mouth found a nipple.

She felt her breast responding.
Once again they were bonded.

Agon knew.

He felt the contractions.

He felt the movement, the birth, the cutting of the cord.

He raced up the escarpment, pausing at the entrance to the cave. The fiery star had long been gone, but now a great shower of falling stars occured, blazing across the sky like sparks from a giant campfire, telling the birth of his son.

He entered.

Eena called from the main hut.

16

Sons of Chieftains

ERAN SUCKED RICH milk from his mother's breast for two years and grew strong as a young bull. He demanded meat on his second birthday and never again nursed. He walked at nine moons, ran at one year, and at two years threw with accuracy the small spear Agon made for him. His raven-black hair grew thick as the mane of a lion, and a central streak of gold shone like the fiery star. His courage and temper coursed strong as the river current, and he impressed all who saw him as being the son of chieftains.

With Agon he held a mixture of admiration and rivalry. He watched with awe as Agon hunted, threw the spear and axe, and wrestled with the young men of Yurok's tribe. But he resented the affection shown between Agon and Eena. Eran possessed such a strong love for Eena that as a child he pushed angrily against Agon when Eena embraced him, and at night insisted on sleeping not only next to his mother, but between her and Agon.

Agon put up with this for two years and three moons before he plucked the enraged child from Eena's side and deposited him in a bed of his own. He looked into Eran's eyes and spoke softly to him: "This woman is my mate. She has nursed you and held you for over two years. Now you will learn to be a man. Find your own mate."

Alar was born three winters after Eran. Eena gave birth alone while Agon and Eran tramped in the snow below Bear Hill.

Alar was born with golden hair, and he was such a handsome child that he seemed somehow fragile. His blue-green eyes resembled his mother's, and while his features showed the same strong lines as his father's, they were tempered with Eena's more delicate features.

One day when Alar was almost two years old, Eran watched as Alar nursed at Eena's breast, then raised his spear. Agon grasped the spear with one hand, Eran's shoulder with the other. He turned Eran so that he looked into his eyes. He spoke quietly:

"You will never raise your spear against your brother."

"He's not my brother."

"He is. Hear what I say."

Eran glared at Agon. "Let him find his own mate."

"After two years. Now he feeds from your mother as you did."

"I'll kill him." Eran raised his spear again.

Agon seized the spear, broke it, and threw it into the fire.

Eran's face showed a terrible anger. "I'll make a new spear, a bigger spear. I'll kill him. I'll kill you."

Agon slipped the axe from his belt. "Do you see the axe? If you move to throw a spear at your brother or at me, the axe will split your head before you throw."

"When I am a man, my spear will be faster than your axe. I will kill you then."

"Anyone who raises a spear against me dies."

Eena stared white-faced at them. "Do not speak of killing each other."

"He must learn," Agon said. "He does not raise his spear against his brother or father." He spoke to Eran: "You are my firstborn son. We will have our own tribe. When I die, you will become chieftain. You will start being son of a chieftain now. Take off all your furs."

Eena gasped. "He is only a child. . . ."

"He will become a man." Agon pointed toward the cave entrance. "Eran, you will go naked into the forest below the hill with only a knife. You will find a young ash tree and cut its trunk for a new spear."

"The snow is deep. Please, Agon, do not make him do this."

"He will do it if he is son of a chieftain."

Eran threw off his furs. "I am son of a chieftain. I will find an ash tree and make a spear bigger than yours."

Agon studied Eran's face. "You have a chieftain's blood. I would not want a son who showed fear."

"Fear? What is fear?"

"A chieftain may know fear, but he must never show it."

"I don't fear. Not you. Not your axe. Not the snow or cold. But I will never forget that you have sent me out into the cold."

Agon's voice was like ice. "Never forget that you will never again raise your spear against your brother."

Eran pulled the knife from his belt that lay on the cave floor. "I will raise my spear against anyone who stands against me." He pushed aside the hide covering the cave entrance and went out into the snow.

17

Alar

ALAR THRIVED ON Eena's milk and grew strong, as had Eran. At the age of two he threw his spear accurately, and he ran and climbed. When he was four years old, he hunted with Agon and Eran. His hair remained golden as Eena's, contrasting with Eran's black mane with its golden streak. Alar's love for Eena was as strong as Eran's, yet he did not show the same resentment toward Agon's relationship with her. Instead, Alar bonded strongly with his father and loved to be held by Agon.

Alar looked on both Agon and Eran as gods. He practiced almost constantly with his spear, seeking to achieve the long throw, the accuracy of his father and brother. He watched with delight as Agon outmatched Yurok's hunters in skill and strength, and when Eran challenged and easily bested boys his age and older in wrestling and spear throwing.

Agon wrestled playfully with the two boys from the time they could stand, and as their strength and agility increased, so Agon increased the hardness of their combats. As they struggled, Agon came to know the singularity of each boy's way of fighting: Eran fought with violent ferocity, fiercely, moving in quick bursts of strength, always attacking. Alar fought just as fiercely, but with an implacable, relentless determination that Agon recognized as his own way. When the two boys wrestled together, Eran always won, yet Alar never gave up, never asked for mercy, fighting on until Eran grew enraged and brutally forced him into a helpless position.

One day as Alar visited Yurok's camp with Eena, three

boys of Yurok's tribe tumbled him in the dirt. Alar was six and a half years old. He smiled at the largest boy. "Will you fight me alone?"

The boy sneered at him. "Run to your mother."

Alar threw himself at the boy and seized his wrists as they went down. His hands never left the wrists as they rolled and twisted on the ground. The boy drove his knees into Alar's body, yet the grip only tightened. Now fear showed in the boy's eyes, for his hands seemed caught in a trap, a trap so strong and relentless that it would never let go its grip. Larger than Alar, the boy kicked and struggled helplessly and finally lay still on the ground. Alar spoke quietly: "Next time I will take you by the throat." He released his grip and came to his feet. He looked into the eyes of the other two boys, and the boys slunk away. Alar's eyes held death.

18

Confrontation

EENA TOLD AGON and Eran of the fight. Eran scowled. "If I had been there, I would have fought all three of them. Why did you let the other two go?"

"Because they didn't want to fight," Alar replied.

"Cowards! You should have broken their arms."

Agon shook his head. "Only fight with men. Fighting with a coward brings no honor."

"What is honor?" Eran asked.

"To have men respect you."

"If I kill them, they'll respect me."

"No. They will fear you. But to be respected, to have honor, you must not kill weaklings or cowards unless they attack you first."

Eran's eyes gleamed with a cold light. "When I'm chieftain, I'll kill them. Cowards and weaklings would be no good in battle. They deserve to die."

"Why always talk of killing?" Eena remonstrated. "Great chieftains show kindness to their people."

"And to strangers," Alar added.

Eran scoffed at this. "Strangers! Haven't you listened to the stories of how strangers brought death to the tribe of Ka?"

"Who told you of this?" Agon asked sharply.

"Hura."

"Hura!" Eena seized Eran's arm. "When has she talked to you?"

"When I visit Yurok's camp."

"Hura told you of our tribe and Ka?"

"Yes. More than you have told me."

"What has she told you?"

"I am of a tribe of great chieftains. The tribe of Grae tried to kill our people. We fought against the strangers and killed many of them, but our chieftain was killed."

Eena stared at Eran, then at Agon. "She lies! And Eran believes her lies!"

"He has heard the truth from us."

"Who knows what evil she intends?" Eena faced Alar. "Has she talked to you?"

"No. I don't like her."

"Never let her talk to you."

"I won't."

"I will kill her if she tells her lies to either of you."

Alar regarded his mother with wide eyes. "You would kill her?"

"Yes."

Eran looked coldly at Eena. "You tell me not to kill. No longer will I listen to you."

"You will listen to her," Agon said. "You will obey her. You will obey me. You will not talk to Hura again."

Eran shrugged. "But I'll kill anyone I want to."

"No. Kill if you have to, but you will not kill otherwise."

"When I am a man, you will not command me. I will kill anyone who angers me."

"Not if you belong to our family, our tribe."

"Then I will leave your family, your tribe."

"That may be. But now you are still a boy. You are still part of our family. You will obey us."

Eran glared silently at Agon.

"Answer me. Will you obey us?"

Eran raised his spear.

Agon grasped the spear with one hand. "Never raise your spear against your family. I have told you that."

Eran's face showed a terrible anger. He grasped his spear with both hands and tried to wrest it from Agon's grip, but Agon held the spear easily in one hand; it seemed imbedded in rock. Eran's voice was thick with hatred. "When I am a man, you will not hold my spear."

"You are not yet a man. You will obey your mother and father?"

"I will obey my real father."

"I am your real father." Agon held out his hand to Eran. "Take my hand, and we will be friends."

"You are not my father."

Eena's face grew pale. Agon kept his hand extended. "I am your father. Take my hand."

"No. Hura told me. My father was chieftain of a great tribe."

Eena stepped between Agon and Eran. "Grae was chieftain of a great tribe. Your father is Agon, son of Grae."

"No."

Agon's voice was cold as the ice fields. "Then who is your father?"

Eran's eyes blazed. "Ka, son of Kaan."

19

Spear Woman

EENA WENT ALONE to Yurok's camp in the pinewoods. She carried her spear.

Yeta met her at the edge of the camp.

"You have not come to weave baskets."

"I come to talk to Hura."

Yeta looked at Eena's eyes. "There are many who would help you kill her."

"If I kill her, I will do it alone."

"I see that. What has she done?"

"She has told Eran lies. Where is she?"

"In her hut, there." Yeta pointed. "Be careful, Eena. Eat or drink nothing she offers to you."

"I would starve first." Eena left Yeta and went toward Hura's hut. As she approached, Hura appeared in the low entrance. She stood leaning against the doorpost with her arms folded, staring coldly at Eena.

"What do you want?"

Eena stopped a spear's throw from the sorceress. "I have come to tell you one thing. If you ever talk to either of my sons again, I will kill you."

Hura laughed. "How many times have you told me that you will kill me? You are like a barking jackal bitch. . . ."

Eena's spear flashed through the air, slashed across the side of Hura's head, and pinned her to the wooden post by one ear. Blood streamed down the side of her head, and she screamed, again and again.

Eena ran forward and pressed the point of her knife against Hura's throat. She pulled the still-quivering spear from the post and ripped the flint point and leather binding back through Hura's ear while Hura shrieked in agony and fear.

Then Eena turned and went through Yurok's camp, into the pine forest, and back to Bear Hill.

20

Ulam

ON A DAY in late summer an old man came along the riverbank from the east. He used his spear as an aid in walking, and his long white hair and beard were tangled and unkempt. He hobbled through Yurok's empty winter camp under the cliffs and proceeded uncertainly along the river toward Bear Hill.

Agon and Eena and the two boys watched him from the porch in front of the cave entrance. Agon studied the bent figure. "Ulam!" he shouted. "Ulam! Come up!"

The old man peered up at the figures on the hill. "Agon!"

Agon ran down the escarpment, followed by Eena and the boys. They met Ulam on the plain between the hill and the river.

Ulam's weathered face crackled with happiness. He embraced Agon, then Eena, gazing in wonder at them, then at the two boys.

"I thought you were dead. . . ." Tears welled from his eyes.

They helped him up the escarpment and sat him in the place of honor by the fire. Eena brought him deer stew while Agon explained to the boys:

"Ulam is from Grae's tribe. He was the greatest hunt leader of all the bison hunters."

Alar moved closer to Ulam, but Eran scowled and drew back.

Ulam looked up from the bowl of stew and spoke to the boys: "Your father was the greatest hunt leader of the bison hunters. But as a boy he was in my rite band. I may have taught him a few things."

"You taught me much." Agon put his hand on Ulam's shoulder. "Why have you come so far from the tribe?"

Ulam's face lost its look of happiness. "Evil has come to the tribe. I came, hoping I might find you, even though I feared you were dead." Tears came to his eyes again. "I followed Alar when Eena led Ka from the tribe. I saw Ka kill Alar. I saw Ka carry Eena across the river. I saw you, Agon, hold off all of Ka's men in the river. And I saw the great wall of water strike you . . . I thought you both were dead. . . ."

"But we live, as you see."

"Thanks to the gods."

Alar stared at Ulam. "I am Alar. I am not killed by Ka. . . ."

"Alar was one of my brothers," Agon explained. "You are named after him." He spoke to Ulam: "What evil has come to the tribe?"

"Zur."

"Zur lives?"

"He is Grae."

Agon's hand touched the handle of his axe. "Then evil has come to the tribe."

"Aye. Great evil."

"What?"

"Zur kills your young brothers. One by one."

Eena made a sound of sorrow as Agon rose to his feet. Agon grasped Ulam's shoulder. "All my brothers?"

"One is left. Alfgar. Zur will kill him next Sunstand Day."

"All my other brothers are dead? All the sons of Grae and Erida?"

Ulam nodded. "All but Alfgar."

Agon seized a huge boulder that lay among the many at the top of the escarpment, a boulder so heavy that no other man could have lifted it. He raised the boulder high above his head and hurled it out over the edge of the escarpment, where it fell crashing down the slope to the flat plain below. Then Agon hurled another great boulder, and another, while Eena and Ulam and the two boys watched his terrible anger.

Agon stood staring out over the plain to the east, his body rigid. The only sound was the crackling of the fire.

A black raven came flying from the west, over the top of Bear Hill and the people on the porch before the cave entrance, then on to the east, down the river valley. Agon watched the raven until it disappeared in the distance.

Eena held her hands to her mouth, knowing now what Agon would do.

Agon turned back toward the fire, his eyes holding death. He said to Ulam, "Tell me how Zur killed my brothers."

21

Ulam's Story

ULAM SPOKE SLOWLY, as old men speak, his eyes looking inward, seeing the events he described.

"Zur had the spear wound in his side from when Ka attacked. We all thought he would die. After Grae fell upon his spear and we buried him and the fallen people, Alar led the tribe toward the safe place. You, Agon, had gone to kill Ka.

"We carried the wounded. Carried them on litters of spears and hides. Zur's men carried him, saying that he was chieftain. Eena led the women and children. Alar was wounded in the shoulder, but he led the people through that night and the next day. Alar wanted to keep on toward the safe place, but Zur commanded that we stop. Zur said that Alar would die for leading the tribe. That next night Spear Mountain leaped into the sky in blasts of fire, and a great wind struck us, then rain and lightning and thunder. Water rose around us; in the storm many died, and Zur seemed dead. Alar and Rok and Eena led us on toward the safe place. Then Ka and his men found us."

Ulam spoke to the two boys. "Your mother saved the tribe. She knew that Ka wanted her, and she led him away from the tribe. Alar followed, weak with his wound, and I followed Alar. When I saw the great wall of water swallow your father and Ka's men, I mourned for him, for I thought he could not live. Huge trees whirled in the water, boulders big as bison were swept before it. Then I returned to the tribe, where they hid in the safe place."

Alar asked Agon, "How did you live when the water swallowed you?"

"The gods must have held me in their hands."

"And how did you find Mother?"

"I crossed the mountains and came down on the other side of the river."

"You crossed the mountains!" Ulam exclaimed. "The peaks of snow and ice that rise into the sky?"

Agon nodded.

"And you took Eena back from Ka!"

"Yes."

"How?"

"I killed him."

"But his tribe . . ."

"We went over the edge of the cliffs. They could not follow us."

Eran spoke: "Why have you never told us of Ka?"

"Because of the evil in him, in his tribe," Eena replied. "We did not want the evil to follow us."

Eran regarded his mother with cold eyes. "Were you the mate of Ka?"

Eena's cheeks flushed, and her hand went to the carved deer totem at her neck.

Agon spoke harshly to Eran: "She was never the mate of Ka. Never say that again."

Alar moved closer to his mother and looked up at her. She took his hand in hers. A drop of blood appeared on her lower lip, and she brushed it away.

"Speak no more of Ka," Agon commanded. "Tell us of Zur."

Ulam looked from Agon to Eena, his old eyes concerned. He pulled at the tangle of his beard.

"I thought Zur would be dead. But when I returned to the tribe, he was alive. When Rok and his men returned to their tribe, it started." Ulam gazed into the fire.

"While Rok was with us, Zur feared to show how he would rule. When Rok left, Zur became cruel, evil. We thought it was because of the pain of his wound. Then a great streaming star appeared in the west, and Zur became even more evil. He grew worse every year." Ulam glanced at Agon. "I knew, you knew, what he was like. I think his mother was evil."

"Erida was not evil!" Eena's eyes flashed.

"Erida was not Zur's mother. He was born of Grae's first wife, a sorceress who came from the forest. Her name was Lilith."

"What happened to her?" Eena asked.

"She disappeared." Ulam's voice became filled with mystery. "Some say she flew away in a thundercloud. She had great power, but she used it for evil." Ulam poked at the fire with his spear. "She never came back. But she left Zur, Grae's firstborn son. Now Zur is Grae, chieftain of the bison hunters. And Zur works his evil upon the tribe."

Agon touched the ibex on his chest. "Tell me of the evil."

"It began six years ago," Ulam said, "and it has happened every year since. Five of your brothers have died, Agon. Zur started with the oldest one. Now only Alfgar is left alive, and he will die this year."

"Why has someone not killed Zur?" Agon's voice was tight with rage.

"Because they are afraid. Anyone who angers Zur is killed. Zur rules by terror." Ulam raised his spear in a shaking hand. "I would have killed him, but I no longer have the strength."

"No one blames you. Tell me how Zur made my brothers die."

"Six years ago, before winter Sunstand Day, Zur told the people that the sun would not come back because of their disobedience to him. He showed then how every day the sun sank lower, pointing to the cliff shadow on the wall. Then Zur told us there was only one hope—someone must offer themselves to the sun, someone of the line of chieftains, as only such would be acceptable to the sun.

"But Zur was clever. He went to Alan, the oldest of your brothers, and told him that no harm would come to him—he must only offer himself on Sunstand Day.

"The day came, and Zur stood in front of the great fire, chanting as the sun approached the noon mark. Then Zur called out, 'Who will make an offering of himself to make the sun stop? What son of Grae is brave enough to come forward?'

"Then Alan came to the fire, and Zur's men, Van and Xo, laid him on a platform of branches before the fire. Now the shadow approached the final mark on the cliff wall, and Zur pointed to it with his staff as he chanted. The shadow rose higher and higher, and Zur chanted louder, struggling with the sun.

"Then the shadow went *above the mark!* Never had it done this before. Zur cried out to the people, 'Now the sun is disappearing! The great darkness and cold will come forever!'

"And Van and Xo cried, 'Save us, Grae! Hold back the great darkness and the cold. Stop the sun!' And the people took up the cry, all shouting, 'Save us, Grae! Hold back the great darkness and the cold! Stop the sun!'

"Then Zur held his knife to the sun. He cried, 'Accept

our offering, Sun! Accept the blood of the line of chieftains!' "

Ulam paused, then he looked up at Agon.

"Then Zur plunged the knife into Alan's chest."

22

Departure

AGON CALLED THE two boys to him and led them to an open glade in the forest below Bear Hill. He held out two small axes like his own—the heads of greenstone, the handles of antler.

"Learn the axe song. Practice with these every day. Throw them spinning toward each other, catch them by the handle, throw them back. Whirl the axes, spinning your bodies. Fight with an unseen enemy: use the little axe song, then the big axe song. Learn to throw the axes so they go blade first into a soft target. Watch."

His own axe suddenly appeared in his hand. "Throw the axes toward each other as I throw this into the sky." He threw the axe spinning high in the air, and as it descended, he caught it by the handle and threw it again, and again. "Whirl with the axe." Now he spun his body as he whirled the axe, faster and faster, and the axe began to sing, a sighing song of death, moving so fast that it was a blur. "The little axe song." He fought with an invisible enemy, swinging and jabbing the axe in the short strokes of the little axe song. "Now the big axe song. This is to kill." Then he swung the axe in long and terrible sweeping strokes. Suddenly he stopped the axe song and hurled the axe into the trunk of a dead and rotting pine tree, where the blade sank deeply into the wood.

Agon retrieved the axe and showed the handle to the boys.

"The ibex is my totem, my brother. Now you must carve your totems into your axe handles. Their magic will strengthen you and guide you."

Eran asked, "Why have you waited until now to give us the axes and show us the axe song?"

"Because you weren't ready. Alar is still too young. But now you both must become men."

"Why, Father?" asked Alar.

"Because you must protect your mother."

"You're going with Ulam, aren't you?"

"Yes."

"When will you come back?"

"As soon as I've killed Zur and made Alfgar chieftain."

"How old is Alfgar?"

Agon held up the fingers of both hands, then one finger. "Eleven winters."

Eran scowled. "How can he be chieftain? I'm almost that old, and you won't let me be chieftain."

"Ulam will help him."

"We should all go back. You would be chieftain. Then I would be chieftain."

"Not until I kill Zur. He's become strong and killed all who are against him. I can't bring your mother and you boys back into his tribe now."

Alar raised his axe. "We would help you kill Zur."

"No. You're too young. Not until you learn to use the axes. And I must go soon before Alfgar dies."

"You tell us we are to protect Mother," Eran said, "yet you tell us we are too young to fight Zur."

"You are too young. But at Bear Hill you will keep watch day and night. You can fight off a tribe by rolling boulders down the escarpment. Your mother can fight like a man. The three of you will be safe here. If I take you with me, you might all be killed. Stay here and protect your mother"

"We will," Alar said, "but I'm not afraid of Zur."

Agon looked at Eran.

Eran scowled. "I'll kill anyone who threatens her."

"Good. Now start throwing your axes to each other."

When they came back up to the cave at Bear Hill, Eena greeted them at the top of the escarpment. "Ulam is asleep. He was tired from his long journey."

She examined Eran's bruised and bloody hands. Agon said, "He fights the axe now, but he will learn if he practices."

Eena agreed. "Of course. Erida told me she was always bandaging your and Orm's hands."

"Who was Orm?" Alar asked.

"My friend and rite brother," Agon replied. "We learned the axe song together."

"Why hasn't he killed Zur if he knows the axe song?" Alar swung his axe in a long stroke.

"He died protecting our tribe when Ka attacked. Four of Ka's men lay dead before him."

Alar's eyes grew wide. "Four men! What was Orm's totem?"

"The red deer."

"Can I have the red deer for my totem?"

Agon regarded the boy. "A totem must be part of your own magic. You and Eran must find your magic, your totems."

"How can we do that?"

"Artron will guide you. Before I leave, we'll talk with him."

Eena stood straight and still. "You're going back to kill Zur."

"Yes."

"Take us with you."

"No. You and the boys will stay here."

She gazed into his eyes. "We have fought side by side. Why will you now fight alone?"

"Because I want you and the boys to live."

"If you die, I want to die."

"And the boys?"

"Let them die with their father and mother, fighting beside them."

Agon regarded her silently. She was as beautiful now as before the children were born, still slender and hard muscled, still fine featured and lovely. Her chin was raised in the gesture he knew so well.

"The line of Grae," he said, "goes back into ancient times. You and I, our sons, and Alfgar are the last of that line. I will not have us all die together. I have decided."

"*You* have decided."

"Yes."

Their eyes held as their wills, their spirits, clashed. The ibex quivered on Agon's chest, as did the leaping doe on Eena's breast.

Ulam staggered from the cave, supporting himself with his spear. He sat down heavily on a boulder by the fire, his face, body, and eyes showing his exhaustion. Eena went to him and knelt, touching his forehead, listening to his breathing. She looked up at Agon and silently shook her head.

Ulam said weakly, "I'm only tired from the journey. Tomorrow I'll help you hunt." He swayed on the rock, then fell sideways onto the ground.

Eena and Agon sat all night by Ulam as he fought with death. They had laid him in his bed of furs, and Eena periodically felt his wrist and put her ear close to his half-open mouth. She said to Agon, "He was so brave when the tribe fled through the storm. . . ."

In the morning Ulam still lived, but the right side of his body seemed frozen, and the old man had only partial use of his left arm and leg. Struggling to speak, he whispered to Agon, "We'll go soon . . . when my strength . . . comes back. . . ."

That night Eena spoke quietly to Agon when Ulam and

the boys were asleep: "Eran is almost a man. Take him with you and kill Zur. Alar and I will care for Ulam."

"No. Both our sons stay with you."

"Alar and I will be safe."

"No. I go alone. I have talked with Eran and Alar. They will stay here to help you defend this place."

"Maybe Ulam will become strong again. Then we all can go."

"There is no time to wait. And Ulam will never become strong again. I've seen this happen with other old hunters."

"Then you'll go alone."

"Yes."

Eena was silent, then said, "Do you remember when we came to the camp of the Red People and you were ready to fight with Ror because he carried me in the dancing?"

"I remember."

"And do you remember how we talked that night about the great birds that take only one mate until they die?"

"I said that I would keep you like the great birds," Agon replied, "until we both should die."

"I have never forgotten that. And I will keep you in my heart. I will have only you for my mate. Wherever you go, no matter how long you stay, I will always be your mate."

Agon held her in his arms. "And I will always be your mate. No matter what happens, no matter how long we are separated, my spirit will find yours."

The next day Agon took the two boys to Yurok's camp. He told Yurok, Emar, and Artron of Ulam and Zur.

Emar said, "Let me come with you to kill Zur."

"I thank you, but I go alone."

Yurok stared hard at Agon. "You go to kill a chieftain. Will you leave his tribe without a leader?"

"If Alfgar is still alive, he will become chieftain."

"A boy cannot rule a tribe."

"I will help him."

"Then you won't return this winter."

"Maybe not."

"You leave your mate and family. Bring them here to our camp where they'll be safe."

"My mate wouldn't live in the same camp as your priestess."

Yurok guffawed. "Nor would my priestess dare live in the same camp as your mate! Spear Woman's weapon would pierce more than Hura's ear!"

Artron spoke: "Warn Spear Woman that she has made a dangerous enemy. Hura can't throw a spear, but she has powerful magic."

"I will tell her."

Artron looked at Eran and Alar. "They have grown like young lions. I haven't seen them since Spear Woman came to warn Hura."

"I bring them to you to ask your help."

Artron nodded. "They need to find their totems."

"Yes."

"The son of Grae honors me." Artron studied the boys' faces. "They both will want totems of great power, but I see differences in what their magic will bring them. I will come to the foot of Bear Hill in three days to get your sons."

"I thank you." Agon looked up at the cliff wall. "Will you tell me one thing?"

"If I can."

"Who made the Sunstand marks on the wall?"

Artron looked curiously at Agon. "They were made long ago, before my father and his father and his father. No one knows who made the marks, but they are ancient, carved into the rock by the hands of men of great knowledge."

Agon thanked Artron, Yurok, and Emar. Then he said to them, "Ulam was a hunt leader. When he dies, I ask that you help his spirit find peace. He was a good man."

Early the next morning Agon set out for the camp of the bison hunters, which lay far to the east. He carried his axe, two spears, a knife, a sleeping robe, and a bag of traveling food that Eena prepared for him. Before he descended the escarpment, he grasped the hands of Ulam, Eran, and Alar in farewell, then he held Eena in his arms. He said to her, "Wait for me. My spirit will find yours though the demons of Hell stand in our way."

23

Eran's Dream

ERAN LIES ALONE on a hilltop above the river valley. He has not eaten for three days. Night comes. Thunder rumbles faintly in the west.

He floats softly in warm darkness, and the mother heart beats with his heart.

He presses against the mother breast, and his mouth consumes the mother, taking in her body, tasting her flesh, her blood, her milk. Warmth and strength flow into him.

The mother smell envelops him. Milky, nurturing, sweet, comforting, animal, feminine, sensual, his.

Mother sounds. Soft, gentle, protective, loving, soothing, caring, tender, kind.

His own sounds. Mewling, gurgling, sucking, whispering, crying, laughing.

His hands, face, lips, feet, body, touch the mother skin, body, hair, lips. Smooth, warm, soft, moist.

The mother hands caress him, stroke, fondle, enclose, clean, hold, lift, turn, wrap, unwrap.

The mother eyes look into his. Large, beautiful, loving, tender.

She is his. To suck, taste, nuzzle, touch, smell, hear, see, command. To feed him, hold him, stroke him, touch his skin, his gums, his genitals, his hair. No other can have her. She belongs to him.

The other. Huge, hard, hairy. Smell of blood and death, of alien beasts, maleness. Deep harsh sounds. Fierce eyes, big hard hands, powerful arms. Between him and the mother. Hate. Extend curved raking claws. Glare from hiding. Creep forward. Leap. Hold. Bite. He forces himself between them. His mouth finds the mother breasts, swelling nipples, warm flesh, hot milk flowing. She is his.

He walks. Clutches the mother legs. Holds her. Has her.

The other above him. Big cold hands lift him. Smell of blood again, of beasts, death, maleness. He glares in rage. Growls silently deep in his throat.

Now another. At the mother breast. He raises his spear. Kill. Spear breaking, burning. He raises the spear again. Big hand holding. He tears the spear away and crouches, ready to spring. His claws extend, his great teeth bare in fury.

Wait.

Thunder rumbles nearer. Eran hears but does not hear. Lightning flashes in quivering tendrils, and he sees but does not see. Wind sighs over the hills. He feels but does not feel.

Storm approaching. Black clouds billowing. She pulls the spear from the baby's side and wraps him in bison skin. The bison horns of chieftain sway above his head.

The sun drops lower. The great fire roars beneath the cliff wall where the shadow creeps up. The other lies before him. He raises the knife, plunges it into the chest.

The black thundercloud drops down, whirling, lightning darting out from it like snakes' tongues. She holds her arms out to the cloud.

The cliffs, the river, the fire, fall away. She is free.

The storm sweeps over the hills. Wind-driven rain lashes over Eran. Lightning cleaves the sky, and thunderclaps crash and roar, shaking the earth.

He runs with her through the storm. Behind them comes the hated other. She comes into his arms, and he carries her. They cross the river as a great wall of water thunders down upon them. He climbs the slope, untiring, strong, triumphant. She holds his face to her breast, and the milk flows hot and sweet.

But the other is upon them.

Fighting. His strength is unlimited. He crouches, leaps, holds, kills. She is his.

The den lies far back under the rock ledge. He pads silently toward the dimming light and looks out upon the plain below. Horses, cattle, and bison feed in scattered herds, gathering together for the coming night.

She joins him and stares out at the herds. Together they descend the wooded slope to the plain. They enter a bush-filled streambed and creep silently toward the horse herd. They pause at the edge of the brush, flat on their stomachs, watching.

A mare nurses a wobbly-legged foal at the edge of the horse herd. They can taste the red-dripping meat, smell the blood. But they wait. Wait for darkness. And as they wait, he feels great muscular coils growing within him, and he hisses with terrible strength.

Eran woke in the darkness before dawn. The hills rose dim and ghostly around him, and the storm rumbled off to the east, lightning flashing intermittently, thunder growling. He was cold, wet, aching with hunger.

Something in the sky. A cloud? Part of the storm? He

watched. An indistinct shape moved, shifted, coalesced, took form.

He knew.

Artron came at sunrise, bringing water and meat.

Eran drank, bit into the meat.

Artron said, "You have found your totem."

Eran nodded as he tore at the meat, his spearlike teeth driving into flesh.

24

The Death of Ulam

EENA KNELT OVER Ulam in the night. He struggled for breath even in sleep, the sound ragged and painful. Ulam was slowly dying, yet the old hunter fought on, his life spirit tenacious as the roots of a storm-swept and lightning-blasted old oak.

If he dies now, Eena thought, I will wake the boys, and we will fill our packs with food and collect our traveling robes and weapons. We will bury Ulam at the foot of the hill, and then follow Agon. He will travel fast, but we will travel faster. We will catch up with him before he is half-way there.

The thought excited her so much that she reached for her pack. Dried venison, blackberries, nut kernels. She would need her sewing kit, two good fire stones, extra spear points. . . .

Ulam stirred in his sleep and groaned. Eena placed her hand gently on the old man's throat, feeling the weak throbbing, the coldness of his flesh. She tucked the deer-skin robe around him and added another log to the fire, then quietly returned to her empty bed. She lay motionless, looking up at the flickering shadows on the rock ceiling, shadows now of loneliness and sadness, of separation and waiting. Shadows that once had been comforting and happy. Agon was sleeping alone somewhere under the stars. . . .

Ulam was still alive in the morning. For seven more days he fought with death. He watched Eena silently as she cared for him, unable to speak, only his eyes able to show his gratitude.

Finally, at the last, his lips trembled, and he struggled to speak. She bent close to him.

"Out . . . put . . . me . . . out . . ." His words were barely a whisper, and so slurred she could hardly understand him.

The old often went alone into the darkness to die. Ulam was helpless, could not go with dignity into the night. Eena stroked his forehead. "Soon you will rest. Your spirit will come again, young and strong. Again you will lead the hunters and bring game home to the tribe."

"Agon . . ."

"He is gone. Soon he will return."

"Best . . . of . . . the . . . hunters . . ."

"Yes. Like you."

Ulam stared up at her. His eyes seemed to look beyond her. For an instant they became again the keen eyes of a young hunter. Then Ulam died.

Artron came with Emar and the two young hunters, Berg and Redon, to bury Ulam. They carried him down the escarpment to a bare hilltop that looked out over the river valley. Eena, Eran, and Alar stood by the grave as Artron spoke the last words:

"You were old, but you came far to seek help for your people. You were of another tribe than ours, but you were a hunt leader, honored by your people. Now let your spirit rest. People of your own tribe live near your grave, and they will remember you and honor you. We ask that your spirit not howl in the night nor scream in the storm or blizzard. Rest now until your spirit is born again."

They laid Ulam's spear beside his body, and Eena placed the liver of a deer in his hands that he might have food in the afterworld. His totem, a bull bison, lay on his chest. They covered him with earth and slabs of stone to protect his body from the beasts of the night.

Eena spoke to the men: "We thank you for honoring one of our people and laying his spirit to rest. My sons have seen this, and they will remember, with me, your kindness. We will tell Agon of what you have done today."

The four men exchanged glances. Emar said, "You'll follow him now?"

"Yes."

Emar shook his head. "Winter approaches."

"We aren't afraid of winter."

Artron spoke: "All the signs tell us the winter will be hard. If you're caught in a storm, you could die. Look at the clouds in the west."

A roll of gray clouds lay on the western horizon, heavy and ominous. Even though the day was bright and crisp, a smell of coming snow permeated the air.

"We have our snow sandals." Eena raised her chin. "If we leave now, we can find Agon before he reaches Zur's camp."

Artron pointed to the sky. "A blizzard comes, earlier than anyone can remember. It is a sign you should not go." He pointed to Ulam's grave. "The old man kept you here by his dying. It is another sign. You are not meant to go with Agon."

Emar smiled at her. "Now we'll help you drag logs into your shelter so you'll be ready for the winter." He spoke to Eran and Alar. "After that we'll hunt. The deer are fat now. We'll bring home three for your mother's meat-drying racks."

Eena saw the excited expressions on her sons' faces. Agon's words came to her: "You and the boys will stay here." She gazed to the east. Agon was there, now far away, approaching the camp of the bison hunters. She longed to join him, to be with him, to fight with him against Zur. Then she looked at the approaching storm clouds, at the grave of Ulam. Was Artron right? Were the signs against her going? Her hand closed around the totem on her breast, the leaping young doe carved by her father. The doe was motionless, silent. She touched the magic belt given her by the women of the Earth Mother. The belt gave her no answer.

Then a black raven came flying from the west. The bird flew over Bear Hill, over the people by Ulam's grave, and continued a little way to the east. Then the raven turned in its flight and circled back over Bear Hill. With a loud, harsh call it settled in the top of a tall pine tree that grew above the porch and the entrance to the cave.

25

Storm

THE BLIZZARD STRUCK in the night. Eena heard the shriek of the wind outside the entrance, smelled the snow, felt the cold. She left her bed of furs and the hut and pushed the fire log deeper into the coals. In the firelight she saw the shaking of the framework of branches and hides that sealed the cave entrance. She drew on her winter hunting shirt and leggings, her warm moccasins, then spread an extra robe of furs over the two boys. They awoke briefly, then curled under the warm furs like two woodland animals.

If they had left to follow Agon yesterday, Eena told herself, they would be caught in the blizzard now. The raven had been right.

Where was Agon? Had he reached the camp of the bison

hunters? Or was he crouched in some hollow, wrapped in his deerskin robe, waiting out the storm? He was strong, but could his strength prevail against the tearing wind, the icy cold?

She drew a robe around her shoulders as she stared into the fire. They had firewood and food to last possibly three moons . . . they could withdraw deep into the cave if the cold became intense . . . they could survive . . . they could wait for Agon. . . .

When morning came, they peered out around the edges of the hide barrier. Snow blew almost horizontally across the drifted porch, and the air and sky were so filled with snow that the plains and the river valley were invisible. The cold was intense, penetrating.

Alar asked, "Does the blizzard cover the whole world? Is Father caught in it?"

Eena reassured Alar. "He's far away now. Winter is not so cold there. Some winters no snow came."

"How can snow come here and not there?"

"It's farther south there. The sun is closer."

Alar considered this. "Then Father will be all right."

Eena touched her deer totem. "Let him be all right. Let him be safe and warm."

"Why do you touch your totem?"

"It gives me strength."

"How can it do that?"

"Magic. Our totems give us magic strength."

"I'm going to carve my totem into my axe handle today while we have to sit around the fire."

"It will be a good time to do it." Eena smiled at the boys. "You haven't told me yet what your totems are."

Alar held up his axe. "When I'm finished, you'll see."

Eran scowled. "Mine is a secret."

While Eena sewed new winter hunting shirts and moccasins, the boys worked with sharp flint burins at the antler handles of their axes. They bent silently and secretly over their carvings, so absorbed that Eena had to remind them to eat the hot stew she prepared.

Darkness came before the handles were finished.

In the white light of the following morning they saw that the blizzard still raged outside. The boys continued their carving. Eena bandaged their cut and blistered fingers, tended the fire, brought food to the boys.

Alar, strangely, finished first. At the end of his axe handle was carved the head and flattened antlers of a male red deer. Eena hugged him in delight. "It's beautiful. And the red deer is a good totem. You'll be strong and fast and brave."

"It's the same as Father's axe brother's."

"Orm. He was so brave. . . ." Tears came to Eena's eyes.

"He protected our tribe. He killed four of Ka's men before he died." Alar stood straight. "I'll protect our tribe."

"Your father will be proud of you." She touched her own totem. Let Alar live. But if he must die, let him die with honor, as Orm died.

Alar looked up at her. "Why do you cry, Mother?"

She hugged him again, hiding her tears. "Because I am happy."

Eran worked silently at his carving. What he carved required great care. The head of an ibex was appearing at the end of the axe handle, a young male ibex with strong, spearlike horns pointing back over its muscular shoulders. But as Eran worked, he periodically turned the axe handle end up and carved at something facing in the opposite direction from the ibex. He carved so well and so cleverly that the axe handle seemed to have only the strong figure of the ibex. Yet there was an ambiguity in the face and form of the ibex that was mysterious and strange.

As Eran carved, he felt himself changing. His spirit, his body, his mind, slowly took on the spirit, the body, the mind of the totem he carved. He grew fiercer, stronger, cleverer. And he felt the weaknesses of childhood leaving him.

When he was finished, he slipped the axe into his belt.

Alar came near. "Show me your totem."

Eran took the axe from his belt and held it up out of

Alar's reach. "Keep your hands off it. Only I can touch it."

"An ibex!"

Eena came from the storeroom. "The same as your father!" A feeling of joy and relief flooded over her: Eran was Agon's son.

"I saw it in the sky. It came in my dreams."

"Your father will be proud and happy."

"It's not his ibex. It's my ibex."

"Of course."

"No one must ever touch it."

"I heard you tell Alar."

"If he touches it, I'll kill him."

"Don't talk like that. Alar is your brother. Remember what your father said."

"I remember. He sent me naked into the snow."

"He should have. Never talk again of killing Alar."

"Agon is not here now."

"I am."

"You?"

"Yes."

Eran laughed. "My little mother. Listen: 'I'll kill Alar.' "

Eena slapped Eran so hard across the face that he spun around and fell back across the fire log. He crouched, glaring up at her. "You hit me!"

"I'll hit you again if you ever talk of killing Alar."

"I'm your oldest son. I'm chieftain. You'll be sorry you hit me."

"You are not chieftain. Agon is chieftain."

"Agon is never coming back. He's dead."

"He is coming back. He is not dead. I would know if he were dead."

"You wouldn't know. You have no magic."

"That may be. But our spirits are always together. We are mated like the great birds that take only one mate for all their lives."

"You have had more than one mate. You are not fit to be mother of a chieftain."

"Who told you that?"

"Hura."

Eena's voice was like ice. "Hura spoke to you again?"

"Not since you tore her ear off with your spear. She told me before that."

"You believe Hura over your father and mother?"

"Yes."

"Why?"

"Because I know already."

"You know what?"

"Who my real father is."

Eena stood perfectly still. She said to Alar, "Take a torch and go into the storeroom. Bring back a pole of dried venison. I will make more stew."

When Alar had gone, Eena came close to Eran. She spoke quietly: "I was fourteen winters old. Ka killed my father and brother. He took me to his cave and raped me. Agon saved me from Ka and brought me to the Earth Mother. Her priestesses washed the seed of Ka from me. You are not the son of Ka. You are the son of Agon."

Eran glared at her. "You think I am the son of Agon. What was Ka's totem?"

"A snake or great cat." Eena's voice trembled. "It had long fangs and a terrible face. . . ."

Eran took his axe from his belt and held the handle up before his mother's eyes. "What do you see?"

"An ibex. The totem of your father. You saw it in your vision. It proves Agon is your father."

Eran laughed harshly. He turned the axe handle so that Eena saw the upside-down view of the handle. "This is what I saw in my vision!"

Eena stared at the handle, then gasped in horror.

Glaring at her from the handle of the axe was a different creature. The long, spearlike horns of the ibex were no longer horns. They were long, sharp teeth. And the face from which the teeth protruded was the terrible face of a great hissing snake.

26

Return to the Bison Hunters

AGON CAME TO the place on the riverbank where, many years ago, he had floated ashore after the wall of water had torn him from his last view of Eena being carried away by Ka. Here he had lain like one dead, his spirit failing, willing himself to die. Here he had felt the magic of his axe bring his spirit back, and he had lived. From here he had gone to cross the mountains and find Eena. From here he knew every step of the way to the great cliff shelter of the bison hunters.

He traveled on to the east, and in time he saw the high cliffs that rose on each side of the river. He approached the camp stealthily, cautiously, along the cliff tops. He came to the ancient black rock, the Stone, the sacred altar of his people.

Memories crowded in: childhood, boyhood, rites of passage, mystic ceremonies at the Stone. Memories of fighting and death, of Eena standing on the black rock, calling for the spirits of her people, of Eena being carried from the black rock by the snakelike killer, Ka.

He crawled through the brush to the cliff edge. The camp lay below him. Smoke spiraled up from evening cooking fires, women tended spits of roasting meat, hunters lounged before the cliff shelter, children tumbled like wolf cubs in play.

There he had stood before Grae and Erida with his hunting band. There he had fought with Horn and killed him. There Zur had demanded his death. There Orm and the hunters had died defending Erida and Ara. There, in the river, he had fought Ka's men until the great wall of water struck.

But why so few people? Why should there be more? Almost half the tribe massacred by Ka. His four brothers sacrificed by Zur. . . .

Where was Zur? And Alfgar?

Someone came from the cliff shelter.

Grae!

Bison horns. Staff. Bison robe. Tall, straight figure. Grae lives!

Grae is dead. Agon saw him fall on his spear. Agon laid Grae in the grave with his people.

The figure turned.

Zur!

Agon drew back from the cliff edge. He would wait until dark. Come silently down the cliff path. Find Zur in the cliff shelter. One blow to the head with the axe. Then he would return to Eena.

Movement in the river valley to the east.

Men in the underbrush beneath the trees.

Not men of the bison hunters. Knobs of hair.

Men of Ka!

Agon scanned the river. It flowed high and fast. None could cross it. Could some of Ka's men have lived? Survived the roaring blast as Spear Mountain erupted into the sky? Lived through the crashing wall of water that swept down the river valley?

He watched the knob-headed men. One climbed a tree. Stared toward the camp. Gesticulated.

How many? Agon counted. Nine? More hidden in the underbrush.

The man in the tree descended. Pointed.

The men looked toward the camp.

They turned back to the east. Agon watched them until

they disappeared in the approaching dusk, in the darkness of the trees.

Why had Zur no sentries? How many fighting men had he?

Agon counted the hunters. Eight. Possibly more on the plain. Four old men. Seven boys large enough to lift a spear. And Zur.

Should he kill Zur that night?

Or warn him?

27

Zur

AGON CALLED FROM the cliff top, the call of the returning hunter. The people gazed up at him in alarm as he came down the path. Zur motioned, and four hunters raised their spears and ran to the bottom of the path. Van and Xo and two other hunters from Zur's hunting band.

Van stared at him with hatred. "You dare to come here!"

Agon said nothing.

Xo scowled. "We thought you were dead."

"I live, as you see."

"Why have you come back?"

"To warn Zur."

"Warn him of what?" Van spat on the ground. "You ran away when Ka attacked."

"I went to kill Ka. Now move out of my way. I want to talk to Zur."

Van bared his teeth. "One word from me and four spears will be in you."

Agon looked into Van's eyes.

Van stepped back. "Talk to him, then. All the hunters will be behind you with their spears."

Agon strode forward past Van and the other men. Zur raised his staff as Agon approached. His voice was strong, stern, authoritative:

"You dare approach Grae with weapons?"

"My weapons are not raised."

"Why have you come back?"

"To warn you."

"Warn Grae of what?"

"Where is Alfgar?"

Zur's eyes burned into Agon. "You betrayed the tribe. Grae could have you killed."

"As you killed my brothers?"

Zur became deathly still. "Who told you that?"

"Ulam."

Zur glanced up at the cliff top. "If you try to attack me, Grae has but to raise his staff. You will die."

"And you will die."

Zur glared at Agon. "You dare to threaten Grae?"

"Where is Alfgar?"

Zur's eyes became crafty. "He is on a long hunt."

"Where?"

"You are not to know."

"If he is dead, or dies, I'll kill you."

"You threaten Grae again." Zur's eyes narrowed. "Try to kill Grae and your brother will die."

"Where is he now?"

"Why should Grae tell you?"

Agon stepped closer to Zur. "Is he alive?"

"Why shouldn't he be?"

"Because you've killed him."

"Killed him? Grae's own half brother?"

"You killed my other brothers."

"Never."

"Then where are they?"

"They died. Grae did all he could to save them."

"Ulam said you killed them. One each winter Sunstand Day."

in the depths of the earth. The Onstean had sent Agon to the Earth Mother. A journey of death.

Beren was right. Alfgar must be dead.

"When did this happen?"

"Three days ago."

"Why?"

"Zur said that Alfgar had offended the gods by not giving a blood offering when he killed a deer."

"Zur lied. Every boy learns about the blood offering."

"Yes."

"And Zur told the people this lie?"

"Yes. He said the Onstean would decide Alfgar's punishment."

Grae would never have even said the word *Onstean* to the people. "Zur should not be chieftain."

"Zur says he is Grae by right of his birth," Beren replied. "Also by the will of the Onstean."

"It was his right by birth. But no more. And not by the will of the Onstean."

"Kill Zur now, Agon."

"Alfgar may still be alive. I have to find him first."

"How?"

"Go to the Onstean."

Beren drew back from Agon. "You would die . . . the Onstean . . . would take your spirit. . . ."

"I must go."

The old man looked into the darkness, then back at Agon. "I came to help you kill Zur. He is destroying the tribe. But the Onstean . . ."

"You would fight alongside me?"

"Yes. I am old, but I can still hurl a spear."

Agon laid his hand on Beren's shoulder. "When I was a boy, you and Ulam were two of the best hunters. Ulam would have come with me, but he is dying. I thank you for coming to help me kill Zur. We'll fight side by side when the time comes. But you need not go to the Onstean with me."

"I came to help. I go where you go. Even to the Onstean." Beren peered into the cave again. "Where are your other men?"

"I have no other men."

Beren clasped Agon's arm. "Now I know that you are the same Agon who led the hunters. You came to Zur's camp alone, just as you fought Ka's men alone. If I die fighting beside you, I will die with honor."

"You already have honor," Agon replied. "Now we go to find the place of the Onstean."

"Now? In the night? How can we find it?"

Agon lifted his second spear from the ground. "Twelve winters ago Horn and I fought."

"I remember. After you killed Horn, Grae said you were to die. He told you to go to the Stone and wait for him. Around midnight."

"Yes. Grae led me to the place of the Onstean."

"You went to the Onstean?"

"Yes."

"You saw the Onstean and lived!" Beren gazed in awe at Agon. "We never knew that. Zur said you had run away."

"Zur lies."

"But no one has ever found the place of the Onstean. . . ."

"Grae knew where it was."

"And you think you can find it again? But you went in the dark . . . Grae led you. . . ."

"We'll find it, tonight."

Beren slapped his spear. "Agon, you're going to track a way you took in the night—twelve winters ago?"

Agon shrugged. "That's why we go now, at night. The way will look the same. Smell the same. Feel the same."

They went through the hills until they came to the place where a small tributary of the river dropped down into the river valley. Agon looked up at the stars, studying them. "Grae and I came here from the Stone. Now we track."

He led the way, turning, stopping, reversing direction, studying the stars, clambering over and under fallen trees, sniffing the air, climbing up gullies, listening, scaling rock faces in the starlight, standing motionless, pushing through growths of young trees. Finally he halted at the base of a hill. He parted the brush to reveal a dark hole in the hillside.

"The Onstean meet here."

Beren drew back, clutching his horse totem. "You have found it! But I would rather fight Ka's whole tribe than go in there!"

"We have to go in."

"Why?"

"The Onstean brought me out of another entrance. When we find that, we'll track Alfgar."

"If he lives."

"Yes. If he lives."

"We'll need torches."

"No."

Beren stared at Agon. "We go in there without torches?"

"I had no torch when I went in. There were many side passages. The Onstean led me out with a hide over my head and eyes. I can remember the way better in the dark."

Beren swallowed. "Agon, what if they . . . what if the Onstean are in there now?"

"Then we die."

The first gray light of dawn shone in the east as Agon and Beren emerged from the cave. Beren raised his arms to the sky. "I thank the gods who have brought us from the darkness. My spirit knew such fear that even now it trembles!" He looked back at the hole from which they had just emerged. "Never could any man remember every passageway in such a place of terror. And the Onstean may have been watching us. More times than my winters I thought we would die, yet you led us through to the light!"

Agon studied the stony ground. "This is the place where

they brought me. When daylight comes, we'll search for tracks."

They hid in thick brush and slept until sunrise. Then they came back to the cave entrance and circled the ground like wolves, moving out from the stony area toward softer earth.

Agon stopped. "Here. Two sets of tracks."

Beren studied the tracks. "Alfgar. I know his prints. But the others . . . another boy?"

"A woman." Agon pointed. "See how narrow."

Beren looked at Agon with terror in his eyes. "Agon, Alfgar is dead. We'll die. Follow this trail no more."

"Why?"

"Because the only woman who could come from the cave of the Onstean is a she-demon. One has taken Alfgar. They tear men and boys into pieces and eat their flesh."

"I have to find Alfgar," Agon said. "Wait for me in the hill cave if you fear the she-demon."

"You'll go on?" Beren stared at Agon.

"Yes."

"Then I go with you."

Agon clasped Beren's arm. "Good."

Alfgar's and the woman's trail led out onto the plain, then toward the shattered remains of Spear Mountain. They followed the trail all that day. The next day, still following the trail, they approached the bend in the river before Spear Mountain.

Agon looked down from the cliff. Twelve years before he had seen Ka and his men kill Eena's father and brother, then carry her off to the cave under the brow of Spear Mountain. Eena. She had wanted to come with him now. He should have let her come. If she and the boys were here, he would go back into Zur's camp, kill Zur, kill any of Zur's men who resisted. He, Agon, would become chieftain, become Grae, by right of birth. He would bring Eena, Eran, and Alar into the tribe. But without Eena and the boys here, he could not stay. Now if he killed Zur, and Alfgar was dead, who would lead the tribe? The people, were without spirit, without leaders . . . the tribe would weaken and die. . . .

Beren pointed down the river valley. "Ka's men hide somewhere to the east."

Agon studied the cliffs. "Have they ever tried to attack the camp?"

"Not yet. But as Zur kills our people, we have become weak. They watch and wait."

"I saw them. They outnumber you in fighting men already."

"Zur scoffs at them."

"Zur is mad."

"Kill him, Agon. We will make you chieftain."

"I can't become your chieftain. My family is with a tribe far to the west. Eena and my two sons. We have to find Alfgar."

"If he still lives. But he is only a boy. Although he is a son of Grae, he can't lead the tribe in fighting Ka's men. We need you, Agon."

"First we find Alfgar."

They left the cliff edge and continued tracking Alfgar and the woman through the great chunks of the shattered mountain that littered the plain. Agon marveled that he had survived the explosion of fire and rock as he killed Kaan and ran from Ka's cave twelve years before.

As they rounded a huge rock, they saw that the trail of Alfgar and the woman turned to the left, across the plain toward the mysterious Blue Hills that showed in dim silhouette on the northern horizon. Agon felt the back of his neck prickle. "I know where the woman has taken Alfgar."

"Where?" Beren asked.

"To the Earth Mother."

Agon and Beren followed the faint trail of the woman and Alfgar across the plain, taking almost the same route that

Agon and Eena had taken twelve years before. As they tracked, Agon relived the events of those nights and days of blood and fighting.

Here, after finding Eena raped and seeking death in Ka's dark lair, Agon had brought her past the bloody heads of her father and brother swaying on poles under the gibbous moon. Here they had fought Ka's men on the cliff edge. Here they had run across the plain in the darkness. Here, hiding in this marsh, Eena had washed her blood and Ka's semen from her body. Here Agon had held her while she grieved for her family. Here, between the marsh and the Blue Hills, they had fought Ka and his men and escaped into the Blue Hills, leaving Ka stunned on the ground and one of his men dead.

Now, when he and Beren entered the Blue Hills, Agon saw gratefully that the woman they followed had taken a different course into the mountains than he and Eena had taken, keeping secret the existence of their glade and cave, a place of magic and love he and Eena could share with no one else. And in the deep recesses of their cave, the ivory figurine of Eena waited, with Agon's ibex spirit and Eena's deer spirit guarding her.

The trail of the woman and Alfgar led across the valleys and pine-covered mountains of the Blue Hills toward two peaks that Agon remembered, the peaks that resembled the breasts of a supine woman. Beren became more and more terrified as they advanced, and when they came to a thick woods that lay under the peaks, the old hunter spoke fearfully. "Agon, men should never come to this place. I was a hunter, not afraid to die on the horns of a bison, but I sense something here that is more terrifying than death."

"The Earth Mother."

"She will kill us and take our spirits."

"She may. But because Eena was with me, she spared us."

"Eena is not with you now."

"No. But I must find my brother. Wait for me here. If I do not return in three days, go back to the tribe."

Beren shook his head. "I told you I would come with you. I will go with you even though my spirit shudders like a dying stag in the jaws of the great cats."

When they entered the deep shade of the woods, they heard the distant voices of women. Women singing, laughing, crying. Agon said, "It is the voice of the waterfall. The women who serve the Earth Mother are near."

They came to the waterfall, and Beren trembled in awe, for the voices of the water were as from a great camp of women, and both men felt the power of the female spirits around them. Agon laid his weapons on the ground. "Now we must wait."

Beren laid his spear and knife next to Agon's weapons. "My spirit tells me of mysteries I have never dreamed of."

They waited, lying on the forest floor, and as twilight deepened into darkness, the voices of the waterfall overcame them, and they slept.

They awoke in the soft light of the moon. A hooded figure stood nearby, eyes and face hidden, mysterious and terrifying.

The figure spoke, and its voice was that of a woman, a voice as old as the rock of the mountains, yet as young as the soft tinkling of the falling water.

"Men of the bison hunters, why have you come here?"

Agon stood up. "We come to find my brother. A boy who has been taken by an evil woman."

"You speak of a woman as evil? Beware."

"She is Lilith."

The hooded figure drew back. "Do not speak her name. Go."

"I need your help."

"Go! Go while you still live."

"The tracks of my brother and the woman come here."

"You will die." The hooded figure turned toward Beren

and pointed back the way they had come. "Old man, leave now or you, too, will die."

Beren came slowly to his feet. "Kill me if you will. I stay with Agon."

The hooded figure lowered her arm. "You are Agon?"

"Yes."

"Son of Erida?"

"I am son of Erida and Grae."

"You came here before with the woman Eena."

"Twelve winters ago."

The figure pointed toward the waterfall. "Wait there."

Agon and Beren sat by the waterfall, and a different hooded figure brought them strange fruit and wooden cups of clear liquid that tasted of moonlight and spring and life.

Then another hooded figure came from the shadows.

"Agon, the woman of the moon knew that you would come back."

Agon felt a surge of remembrance. The woman of the moon had come to him in the golden mist twelve years ago.

He said, "I come asking your help."

"You seek your brother and the woman of evil."

"Their trail led us here."

"They have been here and gone. The woman dared to take one of our young girls from us and has gone to a place of evil."

"Tell me how to find her. I will take my brother and the girl from her."

"You cannot save them by yourself. She will kill your brother and the girl, and you and this old man if you go alone."

"We fear no man or woman."

"She is not an ordinary woman. Listen to what I have to tell you. If, after you have heard, you still dare pursue her, I will help you." The woman motioned toward two low rock benches. "Sit and listen while I tell you of the Earth Mother and of the woman of evil."

Agon and Beren sat, and the woman sat opposite them

and spoke: "Since ancient times, we who serve the Earth Mother have lived in this place. You, Agon, have seen the Earth Mother and lived, a thing happening only to certain men. You were spared because of your bravery and the bravery and magic of the woman, Eena, whom you came to save, but also because the priestesses of the Earth Mother needed you for something else. The Mother is all-knowing and cares for Her daughters.

"At the same time that the Earth Mother came into being, another force was created, a force of evil. Evil that has no mercy. Evil that feeds upon itself, growing stronger as it feeds. The priestess of this evil is one whose magic is as strong as ours. Her name is Lilith.

"Just as I and my sisters serve the Earth Mother, so Lilith serves evil. Lilith never grows old, never dies. She seems always youthful because she and her daughters and their daughters are one and the same—are Lilith.

"We, the priestesses of the Earth Mother, do grow old, do die. But we live through our daughters and their daughters.

"Agon, I told you the priestesses of the Mother needed you for something. We need certain men to mate with us. You were chosen to help keep our line of priestesses alive."

The moon woman, a priestess of the Earth Mother, had come to him in the moonlight, shimmering like light on rippled water, the spirit of all things female, beguiling, seducing, loving, filled with desire and passion, her voice calling, *Come, Agon, favored of the Mother. . . .*

The woman continued: "Because the Mother favored you, you were mated to Spear Woman, and together you saved your tribe from Ka. But know that you are the father of a daughter. A daughter who was to become one of the priestesses of the Mother."

Agon stared at the hooded figure. "I have a daughter?"

"Her name is Ara."

"My sister's name!"

"Ka killed your sister. But your daughter bears that same name."

Agon came to his feet. "Let me see her. . . ."

"You cannot see her. Lilith took her."

"Took my daughter? Why?"

"Because Grae and Erida drove Lilith from your tribe. She loved Grae, but hated Erida. She hates you and all others having the blood of Erida. She has taken your brother and your daughter to the gate of Hell to lead you to your death. It is a place where poisonous fumes spout from fiery craters. Dark clouds of ash are hurled into the sky. Molten lava erupts from black cones. No man or woman can enter there and live unless they are protected by powerful magic. It is a place of doom."

Agon's eyes became cold as ice. "I will go there."

"I would not send you to your death."

"I have come to save my brother. Now I will save my daughter also. Tell me how to find this place of doom."

"I will come with you. Together we will find your brother and our daughter."

Then Agon knew.

The hooded figure spoke proudly:

"I am Ara's mother."

30

Lilith

IT SEEMED TO Agon that he stood under the night sky of twelve years before. This woman truly was the moon spirit with whom he had soared into the lightburst of love.

He asked the woman, "What is your name?"

"I am called Erina."

"You taught me much."

"How to love. Eena needed love to heal her terrible wounds. You wanted to give her love, but needed our help."

"You made her a maiden again after Ka had fouled her," Agon replied. "She wanted to die until you helped her."

"The Earth Mother cares for women who are wronged." Erina touched his arm. "We know that you killed Ka, but you are not chieftain of the bison hunters. Why?"

"Zur is chieftain. He is Grae's first son."

"Where have you been?"

"After we escaped from Ka's tribe, Eena and I went far to the west to start our own tribe. We have two sons."

"Why did you come back?"

"Ulam came, telling us that Zur has killed all of my brothers except Alfgar."

"And Zur gave him to Lilith."

"Yes."

"You know that Lilith is the mother of Zur."

"Yes. How could Grae have taken her for his mate?"

"She beguiled Grae. She feeds on the blood of chieftains."

"Grae lived."

"Only because he was a great sorcerer. By his magic, and Erida's magic, Lilith was driven from your tribe. But she still lives. Lives either as herself, or as her daughter, or the daughter of her daughter. And each is evil."

"She and Zur must die."

"To destroy her will not be easy."

"No."

"What of this old hunter? Why has he come?"

Beren spoke: "I came with Agon to find Alfgar, then to kill Zur. I have seen Lilith. I will help you find her."

"Lilith is as clever as she is evil. She seems to men to be of great beauty. She seems to children to be of great kindness."

"I am old. It may be that I can see beyond her beauty."

"You may die."

"Death does not frighten me."

Erina regarded Beren, then Agon.

"Bring your weapons. I will take you to the gate of Hell."

The trail of Lilith, Alfgar, and Ara led to the northeast, circling the waterfall and leading along the base of one of the two conical mountains. Erina followed the trail as easily and fiercely as did Agon and Beren. She said, "As we thought, she goes toward the gate of Hell."

Beren asked, "How could she make Alfgar and the girl come with her?"

"She can make herself seem the most loving of women. She has deceived them, made them think she is taking them to someone they love, someone who loves them."

They followed the trail on around the base of the second mountain. As the day passed, the thick forest of pines gradually gave way to low brush, and as night approached, they came to a desolate wasteland of bizarre rock formations and strange bare hills that led to the base of a mountain whose upper half was gone. The mountain was devoid of vegetation, its sides composed of glistening black obsidian. Gray clouds hung over portions of the mountainside like a repulsive fungus that crawled down from the pall of dark churning smoke atop the shattered half-cone.

A feeling of evil exuded from the mountain, and Agon and Beren touched the carved totems that hung at their necks.

Erina extended her arm. "The gate of Hell."

They ate travel food, then slept in the thick brush at the edge of the wasteland—Erina at some distance from the two men.

At daylight the hooded figure appeared, and they continued their journey toward the gate of Hell. But now, as Agon studied the trail they followed, something seemed different—a sense of some slight change in Lilith's faint footprints.

They entered the wasteland. Fragmented black rocks lay among streams and pools of hardened lava, crevasses gaped like bestial jaws in the earth, and they saw no plant or animal, no life. As they neared the obsidian mountain, evil-smelling fumes assaulted their nostrils, the air became thick and hot, and gray ash sprinkled their heads and bodies. Their sense of dread increased, and the feeling of evil was like a strong wind.

They climbed up the side of the mountain, following a narrow escarpment, then along a ridge, up another escarpment, and now they stood on the edge of the gate of Hell.

The whole top of the mountain was gone. In its place lay a huge crater filled with black cones, ash, steam, cauldrons of boiling mud, vent holes from which jets of black liquid sprayed, and pools of molten lava. A somber mist of smoke and steam swirled throughout the crater.

They descended the lip of the mountain into the crater, following a tortuous path around the cauldrons and crevasses, gasping in the smoke and heat, the sulfurous mist. Then a hooded figure appeared in the mist, and a woman's voice called, the voice of Erina: "I have found them! They are safe. I came before the dawn. Kill the one beside you, Agon. She is Lilith!"

The hooded figure beside Agon spoke: "Kill her, Agon. I am Erina. I came here with you." The voice was Erina's.

Agon touched the handle of his axe. The ibex was vibrating.

The hooded figure in the mist raised both hands to the hood that covered her face. "I will raise my hood. You saw my face in the moonlight, Agon. Kill me if I am not the one with whom you mated. If I am the one, kill the one beside you."

She lifted her hood and let it drop behind her head.

She was beautiful, shimmering, her face like moonlight, her eyes glowing softly, like stars. Her hair was soft and light as moonbeams. "You know me, Agon. Kill her, and we will love again under the moon."

"I told you she was clever. Do not let yourself be fooled." The figure beside Agon raised her hands to her hood. "I will raise my hood. Choose which one of us you will kill, Agon."

She lifted her hood.

She was also lovely, but her face was no longer that of a young woman. Her hair was lightly sprinkled with gray, and her luminous eyes held a look of ancient wisdom and magic. She said, "We have mated, Agon. Kill Lilith, who stands above us."

Agon touched the ibex on his chest. It lay cold and still. One of the women was evil.

The woman above him spoke: "Lilith is more clever than we thought. She makes herself appear older, a mother, not a maiden."

The woman beside him smiled. "I am a mother. The mother of Ara."

"Which was Grae's mate?" Agon asked Beren.

Beren peered through the smoke at the two women. "One looks as Lilith did then, one as she might look now. I cannot tell."

Ara, Agon's daughter, the daughter of Erina, could tell him which was her mother. Agon said to the woman in the mist, "Take us to Alfgar and the girl. Let the girl tell us who is Lilith."

The woman of the mist replied, "Agon is wise."

The woman beside Agon spoke: "The girl has not seen her mother's face since she was a baby. Priestesses of the Earth Mother never raise their hoods in her presence."

"Take us to Alfgar and the girl!" Agon raised his axe. "Now! Or one of you will die."

The woman of the mist held out her hand. "Who will help me bring the children? They are tired and can walk no more." She smiled at Agon. "Will the father of my daughter help me?"

"Beware, Agon," the woman beside him said. "Go not into the mist alone with her or you die."

"She lies," the woman of the mist said. "Stay with her here and you die."

Agon touched the ibex on his chest. "Lead us to Alfgar and Ara. Unless we find them safe, both of you will die."

They followed the woman of the mist into the swirling smoke, through the heat and steam, the reeking fumes. The only light was the red glow of molten lava flowing through the crater. Both women disappeared in a great billow of smoke, and then reappeared ahead of the two men, one woman before the other.

Beren gasped for breath as he staggered alongside Agon. "No one can live here. Both of the women are demons. See how easily they walk? Kill them both now, Agon."

"Not until we find Alfgar and the girl."

"They must be dead."

"No. We keep on."

Now the darkness grew more intense. In the glow of the lava, the figures of the women became indistinct, blending with the ash and smoke, disappearing and reappearing like intermittent flames in a dying fire.

Now he saw them! Alfgar and a girl standing together on a black rock, fiery lava encircling them, reaching toward their feet. On a rock above the children, below a black cone, stood the older woman. The woman of the mist stood below the two children and reached her arms toward them over the lava.

The woman below the cone extended her arms toward Agon.

"Agon, son of Grae, here are your brother and your daughter. I have saved them from Lilith!"

The woman of the mist spoke: "Do not believe her, Agon. She is Lilith. I am Erina, who came with you from the peaks of the Earth Mother. I am the mother of your daughter."

The lava was rising higher around the rock on which

Alfgar and Ara stood. Agon called, "Ara, which is your mother?"

Ara pointed to the woman of the mist. "She is my mother."

The woman below the cone spoke: "Kill her now, Agon. Ara has been made to believe that Lilith is her mother."

The molten lava surged higher.

The woman beside Agon cried, "Save your brother and Ara before the lava swallows them! There is no time left!"

The woman above them shrieked in hideous joy. "Too late, Agon, son of Erida! Your brother and daughter are doomed! Watch them die, and then die yourself!"

Agon hurdled over the flowing lava, the length of two men, onto the rock that held Ara and Alfgar. He lifted the girl in his arms and jumped across the lava with her to Erina, then back to the rock. The river of lava had widened, risen higher. Agon took Alfgar's hand in his. "Now, my brother."

Together, they leaped across the lava to where Beren and Erina waited with Ara. And now a great torrent of lava erupted from the black cone above them. They ran across the smoking rocks through the smoke and ashes to the crater rim.

They looked back once, and they saw the wall of boiling lava pour down over Lilith and the rock on which she stood. The Earth Mother had vented her wrath on the woman who had dared steal one of her priestesses.

But as the lava poured over Lilith, it seemed to Agon that only an empty cloak stood on the rock.

31

Sunstand Day

ZUR STOOD ON the chieftain's rock under the horizontal sun shadow marks on the cliff wall. He wore the bison horns and carried the long staff of Grae, chieftain of the bison hunters. Today he would show the people that he was merciful as well as all-powerful. He would bring the sun back by his magic alone—he would not need to carry out human sacrifice. There was no need for sacrifice; all the sons of Grae and Erida were dead. Zur, only son of Grae and Lilith, lived. Agon had followed Alfgar's and Lilith's trail, the trail Zur and Lilith had planned. By now Agon's and Alfgar's bones charred in boiling lava. Now no son of Grae and Erida could scheme against him, take the horns and staff of Grae from him. No longer would he dread the coming of Agon.

And now the sun shadow of the rock pinnacle moved toward the mark of noon on the cliff wall, and he would show his magic, his power.

He raised his staff. "Light the fire."

As the women spun the fire stick between their palms in the old way, Zur spoke softly to Van and Xo: "Watch the cliff path, the river trail. If by chance Agon lives, he will try to attack today."

Van spat. "He had no men with him. The old man was nothing."

"Still keep watch. If he comes, kill him. Give him no chance to talk to anyone."

The people shouted, pointing at the shadow on the cliff wall. Noon was almost upon them, and the shadow of the pinnacle moved toward the highest horizontal mark on the wall. Let it go above that mark, and the sun would never return. Eternal winter would rule the world.

But Zur, Grae the chieftain, would stop the sun. Grae would make the sun stand still, then start its journey upward to bring an end to winter. Only through the magic of Grae could the tribe survive.

Zur raised his staff and began to chant. He felt the power of Grae surge within him, mystical and strong. Grae would make the sun stand. Grae would bring back the sun.

An old man in the crowd moved closer to the fire, to Zur. An old man in tattered hides, bent and stooped, his straggly gray hair hanging over his eyes and face. While the people stared at the markings on the cliff, he had hobbled silently into the crowd from the trees that grew along the river. A boy came through the crowd toward the old man, a boy whose unkempt hair fell over his face, a boy so like all the other boys that he attracted little attention.

The cliff shadow crept toward the last and upper mark. Zur chanted louder, his staff pointed at the sun, slowing its descent. The bent old man peered up at him through tangled hair the color of wood ash. Too close. The old man was too close. Who was he? Zur motioned to Van to push him back.

Something was wrong . . . the shadow was going above the line! But Zur had moved the line back up . . . the shadow should have stopped, reversed. . . .

The people began a low howling of fear, a sound of terror. Zur brought his staff slowly, powerfully up, trying to raise the sun, lower the shadow. And the shadow moved higher. Now the people were screaming, tearing their hair, running toward the cliff shelter, then back into the open, their eyes wild, their mouths wide in fright.

Beren appeared on the cliff top. As one person and then another saw him, the terrified people stared up at him. His voice carried down from the cliff top:

"Make Alfgar chieftain! He can bring the sun back!"

"Alfgar is dead!" Zur screamed the words.

"Algar is not dead! Zur tried to kill him, but he lives!"

"Alfgar lives!" The bent old man standing near Zur straightened. He lifted the boy up onto a rock before the people. "Here is Alfgar! Make him chieftain! He can bring the sun back!"

"No!" Zur screamed. "Zur is Grae! Grae is chieftain!" He seized Van's spear. "Alfgar dies!" Zur raised the spear to hurl it into the boy.

So fast that the motion was almost unseen, something spun out from the old man's hand, an axe whirling in a song of death. The axe blade struck Zur in the middle of the forehead, just below the black shiny bison horns, and Zur fell backward from the chieftain's rock onto the ground, dead.

The old man seized the axe and the chieftain's staff from the ground beside Zur's body. He stood up and brushed the hair and ashes away from his face.

"Agon!" The people fell back in astonishment. Then they pointed at the sun, at the shadow on the wall. "Stop the sun, Agon!"

Agon thrust the staff into Alfgar's hands. "Hold it high!"

Then Alfgar raised the staff. And the sun stopped. The shadow on the cliff wall hung motionless on a barely discernible horizontal line on the cliff wall—a line a hand's width above the line the people had been staring at.

Agon shouted, "Alfgar is chieftain!"

And the people cried, "Alfgar is chieftain!"

"Alfgar is Grae!"

The people shouted, "Alfgar is Grae!"

Later that day as the people celebrated and feasted, an old hunter spoke to Beren:

"It's strange. Last night when I had to go piss in the bushes, it seemed that I saw men on the cliff wall, doing something in the darkness."

Beren glanced innocently at the old hunter. "Probably

you were still not awake. On what part of the wall did you think you saw these things?"

"It seemed that they were by the Sunstand marks."

"No man could climb there." Beren smiled. "You saw only shadows."

32

Spring

EENA FELT AN eager, happy expectation. Soon Agon would return. The winter was past, and with spring Agon would cross the great expanse of land and return to Bear Hill.

She and the boys took the screen of hides and branches from the cave entrance to let the sunshine in, and in place of their snow sandals, the family wore high moccasins waterproofed with aurochs tallow when they hunted. The plain was soaked with water from the melted snow, and the creeks and streams ran noisily into the river valley. Trees formed fat buds, and the willows along the river showed red in the sunlight.

One morning Eena visited Ulam's grave and placed the white blossoms of the early-blooming lily on the earth above the old hunter. As she stood by the grave, she thought of the days long ago when she had brought spring flowers to her mother's grave on the hilltop above the river. Thirteen winters had passed since she had placed the fire stones in the earth by the grave and left with Stig and her brother for the camp of the bison hunters. Thirteen winters since Ka had murdered her family and, hissing like a great snake, had raped her.

Eran's totem, the snake carved into the handle of his axe. Could her firstborn be the son of Ka? She had denied it all these years, but as Eran grew more cruel, more filled with hatred, she found it harder to deny. Yet she must deny it. Eran must be the son of Agon. Agon, who would soon return. . . .

The young hunter, Berg, came from the trees below the grave site. He waved his spear at Eena and then ran lightly up the slope to the grave.

"I came to bring you to the camp." He smiled at her. "Tonight we have the spring hunt festival."

"I know. But I don't come to your camp."

"Because of Hura?"

"Partly."

"What else?"

"I want to be here when Agon returns."

"Agon has been gone many moons."

"The winter storms kept him."

"The winter is long over." Berg moved a step closer. "You need a man."

"A man?"

"Me."

"My sons and I can protect our home."

"I didn't mean that."

"What did you mean?"

Berg shuffled his feet. "In our tribe the women choose the man they want to mate with."

"So?"

"So you need a man. Agon is gone. I'm here. Choose me."

"You want me to mate with you?"

"I'm the fastest runner in the tribe. I'm the best of the hunters, except for Emar, and he's too old for you. . . ."

"How old do you think I am?"

Berg studied her. He held up the fingers of both hands twice. "But you don't look like you're that old."

"You know I have had two children."

"That doesn't matter. Yurok always gets to break the maidenhead on our girls."

"Then he wouldn't want me."

"No, but I do."

"Why? There must be many girls in your tribe who want you."

"There are. But they're not like you." Berg's breathing became faster. "You're like a deer—everything slender and strong. You can run and throw a spear like a man, but you aren't like a man. You're like a goddess." He moved closer to her. "Let me hold you! Let me take off your tunic!"

"No!"

"We can go into the trees or up to your camp."

"My sons . . ."

"They're still boys. And they're gone. Come. I want you now."

"You'll die."

"Die? Why should I die?"

"Because I'm Agon's mate. Agon will kill any man who has even tried to mate with me."

"Even though he has left you alone? Gone back to his tribe? What claim does he have on you?"

"Agon and I belong to each other as long as we live. When we die, our spirits will be together."

"I am younger than Agon. The mare favors the young stallion."

"I favor the man I love."

Berg placed his hand on her arm. "What if Agon never comes back?"

"Even then I'll wait for him."

Berg looked into her eyes. "I'll wait for you."

"No. You must not."

"I will. Until I die."

Eena's eyes showed her concern. "Find a girl in your tribe. If you love her, mate with her as Agon and I have mated."

Berg slowly let his hand drop from Eena's arm. "If I can't have you, I don't want any woman."

Eena smiled. "I've seen your hunt festivals. Tonight, when the drums speak and the people dance under the moon, you'll change your mind. Then all women are beautiful, all hunters are strong. You'll find that a girl you have known all your life has become a goddess in the moonlight."

Berg's face lost some of its despondent look. "Is that how Agon found you?"

How Agon found her. Agon, kneeling over her in Ka's dark cave as she asked for death . . . Agon, holding her gently as she wept for her murdered father and brother . . . Agon, rescuing her as under a gibbous moon she was carried above the heads of the screaming dancers of Ka's tribe . . . carried toward Ka.

She smiled. "Yes, that is how Agon found me, dancing in the moonlight."

After the death of Lilith, Erina had told Agon that he must return immediately to Zur's camp:

"Go now with Alfgar and Beren. The time of the shortest day is almost here. Make Alfgar chieftain before Zur murders more of your tribe."

"We go. Can you return to your waterfall home by yourself?"

"Of course."

"A woman alone in the mountains?"

"Those who serve the Mother learn many things."

"You told us that Lilith never dies."

"You saw the lava cover her."

"I saw the lava swallow her robe."

"Those whom the Mother destroys will not live again."

"Even through their daughters?"

"We know of no daughter of Lilith. We will be safe."

"We?"

"Ara and myself."

"Ara goes back with me."

Erina's eyes flashed. "She's my daughter, consecrated to the Mother. She goes back with me!"

"That's over now."

"It's not over. She's given her life to service of the Mother!"

"*You* have given her life to the Mother. Not Ara. Not I."

"She was born to serve the Mother. You were part of that. Have you forgotten, Agon?"

Shimmering moonlight . . . the spirit of all things female . . . he had not forgotten. . . .

"Return to Eena. She waits for you. But she does not wait for the daughter of another woman."

Could he bring Ara back to Eena? Could Eena accept her? Could Ara accept Eena as her new mother? And would she become like the girls of Yurok's tribe, mating with one man, then another? But first with Yurok . . .

"You are right. Ara should stay with you." He held his hand out to Erina. "You helped Eena and me when we came to the Earth Mother to die. And you helped me find Alfgar and destroy Lilith. Ara is yours."

"And yours." Erina took his hand. "Ara must now begin a time of learning. Not every daughter of a priestess is suited to serve the Mother. If Ara cannot or will not accept the life of a priestess, I'll send her to you."

"My home is far from here."

"Yes. But you will stay here for a long time."

"No. Only until Alfgar is strong enough to rule. Zur's men would kill him if I leave now."

"What about the men of Ka?"

"They must be killed."

"And you need Zur's men to fight Ka's men."

"I would kill Van and Xo now, but the tribe is so weak from the battle with Ka that it needs every man. I may have to stay here until next summer, but no longer than that."

"Eena and your boys will miss you."

"Yes. But not for long."

Erina's eyes were sad. "Ara and I will leave tonight." She held out a small wrapped object to Agon. "When you return, give this to Eena. It will help her bring the power of the Mother to the place where you live."

He took the object, and he felt the magic in it.

"Do not forget me, Agon." She smiled. "We will meet again."

Erina's eyes were like moonlight, but it seemed to Agon that for an instant he saw death in her face.

33

The Second Year

A YEAR PASSED, and still Agon could not leave the bison hunters. Ka's men were no longer seen by the the bison hunters, yet the threat of attack was always present.

Agon took hunters up the river valley in search of the men, but they found only the filth and litter of abandoned camps. They went as far as Spear Mountain and carefully investigated the shattered cone for any cave entrances that might have survived the volcanic blast. They found nothing but lava beds and destruction.

The canyon down which Agon had raced after killing Kaan was so filled with solidified lava and the raging waters of the river that no man could traverse it. Evidence of the violence of that eruption and the subsequent flood was seen in the grotesque forms of lava that had poured in boiling waves into the river and then been struck by the great wave of glacial water roaring down the river valley after the ice dam had broken.

Every hunting party that went out on the plain watched for signs of the men of Ka, but none were found.

Agon talked with the people of the tribe about the threat:

"We cannot find the men of Ka, but they still must be

on this side of the river—no man could cross it now. They have either gone across the plain or are hiding somewhere beyond Spear Mountain. Unless we find and destroy them, we have to be ready for an attack at any time."

Alfgar, now thirteen years old, spoke confidently: "Let them attack! Then we can kill them."

Beren shook his head. "You're too young to remember. When Ka attacked the camp, you were only a baby. We lost half the tribe in that battle." He pointed to the ground in front of the cliff shelter. "Here Agon's hunters stood. They died fighting, each killing two or three men. But in spite of their bravery, Ka broke through and killed your mother and sister."

"But Ka is dead. Agon killed him. They have no leader like Ka. And part of the attack came from across the river. The river was low then. Now no one can cross it."

Agon watched the old man and the boy as they spoke. Alfgar would make a good chieftain, if he lived. Could Beren help Alfgar enough so that he could rule now? If it were not for the threat of Ka's men, the danger of revolt by Van and Xo . . . Alfgar was gaining confidence—almost too much, and he was growing, becoming stronger, bigger—but at only thirteen years old, he could not yet stand up to Van and Xo. And Beren? The old hunter seemed thinner, more fragile, his skin more transparent, his eyes lighter in color—how long could he help Alfgar, and how much?

"Alfgar is right—without Ka to lead them, his men may not be as dangerous as they were," Agon stated. "But Beren knows how hard it is to defend this camp. And we haven't been able to send enough men out to fight Ka's men. I believe we should take the women and children to the safe place you went to in the time of Ka. We'll leave four men there to guard the camp. All other men will form a war party and track Ka's men down. Go beyond Spear Mountain, into the mountains, across the plain. Find them and kill them."

Van scowled. "War party!" He held up the fingers of

both hands. "We have this many men who can lift a spear. If you leave four hunters with the women, the 'war party' would have only six hunters. Agon tells us he saw more men than that watching the camp! And how many more might there be that Agon did not see?"

"Six good men are enough," Agon replied.

"And who will lead this 'war party'?" Xo asked. "The boy chieftain, Alfgar? Or Agon, who ran away when Ka attacked?"

Van spoke to the hunters: "Agon would kill all of you, taking you into the snow and ice of the mountains to search for men who are no threat to us."

The seasoned hunters had all been part of Zur's hunting band, as had Van and Xo. They would follow Van and Xo. Every one of Agon's hunters had died defending the tribe; Agon could only hope to gain support from the old men, the women, the young hunters. And of these, only from those who remembered him favorably, or had not been influenced by Zur's lies.

"Since Van and Xo scorn our leadership," Agon said, "they can remain behind with the women and children. We will leave two other hunters to protect Van and Xo."

Now Van and Xo will challenge me, Agon thought, and I can be rid of them and return to Eena. His fingers touched the handle of his axe.

Van smiled sourly. "Agon tries insults so he can kill us as he did Grae."

Agon turned his back on Van and faced the people. "To survive you must be strong. How many men will come with me and Alfgar to find and kill Ka's men?"

Beren and three other old men stepped forward.

Agon looked at the hunters. "Who will come?"

Not a single hunter came forward.

"None? Only four old men are brave enough?"

Another of Zur's hunters, a big man called Stag, spoke: "You have the six men you wanted, Agon. Go and show us how you will kill Ka's men, who stay invisible."

Van shouted, "Kill the hunters of our tribe in the snow,

Agon. This is what you came back to do. You came to destroy the tribe."

Agon looked around at the people. "I came to save the tribe, not destroy it. Now I wonder if it's worth saving. You all watched and did nothing as Zur killed my brothers. You listen to men like Van and Xo, who are afraid to leave the camp, and you wait here helplessly like sick bison calves while Ka's men stalk you. Where are the people of Grae? Where are the bison hunters who feared no man, no tribe?"

The people stared silently at the ground.

"Where are the ancient people whose power lies in the Black Stone?"

The people shifted their feet uneasily. Some looked up at Agon, then away.

An old woman moved forward in the crowd. "Agon, I'm ashamed to see what kind of people we have become. When your father was chieftain, we feared no one. Now our men are like frightened children. Kill the cowards, Agon. Then take these brave old men and track down Ka's men. We women and the children will wait in the safe place. We will defend ourselves!"

Van hooted in scorn. "Be silent, old hag. Who will bring you meat now?" He shoved the woman back so forcibly that she fell. "Go pick your food from the rubbish heaps!"

Now the women of the bison hunters showed their anger. They lifted the old woman to her feet and gathered around her protectively. They shook their fists at Van and the hunters. "Cowards! Children! Half-men!" they shouted. "Go and hide! We will protect you!"

Agon motioned to Alfgar, Beren, and the three old men, and they left the crowd. Agon clasped the arms of each of the old men in turn. "You were the best of the hunters. You are still the best of the men. But I can't ask you to go as a war party."

"We are ready, Agon. Lead us and we'll go." Beren raised his spear. "We can still fight."

"I know you can. But if we go into the snow and ice of the mountains, you will die."

"Better to die as men than to live as cowards."

"Yes. But the tribe must live. We have to wait."

"Wait for what, Agon?"

"Until Zur's hunters see that they must fight. The tribe will die unless everyone joins together."

One of the old men chuckled. "Listen to the women. Zur's hunters may change their minds sooner than we think."

Beren contemplated the shouting people. "They may, but I doubt it. Zur made Van and Xo think that they were better than the rest of the people—they will never change. I see only one answer."

"What is that?" Alfgar asked.

"Kill Van and Xo. Without them, the other hunters would soon follow you."

"Follow me? You mean follow Agon."

"You are chieftain," Beren replied. "Agon should return to his family. He has helped the tribe enough."

Alfgar considered this. "Agon should be chieftain. He is the oldest son of Grae."

The old men turned their eyes on Agon.

Agon shook his head. "I left the tribe. My family is far away. As soon as Alfgar is old enough to rule alone, I'll return to my family."

"When will I be old enough, Agon?"

Agon touched Alfgar's spear. "When you are strong enough to kill Van and Xo."

On a cold day in autumn, Emar came to Bear Hill, where Eena and the two boys were bringing in winter firewood. He helped them drag logs and branches up the escarpment until the cave would hold no more.

"Now you're ready for winter. Soon the storms will come, but you'll be warm." He looked around the cave. "Agon has been gone more than two winters."

"He could still come before the storms." Eena gestured toward the skin bag of stew by the fire. "Sit and eat with us."

Emar accepted the wooden bowl of stew and sniffed it appreciatively. "No one can make deer-and-onion stew as you can."

"Agon will be hungry when he comes back. I always have stew ready."

"He's not coming back." Eran, now almost as big as a man, spoke from the other side of the fire.

"He *is* coming back," said Alar. "I dreamed last night about him."

Eena glanced hopefully at Alar. "You saw him coming back?"

"No. But I knew he was coming back."

"How did you know?"

"He talked to me. He said, 'I have to come back.' "

"His spirit talked to you! He will come back." Eena's eyes showed her happiness. "What else was in the dream?"

"He was fighting. Fighting against evil men."

Eena's eyes lost their look of joy. "Who were the men?"

"Men with big heads."

"Ka's men!" Eena held both hands to her breast.

Eran's eyes seemed to reflect the fire. "Agon won't come back. Ka's men will kill him."

Eena glared fiercely at Eran. "Be quiet. Agon will scatter Ka's men like quail. He will come back."

Eran laughed scornfully. "Two winters he has stayed away." He looked out over the plain to the east. "I see no one. Agon is afraid to come back, knowing I am now chieftain of our family."

Emar had been watching and listening quietly. He said to Eena, "In our tribe, a hunter sometimes shows a boy that he is not yet a man."

Eena looked quickly at Emar, then Eran. "I am shamed that you have seen and heard how Eran feels toward his father. But I am still able to show Eran that he is not yet a man."

"He grows large and strong. You may need a man's help."

Eena regarded Emar silently. "You bring game to us, you help us with the firewood. Now you are ready to help me with Eran. You are a good man."

"Agon was my friend. I want to help you."

"We don't need your help." Eran came around the fire. "And if you want to try to show me I am not a man, I will fight you any way you want. Spear, knife or the neck-strap way."

Emar calmly speared a piece of venison from the bowl with his knife. He looked up at Eena. "Tell me if you want help with this boy. I am becoming ever more eager to give it."

Eena stepped between Emar and Eran. "I thank you. But Agon will soon come home. He will show Eran that he is not yet a man. It is best that he should do this for his son."

Eran grimaced. "I'm not his son. And I'm not the son of this hunter who sniffs around you like a rutting stag."

Eena put her hand on Emar's arm. "I ask you not to hear him. He's still a boy."

Emar stood up. "For that reason I will not hear him now. But I tell you this as your boys listen: If Agon never comes back and you want or need a man, I'll be ready. I would do anything for you. I could never take Agon's place, but I would love you as I do now and always will. And if you need help with Eran, I am ready for that, too."

34

The Plot

FOR YEARS HURA had schemed for revenge. Since Eena's spear had sliced through her ear, she had plotted how she could harm the woman who had shamed her.

Every morning she left Yurok's camp and watched Bear Hill from a cave in the hills. She had noted that one member of the family always guarded the escarpment when the other two hunted or brought food and firewood. On a day when Eena and Alar hunted together, Hura waited until they were in the far hills, then came to Bear Hill. Eran watched her approach the escarpment.

She called up to him: "Let me come up."

"Do you want to die? My mother will kill you."

Hura glanced nervously behind her. "She's away now."

"For a while. But if she comes back and finds you . . ."

"I want to talk to you."

Eran laughed. "You want to lose another ear?"

Hura looked behind her again. "Come down, Eran, where she can't see me."

"Why should I? You told me you'd help me become chieftain. You're so afraid of my mother I haven't seen you for years."

"That's why I came today. Either come down or let me come up. We have to talk."

Eran gestured. "Come to the top of the slope. Walk in the water. If my mother sees your tracks, she'll come after you."

"The water's cold."

Eran turned away. "Stay down there, then."

Hura stepped hesitantly into the stream and climbed up

the escarpment. Eran stopped her at the top. "Stay there."

"In the water?"

"It'll make you talk faster." Eran looked out toward the hills. "She'll be coming soon."

Hura shuddered. "Tell me if you see her."

"I might."

"Listen, Eran. Your father, Ka, was chieftain of the most powerful tribe in the east. He was the most feared of any man. No tribe could stand against the tribe of Ka. No man could stand against Ka. When you are a man, you will be like Ka. But you will be even greater than Ka."

Eran fingered his spear. "I'll be greater than Ka?"

"You will. Because of Agon."

"Agon? I hate him."

"But think. Who killed Ka?"

"Agon."

"How could he do that?"

"Some sort of magic. Otherwise he couldn't have done it."

"Of course not. And what was Agon's magic? What did Agon teach you?"

"Nothing."

"He didn't teach you the axe song?"

"I hate the axe song. I fight with the spear. I can kill Agon with my spear, the spear of Ka!"

"Of course. You can be be the greatest warrior of all men. You have the courage, the strength, the fierceness of Ka."

"I'll kill Agon if he ever comes back."

"You could do that. But when the leopard takes its prey, does it kill the prey at once?"

"It plays with it."

"So you must do with Agon."

"But how can I do that? We fight. I kill him."

"What does Agon care about most?"

"My mother! He took me from her. Pulled me away so he could have her." Eran glared at Hura. "But I'll kill you if you try to hurt her!"

"No, no. I wouldn't hurt your mother. Even though she hurled her spear at me, I try not to remember it. But what we want to do is hurt Agon through your mother."

"Through my mother?"

"Yes. What would hurt Agon the most?"

"To have him fear me."

"He'll never fear any man. But what else would hurt him?"

"Ah! My mother. If I took her away from him, hid her. . . ."

"He'd find you. Think. What would hurt him the most?"

"If I made her my mate."

Hura shook her head. "That would hurt him most, but Kala, goddess of death, forbids that above all other things. A son cannot mate with his mother. But what if another man . . . ?"

Eran's eyes grew hot with anger. "No other man can ever mate with her. I'll kill whoever tries."

"Of course you will. But what if Agon *believed* another man had mated with her?"

"How could we make him believe that if the man doesn't mate with her?"

"People would have to see the man coming and going from Bear Hill when your mother is alone. They would have to tell Agon of this when he returns."

Eran scowled. "I won't let any man go there when she's alone."

"The man wouldn't try to mate with her. No one would dare do that. People just have to believe he tried."

"No. I won't let you do it. Agon might hurt her if he found out."

"He would never hurt her. Have you ever seen him strike her?"

"No."

Hura smiled. "He's always gentle with your mother."

"He wants her only for himself."

"Of course. That's why we can hurt him."

"As long as she doesn't get hurt . . ."

"She won't be hurt. We just have to find a man that Agon would suspect; a man Agon thinks is his friend. . . ."

"Emar's already been sniffing around her. He said he wanted her."

"That's good. Emar mating with your mother would hurt Agon most."

"It won't work. She told Emar Agon would kill him if he mated with her. Alar and I heard her."

Hura frowned. "No, Emar's not the one then. . . ." She clapped her hands. "I know the one!"

"Who?"

"Who else? Yurok. Yurok the chieftain."

In the camp of the bison hunters Agon chafed in impatience and frustration, wanting to return to Eena, yet knowing that he must remain with Alfgar's tribe. Van and Xo, without giving him cause to kill them, still kept the people from obeying Alfgar. The whereabouts of Ka's men remained a mystery, yet Agon knew they were preparing for a surprise attack on the camp. His greatest disappointment was that he could not muster a war party to track down the men of Ka. The spirit of the tribe seemed broken.

Agon spoke with Alfgar about a possible course of action:

"The tribe will die unless we can bring back its courage. We must teach the boys to be warriors. They're your friends; they don't follow Van and Xo. We'll form a band of the boys. We'll call it a hunting band, but I will teach them how to fight."

"Teach me to fight, too, Agon. Teach me the axe song."

"I will. We'll have all the boys make axes. Not everyone can learn the axe song or finds the axe to be their best weapon, but all of you know how to throw a spear. What I will teach you and the other boys is how to fight with axe and spear against Ka's men. Spearing a deer or a bison is not the same as fighting with a man who carries two spears and knows how to use them."

"Teach us, Agon. Start now."

"I will."

"How long will it take? How soon can we form a war party and find Ka's men?"

Agon regarded the boys of the camp who were idly throwing stones into the river.

"One year. You will be warriors in one year."

35

The Fourth Year

HURA HAD ATTEMPTED for a year to convince Yurok that Agon was never coming home, and that Eena longed for a man. Not any man. Yurok. Finally she seemed to be succeeding. She spoke to him in his hut late one night.

"She's wanted you since the day they came here. I could see it—standing behind you with her spear while Agon fought Buner, running before you in the races, showing her skill with the spear . . ."

Yurok grinned from his hide couch. "She showed you her skill with the spear."

"That's past and forgotten. Now I feel sorry for her. Her man is gone, and she's too proud to show her desire for you."

"How do you know she desires me?"

Hura lowered her voice. "Eran told me. Never tell her that he has spoken to me. And Eran would never tell you, of course. But she cries in her sleep for you."

"For me? Not for Agon?"

"No. For you. She longs for you."

"Agon is my friend. In his tribe they take their mates for life. I would not take his mate."

"Of course not. But Agon has been gone almost five winters. He must be dead."

"I don't know that. Agon went back to help his young brother become chieftain. He may be staying until the boy is old enough to rule."

"And not send a message? He must have many hunters—he could have sent one of them to tell the woman."

Yurok scrutinized Hura's face. "Why are you telling me this?"

"Because I know that you want the spear woman. I saw it in your face when she threatened you with her spear."

"I wanted her. Every man wanted her. But she's Agon's woman."

"Remember, I told you many winters ago that the man who lies with a spear woman would never be satisfied with another woman."

"I remember. But she's older now. You know that I find the young girls of my tribe most to my liking. Why should I want Spear Woman more than them?"

"Because she knows the magic of love. She knows ways to please a man that your young girls have never heard of. And she has the strength of a man. She will not be like your frightened maidens who lie under you like dead fish. You will know passion such as you have never dreamed of when she pretends to fight against you."

Yurok sat up on the couch. "She would pretend to fight against me?"

"How else? She must keep her honor. She will tell you that she only loves Agon, that she waits for him, that she doesn't love you. But all the time she will want you to overpower her, force her to your will. That is the only kind of man a spear woman can respect."

"And afterward. What then? What if Agon comes back?"

"He need never know. Who would know? Who would tell him?"

"The two sons. They would tell him."

"Eran hates Agon. He would never tell him. The

younger son, Alar, might tell his father. But he need never know. The three of them at Bear Hill always leave one person to guard the cave when the other two go out to hunt. When the two boys go out, you come to Bear Hill. Spear Woman will be waiting for you."

Yurok stood up. "You hate Spear Woman. I think you're trying to make me believe things that aren't true. Before I listen to any more of your talk, I have to know that she really wants me. I won't make a fool of myself."

Hura smiled. "If you need that, I have ways to help her show her desire for you. It may take a few moons, but when I tell you she is ready, go to Bear Hill. Her passion for you will be like that of a lioness in heat."

Agon found a strange thing as he trained the boy warriors. While the boys became skillful in the use of their spears for fighting, none of them except Alfgar could learn the axe song. They threw their axes clumsily, were unable to catch a thrown axe, and worse, they had no feeling for the magic of the whirling axes. Alfgar, however, felt the magic and practiced so assiduously that within a year he was able to do part of the axe song with Agon.

Now sixteen winters old, Alfgar had increased so much in strength and judgment that Agon felt the young chieftain could soon rule the tribe. And once Agon and the boy warriors found and killed Ka's men, Agon would return to Eena and his sons. Four winters had passed since Agon left Bear Hill.

But one day when Alfgar and Agon were almost through practicing the first part of the axe song, Alfgar called out, "Keep on, Agon! We'll do the whole song! Throw faster! I want to spin with the axes!"

"You're not ready." Agon continued throwing the axes at the same speed. "You have to practice spinning without the axes first."

"I've done that!" Alfgar spun around once as he threw

one axe and caught the one thrown by Agon. "Throw faster, Agon. Spin with me."

The boys who were watching called, "Show us, Alfgar. Do the big axe song."

Agon threw the axes at the same rate. "He's not ready." But Alfgar spun his body, caught the axes, and threw them back so skillfully that Agon had to increase his speed. Faster and faster Alfgar spun and threw until the whirling axes began to sing. Alfgar shouted in joy as he whirled: "Faster, faster!"

Something made a small cracking sound, and Alfgar's axe spun wildly off to one side. Alfgar stopped spinning and looked down at one arm. He raised his arm; his wrist and hand hung limply down.

Agon went to him. Alfgar's arm was broken. The blade of a spinning axe had struck him just above the wrist and broken both bones in his forearm. The skin above the break was cut and bruised, but no bones showed.

Alfgar looked at the ground in shame. "I thought I could do the big axe song with you, Agon. I'm sorry."

Agon felt the broken bones. "The breaks are clean. Stand on your hand and pull up."

Alfgar bent down and laid the limp hand on the ground. He placed his foot on it then straightened his body. The bones in the arm came into place with a small sound like rocks grating together.

"Take off your belt. Then get your axe."

Alfgar unfastened his belt with his good hand, then retrieved his axe from the grass.

"Take your axe handle in your teeth. Hold it against your arm and wrap your belt around the break."

Alfgar gripped the axe handle with his teeth and held the axe against the broken arm. With the other hand he wrapped the belt around the handle and his arm.

"Now hold the belt tight with your good hand while we go back to camp."

The other boys had watched silently. Agon spoke to them: "When you're hunters and warriors, you'll have many broken bones. If you're alone, you have to put the bones back in place by yourself. Remember how Alfgar did this."

Later that day Alfgar came to Agon. The healing woman of the tribe had bound Alfgar's arm with thongs, rabbit skins, and wooden splints.

"She says I can't throw the axe again for four moons."

"Listen to her."

"But we were going to go find Ka's men. . . ."

"We will. In four moons."

"But you wanted to go back to your family before winter comes."

Agon laid his hand on Alfgar's good arm. "I can't go back to my family until you're a man. Yesterday you were still a boy. Today you became more of a man."

36

Magic Powder and Death

Hura came to Bear Hill one day late in summer when Eran was alone. He let her come to the top of the escarpment.

"You must never tell your mother I've been here." Hura looked back apprehensively at the plain. "She might see me."

"She won't see you. She and Alar are hunting on the other side of the hills."

"I saw them go. But they might come back. Let me come in." She smiled. "I have something I want to give you."

"What?"

"Something that will help you hurt Agon."

"Give it to me."

"In the cave. I need to show you how to use it." Hura pushed by Eran, went through the porch, and entered the archway of the cave entrance. She scrutinized the comfortable furnishings: the cheerful fire with its nearby cooking bag of stew, the ample pile of wood, the sleeping hut with its fur robes, the log seats by the fire, the weapons leaning against the walls.

"Spear Woman is lucky to have a son like you who cares for this place while she hunts."

"She cares for this place."

"Of course." Hura peered into the storage room with its racks of food and clothing, then into the dark recesses of the cave. "It must go deep into the hill."

"It does."

"What is back there?"

"Just some things?"

"What kind of things?"

"Long passages. Chambers."

"What kind of chambers?"

"Big. Little."

"There must be more."

"Just some animals."

"What kind of animals?"

"Just animals."

"Take me back there. I want to see them."

"No."

"Why not?"

"They're the animals of my family, of my tribe when I'm chieftain."

"Of course. And you will be chieftain soon."

"As soon as I kill Agon."

"After he suffers. I have something here that will help us make him suffer." Hura held out a small leather pouch. "These are magic herbs. You must secretly sprinkle a little bit each day into your mother's food."

Eran stared at Hura suspiciously. "You want to poison her. You hate her for spearing you."

"Oh, no. I don't hate her. This is to help her. The herbs won't poison your mother. They'll make her younger and more beautiful."

"I don't believe it."

"Yurok won't be able to stay away from her. Agon will suffer more every time you put the herbs in her food."

"If you're lying to me, if she gets sick or dies, I'll kill you."

"I wouldn't lie to you. Yurok will come soon to see your mother. I've told him she wants to talk with him. He must see her beauty, or he will never come back. To make Agon suffer, people must see Yurok come up here again and again."

"Show me the herbs won't hurt her. Eat some yourself."

Hura moved closer to him. "Would you like to see me become more young and beautiful?"

"I want to see if you die or not. Eat some."

Hura opened the pouch and took out a small portion of brown powder on her finger. "This is how much you will put in her food each day. Watch. I will eat it and live." She placed the powder in her mouth. "It has no taste. But already I feel younger, more beautiful." She smiled again. "Taste it yourself. The girls of Yurok's tribe will gather around you like does around a stag."

"I need no women's magic."

Hura touched his arm. "Your magic is strong. I can feel it. The magic of a chieftain." She moved her hand up his arm. "Do not taste the powder. Your magic would make me forget that I am older than you."

Eran struck her hand away. "Leave here! Send Yurok, but never come here again. And if the powder harms my mother, I'll seek you out and kill you. Now go!"

On a summer afternoon when Agon and his band of young warriors returned from the plain with meat, they found the women of the camp waiting for them with concerned faces and angry eyes.

The old woman explained to Agon: "Mia has been taken by the men of Ka!"

"The daughter of Mara? The woman who died last winter?"

"Yes. Mia was picking berries with the other girls. They saw her carried off!"

"Where? When?"

The old woman pointed to the east. "In the river valley. The girls came running back at noon."

"Where is Van?"

"In the cliff shelter with his cowards!"

Agon entered the cliff shelter. Van and his men lounged against the cool stone walls.

Agon looked at Van with cold eyes. "You would not save a girl from your tribe?"

Van shrugged. "Girls are not worth saving."

"Have you followed Ka's men?"

"They were gone long before we were told."

"I will take my hunting band and track them. Will you come with us?"

"Someone must guard the camp."

Agon turned his back on Van and went to his young hunters.

"Each bring one bag of traveling food and your weapons. We go to kill the men of Ka."

They ran through the river valley to the berry patches and found the tracks of Mia and those of two men, and the place where Mia had been taken. They followed the trail along the river valley until night. They slept, and the next day they followed the trail up out of the valley onto the plain, where they skirted the ruins of Spear Mountain. The tracks led into high grass that had been trampled by men, and they found blood and marks on the ground where Mia had struggled under heavy bodies.

The boys of the hunting band became wolflike, and their eyes took on the look of death. Agon led them to hunt a bull bison on the plain, and they ate the liver and heart raw and wiped the blood on their bodies. They ate great slabs of meat, and they gained in strength and fierceness each day as they followed the tracks of the men of Ka.

They found Mia's body in thick brush. She had been raped, mutilated, and beaten to death.

They buried her, and Agon spoke to his hunting band.

"It is better that she died before they took her to their camp. She will suffer no more. Now we will find these men of Ka and destroy them all."

They followed the tracks along the cliff top until they came in view of the great waterfall that dropped down from the river mother, the huge, glacier-fed lake that lay in the mountains. The tracks led to a game trail that snaked down the cliff face into the river valley.

Agon stopped his hunters at the cliff edge. They lay in thick brush and studied the valley below. No smoke of cooking fires was visible, no sign of a camp. Yet the men had to be somewhere below the cliff—there was no way to go beyond the falls.

Alfgar turned a puzzled face toward Agon. "Where are they?"

"Where did Ka bring his people?" Agon asked.

"To a cave."

"So?"

"We find the cave and attack."

"Will we go down the trail, or the face of the cliff?"

Alfgar considered. "The cliff face. If we go down the trail, we could track them, but we couldn't surprise them. If we go down the cliff face, we can find the cave without being seen. Then we attack."

"Will we attack in darkness or daylight?"

Alfgar thought again. "Darkness. We find their cave entrance during the daytime, wait until night, then attack."

"Good." Agon spoke quietly to Alfgar and the other boys. "If we rush into their cave, many of you could be killed. Here is how we will destroy the men of Ka."

Eena felt that if Agon were to return to Bear Hill now she would send the boys out and have Agon mate with her throughout the day and night. And this would not be enough. She and Agon would go back into the great painted chamber of the animals, and they would make love with the magic of the animals, giving Agon the strength of the stags, the bulls, the stallions. . . .

Something had changed within her. The hot blood in her body excited her spirit until it called for Agon with the strength of a demon. She must have Agon now. . . .

Alar watched her with worried eyes. "Mother, are you sick?"

"No. Why?"

"You look kind of wild."

Eran scowled at Alar. "Be quiet. She looks the same as she always does." Eran's face and throat looked bruised, as though he had been fighting again with the boys of Yurok's camp.

"No, she doesn't," Alar replied. "Look how red her cheeks are."

"They're just warm from the fire." Eena heard her voice as though a stranger spoke; a strange woman who was filled with passion. Passion for Agon.

Eran looked at her, his eyes contemplative. "You aren't sick, are you?"

"No, of course not. You know I'm never sick."

"If you do get sick, tell me."

She smiled at Eran. "I'll tell you. You've been good to me lately, even helping me with the fire and the cooking bag. When Agon comes home, I'll tell him how you've changed."

His eyes darkened. "Five winters he's been gone. Still you wait for him."

"I wait for him because I know he'll come back." By force of habit she looked out across the river valley, searching for the approaching figure of Agon. "Something has made him stay with his tribe, but soon he'll be coming back. . . ." Eena half rose from her sitting log. Someone came across the plain. The solitary figure of a man striding toward Bear Hill! Eena stared at the figure. Agon? She felt her nipples rise up hard under her deerskin tunic.

"It's Artron." Eran's voice was angry. "I'll go send him back home."

Eena sank back on her log. Tears of disappointment were forming under her eyelids.

Alar touched her arm. "You thought it was Father, didn't you?"

She turned away to hide her tears. "Yes."

"He will come back."

"He will. I know he will."

Eran spoke scornfully: "He won't come back." He took his spear from the wall. "I'll just roll a few rocks down on Artron to scare him away. I don't want him up here with his silly magic."

Eena came to her feet. "You won't roll rocks on him! You could kill him!"

Eran glared at her. "I told you I don't want him up here!"

"You are not chieftain here." Eena pushed by Eran and went to the top of the escarpment. She called down to Artron, "Come up."

Artron looked up at her. "Will you come down and talk with me? Alone?"

Eena looked back at Eran and Alar. "Stay here." She descended the escarpment to where Artron waited, her feet as light and clever on the rocks as when she first came to Bear Hill.

Artron's face, his eyes, were distraught. "Eran must flee. Have him go at once."

"Eran? Why?"

"Because Yurok will have him killed."

Eena's face became pale. "Why?"

Artron stared at Eena. "You don't know?"

"Know what?"

"Eran killed one of the boys in the tribe."

"Killed?" Eena held her hands to her mouth. "How?"

"In the thong wrestling. They were wrestling as boys do, for fun. The boy was bigger than Eran and started to taunt him. Eran killed him."

Eena's hand grasped the deer totem at her throat.

Artron looked up the escarpment. "The other boys say that Eran became terrible."

Eran, son of Agon? Or of Ka? Each of them became terrible when they fought. Eena saw Ka as he killed her father and brother, hissing in fury, his powerful body moving with the quickness of a striking snake. She saw Agon as he killed Ka, even more terrible in his anger, smashing Ka's arms and legs with the axe, raising him high above the cliff top and hurling him out into space. . . .

"Tell Eran to go, now, fast."

Eena looked up the escarpment. "He'll never leave . . . he'll fight. . . ."

"Then Yurok will kill him. They'll wrap him in hides and throw spears into him."

"No! They can't! Yurok is Agon's friend!"

"Agon is gone."

"I'll talk to Yurok—ask him to spare Eran."

"It won't do any good. Death debt must be paid."

"How?"

"Blood or banishment. Blood of the murderer or his closest relative. Or banishment of the murderer. Either Eran flees, or he dies."

"There is no other way?"

"None." Artron stroked his chin. "Except . . ."

"What? Tell me."

"If the dead boy's mother would agree to have Eran bring her game and furs and wood for the rest of her life. Be her slave."

"Who was the boy?"

"Drom."

"No! Drom, son of . . ."

Artron nodded. "Son of Hera. Hura's sister."

37

Battle

THE CAVE OPENING yawned like a black mouth in the face of the cliff. As darkness enveloped the river valley, the faint glow of a fire shone from the opening. A lone sentry stood silhouetted against the glow.

Agon motioned to his boy warriors, and they crept silently through the undergrowth until Alfgar and four of the boys were on one side of the opening, the remaining on the other.

Then Agon slipped through the darkness until he was directly in front of the opening. The sentry stood two spear-throws away. Agon crawled silently forward with two spears in each hand.

At least ten men were in the cave. Agon and the boys had counted them that afternoon from their hiding places in the bushes, watching the knob-headed men carry game down the trail and into the cave, watching other men drag in logs and branches, watching them go to the river to drink. The men were older than Agon, but still powerful-looking, still armed with two spears each. Agon knew that, man for man, his boy warriors could not stand up to Ka's fighters. One man appeared to be chieftain, the tallest of the men, a man who wore a bone in his hair, a man who reminded Agon of Ka.

One spear-throw away.

Agon threw a stone toward the cliff face. The stone made a sharp noise of striking, then dropped onto the platform behind the sentry. The sentry turned and stared up the cliff face, his spear raised. Agon rose silently and threw his first spear.

The sentry's arms flew up as the spear thudded into his back. He uttered a hoarse cry, turned, and staggered toward Agon with his spear raised, then fell facedown.

Spears clattered, and men rushed from the cave opening. Agon's second spear sliced through the night and into the chest of the leading man. Then the boy warriors hurled their spears from either side into the dark forms, and Agon threw his third spear and ran forward with the fourth.

The men of Ka fought as they had always fought, like demons. With spears bristling from their bodies they screamed in rage and charged at Agon and the boys.

Now Agon shouted, and the boys fell back, circled in the darkness, and came in behind him. Like a spear, Agon and the boys plunged straight into the mass of screaming men. The tall form of Bone Man loomed in front of Agon, and Agon gutted him with an upward slash of his spear. Then Agon threw the spear into the throat of another man, ripped the axe from his belt, and with the axe whirling a song of death led Alfgar and the boy warriors in a bloody path through the men of Ka. Every crunching bone, every slash of flesh was sweet vengeance for the death of Mia and the massacre of the bison hunters seventeen years before. Vengeance for the slain fathers, mothers, brothers, sisters, grandfathers.

Finally every man of Ka lay dead. The surprise attack and strategy of Agon and Alfgar had succeeded.

Agon led the way into the empty cave, and in the firelight they saw the debris of bones and hides, smelled the stench of rotting meat and human waste, and felt the dying evil of the men of Ka.

Eena went alone and unarmed to Yurok's camp in the pine forest. She asked for the hut of Hera and found the woman and Hura preparing the body of Drom for burial. The people of the camp gathered around the three women.

Eena bowed her head before Hera. "I come to ask you to spare my son. Let him live, and my sons and I will bring you game, clothing, and wood for as long as you live."

The two women stared murderously at her. Hura spat on the ground. "You! Have you forgotten how you wounded me?"

"I remember."

"You think you can pay for the murder of my sister's son by begging before us?"

"I want my son to live."

"*You* want? You, whose man has left you? You, who know not the fathers of your sons? You, who came in your pride and threw your spear into my flesh? You, who have tried to lure the men of our tribe to your filthy den?"

"I will be your slave. Let my son live."

"The slave of both of us? My sister and me?"

"Yes."

"You aren't worth it. What more can you give?"

Eena was silent, then she looked up at the two women. "My blood."

The two women closed on Eena as lionesses approach a wounded and fallen deer. They pushed her back against the wall of Hera's hut and held her there. Hura drew a flint knife from her belt.

"Five years ago you hurled your spear through my ear. Now your son has killed Drom. I will cut off both of your ears and your nose, then give Hera the knife. Show us how brave you are, Spear Woman." Hura roughly jerked Eena's hair back and seized her right ear. Eena stood motionless as Hura raised the knife.

"Stop!" Artron stepped forward from the crowd.

Hura turned her head and glared at Artron. "It is my right. Hera's right."

"Hera's right. Not yours."

Hura drew her own hair back. "Look at my ear!"

"Your ear is another matter. Spear Woman comes to pay death debt for the son of Hera."

Hura spat on the ground. "She will pay death debt. Hera can cut her when I am finished." She brought the knifepoint to Eena's face. "Show us now your magic, Spear Woman. Show us how you do not bleed."

A spear sliced through the air and quivered in the wall of the hut just beside Hura's arm. A voice came from behind the crowd. "The next spear will be in your gut. Get away from our mother." Death was in the voice.

The people turned and gaped. Eran and Alar pushed through the crowd, spears and axes in their hands. They hurled Hura and Hera aside and stood on either side of Eena, facing the crowd.

"We'll kill the first one who touches her." Eran stared scornfully at the people. "You cowards. You would stand here and let these two witches cut my mother into pieces. My mother didn't kill Drom. I did! I killed him in a fair fight. If anyone wants to try to kill me, let him try. Here I stand before you!"

Alar reached back, pulled the spear from the wall, and gave it to Eena. "Our mother came without weapons, without telling us. She offered you her blood. Now she has her spear. Now all three of us are here. We offer you our blood, but know that we will take more blood than you can spare. Who will come first to take our blood?"

The people stood silent.

Then Artron spoke: "Yurok hunts with Emar and his band on the plain. I cannot speak for Yurok, but I say this: Let Spear Woman and her sons return to Bear Hill without spilling blood. When Yurok returns, he will decide what should be done."

"Kill them!" Hura screamed. "Kill the evil woman and her whelps!"

Artron stared coldly at her. "Will you kill Spear Woman? Come now with your knife!"

Hura shrieked in rage. "I go to find Yurok! The law of the tribe must be followed! Blood for blood!" She ran wildly from the camp into the pine forest, and her cries grew fainter and fainter: "Blood for blood! Blood for blood!"

Artron spoke to Hera: "If Spear Woman and her sons

will bring you game, clothing, and wood, will you forgive the death debt?"

Hera scowled. "Let Yurok hear what has happened here today. Game and wood will not bring back my son."

"You'll let Yurok decide?"

"Maybe." Hera pointed menacingly at Eran. "He was the one who killed Drom. Let him die."

Artron spoke to Eena: "You and your sons have shown us your courage today. Go back to Bear Hill and wait for Yurok to decide."

"Yurok," Eran said, "will decide nothing."

Artron regarded him with a strange expression on his face. "Be careful what you say. Yurok has powers you know nothing of."

Eran shook his spear. "His powers are nothing to me. Tell him that anyone who tries to kill me or my mother will die."

38

Alfgar

ON THEIR RETURN journey to the camp of the bison hunters, Agon's boy warriors were jubilant. They gloried in their wounds, and in their eyes Agon saw rekindled the fire of courage and pride.

Alfgar, bearing a spear wound in one shoulder, spoke quietly to Agon as they neared the camp: "You taught us how to use our weapons and how to fight. You led us and showed us how to win a battle. You should be chieftain."

"Eena and my sons are far from here. You are chieftain, Alfgar."

"I wouldn't be chieftain without you. You killed Zur. You led us in killing the men of Ka."

"Zur was my enemy. I showed you how to fight, but it was you and the other warriors who killed most of Ka's men. Now you are ready to be chieftain without me."

Alfgar walked silently along for a time, then said, "I'm not ready, Agon."

"Why not?"

"I don't know what to do about Van and Xo."

"What do you think you should do?"

"Kill them?"

"If they break the laws of the tribe, yes."

"What if they keep on telling the people not to follow me? What if they cause trouble?"

"Then show them you are chieftain."

"I don't know if I can."

Agon touched Alfgar's healed arm. "You didn't think you could put your bones back in place, did you?"

"No . . . how did you know?"

"Because the same thing happened to me when I was learning the axe song. Grae or Erida could have set the bones for me. But they made me do it. Hunters must be able to do hard things."

"And being a chieftain is like that?"

"Yes. You do what you have to. No matter how hard it is, you must always do what is best for your tribe."

"How many men have you killed, Agon?"

"Many."

"Did you ever fear any of them?"

"No."

"Have you ever been afraid of anything?"

"Why do you ask that?"

Alfgar swallowed. "Because I have fears. I'm not like you, Agon."

"The man who has never been afraid has never lived."

"I thought I was the only one . . ."

"Who feared? You've been thinking you shouldn't be chieftain because you had fears?"

"Yes."

"If you had told me you feared nothing, I would have had to become chieftain."

Alfgar considered this. "What do you fear, Agon?"

"To offend the gods. To bring dishonor on my tribe. Demons. What do you fear?"

"The gods. Evil. That I'll not be a good chieftain. That I'll show fear before the people."

"Then you'll be a good chieftain. Keep your fears. They give you no dishonor."

They approached the ancient black rock, the Stone, the shrine and altar of the bison hunters. Agon said to Alfgar, "Lay your hand on the Stone."

Alfgar did so.

"What do you feel?"

"Something coming up my arm . . . strength . . . power!"

"It gives you power now because you've become a true chieftain. Magical power. In the beginning, the Stone was here. The first Grae touched it and received his power. Every Grae since then has been given power by the Stone. When you need it, the Stone will give you power."

Alfgar gazed in wonder at the black rock. "I've touched it many times before. Never has it done this!"

"Lay your weapons on the Stone."

Alfgar placed his axe and spear and knife on the rock. "They glow!"

"Now take them up. You are Grae, chieftain of the bison hunters. Go down to your tribe with your warriors."

Alfgar stood straight and strong with his weapons. "You go first, Agon. You are the war leader."

"No. You are war leader now. And chieftain. Go down to your people."

"They are your people, Agon. Come beside me."

Agon clasped Alfgar's hand. "I have been away from my family too long. Now I return to Eena and my sons."

Alfgar looked sadly at Agon. "You have been my brother, my father, my friend. But I know you must go."

"Yes."

Alfgar embraced Agon. Tears were in his eyes as he spoke: "Will we see each other again?"

Agon smiled. "We have seen each other in every generation, every chieftain, since our tribe began. We will see each other again." Agon turned toward the west.

Just then a shout came from below the cliff: "Agon, wait!"

Beren waved his arms from the bottom of the trail, a slender, dark-haired woman standing beside him.

"It's Ara!" Beren called. "She's come to go home with you!"

39

The Demon Among the Aurochs

HURA MET EMAR and the hunters at dusk as they came from the plain carrying game. She spoke so incoherently they could hardly understand her:

"Yurok! She's mine! Her blood is mine! Kill her! Spears! They threw spears at me! Give her to me!"

Emar tried to calm her. "Yurok isn't with us. Who threw spears at you?"

"Find Yurok! Make him give her to me!"

"Who? Why do you want her?"

"Blood! Her blood! Mine! Find Yurok!"

Emar touched his bear totem. "You want someone's blood?"

"My ear! Look!" Hura frantically pulled back her hair. "Blood for Drom! Find Yurok!"

"Drom! You want someone's blood for Drom?"

"She came! She offered her blood! They threw spears at me!"

"Who threw spears at you?"

"Her whelps! Spear Woman's!"

"You were going to take Spear Woman's blood?"

"Blood for blood! Her ears! Her eyes!"

Emar drew back from Hura in loathing. "You hag. Spear Woman's sons should have killed you." He raised his spear. "Did you cut her? If you did, I'll kill you."

"Too soon! They came too soon! They threw spears at me! Find Yurok!"

Emar turned away. "Find Yurok yourself." He pointed back at the darkening plain. "He's out there, waiting for you."

Hura ran across the plain in the gathering darkness. Yurok would listen to her. Yurok would give Spear Woman to her. She would cut her slowly, moving the knife blade gradually through the skin, the tissue. Blood would flow in a little trickle at first, with the little cuts, then faster. . . .

Cutting her eyes would require a delicate touch. Just the point of the flint blade gently piercing the eyeball, then slowly pushing in . . .

Would Spear Woman draw back and scream? Or would she try to show her pride and strength? At first she might do that. But not later . . .

A dim mass of moving forms lay ahead in the dusk. The smell of dung, sweat, and milk came to Hura's nostrils. The aurochs herd. Hura shivered. The great bulls surrounding the herd would see her and raise their wide-horned heads. They would run toward her, their huge hooves pounding the earth, great cloven hooves that would trample her into red mush. . . .

Hura crouched down in the grass. She started to back silently away, back toward the shelter of the hills and trees.

But Yurok. She must find Yurok. Yurok, who would give Spear Woman to her.

Something tall, white, and horned moved in the center of the herd! The giant and terrible aurochs demon she had seen so many years ago! Hura felt her heart pound. The demon still lived!

Something was happening—the herd was moving, milling, coming toward her. Hura turned and tried to flee, scrambling on her hands and knees in the long grass, falling, gasping, moaning in terror.

The herd closed on her like a sweeping storm. Hura came to her feet and ran screaming across the plain in the darkness as the pounding hooves of the aurochs thundered closer behind her and then upon her. But as Hura fell under the aurochs, it seemed that the god Kaan came to her, and she felt no pain of death but only a great joy.

40

Yurok

YUROK CAME TO Bear Hill the next day while Eran and Alar were hunting. He called up to Eena from the bottom of the escarpment and then climbed up to where she stood. He wore the aurochs horns and white robe of chieftain.

"You were willing to give your blood for Hera's son."

"Yes."

"Hera still demands death. Eran's or yours."

"Eran and Alar will fight all your hunters."

"They'll both die, then."

"Yes. I'll die with them."

Yurok regarded her searchingly. "I don't want that to happen."

"There's no other way."

Yurok frowned. "I've seen Eran and Alar fight. I've seen you throw the spear. I could lose half my hunters."

He glanced at the pile of boulders at the top of the escarpment. "Maybe more."

Eena made no reply.

"You offered to bring Hera game and wood. I think she might have accepted if Hura hadn't been there."

"Hura wants vengeance for her ear."

"You were going to let her cut you."

"I want my son to live."

Yurok moved closer to Eena. "Your son could live."

Eena stood motionless. The male scent of Yurok made the nipples of her breast rise up firm and hard under the deerskin of her tunic. Her desire for Agon was like fire. Desire for the male being. Desire for Yurok. Yurok was here. Yurok was chieftain. One word from him and Eran would live. Agon would never come back. . . .

"I have been told," Yurok said, "that a spear woman can arouse such passion in a man so that he never again can be satisfied with any other woman."

Her body was flushed, hot. It seemed that Agon stood before her. They would go back into the great hall of the animals. . . .

"I have been told that a spear woman would pretend to fight me. Would you do that, Spear Woman?"

Eena leaned toward Yurok. His aurochs horns curved up like two great male organs. . . .

Her fingers found the lacing of her tunic. Slowly they began to undo the lacing. . . .

Her hand touched the belt at her waist. The wedding belt given her by the priestess of the Earth Mother. Slowly her fingers began to unfasten the belt. . . .

Yurok seemed to grow taller. He was the spirit of all things male. . . .

Eena's other hand touched the ivory totem at her throat, the young female deer given her by her mother. . . .

She stood as if frozen. Then she fastened the belt back around her waist, and she felt its magic strength flow into her body.

"No."

Yurok's eyes glinted. "You pretend to fight me."

"No." Eena drew the small knife from the belt and crouched in a fighting position. "I'll kill you."

"I kill hard."

"Maybe. But you won't have me."

"You wanted me."

"Yes."

"You need a man."

"Yes."

"If you give yourself to me. I can save your son."

"My son and I will die fighting."

"You would die for your honor?"

"For Agon."

"Agon is gone."

"Agon will come back."

"He doesn't need to know. . . ."

"He will know. Agon and I will only take one mate until we die."

Yurok looked into her eyes. "I want you as I have never wanted any other woman."

"And I wanted you. But it cannot be."

Yurok's eyes held a strange expression, a look of desire, of power. But something else—a look of death. Suddenly he smiled. "Agon is a friend of mine. I'm glad for my friend." He held his hand out to Eena. "When Agon fought Buner, you stood behind me ready to kill me with your spear. Now when Agon is away, you are ready to fight me with your knife. You are all woman and all warrior. Give me your hand."

"You are too strong. Keep your hand back."

Yurok laughed. "Good. Don't trust any man." He stepped back away from her. "Look. I go below your pile of rocks. Roll them down on me if you fear me. Let us talk."

Eena came out of her fighting crouch and stood beside the pile of boulders. "I listen."

Yurok gazed out at the plain, then at Eena. "Neither you nor Eran have to die. I talked with the boys who saw the fight. Drom tried to kill Eran first. I think I can keep Hera from claiming death debt in blood."

"But Hura . . ."

"She has no death debt on you or your son."

"She hates me. . . ."

Yurok shrugged. "Emar told me that Hura went out on the plain last night searching for me. She hasn't come back."

"She roams the hills and plain, watching us. I have felt her eyes at night."

Yurok's eyes held a mystery. "Strange things happen on the plain at night."

"What do you mean?"

"Hura will never watch you again."

Eena stared at him.

Yurok spread his hands. "A herd of aurochs must have stampeded. Hura prowled at night on the plain. The hunters found what was left of her this morning."

Eena made a little sound of horror.

Yurok smiled. "I won't miss her."

"The poor woman . . ."

"Don't feel sorry for her."

"But alone on the plain . . ."

"She was evil."

"Not so evil as to deserve that. . . ."

"She was. She went there to find me, get me to give you to her. You know she would have blinded you, crippled you, mutilated you. And before Eran killed Drom, she was going to secretly give you her witches' mating herbs."

"Witches' mating herbs?"

"Herbs that would make you give yourself to any man."

Eena gasped.

"She hated you so much she wanted you to be unfaithful to Agon. When he comes back, she wanted him to kill you."

"No one could be that evil!" Then Eena looked at Yurok in anger. "You came up here knowing that!"

Yurok shook his head. "She had no way of giving you the witches' herbs. I came up here to talk with you about saving your son's life." He looked into her eyes. "But when I was alone with you, I knew I had to have you, had to mate with you. No man could feel otherwise. I forgot everything except you."

"How can I believe that?"

"You can't. But you should know one thing."

"What?"

"If you had mated with me, I would have killed you afterward."

Eena looked at Yurok in quick disbelief, then in understanding. "If I had mated with you, you should have killed me."

Yurok nodded. "Agon is my friend."

41

Return

THE FOLLOWING DAY Eena saw two figures coming toward Bear Hill from the river.

Agon!

42

Ara

ARA WATCHED AS Agon and the golden-haired woman held one another. The woman was Eena, Agon's mate. She had come leaping down the escarpment and running like a deer across the plain to Agon. Now she was crying and laughing and holding Agon as he held her. The woman was like a young girl, and she was lovely.

Now a man ran across the plain toward them. A young man, his dark golden hair flying behind him. As he approached, Ara saw that except for the color of his hair he was another, younger Agon. He stopped a spear's length back from Agon and the woman and gazed at them with an expression of happiness and delight. He glanced once at Ara, and she saw that his eyes were beautiful.

Finally Agon and the woman drew apart, and as they did so, the young man rushed into Agon's arms.

The woman watched the two men with the same delighted expression that had been on the young man's face. Ara saw that beyond them, high on the hill above the escarpment, another man watched them.

Agon led the woman and the young man toward her. She almost turned and ran, but then she faced them, standing erect and proud. The faces of the woman and the young man were somehow alike, and they both had expressions of wonder and surprise. But the woman's face held something else—a look of challenge.

"This is Ara, daughter of Erina, priestess of the Earth Mother. Erina is dead." Agon's voice was strangely husky.

The woman's face changed, the look of challenge

changing to one of compassion. She held out her arms to Ara.

"I am Eena. Will you be my daughter now?" Her voice was soft and kind.

Ara hesitated, looking into the woman's eyes. Then she saw such love there that she came into the woman's arms, and she cried in her happiness as the woman hugged her and stroked her hair.

Eena said softly, "I've always wanted a daughter. We can weave baskets together, and I'll teach you the names of the flowers that grow here. We can pick berries together and make clothing for our men." She looked into Ara's eyes. "Will you be my daughter?"

Ara replied through her tears, "You're like my mother. If you want me, I'll be your daughter."

"I want you." Eena took her arm and turned toward the young man. "And this is our son Alar. He'll be your brother."

Ara felt a strange thrill of excitement as she took Alar's hand. Agon and Alfgar were fine-looking men, but Alar was beautiful. He smiled at her, revealing his even white teeth. "I'm one of the men you'll make clothing for. And we can go hunting together."

"Agon showed me how to throw a spear and hunt deer as we came here, but I had never lifted a spear before."

"I'll show you how to hunt aurochs and horses."

"Would you? I'd like that."

"I can show you how to trap for furs, too. When winter comes, we can go on our snow sandals to visit the traps."

"Agon told me of snow sandals."

"You don't have them where you came from?"

She looked down at her feet. "I've always gone barefoot in the forest. Agon made these sandals for our journey here. Are they snow sandals?"

"No." Alar laughed, pleasantly, not scornfully. "We'll make you snow sandals. Just wait until winter comes; we'll skim over the snow like blowing leaves."

Eena took their hands. "You'll be good friends." She asked Ara, "How old are you?"

Agon spoke: "Sixteen years. The same as Eran."

Ara pointed to the top of the escarpment. "Is that Eran up there?"

Alar answered. "We always leave one of us to guard the trail. Otherwise Eran would have come to meet you and father."

Eena tried to hug Ara, Alar, and Agon at once. "Come home now!"

Agon studied the still form at the top of the escarpment. "Eran has grown tall."

"And strong," Alar said. "He can beat anyone except Yurok and Emar in wrestling and spear throwing."

"Thong wrestling?"

Alar looked quickly at Eena. "He doesn't do that anymore."

"Good," Agon said. "It is not a man's way to fight."

Eena said quickly, "Come. You must both be hungry. We have venison-and-onion stew by the fire."

Agon gave Eena a small object wrapped in white leather. "Ara's mother gave you this. Five years I have carried it."

Then Ara felt the magic of Eena join with the magic of the Earth Mother, and she knew that the women's magic, the Onerana, the Invisible Earth Spirit Women, lived in this place far from the Earth Mother. Eena placed the object in her belt pouch, and then took Ara's hand. "Your mother's spirit is with us now."

As they came to the escarpment and climbed single file up the slope, Ara sensed the love of Agon and Eena and Alar for one another, and she shared the happiness of coming home. After the death of her mother, the trip across the plain to the bison hunters, the waiting with the people of the bison hunters for Agon's return, and the long journey across a land so immense and strange as to almost overwhelm her, it was good to come to a place called home.

When Ara came to the top of the escarpment, she saw the comfortable and protective porch, the graceful and airy entrance to the cave, and, standing with a spear in his hand, Eran.

Never, except for Agon, had she seen such an imposing, magnificent man. And never such a beautiful yet terrifying face, such a mane of black-gold hair, such fierce eyes, such a posture of pride and arrogance. Once on the journey with Agon she had seen a pride of lions resting after a kill. Eran was like the great tawny male, supreme in power, overwhelming in strength, awesome in his beauty and savagery.

Agon and Eran faced each other.

Eran spoke first: "After five years you come back."

"Yes."

"You expect to sit in the chieftain's place at the fire after leaving my mother for that long?"

"I will sit in whatever place is empty."

Eena came between them. "Agon will sit in his place as chieftain of our family." She placed her hand on Agon's arm. "Come into your home. Sit at your fire. Eat the food I have prepared for you." She smiled at Ara and took her hand. "Come into your new home. Always there will be a place for you here: Your own place at the fire. Your own bed of furs. Your own clothing and tools and weapons. Your own family around you."

Eran's eyes blazed. "For five years I have protected this place. For five years I have brought game for your food. For five years I have trapped furs for your robes. For five years I have dragged logs up the escarpment for your winter fire. Am I now to sit like a child at the fire, begging for morsels of food from the game I have killed? Begging from the man who left us for five years?"

Eena replied, "You have not done these things alone. Alar and I have also protected this place, brought game, trapped furs, dragged logs. Before that your father and I did these things for ten years while you grew from a helpless baby to a boy. Do not talk of what you have done for us, or of your father being away five years. He is home now."

Eran glared at her. "You have always favored him over me."

"And I always will. But you are my firstborn son. Come now and be happy with us." Eena put her arm around Ara. "This is our new daughter, your sister, Ara."

Eran glanced at Ara. "She's not my sister. I have no sister."

"Now you have. Ara's mother did things for us that we can never repay or forget. Now her mother is dead. Ara has come to live with us as my daughter." Eena took Eran's hand. "Come in with us. While we eat by the fire, your father will tell us of his tribe."

Eran jerked his hand away. "I stay out here to keep watch."

Ara smiled at him. "My new brother will protect us."

Eran looked again at her. "Bring me a bowl of stew, then. As a sister should."

43

The Painted Chamber

As the family sat around the fire eating, Agon told them of his journey to the bison hunters, of Zur and Beren, Alfgar and Lilith, Erina and Ara, the boy warriors, the men of Ka, and Alfgar's rise to power.

Alar was fascinated, and he asked so many questions that Agon was forced to reveal details he would ordinarily not have mentioned. When he described the gate of Hell and the death of Lilith, Eena shuddered and held Ara's hand, and when he told of the battle with Ka's men, Ara saw that Eran stood listening by the cave entrance.

The details of the murder of Agon's brothers and the death of Zur on Sunstand Day brought a hush to the chamber. When Agon had finished telling of this, Alar spoke: "Zur was son of Grae, a good chieftain. Yet Zur was evil. How could that be?"

Agon replied, "Grae's mate before Erida was Lilith. Zur was son of Lilith. I think her evil came to Zur."

Eena held her deer totem. "The blood of the mother is the blood of the son. Those who see birth know that."

"Nothing comes from the father?" Alar asked.

Eena's face was pale. "Not evil."

Alar's face showed his puzzlement. "But what does come from the father? And why is the oldest son of a chieftain always a chieftain?"

"The oldest son of a chieftain should not always be chieftain," Agon replied. "Zur showed that."

"But what about good chieftains?"

Agon paused, thinking, before he replied. "Magic. The good chieftain gets his magic from his father. He cannot be chieftain without strong magic."

Alar smiled in agreement. "That's so. Just like the magic of the axe song."

Agon regarded Alar. "Have you learned the axe song?"

"I think so."

"The axe sings for you?"

"Yes. And when it sings, I feel its magic growing stronger and stronger."

"Good. Let me see your axe."

Alar took his axe from his belt and handed it to Agon. Agon inspected it, felt its balance in his hand. "Your totem is the red deer."

"Yes."

"Like Orm's."

"I saw it in my spirit dream. Is it all right, Father?"

Agon placed his hand on Alar's shoulder. "Orm was my friend. It's all right. I'm proud to have you find the same totem." Agon smiled at Alar and gave the axe back. "We'll do the axe song together. Have you practiced with Eran?"

Alar hesitated. "Sometimes."

Eena spoke: "They are so busy hunting and bringing wood that they have little time for the axe song. Maybe now they can practice with you."

Agon nodded. "We'll do that." He touched the handle of his own axe. "I noticed a strange thing when I tried to teach the axe song to Alfgar and the boys of his tribe. Only Alfgar could learn the axe song."

Alar spoke excitedly: "Because they weren't sons of a chieftain! It's as you said, Father; the good chieftain gets his magic from his father!"

Eran spoke from the entrance. "The powerful chieftain gets power from his father. Not magic, but power and strength and courage."

Agon turned to look at Eran. "You don't believe in magic?"

"Magic is for women and half-men like Artron."

Agon was silent for a moment. He said, "Come and sit with us, Eran. It is good that you believe in power and strength and courage. No chieftain can rule without them."

"I'll stay outside."

"You carry an axe. Will you let me see it?"

"No one touches my axe but me."

"Good. Only let the axe leave your hand when you throw it or when it rests in your belt." Agon smiled at Eran. "What totem is carved in your axe handle?"

Eena replied before Eran could speak. "It's the same as yours, Agon."

Agon's eyes lighted with surprise. "Eran's totem is the ibex?"

"Yes."

Agon spoke to Eran: "When we do the axe song together, the axes will be brothers."

Eran made no reply.

"I'm glad that he has pleased you," Eena said. "It's been hard for him to have you away so long."

"It's been hard for all of you." Agon studied Eena's face

and body. "The boys have grown to men, but you look the same. Do you still hunt?"

Eena nodded. "We take turns. Two of us go out while one stays to guard the camp."

"That's why you could run so fast when you came to meet us."

"It's why I could run so fast, but not why I did run so fast."

"Tell me all the things you did while I was gone. I often imagined what you were doing."

Alar answered first. "She waited and watched for you, Father. Every day."

"I believe that."

Eran spoke again from the entrance. "She waited and watched not only for Agon."

Agon looked sharply at Eran. "What?"

"When a man stays away for five years, he shouldn't be surprised if someone had been sniffing around his mate. Berg. Emar. Yurok."

Agon came to his feet. "Berg? Emar? Yurok?" He stared at Eena. "Is this true?"

Eena's voice was low. "It is true. Each of them came, thinking you would never return, thinking I needed a man."

"Did you mate with them?"

"No." Eena touched her deer totem. "I never mated with anyone."

"Ask her about Yurok!" Eran stepped through the entrance. "Tell Agon why Yurok came here, what he did!"

Eena said to Agon, "I am ashamed that our son talks as he does. Nothing happened between me and Yurok."

"Tell me why he came here."

"Only to talk. . . ."

"He came because I killed Drom." Eran's voice was filled with malice. "He came to tell my mother that if she would mate with him, he would let me live! Look at me! I'm still alive!"

Agon's voice became cold as ice. "Watch what you say, Eran."

Eena came between them, facing Agon. "Please don't be angry at him. He and Alar kept Hura from taking my blood."

"Taking your blood!" Agon ignored Eran. "Why your blood?"

"For death debt."

"I'll kill her! Where is she now? Which camp?"

"She's dead." Eena placed her hand on Agon's. "That's what Yurok came to tell me."

"But you were going to give your blood, your life, to Hura because Eran killed Drom?"

"Drom was the son of Hura's sister."

Agon took a long burning branch from the fire. He held it in one hand and his spear in the other. "Alar, take care of Ara." He said to Eena, "Come with me."

He led Eena back toward the rear of the cave, toward the long passage that led back into the hill. Just before they entered the dark passage, Agon turned back to face the entrance where Eran stood.

His voice echoed in the depths of the cave.

"If anyone follows us, they die."

Agon led Eena back through the winding passageway until they came to the great painted chamber of the animals. In the flickering torchlight the bison still pawed the ground, the bulls held high their widespread horns, the horses galloped over the plain.

Agon placed the end of the torch in a crack in the wall, and with his spear, faced Eena in the dim light.

"For five years I have dreamed of you. For five years I have wanted to hold you in my arms. For five years I have wanted to mate with you in this place."

Eena stood silent and motionless before him.

"We promised," Agon said, "to have only each other."

"Yes."

"Now I find that other men came to you while I was gone."

"Yes."

"And you would have let Hura kill you because of Eran."

"He is my son."

Agon looked into her face, her eyes. "Now this spear calls for blood."

Eena made no sound.

Agon held the spear out to her. "Take it."

She stared at him.

Agon said, "You have been faithful to me. I have not been faithful to you."

"No . . ."

"Ara is my daughter."

Eena drew in her breath.

"When you and I went to the Earth Mother, I mated with Erina. I knew nothing of Ara until Beren and I followed Lilith and Alfgar into the Blue Hills. Erina told me then."

Eena's eyes were luminous in the torchlight. Agon took one of her hands and put the spear in it. "Kill me if you wish."

Eena gazed at him, gripping the spear. Then she let the spear drop to the floor. She moved close to Agon and laid her head against his chest. "You mated with Erina before you and I were mated, while I was still unclean from Ka. There is no blame in what you did. Hold me, Agon; I could never kill you!"

He held her, and he knew that she was softly crying. He gently stroked her hair.

She whispered, "I am the one who should be killed. I let the men come to me, talk to me."

"No. You have been faithful to me. I know that."

"I was faithful. Don't kill the men, Agon. They are your friends."

"I won't kill them."

They clung silently together, feeling their love for one

another rekindle and burn, as glowing coals that have been buried in ashes ignite the hearth fire.

Agon felt that Eena was untying the lacing of her tunic, and his hands moved to help her. She moved his hands to the belt that circled her waist. She said softly, "The belt is for you to take off. No other man has ever removed it. No other man ever will."

There under the great painted ceiling, while the good spirits of the animals watched over them in the flickering torchlight, Agon and Eena came together in their love.

44

Two Brothers, One Sister

ARA'S ENTIRE LIFE had been spent in training for service to the Earth Mother. She knew little about tribal and family life, could only throw a spear because of Agon's instruction during their journey, and was almost overwhelmed by the presence of men, especially men of the strength and fierceness of Agon and Eran.

But the rigorous training of the priesthood had disciplined her mind and body in such a way that she could cope with her new way of life, with any situation. The long trek across the great landmass had toughened her body so that she was slender and hard muscled as a young deer, and she soon learned to hunt and fish, to skin and butcher game, and to run like a she-wolf with the wolflike family of Agon and Eena.

The mystery of her training to be a priestess, her physical ability, her attractiveness, and her loving nature caused Alar to fall in love with her. With Alar she was happy, laughing, playful. She let him show her how to stalk game, how to throw the spear accurately while running at full speed, how to catch fish in the river, how to snare rabbits, how to trap muskrat and mink. But she felt for Alar only the love of sister to brother.

With Eran she felt a strong physical attraction, not only because of his savage beauty, but also because of an unspoken fear of his strength, his anger, his violent nature. In his presence she was reserved, shy, never making eye contact with him, careful never to anger him. On Eran's part, he seemed to show only antipathy toward her, speaking curtly to her, often ignoring her, treating her as an unwelcome stranger.

But with the return of Agon and Ara, the hunting pattern of the family had changed, and this led to Eran's revelation of his true feelings toward Ara. Now, with five family members instead of only three, larger groups could hunt or guard the camp. On a day when Agon, Eena, and Alar hunted together, Eran and Ara were left to guard the camp.

Ara worked by the fire sewing winter moccasins for the family, while Eran watched the plain from the porch at the top of the escarpment. At midday Ara brought him a bowl of venison stew. She looked out over the plain as Eran ate.

Eran put the empty bowl on a ledge. "What are you watching for? Agon?"

"Not just Agon. All of them."

"I wish he had never come back."

She glanced quickly at him. "Because he brought me?"

"No. Because of Agon. I hate him."

"Because he stayed away so long? He had to stay with his tribe until Alfgar could rule as chieftain."

"That's what he says." Eran glanced at her. "I'm going to kill him someday."

She looked at him in horror, then turned her eyes away. "Please don't say that. Agon is your father."

"He's not my father. Ka's my father. I come from the people of Kaan."

"Who is Kaan?"

"The god of my people."

"The bison hunters don't worship Kaan. Agon is son of their chieftain. You are son of Agon."

"No. I am son of Ka."

"You can't be. Ka was evil. He killed half of Grae's tribe. He killed your mother's father and brother."

"Agon told you that. I don't believe it."

"Agon killed Ka. Why else would he kill him?"

"Because he wanted my mother. She was Ka's mate, and Agon wanted her."

"Eena was Ka's mate?"

"Hura told me."

Ara shook her head. "Hura was an evil woman. She would tell you lies. Alar told me how she was going to cut your mother. I'm glad you stopped her."

"Nobody cuts my mother."

"You're a good son to her. Why can't you like Agon as you do your mother?"

"Because he took her away from me. He wants her all to himself. Agon is bad."

"Agon is good. If you had seen him rescue Alfgar and me from Lilith, you'd be proud of him."

"Saving you from a woman is nothing."

"Lilith wasn't a woman. She was an evil spirit."

"So Agon says. If she was so powerful, why didn't she make him die in the lava?"

"Because his magic was stronger then hers."

"Magic is for women."

"He had to leap over boiling lava with me in his arms to save my life."

"He probably liked that."

"What? Leaping over boiling lava?"

"Holding you in his arms."

"He's my father."

Eran stared at her. "Agon's your father?"

"Yes."

"I don't believe it!"

"Didn't you know? Eena knows."

Eran lifted a boulder and hurled it down the escarpment. "Now I will kill him!" He glared at Ara. "You said my mother knows!"

"We talked about it. Agon told her."

"She should have slit his throat."

"No. She knows how it happened."

"How what happened?"

"It's a mystery. I can't tell you."

Eran stepped angrily toward her. "You knew and didn't tell me!"

"I thought you knew."

"You schemed with Agon to keep it from me!"

"No, I didn't. But I'm glad you know. Agon is my father. Don't talk anymore about killing him!"

"I will kill him! I ought to kill him!" Eran's eyes blazed in rage.

She shrank away from him. But then she stood straight before him. "I'm Agon's daughter! Try to kill me!" Her hand held a small flint knife.

Fast as a striking snake Eran seized both her wrists. "Drop it, or I'll crush your bones." He tightened his fingers.

She gasped in pain, but she held on to the knife.

Eran looked into her eyes. "Drop it."

"No."

Slowly he tightened his grip. Ara looked beyond him, her eyes calm.

He looked at her in disbelief. "You'd let me break your wrists before you drop it?"

"Yes."

For a long moment he gazed at her, his fierce eyes burning. Then he loosened his grip on one wrist and took the knife from her numb hand. "You stand pain like a hunter."

"I don't feel pain."

"Everybody feels pain."

"No. Not if I don't want to."

He touched her wrists. "You didn't feel it?"

"I did. But I made it go away."

"You should have dropped the knife." Eran slowly put out one hand and touched her hair. His fingers felt the curve of her neck, then he took his hand away. "I hurt or kill people when Kaan enters my spirit."

She touched his hand. "You wouldn't hurt me."

He looked at her hand. "I liked that, when you touched me."

"I liked it, too."

He looked into her eyes. "When Kaan enters my spirit, don't be afraid. He comes when people make me angry." Eran touched her wrists again. "How did you make the pain go away?"

"Erina taught me."

"Your mother."

"Yes."

"How could your mother teach you to make pain go away?"

"She was priestess to the Mother. They know many things."

"What kind of things?"

"Secret things I can't tell anyone."

Eran circled her waist with a powerful arm. "I could make you tell. I can make people do anything."

"You are strong."

He held her and forced his hand under her garments and against her breasts. She made no movement, no response.

He brought his hand lower. "You will mate with me, now."

"You would not force me."

"Unless you mate with me, I will kill Agon."

Her body stiffened. She said, "Agon will kill you."

"No. I will kill him while he sleeps."

"Alar will kill you if you kill Agon."

"Alar will die, too. I will kill both of them."

"You would kill your father and brother?"

"Agon is not my father. I have waited long to kill him. Alar is not my brother. I have seen him with you, laughing. I hate him."

"If I let you mate with me, will you let them live?"

"If you satisfy me whenever I wish, they will live."

Ara's voice was without emotion. "I will mate with you."

Eran lifted her unresisting body in his arms and carried her to his bed of furs. "Fight with me. I like women who fight."

"I will not fight with you."

"Don't make Kaan come to me."

"Let Kaan come."

He tore at her garments. "You will learn to fear me."

"I will never fear you."

He stared at her. "You will see."

She looked beyond him. "Do what you will with me. The Mother will protect me."

45

The Law of the Tribe

ONE BY ONE, the men who had courted Eena came to Agon and told him of her fidelity. But because Yurok's tribe was away at the summer encampment when Agon returned, three months went by before all of the men talked with Agon. Emar came first, and because his friendship for Agon was so sincere, his account of his desire for Eena and her response so honest, he and Agon parted better friends than ever. Berg came next, fearing that Agon would kill him. Agon listened to his embarrassed confession with cold eyes and then informed him that he would die if he ever again attempted to seduce Eena. Yurok did not come until his tribe had returned to the winter camp in the cliffs along the river valley. The chieftain sent Emar to arrange a meeting with Agon on neutral ground between Bear Hill and the cliff shelters. Yurok asked that Eena, Eran, and Alar also be present.

Yurok did not wear his chieftain's horns and robe, but came dressed in a leather hunting shirt. He carried his huge spear.

Yurok began: "I wanted your sons to hear me. If after I have spoken, any feel they have been wronged, I will give them satisfaction. If they wish to fight with the axe, let them use it against my spear."

"Eena has told me she was faithful to me," Agon replied. "I need to hear nothing more."

"And your sons?" Yurok looked at Eran.

Eran glowered. "You came, unknown to me, to try to mate with my mother when Agon was gone. I need to hear nothing more. If Agon is afraid to fight you, I am not."

Yurok's eyes glowed. "My spear is ready." He looked at Alar. "Will you fight me, too?"

"I'll fight you if my father or my brother don't kill you first. But my mother says she was faithful to my father. I see no need for killing."

"I am told that you stood beside your brother and mother against my tribe."

"Yes."

"How old are you?"

"I have seen thirteen winters."

"And you would fight me."

"Yes."

"What weapon?"

"My axe."

Yurok studied Alar's face. "I think when you are older I would not like to fight you." He spoke to Eena. "If you wish, I will tell Agon and your sons everything that happened between us."

"Only if Agon wishes it."

"What do you say, Agon?"

"I have spoken. I need to hear nothing more."

Yurok said, "Good. But so that none can doubt it, I will say this: I give you my word as a hunter that Eena was faithful to you. I came to her thinking you were dead. She was ready to give her life for her son, but she would not give her honor, If it was the way of my tribe to take mates, I would hope that I could find a woman as faithful as Eena."

Eran hissed, "She should have killed you."

Yurok turned to look at Eran. "I respect you for defending your mother. But know that if you kill again in my tribe without reason, you will die."

"I'll kill anyone who challenges me."

"Challenges, yes. But what starts as a game for others becomes a fight to the death for you. Hear what I say: Kill no more in my tribe without reason, or you die by my spear."

"Your spear! You're too old to lift it."

"Not yet. And I can use the weapon I carry." Yurok glanced at Eran's axe.

"Now I will kill you!" Eran raised his spear.

Agon moved between Yurok and Eran. "Lower your spear."

"You coward! If you won't fight him, I will!"

Agon's eyes became cold as the ice fields of the north. "Lower your spear, or take the axe from your belt and fight me."

"I will fight and kill you with my spear, the spear I went naked into the cold to make. But keep away while I kill this chieftain who tried to steal my mother's honor and insults me."

"Lower your spear, or you will fight me now." Agon's hand touched the handle of his axe.

Eena ran to Agon. "Not the axe! Let Eran live!"

Eran grimaced. "You need not beg for my life. Better you should beg me for his."

Eena turned on him. "You have never seen your father fight. No man can stand against his axe. You would die."

Yurok spoke: "I would not see Agon kill his son because of me." He lowered his spear. "I will not fight Eran now."

"No! Now!" Like a springing lion Eran leaped to one side and threw his spear in the same deadly motion. The spear struck Yurok in the chest and sliced through the hunting shirt, skin, muscle, and bone, deep into the chieftain's body.

Yurok lifted his spear and drew his arm back. Then the spear seemed to be giant, as heavy as a tree, and Yurok slowly let the spear come down until its point touched the ground. He gazed at Eran, then at Agon. "I didn't think he was that quick and strong." His legs gave way, and Yurok fell to the ground like a bull aurochs who has been pierced to death by the hunters' spears.

Agon rammed the point of his spear against Eran's throat. "Don't move." He spoke to Emar. "See if Yurok still lives."

Emar knelt over Yurok. "He's dead." He looked up at Agon. "Eran is your son. If you find it hard to kill him, I will gladly do it for you. Or he can die by the ways of our tribe."

Eena stood motionless with her hands pressed to her mouth.

Agon looked at her before he spoke: "I can do what I have to." He spoke to Eran: "How will you die? By stone or water?" Grae had said those same words to Agon seventeen years ago after Agon had killed Horn.

Eran stared insolently into Agon's eyes. "Use your spear. Since I have none, you need not fear me."

Eena spoke: "The law of Yurok's tribe is different than the bison hunters' law. Let Eran live."

"I live by the law of the bison hunters." Agon tightened his arm and shoulder muscles for the thrust into Eran's throat.

Eena said to Emar, "You are chieftain of the aurochs hunters now. Let my son live."

Emar thrust his spear against Eran's side. "Kill him, Agon, or he will be judged by the law of our tribe."

"Tell me the law of your tribe."

"You saw it with Buner. One who kills another by treachery or without good reason is tied and sewn inside an aurochs hide. The chieftain and the hunters throw spears into the hide until the killer dies. That is the law."

Eena cried, "Must he surely die? Is there no other way?"

Emar looked into Eena's eyes. "The chieftain can give the killer one chance to live. He can try to outrun the hunters. He is given a headstart of half the distance from the cliffs to the hills. If he is caught, he is slowly killed by ways I will not tell you. If he is not caught, he can never return to the tribe. Anyone who sees him can kill him."

Agon said to Eran, "Which do you choose?"

"I run from no man."

"Then you will die in the aurochs hide."

"Never. Kill me now, if you're going to. Or are you such a coward you can't do it?"

"You will die by the law of this tribe."

"No!" Eran spun out and away from the spear points and crouched like a cornered wolf, his teeth bared, his eyes wild. Blood ran from his throat and side.

Agon said, "Everyone back away from him. Emar, go and bring your hunters."

Eena stared after Emar, then at her son. "Go, Eran. Find a home in a new land."

Eran screamed in rage.

"Now," Eena implored, "before the hunters come."

Foam dripped from Eran's mouth. He stared wildly at the faces around him. "Give me a spear!"

"No." Death was in Agon's voice. "You will kill no more."

Then Alar pulled Eran's spear from Yurok's chest. He threw it to Eran. "Go, Eran!"

Eran caught the spear, then like a wounded wolf he raced toward the hills as Emar's hunters ran from the cliffs.

46

One Against the Tribe

ARA CRIED SILENTLY as she lay on her bed of furs. Somewhere in the night Eran ran from the hunters. An outcast, homeless, hunted by every man. The bleak face of Agon and the sorrow of Eena and Alar added to her misery. She knew now that she loved Eran, had loved him since his hand gently touched her wrists. Now he would die. His fierceness, his anger, his love for his mother had made him kill Yurok, chieftain of the aurochs hunters.

The sky outside the entrance of the cave lighted up spasmodically, and the ominous rumble of thunder in the west warned of an approaching storm. Ara slipped from her bed and crept past Eran and Alar's empty piles of furs. Agon and Eena sat on the other side of the banked fire, their heads bowed in grief, and Ara hesitated, studying their still forms.

She moved silently past the fire and out through the entrance onto the porch where Alar stood guard, his dark form lighted by the intermittent flashes of lightning. She walked softly toward him.

He turned, his spear coming up, then recognized her and lowered the spear.

She spoke quietly: "I couldn't sleep."

"No."

"Eran is out there somewhere. A storm comes."

"He knows caves in the hills."

"What if the hunters find him?"

"They won't."

"They might."

"If they do, many of them will die."

"How? He has no weapons."

"He has his spear."

"Your father let him have it?"

"No."

"How, then?"

Alar looked toward the cave entrance. "I gave it to him."

She gazed at him in the glare of the distant lightning. "I'm glad."

"Eran told Yurok he would fight him."

"Then it was fair. Why do they hunt him?"

"Because he killed the chieftain."

"It's not right! They'll kill him!"

"Not Eran. He's stronger than any of them."

"But with all the hunters against him . . ."

"They'll never take him. Eran knows a place in the hills where one man can stand off a whole tribe."

"Do you know this place?"

"Yes."

"Do you think he might go there?"

"If they follow too close."

"But mightn't he go there before they can find him?"

"Maybe."

Ara clasped her hands. "Take me there!"

"Take you there? You might get killed!"

"I don't care. I want to go there. Now."

"No."

"I thought you liked me."

"I do."

Agon spoke from the cave entrance: "No one goes to find Eran."

Ara started like a frightened deer. She gazed toward Agon's dim form. "But they'll kill him. . . ."

"Eran killed Yurok without warning."

"But he told Yurok he would fight him."

"Yurok had lowered his spear."

Ara stared at Alar. "You didn't tell me that!"

Agon advanced to the middle of the porch. "Alar has not pleased me today."

Eena spoke from behind Agon. "Alar wanted to help his brother. I see no wrong in that."

"Tribal law must be obeyed."

"You put the law above the life of our son."

"The sons of chieftains must be ready to die if they harm the tribe."

"It's a cruel law."

"It's an ancient law. No tribe can survive if they disobey the law." Agon spoke to Ara: "Why would you go to find Eran?"

Ara hesitated. "He is like a brother to me."

"You can't help him. Don't leave here."

Eena took Ara in her arms. "Come back inside. A storm approaches."

Ara sobbed against Eena's breast. "They'll kill him. . . . He's all alone. . . ."

Eena held her close. "Eran is strong and fast. The hunters won't follow him beyond the hills. He can go to a new land. . . ."

"Where? Where can he go?"

"To the west. . . ." Eena made her voice strong and confident. "He'll be safe there."

As Eena spoke, a red glare of lightning filled the night sky, and thunder boomed and echoed back from the hills. And in the rumbling echo it seemed to Eena that she heard the hoarse shouts of the chase and the battle cry of fighting men.

Eran turned in the lightning glare and saw the hunters scrambling up the game trail below him. He crouched with his spear in both hands, and as Berg leaped toward him, Eran drove the spear into Berg's chest. Eran yanked the spear out and hurled Berg down upon the hunters, then ran like a cave lion up the slope as thunder crashed and wind and rain struck the hills. In the darkness following the next flash of lightning Eran suddenly turned to his left, ran along the hillside, and dropped to earth. He lay panting until the next flash of lightning, then ran back down the hillside and dropped down again. In the lightning flash he saw the long line of hunters running up the slope, their spears raised. Eran waited until the sound of the running men grew faint above him, then ran through the darkness and the storm toward Bear Hill.

47

Murderer's Hands

THE STORM RAGED half the night, lightning flashing and crackling, thunder crashing, wind and rain roaring. The people at Bear Hill suffered agonies of remorse and grief as they thought of Eran fleeing from the hunters, pictured him wounded and bleeding, imagined they heard his dying screams of defiance.

Eena spoke hopefully from the cave entrance as the storm rumbled on to the east. "The hunters would have come back if they had found him."

Agon sat looking into the fire. "Yes."

"He must have gotten away."

"Yes."

"He hasn't gotten away. They'll kill him," Eena said.

"I can't call the hunters off."

"I know that."

Agon said, "If I go to his secret place in the hills, I might lead the hunters to him."

"You might."

"Then what do you want me to do?"

"Help him."

Agon put his axe in his belt and took his spears from their place against the wall.

Eena came to him. "You'll go to help him?"

"I go."

"I'll come with you."

"No. It is the middle of the night. Stay here with Ara."

"Alar can stay with her."

"No. I go alone."

"I'm coming."

Alar spoke from outside the cave entrance. "Let me go, Father. I know Eran's secret place."

"I know it, too. I showed it to him when he was little."

"Then let me come with you."

"No. I'm going alone."

Eena took her spear from the wall. "I know the place. Go alone if you wish, but I'm going there, too."

Agon shook his head in frustration. "Come with me, then." He spoke to Alar and Ara. "Neither one of you is to leave here. Do you hear me?"

"We hear you."

"Eran might come here. If he does, have him hide deep in the cave."

"Yes, Father."

Agon clasped Alar's hand. "You did right today in giving Eran his spear. We go now. Protect Ara. Help Eran if he comes."

"I will, Father."

Eena embraced Ara, then Alar. "Keep our home safe until we come back."

"We will." Alar smiled at his mother. "I would like to fight at the side of my father and Eran. If I cannot, then they cannot have a better spear fighter than you!"

Eran crouched in the undergrowth at the base of Bear Hill. In the dim light of the cloud-streaked gibbous moon, he saw his mother and Agon descend the escarpment and run at the hunters' traveling pace toward the hills.

Agon should die. Agon had held his spear point against Eran's throat. Agon had refused to give Eran a weapon. Agon had sent Emar for the hunters.

Eran ran silently behind them. The spear would slice in between Agon's shoulder blades. . . .

But his mother loved Agon. . . .

Eran stopped. He watched the two forms as they disappeared in the darkness. He would kill Agon another time.

Eran ran back toward Bear Hill, to the base of the escarpment. He waited, listening for any sound of Emar's hunters, of his mother and Agon returning. He climbed carefully, avoiding the thongs that tripped Agon's alarms. Silhouetted against the firelight, he saw Alar standing guard at the top of the escarpment.

Eran made the sound of the owl, the signal of the family.

Alar stared down at him. "Eran!"

"I'm coming up."

Alar rushed to meet him as he reached the edge of the porch. "You're safe!"

"For now. Get me food and more spears."

"I will! Are you followed? Where are the hunters?"

"Running through the hills like horse-kicked hyenas."

"Father said if you came you should hide far back in the cave."

"I hide from no one. I came for Ara."

"Ara?"

"She's coming with me."

"Where?"

"Wherever I go. Someplace away from here."

"Why? Why take her?"

"She will be my mate."

Alar stared at him. "Your mate? But you can't . . . you're her brother. . . ."

"I'm not her brother."

"You're son of Agon. He's Ara's father."

"I'm not son of Agon. I'm son of Ka."

Ara ran from the cave entrance. "Eran! Come into the cave! The hunters might see you!"

"Bring traveling food while I get more spears."

"I'm going with you!"

"Yes. Quick! Before they come back!"

Alar stepped in front of Eran. "Ara can't go with you. She'll be killed."

"Get out of my way."

"No." Alar grasped Eran's arm.

"Take your hand off me!"

"Ara stays here."

"I'll kill you. Let go!"

Alar tightened his grasp on Eran's arm.

Eran pulled his arm back viciously, but still Alar held his grip. Eran raised his spear in his free hand. "You will die."

"No."

Eran hissed like a snake, and his face became terrible in his wrath. He drew his spear back, then drove it into Alar's throat. He ripped the spear out and drove it in again. "Son of Agon! Die!"

Ara screamed in horror. Alar looked into her eyes as he died. Blood gushed from his throat, from his mouth. But as he sank to the ground, his hand still grasped Eran's arm.

Eran tore Alar's hand away. He seized Ara's arm. "Now! We go!"

Ara stared at him. "You are the son of Ka."

"I told you that."

"I can't go with you."

"You will." Eran seized Ara's arm and dragged her toward the cave mouth. "Fight me and I'll kill you."

"Let her go." Agon's voice came from halfway down the escarpment.

Eran threw Ara back into the porch and rushed to the pile of boulders. He lifted one high above his head to hurl it down the escarpment upon Agon. Then he saw Eena running up the narrow trail behind Agon.

Eran screamed as he held the boulder poised: "Get away from him!"

Eena continued up the escarpment behind Agon. They were coming fast.

"You'll both die! Get away from him! You can come with me and Ara!"

Agon was nearing the top.

Eran shrieked in rage. He dropped the boulder and seized his spear. "I'll kill you, Agon. We're coming down."

Agon and Eena gained the top of the escarpment.

Eran raised his spear for the killing throw. But Ara seized the spear handle in both hands and fell sideways, pulling the spear down as Agon leaped up onto the porch. Agon thrust his spear point against Eran's throat. Then in the firelight he saw Alar's body and blood. Eena saw the body in the same instant.

She ran to Alar and knelt over him, her hands gently touching his face, his hair, his torn throat. She looked up, her face contorted with grief and horror. "Who did this?" Then she saw the bloody spear by Eran's feet, the blood on his hands. "You murderer! Now I know who you are!"

Agon said, "He is our son."

"My son. Not your son."

"Not my son?"

"Look at his axe handle."

Still holding his spear point to Eran's throat, Agon pulled Eran's axe from his belt. He studied the handle in the firelight. "Not an ibex. A great snake."

"Yes. The snake of Ka! He is the son of Ka!"

"Ka?" Agon stared at her. "The priestesses of the Earth Mother washed Ka's seed from you!"

Eena bowed her head. "Ka took me again, after the massacre of your people. Before you found me."

"He is my son!"

Eena's face, her eyes, showed her agony. "He could not learn the axe song. I knew it but could not believe it, because he is my son. But he is the son of Ka, and he has killed Alar."

Agon said to Eran, "If you can sing the axe song with me, you live." Eran laughed wildly. "I am son of Ka!"

Eena's voice held all the sorrow of the world. "Kill him."

Agon held out Eran's axe. "Take it. He dropped it by Eran's feet and stepped back three steps as he slid his own axe from his belt. "Take up your axe."

"My weapon is the spear. I'll kill you as I killed Alar."

"My weapon is the axe. My son's weapon is the axe. Pick it up."

"Give me a spear."

"Will you fight me with your axe?"

"The axe is for women to break wood. Give me my spear."

Agon backed away three more steps, moving toward Eena and Alar's body. He looked down at Alar silently, then lifted Eran's bloody spear from the ground. "Whose son are you?"

"Son of Ka!"

Agon tossed the spear toward the axe that lay beside Eran.

"Son of Ka, take your spear."

Eran seized the spear and came up like a striking snake. In a motion almost too quick to follow he hurled the spear at Agon's chest.

But before the spear left Eran's hand, Agon leaped upon him, and his whirling axe cracked into Eran's spear hand with a sound of breaking bones. Then Agon struck Eran's head twice with the axe, just hard enough to stun him. Agon bore Eran to the ground, held his hands out flat, and with his knife cut off both of Eran's thumbs. Then he castrated him. Agon stood up and threw the bloody thumbs and testicles over the edge of the porch. "Son of Ka, follower of Kaan, killer of your brother, you will never hold a spear again or rape a woman. As you wander the earth, every man's spear will be against you when he sees your murderer's hands. Never come here again."

Agon dragged Eran by his belt to the top of the escarpment and threw him down the slope.

In the darkness Ara crept from the cave entrance and went silently down the escarpment. She carried rabbit-skin bandages, thongs, a bag of traveling food, a small bladder of water, and a spear. She found Eran lying among the rocks, and carefully, gently, she bandaged his wounds and gave him water to drink. Then she led him to the river where a fallen ash tree had floated against the bank. She helped him lie hidden among the branches, then pushed the tree into the current and drew herself up beside Eran. They floated away from Bear Hill, away from the aurochs hunters, away from their family, letting the river carry them westward through the night.

48

Eena

AFTER THEY BURIED Alar, Eena went alone into the depths of the cave at Bear Hill with a pine torch and a small bundle of faggots. She carried in her belt pouch the wrapped object that Agon had brought her from the Earth Mother. In the flickering light she gazed up at the great ceiling of painted animals.

Here she and Agon had come more than seventeen years ago. Here she had come every moon during Agon's absence to pray for his safety. Here Agon had brought her after his return from the bison hunters.

Now Alar was dead. Buried on a lonely hilltop. The only son of Agon, the only son of Agon and herself. The son who had been a joy to them since his birth, who would have been a joy in their middle years, their old age.

And Eran, her firstborn son, was worse than dead. Murderer of his own brother, mutilated, outcast, hated by his family, his tribe. Now dead or wandering homeless, unable to grip a spear or axe, his heart filled with hatred and anger.

Ara, daughter of Agon and a priestess of the Earth Mother, gone in the night. Could she be with Eran?

Agon. The only man she had ever loved, could ever love. Now Agon was without a son, a son to carry the line of Grae into the future.

Eena touched the deer totem at her throat, the totem given by her mother. Now it seemed that her mother called, speaking as softly and clearly in the painted chamber of the animals as on the grassy hilltop far away where her mother had combed Eena's hair in the sunlight. Where her mother's grave now lay.

The torch flame flickered and weakened.

A sign. Death called her.

Eena lighted a new torch from the dying one. Then she walked slowly, dreamily, from the painted chamber. She entered the long passageway that led to the end of the long cave, to the airless tunnel where death waited.

Yeta came to the foot of the escarpment at Bear Hill with a basket of food. She called out, and no one answered from above. She slowly climbed the escarpment. She would leave the food at the cave entrance.

She came onto the porch before the entrance and sensed the emptiness of the cave. She called out again and then turned, looking out over the plain and the river valley, and she saw Agon below her, walking slowly toward the escarpment.

She called to him and waited on the porch as he ascended the escarpment. The lines of sadness on his face made Yeta long to comfort him.

"Where is Eena?" she asked.

"She stands by Alar's grave. I went to walk in the hills where we used to hunt with our sons."

"That's strange. After the burial I went back to my hut to get this food. She was not at the grave when I came back."

"She may have gone into another part of the hills."

"Yes, maybe she has." Yeta opened her basket. "I brought you some smoked aurochs and dried mushrooms. The mushrooms will taste good in Eena's venison-and-onion stew."

"Eena no longer makes stew. Her sadness is so great I think she will die." Agon sniffed the air in the cave entrance. "Pine smoke! Did you take a torch in here?"

"No. I would never enter your home unless someone was here."

As Yeta spoke, Agon ran to the woodpile where the torch faggots lay. "She's in the cave! Half of these are gone!" He gathered up the remaining faggots, rushed to the fire, and held the end of one in the flames until it ignited. "Stay here! I'll find her!" He ran back through the cave entrance and into the dark passageway with the torch flame streaming behind him.

Eena lay in the darkness. Her last torch had burned out as she reached the opening of the tunnel of death, and she had crawled blindly into the tunnel, feeling her way with her hands as she went deeper into the earth. Now she had reached the end of the tunnel. Already she could feel her lungs struggling for air. She held her deer totem in one hand as she waited for death. Weakly, her other hand went to the belt that circled her waist—the belt given her by the Earth Mother. And now she felt the object in her belt pouch, the object sent to her by the Earth Mother.

Agon ran through the cave, the wide passageway, the great hall of the animals, into the winding and narrowing passage that led to the tunnel of death, pausing only to light new torches.

He shouted as he ran, his voice echoing like the cry of spirits of the dead.

Eena felt the movement within her, beneath the magic belt. Now she began to crawl backward in the darkness, back out of the tunnel of death. Faintly she heard Agon's voice. The sound of her breathing roared in her head. Her arms and legs were heavy weights dragging her down, down into the arms of death. She struggled in the darkness, forcing her body back toward the sound of Agon's voice.

They came together in the light of Agon's torch, in the precious air of the open passage. He held her to him, stroking her hair, kissing her eyes, her lips, her throat.

Finally he spoke: "You cannot leave without me."

"No."

"We are mated like the great birds."

"Yes." She took his hand and held it against her body, below the magic belt. "Feel."

"What?"

"Can you feel him?"

He stared at her. "It can't be. . . ."

"It is. I am with child." Her eyes were luminous in the torchlight. "I felt him as I lay in the darkness."

"A child? We are too old!"

"He is a gift from the Earth Mother."

He felt of her body again. "I feel him!"

She placed her hand over his. "He is our son. I know this."

"Our son."

She smiled, her face beautiful.

"His name will be Sagon—Son of Agon."

Together they went through the darkness toward the light of the open sky, toward the plain with its herds of animals, toward the green hills, the winding river valley, and the great river that flowed like their lives: filled with power, with rapids and raging waves and currents at its beginning, now still flowing strongly, but calm and serene as it moved toward the sea.

Part III

The Cave Painter

1

Sagon

SAGON WAS CONCEIVED and born in the great chamber of animals that lay far back in the cave at Bear Hill. There Agon took Eena when he returned from his five-year journey to the tribe of the bison hunters. Under the painted bulls, stallions, and stags, the magic of Axe Man joined the magic of Spear Woman. There, nine months later, Eena came alone and gave birth to Sagon while the pregnant cows, mares, and does watched in the flickering torchlight. There, Sagon's first sight was the great ceiling of animals, and their magic and Sagon's magic were one.

Bear Hill rose almost perpendicularly from the forested slopes that lay beyond the floodplain of the river. From the open porch at the cave mouth, Sagon could see the river winding from east to west between steep cliffs. His parents had told him how, far to the east, lived their people, the tribe of bison hunters. Farther east the river tumbled out of an immense lake high in the snow-covered mountains, and across the plains to the north lay the mysterious Blue Hills. The river flowed to the west into an unknown land. Many winters ago a huge flaming star had floated above this land in the dark blueness of the evening sky. At night when Sagon lay on his bed of ferns and furs, he looked up at the immensity of the sky, a sky filled with the twinkling campfires of the spirits, and he longed to fly like an eagle into the heavens and swoop with great feathered wings down through the ringing silence of the universe.

Ever since their discovery of the cave many winters before, Axe Man and Spear Woman had protected their home by always leaving one person to guard the narrow pathway that led up the escarpment. Here Axe Man and Spear Woman had killed six murderers and rapists who had tried to creep up the escarpment in the night. Here Spear Woman and her two sons, Eran and Alar, had guarded their home while Axe Man was helping Alfgar become chieftain of the tribe of bison hunters. Even now, when all danger seemed past, the path was always guarded, and at night Agon set trip lines to warn of intruders.

When Sagon was one year old, he began to draw with charcoal on the cave walls—drawings of strange, unknown beings. He demanded to be taken into the painted chamber each day, and in the torchlight he held out his arms to the animals in ecstasy. As he grew older, he painted replicas of the animals of the painted chamber, but he was never satisfied with his efforts. Then, when he grew strong enough to accompany his father or mother when they hunted, he began to paint the animals of the plains and forest, using red and yellow ochre and charcoal. His perception and memory of the animals was such that the paintings with which he covered the walls and ceiling of the entry chamber of the cave truly seemed to be ibex, bison, aurochs, deer, mammoth, and bear. Every detail of each animal was portrayed, and Sagon's paintings equaled or surpassed the skill of the ancient ones whose paintings lived in the great hall of the animals. But Sagon was still not satisfied.

"I must show the spirit of each animal," he told his parents. "I must know their magic. I must know the magic of all animals, storms, clouds and sky, of the river, birds and trees, and the moon and stars."

The youthful Sagon, nine winters old, decided to first learn the magic of the cave lions, those huge predators who were the terror of all living creatures. Sagon told his parents one day that he would hunt alone, and he crossed the river at the shallow fjord and went far out across the plain to the water hole where the grazing game came to drink. A long line of ancient cliffs rose beyond the water hole, and in these cliffs lived the cave lions. Sagon climbed into an oak tree between the cliffs and the water hole and waited.

A horse herd approached the water hole, and as the stallion led the mares and colts to the water's edge, Sagon saw two cave lionesses creep from the base of the cliff into the high grass near the water hole.

Sagon lay motionless on the branch of the oak tree and studied the huge lionesses. He noted the muscles rippling under their tawny hides; their fierce, yellow eyes; small, round ears; powerful jaws; and long, sharp fangs. The killing magic of the lionesses emanated from them like light from a fire—magic filled with savage action, tearing claws, ripped flesh, bloody jaws, and quivering death. Sagon was downwind from the lions and horses, and he smelled the rank blood and dead meat odor of the lions, the strong manure and breeding aroma of the horse herd.

The stallion raised his head, his nostrils wide, his powerful neck arched below his stiff mane, his ears and eyes searching. Then he reared, and with his ears laid back, his eyes flaming, his mouth open in dominance, he drove the mares and colts back from the water hole. The stallion's magic came strongly to Sagon, a magic of power and speed and pounding hooves on the plain.

The lionesses burst from the grass, their spread-clawed forefeet reaching toward the horse herd, their hard-muscled hind legs driving their flattened bodies forward in great leaps. The horse herd, driven by the stallion, fled from death as a whirlwind sweeps across the plain before a storm, yet the terrible charge of the lionesses brought them into the flank of the herd, their eyes fastened on a newborn colt racing beside its mother. The leading lioness leaped onto the colt, and it struggled under the claws and weight of the lioness as the other lioness closed in. The young horse died in a tumbling swirl of dust and heaving tawny bodies.

Sagon heard the lionesses tear the flesh from the colt, saw them raise their bloody jaws in ecstasy, watched them drive hyenas and vultures away in short, savage charges.

A huge male cave lion came through the tall grass, snarling his dominance, driving the lionesses back with blows from his great paws. He crouched and tore at the colt's flesh, and his eyes told the females they would die if they came near him.

One of the lionesses stared after the horse herd, then saw Sagon lying on the tree branch. Slowly, she began to stalk him, moving on her stomach through the grass. The other lioness watched, then saw Sagon and crouched low in the grass, creeping toward the oak tree.

Sagon dropped from the branch and ran toward the cliff. As the lionesses charged, he scrambled up the cliff wall, and they leaped at him, grasping at him with bloody claws, snarling in their bloodlust, their curved claws slashing just below his bare feet.

The lionesses dropped back and leaped again, clawing at the cliff face, then one ran up a dry arroyo that led to the cliff top and followed a sloping ledge down toward Sagon. Sagon climbed across the ledge and up, racing with death as the lioness neared.

A small opening in the cliff face appeared above Sagon's fingers, and he pulled himself up and into the hole as the lioness swung her powerful arm at him from the ledge. Her talons raked his leg as he squirmed into a narrow tunnel, and as he crawled forward, he heard her snarling and the scraping of her claws on the tunnel walls as she reached for him with her probing paw. Sagon knew that he lived only because the tunnel was too small to admit the massive shoulders of the lioness.

The tunnel led upward, and Sagon followed it in the darkness. He came to a place where he felt the tunnel walls and ceiling draw back, and he sensed that he was entering a huge chamber. Powerful spirits lived in the chamber, and Sagon felt their cold breaths on his back, their icy eyes staring at him.

A red, flickering light shone ahead of him, and he heard a sighing like the wind in the forest before a storm, and with the sighing was the sound of moving bodies and a whistling like some great bird. He heard rushing water, the crackling of fire, and unknown and terrible beings shuffling in dance. Something whirled wildly as stone cracked on stone, and he heard sounds—half animal, half man.

Then Sagon knew fear as never felt before, and he knew that the death spirit was near. He could not move forward, he could not turn back. His spirit trembled inside him, and his spirit said *death.* But a second, hidden spirit spoke to Sagon: "Learn the magic of all things."

Sagon crept silently toward the sound and the light. He stopped at the edge of the light, and he saw seven creatures dancing in a circle around a fire and a spinning thing, and outside the circle a giant and grotesque bird perched on a slab of rock.

One of the dancing creatures was part owl, bear, wolf, stag, horse, and man. As it danced, the creature went from one wall to another of the chamber, and quick small paintings of bison and deer and ibex appeared on the walls.

Another creature was a slab of stone dancing; another, a red, flickering fire; another, half bison and half man. A hooded figure moved like waves of water, and another dancer held a blazing torch and swung it in sweeping movements from back to front.

The spinning thing in the center of the circle was covered with a white robe that flared out almost flat as the creature turned faster and faster, and the bird creature on the rock held fingers to its long beak and made sounds that were part of the dancing and part birds singing, children laughing, and women crying.

Sagon's heart hammered against his ribs, and his spirit shook with fear, yet as he watched, he felt the dancing creatures draw him toward them as a whirlwind draws fallen leaves into its center. He rose to his feet and slowly approached the wild circle.

Something moved behind him. A paw covered his face, and he struggled briefly. Then all was black, and he knew no more.

Sagon stood on the plain in the sunlight.

Bear Hill rose above the forest, and he walked toward it, watching and waving as his mother and father waved to him from the top of the escarpment. He climbed the escarpment, and they met him as he came onto the porch before the cave mouth.

They saw the back of his leg. Agon said nothing while Eena cleaned the long furrows with fresh water and bound the wound with rabbit skin and a poultice of healing leaves.

When Eena finished, Agon said to Sagon, "You saw things today of which you must not speak." He lighted a torch and took Sagon far back in the cave. With charcoal, Agon made marks on the cave wall in the torchlight:

1.	1. .	1 . . .
11.	11. .	11 . . .
111.	111. .	111 . . .

"These are part of the mystery. These are the male spirits. I learned them from Grae, my father, chieftain and shaman of the bison hunters. Know them now." Agon touched each of the marks in turn and named them:

Fire	Stone	Water
Animal	Sun	Dance
Hunt	Bird	Dream

"They are the Onstean, the Invisible Stone Spirit Men. *On,* invisible. *Ste,* stone. *An,* male. They are all-powerful. Never say the word 'Onstean' to anyone except your father or your sons."

Sagon studied the marks and repeated the names to himself. He said to Agon, "I saw these spirits today."

"In the cliff of the lions."

"Yes."

"The Onstean could have killed you and taken your spirit for seeing them. For a reason I do not know, they let you live."

"Have you seen them?"

"Yes."

"You live."

"I was sent on a mission of death."

"But you lived."

"I was spared by the great spirit of the earth."

"What is the name of this spirit?"

"I may not tell you. For a man to say Her name is to die."

" "Why do you say 'Her'?"

"Because she is the supreme goddess of the women. Ask me no more about her. She is part of a great mystery."

"I feel a great mystery when I paint, but I do not know what it is."

"Once, long ago, your mother and I painted our totems on the wall of a secret cave. When I painted my totem, the ibex, I felt the mystery."

"You know! When I paint, I feel the mystery so strongly that I think I will die!" Sagon stared at his father. "Is this mystery part of the great mystery of the women?"

"I do not know."

"Would my mother tell me?"

"Men must not know the mystery of the women."

"But I must know it. When I paint mares, does, cows, lionesses, I must know their mystery to find their spirit."

Agon shook his head. "You will never learn the mystery of the women. It is enough if you learn the mystery of even one male spirit."

"Then I cannot paint."

Agon studied his son silently, then spoke: "I will tell you of one of the Stone Spirit Men. While I waited for death many years ago in the secret cave of the Onstean, the Invisible Stone Spirit Men danced. One spirit, Animal Man, had the antlers of a stag, the tail of a horse, the eyes of an owl, the body of a bear, and the paws of a wolf.

Animal Man's magic was so strong that his spirit could call the spirits of all animals. While he danced, he painted a bison, a bird, and a falling hunter on the cave wall. They were filled with magic. I can tell you no more."

Sagon listened intently. He said, "I thank you, my father, for telling me of these things. I saw that spirit today, and he did the things you tell of. He, above all others, called to me."

Agon said, "You are old enough now to go through the rites of manhood. Artron, shaman of the aurochs hunters, will guide you. You have learned much today, but you must learn more. It may be that you have in you the spirit of Animal Man. But only the gods can decide whether you are to become a spirit man."

"Who are the gods?"

"The ones who created all things."

"Can we see them as I saw the spirit men?"

"No one can see them. But they are all-powerful."

Sagon said, "How can we live? How can we know what the gods will have us do?"

Agon placed his hand on Sagon's shoulder. "Sometimes our spirits must leave us to know the will of the gods. I can only tell you three things I have learned that may help you."

"What are these, Father?"

"Never act as if you are a god. Fear no man. Protect your family and tribe as the stallion protects the horse herd."

Sagon was not only a painter of animals. He became a hunt leader in Emar's tribe of aurochs hunters. Tall and strong as his father, he was fearless and respected in the hunt and in the rough games of the hunters.

He also became an axe man.

Agon had begun to teach Sagon the mystical axe song after he entered the cave of the lions. The teaching continued until Sagon mastered the little axe song with its short strokes for close fighting, the big axe song with its deadly whirling and strokes, and the song of two axe men. Sagon had learned and loved the axe song from the time Agon gave him his first small axe, and now, after eight years of practice, he knew all that Agon could teach him. Except for one thing: Sagon had never fought and killed a man in battle.

When Sagon was seventeen winters old, he dreamed of strange and horrible beings. In the morning he said to Axe Man and Spear Woman, "I dreamed of the moon. Something evil comes with blood and death. I must find it and kill it."

Eena stared at her son. Spirits of blood and death and the moon belonged to the Onerana, the Invisible Earth Spirit Women.

Agon touched his axe. "Tell us of your dream."

"They came with the rising moon. Blood covered them, yet they came on, like a great snake, bringing death with them."

Eena sensed a cold wind on her back.

Agon touched the ibex at his neck. "Who were these beings that came?"

"They were men, but their heads were huge, as though giant ants ran upright like men. A man bigger than the rest led them. He carried a great spear, and his face was like a hissing snake."

Eena drew in her breath. "Ka!"

Agon's hand closed on the handle of his axe. "Ka is dead."

"Yet he comes again!" Eena grasped the deer totem on her breast with one hand while the other touched the pouch from the Earth Mother that hung from her belt.

Sagon asked, "Who is Ka?"

Eena took Agon's hand. "We must tell him now."

"Yes." Agon's face was grim. "We never told you of Ka."

"Why not?"

"We hoped to keep his evil spirit from our home."

"How was he evil?"

"He murdered your mother's father and brother, and my mother and sister; with his men, half our tribe. I killed him."

"How did you kill him?"

"We fought on a high cliff top. I broke his bones with my axe and threw him from the cliff."

Sagon grasped his own axe. The head of a wolf was carved in the end of the antler handle. "Did you sing the axe song?"

"Yes."

"I am glad you killed him."

"I killed him. But his evil came again." Agon did not look at Eena.

"How could his evil come again?"

Eena said, "He came as my son, Eran."

"Eran?"

Agon placed his hand on Eena's. "When Ka took your mother to his cave, he hurt her and forced her to mate with him."

Sagon felt a terrible rage surging in his spirit as he thought of his mother being taken by the monster in his dream. "Eran was son of Ka?"

"We did not know at first. We thought he was our own son."

"How did you find out he was son of Ka?"

"He killed our true son, Alar. Then we saw Eran's totem. It was the same as Ka's: a snake."

"The son of Ka killed my brother?"

"Yes."

Sagon came to his feet. "He cannot live! Emar's hunters told me Eran drowned in the river! Did you see him die?"

"We did not see him die," Eena replied. "But even if he lived, the spirit of Ka died. Your father killed that spirit."

"You killed Ka's spirit? How?"

Agon's voice was like glacier ice. "I cut off Eran's thumbs and ripped out his testicles."

Now Sagon's voice was like ice. "If you had not, I would find him and do the same."

Eena regarded her son. His long, dark golden hair, his face fierce and hawklike as Agon's, his eyes luminous with intelligence, his body muscular and lithe—he was the son she had dreamed of having. She said, "I would not have you look for Eran."

Sagon replied, "I go to the west to find the meaning of all things. But if I find Eran, I will kill him. If I find the men of Ka, I will return to help you fight them."

Sagon waited to start his journey until the coming of the new moon, a propitious time to begin anything. On the day before his leaving he went to the camp of Emar's aurochs hunters in the cliff shelter by the river.

As Sagon spoke with Emar and told him of his leaving, Artron hobbled toward them. He was so old that his skin was like the wrinkled hide he wore over his shoulders, and his long white hair straggled down from beneath his reindeer antler headpiece like icicles hanging from a cliff edge. He carried a rolled white aurochs hide.

"You go on a journey."

"Yes."

"Beware of the two from one."

"I know of no such thing."

"The stars tell of it. When Axe Man and Spear Woman first came here, many years before you were born, a great star streamed across the sky."

"They have told me of the star."

Artron bent with creaking joints and unrolled the hide. "When I saw the star, I showed it here." He pointed with his staff to a charcoal drawing of the star with a long tail of fire trailing behind it. "I made its tail with many parts, so many that it was like one stream of fire. Look now. How many parts does the tail have?"

"Two."

"It is an omen. Two parts have come from one. For

many years I have tried to understand the meaning of the star. Now you go to the west, where the star filled the sky. You will find its meaning."

"I go for another reason."

"You have had a dream."

"I saw men with great heads coming to kill my father and mother."

"You go for another reason, too."

"I must know all things."

"You go because you will become Animal Man."

"I would bring all animals from the rock, but I could not be Animal Man."

Artron studied Sagon with his ancient eyes. "My spirit will leave soon. Will your spirit go with mine now before I die?"

"I am only a hunter."

"Do you fear what you may learn?"

"I would not offend the gods."

"Nor I."

"Then my spirit will learn from yours."

Artron nodded. "Come. We go to a place of strong magic."

"Learn from him; he has great wisdom." Emar clasped Sagon's arm in farewell. "The aurochs herds are moving to the hills early this year. The tribe will follow them in a few days, and will not return until fall. Go with the gods on your journey."

Artron led Sagon through the forest until they came to a place where three game trails crossed. As they neared the spot, Sagon felt a strange warmth, as though a fire burned beneath the ground. Artron motioned. "Lie on your back here with your heart over the point of crossing."

Sagon lay on the ground. Artron gave him a strange leaf, dried and brown. "Eat this. Sleep as the bear dreams deep beneath the snow. See as the great owl watches in the night. Taste the air as the wolf smells the hidden lion. Dance as the stag prances in rut. Run over the plain as the stallion gallops with his mares. Learn to think and do as the shaman."

Sagon chewed the leaf. It tasted of sunshine and old bones, of spring water and blood. The ground beneath his back grew warmer and warmer, and a soft drowsiness crept over him, a womb-dwelling peacefulness, as his spirit left him.

She curls, sleeping, paws over her face in her den. The trees in the forest above her crack in the cold, and the ice winds of the glaciers sweep down from the north. She feels new life in her as the storms howl through the forest. Searching mouths find her nipples as she senses the snow deepening above, and she lets her life fluid flow into the tiny spirits, waiting for spring.

He sits on a branch in the warm darkness of the summer night while his round eyes and feathered ears search the forest. His taloned feet grasp the oak wood, waiting until they close on warm, fleeing life. He pushes with powerful wings and floats in air, gliding easily, soundlessly, between the dark trees.

The lions are there, hiding in the tall grass. Their smell of bloody jaws comes to him on the light wind. He crouches, and his mate drops into the dry grass beside her. Her red wolf tongue flashes out, and she licks the side of his face in one quick motion. The grass is filled with death, but they must bring food back to the pups.

His antlers swing easily and powerfully atop his head. The smell of does draws him from the protection of the forest into the open glade. Sunshine glows warm on his hide, and he raises his upper lip and draws in the love-laden air. He stamps his hooves on the earth and calls the does, his open mouth raised toward the sky, his forked antlers touching his shoulders. He stamps again, his body strong and filled with desire.

The mares and colts circle as he drives them from the water hole. All morning the young stallion has followed them, calling the mares, making short runs toward them, then wheeling away. He waits until the young stallion runs in again, then he charges, ears laid back, jaws open, eyes white with fury. Rearing, slashing with sharp hooves, whinnying his leadership, fighting for his herd, he drives the young stallion away.

He is bear, owl, wolf, stag, stallion. And man. Animal Man. Shaman. Magician. Leader. Prophet. Healer. Dancer. Painter? He must know. Know life.

Sagon's spirit comes back to him, and he awakens. He is spent, yet strong. Artron smiles at him. "Your spirit has gone far. Now, as Emar said, go with the gods."

Sagon departed Bear Hill with the coming of the new moon. He carried a small leather bag of travel food, fire stones and tinder, a light deerskin robe, two spears, a flint knife, and his axe. He embraced his mother and father, forded the river, and began his journey.

2

Blood of Ka

ERAN, SON OF Ka and Spear Woman, lived for one thing only: revenge on Agon, called Axe Man. Eran had been as powerful as Ka, as fierce as Ka. But Axe Man, son of Grae, mutilated Eran and threw his bloody body down the escarpment at Bear Hill. Now Eran could not hold a spear. Now Eran had no desire for women. Now Eran had lost his strength. Eran held such hatred in his heart that he was like a huge spider waiting to strike.

Ara, Eran's mate, daughter of Agon and Erina, priestess

of the Earth Mother, knew of Eran's hatred, and she sorrowed that Eran wished to kill her father.

She thought of the first time she saw Eran, standing guard at Bear Hill as Agon brought her from the tribe of the bison hunters.

Eran had been beautiful in his strength and young manhood, hard muscled as a lion, noble in bearing as the line of chieftains from whom he was descended. She fell in love with Eran, and he took her in all the passion of their beings. Then came the terrible night when Eran murdered Alar, his only brother.

She had come secretly down the escarpment in the night with water, dried food, and soft skins. She found Eran huddled in agony, bleeding to death at the base of Bear Hill. She knelt and spoke softly to him: "Let me wrap your wounds."

His voice was weak. "Kill Agon."

"I carry your son."

"My son . . ."

"Yes. But Yurok's hunters search for you. A tree has washed against the shore. We will float away and be gone before morning light. We will go to a new land." She held a rabbit bladder of water to his lips. "Drink. I will stop your bleeding."

He drank, and she bandaged his thumbless hands with soft skins. In the dim light of the stars she gently explored the blood-sticky area of his male parts. Agon had butchered Eran as a hunter does a bison, slitting the scrotum and severing the cords of the testicles as he ripped them from their sack. She held a rabbit skin against the bleeding scrotum and wrapped long strips of hide around Eran's hips and between his legs, holding the rabbit skin tightly against the wound.

She had given Eran a handful of traveling food—a mixture of dried meat, fat, and berries. "Eat this for strength. Then drink again, and we will go to the tree." He ate and drank. Then slowly, agonizingly, she helped him stand. He made no sound except the sucking in of air. With Ara supporting him, they crept to the riverbank.

The floating tree had lain motionless against the shore. She led Eran into the shallow water and helped him climb painfully into the branches. Then she pushed the tree away from the land and out into the swift current. She climbed into the branches and held Eran all that night as the tree carried them silently away from Bear Hill and the men who searched for Eran.

When daylight came, Ara had tightened the bandages on Eran's wounds and given him more of the strengthening travel food. They hid in the sheltering branches and leaves of the tree, and for three days and nights the river carried them to the west between cliffs, forests, and plains. Then the river turned to the south in a great curve. Strange animals galloped heavily on the plain: huge creatures with horned noses and sides like gray slabs of rock, and great antelope with long horns that curved up and back over their massive shoulders.

Eran had grown stronger each day, and when Ara changed his bandages, she saw that his wounds were slowly healing, but she also saw how terrible was his mutilation. His thumbless hands were long, helpless paws, and his scrotum was shriveled and empty below his limp penis. Eran's spirit and body had changed, too. The fierce look was gone from his face and eyes, and his body seemed softer, rounder, almost like a woman's.

When the tree had finally washed ashore in a place far from Bear Hill, Ara led Eran up a tributary of the river and made a home for them in a cave under an overhanging cliff. She gathered nuts and berries, dug tubers from the marshes, found nests of birds' eggs, and learned to trap and hunt small animals for their food as Eran's wounds healed. Knowing that she would soon bear a child, she dried food for the time when she could not hunt, and she prepared for winter by making garments of fur and hides for the child and for Eran and herself.

Nine moons from the time that she had mated with Eran,

Ara gave birth to a boy. The birth was difficult because of the child's size and strength. His eyes shone dark and fierce beneath a mane of black hair, and his bellows of hunger and rage were deep and strong as a young bull.

Ara had shown him proudly to Eran. "He will be a great hunter."

Eran held the kicking, struggling boy with his mutilated hands. "He is fierce and strong. He will do more than hunt. He will be a chieftain of men and a great warrior. A warrior as fierce and strong as Ka, his grandfather."

"Not like Ka. Let him be brave, but not cruel."

"Yes, like Ka! No man will stand against him!"

Ara bowed her head. "I will pray to the gods that he is not cruel."

"The boy must become the best spear fighter of all men. See that you teach him well."

"You can help teach him."

Eran grimaced. "With these hands that cannot hold even a stick? With these arms that have lost their strength?"

"You can tell him how to make a spear, how to throw the spear." Ara smiled at him. "You can teach him how to track game, stalk as the great cats do, find the life spirit of each animal so that the spear may kill it with the first throw."

"And kill men. His name will be Kane. He will slay men as a cave lion slays deer."

"I hope he will never have to kill men. Our people have seen too much killing. I will ask the gods to give him no cause to kill."

Eran raised Kane high in the air. "Enough of your asking the gods! Do not try to make Kane weak! He must become a mighty warrior! He will go to kill Agon!"

For seventeen years Eran waited, waited until his son was fully grown. Kane, now powerful as two men, muscled and sinuous as a great serpent, was the reincarnation of Ka, his bloodthirsty grandfather, who led his tribe of killers from the south to massacre Grae's tribe of bison hunters. For seventeen years Eran instilled hatred of Agon into Kane. Now they plotted to kill Agon.

"You must have many fighting men," Eran said. "Agon lives with the aurochs hunters. He will have the whole tribe to help him."

"I will get fighting men."

"How?"

Kane showed his teeth. "I will kill Barhunder, chieftain of the horse hunters. His men will follow me."

"Barhunder is a mighty warrior."

"My spear will rip out his guts."

Eran nodded. "I have seen you fight. You will kill Barhunder. But Agon is not so easy to kill. He has strong magic and has killed many men."

"I should fear an old man?"

"Agon is an axe fighter."

Kane laughed. "I fear no man."

"He killed Ka with his axe. He struck me down before he mutilated me."

Kane spat. "My spear will rip him open before he can lift his axe."

Ara heard them plotting, and when she was alone with her son, she pleaded with him to spare Agon.

"Agon is my father. Now he is old. There would be no honor in killing him when he can no longer fight."

"He deserves to die."

"Agon could have killed your father, but he spared him because your father was son of Eena."

Kane scowled. "It would have been kinder if he had killed my father. Cutting off a man's thumbs so he can no longer fight or hunt is worse than death. Cutting his manhood away kills his spirit."

"Agon lived by the laws of his tribe. Your father killed his own brother without reason."

"Alar was not my father's brother. Alar was son of Agon and Eena. My father is son of Ka."

"And Eena. Ka killed her father and brother and took her against her will."

"Ka was a great chieftain. He would have made Eena high priestess of his tribe."

"She loved Agon. Not Ka."

"Father told me. She was Ka's mate, but Agon killed Ka and took her."

Ara's face became sad. "You have listened to your father too much. He was told lies by an evil woman of the aurochs hunters when he was a boy. Now you believe these lies and will do evil things. Forget about killing Agon. Find a mate and make your own tribe here. Be a great chieftain for your people."

"I will be a great chieftain after I kill Agon."

"Your father has poisoned your spirit with his hatred. You have the blood of my people, of Agon and Eena, and of Agon's father, the great chieftain, Grae. Have you no feeling of their greatness? They fought only to save their tribe against Ka, a man of evil."

Kane's face grew dark with anger. "I have the blood of Ka, the chieftain of the great tribe of the south. Do not talk to me of Grae and his people. Grae was a weak chieftain who fell upon his own spear when he failed to protect his tribe. I have none of his blood, only the blood of Ka!"

Barhunder, chieftain of the horse hunters, watched with angry eyes as Lazor brought his hunters back to the cliff shelter.

"Again you return with no meat and carrying a body!"

"He killed Radun."

"And none of you saw it happen?"

"Radun was last in circling the horse herd."

"As before."

"He watches us, kills the last man, and is gone."

"I told you to track him and kill him."

"He leaves no tracks."

Barhunder scowled. "Every living thing leaves tracks."

Lazor looked uneasily over his shoulder. "See Radun's wound. The same as Hodren's."

Barhunder examined the bloody corpse the hunters laid before him. A spear thrust had been made with such force that Radun's body had been torn open as by the claws of a cave bear. Yesterday the hunters had returned with the body of Hodren, torn by the same powerful spear thrust. Barhunder stood up. "We will kill the man who did this."

"How? He kills our men before they can raise their spears."

"Can a single hunter kill a cave bear? We will kill this man as we kill a bear."

Lazor touched his stag totem. "He comes unseen, he leaves no tracks. He is an evil spirit."

Barhunder grasped his huge spear. "He is no evil spirit! Tomorrow we will find him, and I will gut him as he has gutted our men!"

"How will we find him?"

"As we find a cave bear! We set a trap!"

"A tree trap? We set bait out and kill him with a falling tree?"

"We will set bait out, but we will not kill him with a falling tree. Listen."

That night Barhunder sent ten of his best spearmen to the low hills where the horse herds roamed. The men formed a large circle near a sleeping herd, each man a spear-throw apart, then hid themselves in the high grass.

In the morning Barhunder and Lazor led ten more men into the hills. When they sighted the horse herd, they began to close around it, the men following Lazor in a long, circling line through the hills. The last man in the line was Barhunder, the chieftain, mightiest spearman of all the people.

Lazor led the line of hunters through the place of the hidden men, and as Barhunder entered the circle, the line spread out so that Barhunder appeared to be alone in the hills. Barhunder walked slowly, carelessly, looking neither to the right nor left.

A giant of a man rose out of the grass in front of Barhunder. His face was almost beautiful in its fierce awfulness, his body rippled with muscles, and he held his spear low in both hands, point forward. His eyes burned with a look of insane hatred.

"Ten of my men surround you," Barhunder said. "Put down your spear, and I may let you live."

The man spoke, his deep voice filled with menance and power. "Your men are dead. Chieftain of the horse hunters, you have come to me."

Barhunder had killed more men than he could remember, and he was taller and heavier than the man who had risen from the grass. Barhunder shouted in triumph as he ran forward with his spear raised. The man moved like a striking serpent, a serpent of such quickness and terrible strength that his spear pierced Barhunder and ripped open his body from crotch to throat, spilling out his intestines and stomach like a butchered horse before Barhunder could make the first thrust of his spear.

When Barhunder's hunters, hearing his shout, ran back into the circle of dead men, they stopped in terror at what they saw.

The man spoke to them: "I am Kane. Your chieftain. If you obey me, you will become the most powerful tribe in this land. If any man will not obey me, he will die. Who will die? Come forward. I will fight all of you at once or one at a time."

None of the men came forward.

In this way, Kane became chieftain of the horse hunters.

3

Elina

SAGON FOLLOWED THE river to the west for two moons, and he saw the dim peaks of a mountain range to the southwest. The river turned south, and he followed a tributary of the river that flowed in from the west, entering a deep river gorge with high white cliffs on either side and a stone arch that bridged the river.

During his journey he saw no other people, but as he explored the gorge, he felt the eyes of someone watching him.

Sagon made no sign that he sensed the watcher, but continued along the gorge, his two spears laid casually across his shoulder, his hand not touching his axe. The cliff's chalky walls held crevices, overhangs, terraces, clumps of brush, shrub-filled fractures, and cavelike openings, while the floodplain of the river was heavily wooded with junipers and evergreen oaks. The watcher could be hiding in any of these places.

When the sun was directly overhead, Sagon entered an oak grove and disappeared.

When the sun was halfway down the sky, Sagon came silently behind the watcher who lay on a terrace near the cliff top. The watcher was a girl, lying on her stomach, studying the river valley. She wore a short deerskin tunic and light sandals. Her hair, dark red and curly, was cut just above her shoulders. Sagon thought at first that the watcher was a boy until he saw the shoulder straps of her tunic. A small spear lay by her side, and a flint knife was in her belt.

She spoke without turning her head: "Three men are following you."

"Yes."

She whirled on the ground and came up in one motion, her spear ready, facing him. He thought, My mother must have looked like this when she was a girl. She said, "Why didn't you keep on through the valley? Now they will track you up here."

"I felt you watching me."

"Why did you come behind me?"

"I would rather watch the watcher than have the watcher watching me. I travel to another place. If this is your hunting ground, I will leave without taking your game."

"You have brought those men here. Go now."

"They will not track me. But they will feel your eyes. Then they will find you."

"They will not find me."

"I found you."

"I let you."

"Why?"

"Because you are a shaman."

"I am not a shaman."

"You don't know it yet."

Her eyes had little sparkles of gold in the dark blue centers. She said, "Put your spear down."

"And let you kill me?"

She glared at him. "I can kill you whether you let me or not."

"You are like a she-wolf. I mean no harm to you or your people."

"Go on your way."

"I must go by you. Will you kill me?"

"No."

Sagon studied the river valley. "They will come below us before sunset."

"We will kill them."

"Why?"

"They will try to kill us. I feel it."

Sagon smiled at the girl. "You are fierce."

"I have to be."

"Why?"

"I don't want to be raped."

"You have been raped?"

"I will kill any man who tries."

"Of course."

She pointed at Sagon's axe. "What is that?"

"My axe."

"Why does it have a wolf on the handle?"

"The wolf is my totem." Sagon lifted the carved wolf head that hung on his chest. "This, too."

"My father had a bear totem."

"Bears have strong magic." Sagon glanced at the valley again. "The men search like hyenas. Will they find your camp?"

"No."

The men were steadily coming closer. Sagon said quietly to the girl, "Don't look at them. I felt your eyes."

They lay flat on the terrace, listening. Sagon heard their breathing, their feet swishing through the long grass. He felt their coming like the approach of bad spirits.

Now the men were directly below them. One of them grunted, and the sound of their feet ceased. The man grunted again, and the sound of their walking came and then slowly faded away. The feeling of bad spirits gradually lessened, but still remained in the river valley like a faint odor of rotting meat. Sagon carefully raised his head and peered over the edge of the terrace. The three men were almost out of sight.

He said, "You can look now."

The girl raised her head and gazed down the valley through her fingers. "They look for you."

"Yes."

"Why?"

"I don't know."

She took her hand from her eyes. "What is your mother's name?"

"Eena. She looks like you, but her hair is the color of the sun."

"She must have strong magic."

"Yes."

"Does she have another name?"

"Spear Woman."

The girl's eyes changed, a look of recognition coming into them. "What is your father called?"

"Agon. Axe Man."

"My mother told me of Axe Man and Spear Woman. They killed Ka."

Sagon stared at her. "What was your mother's name?"

"Erila."

Erida, Agon's mother. Erina, Ara's mother. Eena, his own mother. Priestesses of the Earth Mother. Sagon sensed a mystery of women, of the moon, of the earth. A name: Onerana. The Invisible Earth Spirit Women. A name that no man could speak without fear of death.

He asked the girl, "What is your name?"

"Elina."

Her mother knew of Axe Man and Spear Woman. The girl's name came from the Earth Mother. Sagon looked into her eyes. They were filled with mystery.

She asked, "What is your name?"

"Sagon, son of Agon."

She looked curiously at him. "Why do you say you are not a shaman?"

"A shaman speaks with the spirits. He can fly through air or rock. He can drive bad spirits away, but he must die to do it."

"Really die?"

"He dies for a while. Then his spirit comes back to him."

"Is that why you say you are not a shaman? You are afraid?"

"I say it because I am not a shaman."

"Maybe. You have strong magic. I feel it. Animals come to you."

"I try to find the magic of animals in certain caves. I help the animals come from the rock."

"My father did that. With bears."

"I would like to see him do that."

"You can't. He died."

"Where did he bring the bear spirits?"

"Inside the cliff."

"I feel the spirits. All the spirits of the animals."

"You will help them come from the rock."

"If the bear spirits wish it."

"Bears lived there once."

"Not now?"

"Rocks fell from the cliff. The bears are too big to come under the rocks." She motioned with her spear. "Come with me. Let the bear spirits know you."

Elina led Sagon down the cliff and across the scree and slabs of fallen rock at the base of the cliff. She went flat on her stomach and crawled into the pile of slabs, and Sagon followed, squeezing through a labyrinth passage that led under and around slabs, down through crevices, deep into the debris until the daylight was almost gone. Elina stopped at a dark hole in the solid rock of the cliff face. She knelt, took two stones from her belt pouch, struck the stones together, and ignited a small handful of tinder and twigs. She pulled pine faggots from a niche and lit one. "Leave your weapons here."

"I do not leave my weapons."

She held the torch up and looked at his face. "The spirits are powerful."

"Even so."

"Then follow me."

They went through the entrance. In the torchlight an immense chamber opened before them, a chamber whose walls sparkled white like sunshine on snow, a chamber with great columns of white stone, a chamber whose ceiling sparkled like the stars.

Sagon's spirit trembled. He touched his totem, and the wolf was quivering. Then Sagon sensed animals swirling around him: bears, horses, rhinoceroses, aurochs, deer, lions, hyenas, leopards, mammoths. A round-eyed owl circled him, and a creature, half bison, half man, pranced deep in the rock in the smoky light of a magic fire. Then, as he stumbled toward the entrance, the spirits of the animals swirled closer around him, and Sagon's spirit cried out in terror and fled from him as a torn fragment of storm cloud races across the face of the moon and disappears in the night sky.

Sagon awoke in the dim light under the huge blocks of stone that hid the cave entrance. Elina sat watching him.

She said, "You died. Now your spirit has come back. You are a shaman."

He spoke weakly. "The spirits of the animals took my spirit from me."

"Yes."

"The cave goes far back into the earth. All the animals on the walls came and circled around me."

"There are only two bears on the walls. My father brought their spirits here."

"The walls are filled with animal spirits."

"The spirits of the animals wait to be called."

"I saw them."

"My father saw them. But they do not yet live. You must bring them from the walls so that they will live forever."

"I cannot bring them."

"You can. You have brought the animal spirits to the cave of your people. I knew it when I saw you."

"I am a stranger here, far from my people. My magic is weak here."

"What will make your magic strong?"

"The gods."

"What gods?"

"I must not name them."

"My mother told me of secret things."

"The women of her tribe have many secrets. So do the men."

"I have no tribe. We lived here by ourselves."

"My mother, Spear Woman, lived alone with her family. But each year they would come to the hunt festival of her tribe."

"My mother told me of a tribe, far to the east, the tribe of Grae."

"My grandfather's tribe."

"You should be chieftain."

"My father left the tribe. His brother is chieftain."

"My mother and father said they would take me there. They died before we could go."

"How did they die?"

"A cave lion came. It tried to crawl through the rocks. My father and mother fought it and died."

"They were brave."

"Yes. They killed the lion." She pointed. "Its bones are still there. Other lions see the bones and keep away."

She led Sagon to the opposite edge of the great pile of rock slabs. The white bones of a huge cave lion lay near a crevice in the rock pile. Sagon examined the spearlike teeth, the curved talons. "They are the fiercest of all the animals. But the great bears are stronger."

Elina nodded agreement. "There are bones of bear in the cave. They made nests in the dirt and marked the walls with their claws."

Sagon gazed at the cliff. "Someday the bears will come into the cave again."

"How can they do that? They are so big the rocks block the entrance from them."

"Something will take the rocks away."

"You are a shaman. Only a shaman can see what will

happen. If you come into the cave again, your magic will become strong."

"I almost died in the cave."

"Because you are a shaman. Shamans do not carry weapons when they speak with the spirits."

Sagon shook his head. "I will leave my spears, not my axe. An axe man never lets his axe leave his belt or hand unless he throws the axe in battle or in the axe song with another axe man."

"What is the axe song?"

"A magic song. The spirits of the axes and the men sing together."

"Have you ever killed an animal with your axe?"

"No. It is not for killing animals."

"Then leave your spears outside the cave. Bring your axe but do not touch it."

"How do you know these things?"

"The animal spirits talk to me."

"Do you see them?"

"I feel them."

"Yes. I can see that."

"How?"

"Your face. Your eyes."

Elina turned her face away. "Don't look at me."

"Why not?"

"It makes me feel . . ." She stopped.

Sagon said, "I won't look at you."

She pointed to the cave entrance. "I want to show you the bears."

Sagon shook his head. "I cannot go in there again. I have to leave."

"Why?"

"I go on a journey."

"What for?"

"I cannot tell you."

Elina stared at the ground. "You seek a mate."

He asked her, "How many winters have you seen?"

She held up the fingers and thumbs of both hands, then four fingers.

"Have you been through the women's rites?"

Elina shook her head, still looking down.

"When I return, I will take you back to my home at Bear Hill. My mother will take you to the women of the tribe of Emar. There you can learn the things that you must know; you can go through the rites."

She raised her head, her eyes alarmed. "The men are coming back!"

"Which way?"

"Along the cliff top. They have seen us."

Sagon gathered up his spears and loosened the axe in his belt. "Go into the cave. Hide in the darkness."

"Come with me."

"No."

"You cannot fight three men."

"Neither can the two of us."

"Better than you alone."

Sagon peered into the jumble of rock slabs. "They will follow us under the rocks. Can you find your way back into the cave without a torch?"

"Partway."

"Good. Quick. Take all your faggots in. I will follow you."

They dived back into the slab pile, and Sagon followed Elina through the maze to the cave entrance. They carried the faggots in and stopped in the dim light. Sagon said, "Go in. I will stay here."

"I will stay with you."

"No. Go. Now!"

She ran into the darkness. Sagon slipped behind a pillar of rock a spear-length from the entrance, the animal spirits of the cave swirling behind him but not upon him as they had before. He held a spear in each hand, waiting.

The men came to the rockfall. Sagon could smell them,

hear their breathing, sense their evil. Now they came crawling into the pile, grunting, whispering, sniffing, ominous as hyenas. They stopped, came forward, circled, then spread out. Sagon waited.

One of the men gibbered triumphantly, and they converged on the entrance.

They stopped. Sagon sensed that they were peering into the cave. One of the men grunted, and Sagon heard the sound of a man leaving the rock pile. The man came back, and Sagon heard dry branches being dragged through the rocks. The sound of stones striking together came, then the smell of smoke, and a burning branch was thrown in through the entrance. It lay on the stone floor, its flames reflected from the white walls and ceiling. Now the men came through the entrance, hulking figures crouched with spears ready, their bestial faces speaking of rape and murder.

Something roared from the darkness behind Sagon, the fearsome growl of a cave bear. The men stopped, staring toward the sound.

Sagon stepped from behind the pillar and threw his first spear into the lead man's thick chest, his second spear into the throat of the next man as the man hurled his spear. Even as he threw the second spear, Sagon slipped the axe from his belt and threw it at the forehead of the last man as the man's spear flew toward him. Sagon leaped to the side, and the two spears hissed by him as the blade of his axe split the man's skull cleanly between the eyes.

Elina ran into the firelight with her spear raised. She gazed at the three bodies on the floor. "I wanted to kill one of them."

Sagon wiped the blood from his axe on the fur loin cover of the last man, then he pulled his spears from the other men and wiped the blood from their flint points. He smiled at Elina. "Your totem will be the cave bear."

Elina's voice was hushed. "I was going to make the bear sound . . . but it came from the back of the cave. . . ."

"From the back of the cave? You did not make the sound of the bear?"

"No."

"But there are no live bears in the cave. . . ."

"No." Elina's eyes held a look of wonder. "The bear spirit made the sound."

They dragged the bodies of the three men out of the cave and hauled them through the rock pile to the scree at the cliff base. They covered the bodies with scree and dirt and wiped the streaks of blood from the rocks with wet leaves. The pools of blood on the cave floor they left as an offering to the animal spirits.

Sagon said to Elina, "You were ready to fight alongside me. You have no tribe or clan. Will you come back with me to Bear Hill and become part of our family?"

Elina shook her head. "I belong here."

"If you were older, I would ask you to be my mate."

"I am not older."

"No."

"You seek a woman with strong magic."

"Yes."

"Go, then."

Sagon held up a piece of charcoal from the burning branch the three men had thrown into the cave. "If the animal spirits will let me, I want to go back into the cave with you. I want to touch this to the wall in the deepest part of the cave."

"Will you bring the animal spirits from the stone?"

"I don't know."

"I know. They wait for you."

"Will you take me into the cave?"

She looked up at him. "I will take you."

Sagon left his spears just inside the cave entrance and followed Elina around the pools of blood on the floor. She raised her torch, and to their left the white walls of a huge chamber gleamed like snow. Elina led him to their right through a narrow gallery and stopped in front of a white wall. She held the torch up before the wall, and the flame illuminated a large red cave bear with bulging brow and powerful neck and shoulders.

"My father brought the bear's spirit from the rock."

Sagon's spirit quivered in such excitement that he could not speak.

Elina asked, "Will you touch your charcoal to the wall?"

"No. I cannot." His voice was weak.

"You will not die again."

"It is not that."

"What, then?"

"I cannot make the smallest mark on these walls."

"You have the power to bring all the animal spirits from the rock."

"No."

"Why not?"

"I have not lived enough."

She regarded his face in the flickering torchlight. "What is to live enough?"

"To be one with the spirits of all things."

"No man can be that."

"No."

"You try to do too much."

"What would you have me do?"

"Make something beautiful."

"Just that?"

"Yes."

Sagon sensed the wolf totem on his chest vibrating. The lump of charcoal in his fingers grew warm as if it glowed within. He raised the charcoal toward the smooth stone of the wall, then he drew his hand back. "I cannot do it here. This is the spirit place of your father."

"There are other places."

"Show me."

She led him back into the first chamber, then to the left

into a huge second chamber, through that deep into the earth, past rockfalls, great rows of hanging stalactites, walls grooved by ancient bear claws. They came to a great wall beyond which a narrow passage led to the right and a wider passage to the left.

Sagon could not move past the wall. He stood motionless in front of it, staring at the smooth rock.

Elina held the torch high in front of the wall.

A stallion's high challenging cry sounded, and a mare answered, then another, and another, and Sagon's spirit cried with the horses, cried in the strength of the rearing stallion with wild eyes and flying mane, cried in the longing whinnying of the mares, cried in the pounding hooves of the horse herd as it galloped across the plain in the wild free exaltation of strength and speed and joy.

Sagon's hand brought the charcoal to the wall, and the head and neck of the stallion came from the rock, the neck arched in power and desire under the rising mane, ears laid back in domination, eyes hot and fierce, nostrils flaring, mouth with the extended lip of mating.

Elina cried out in wonder, and Sagon's spirit rose like the stallion and carried Sagon up through the rock and the cliff and burst into the high blue air of the sky and flew toward the sun as a meteor flashes through the firmament. Then he knew no more.

He awoke in absolute darkness. He lay on stone. He reached out, and his fingers brushed a stone wall. Above him, he sensed the horse herd, and he remembered. The stallion had come.

He lay in the darkness, and he felt no fear. He said to the stallion, "The mares will come to you."

A light shone in the distance like the reflection of a star on still water, moving gently up and down, from side to side. The star grew brighter, larger, came toward him. Elina spoke from the light. "You live."

"Yes."

"I had to go back for more torches."

"Yes."

"Can you walk?"

He rose slowly to an upright position. "I think so."

She came near him, and the fragrance of her body was like wildflowers and musk. She held the torch in front of the wall. "The stallion waits for the mares."

"Yes."

"Will you bring them?"

"I cannot."

"You can."

"I would die if I tried. A woman should bring the mares."

"There is no woman here."

"You are a woman."

"I am a girl. You told me. I have not been through the rites."

In the torchlight she was beautiful. He saw that she would become more beautiful as she grew older, like his mother. He said, "You can bring the spirits of the animals from the walls. Bring the mares to the stallion."

"I cannot do that."

Sagon took an unsteady step and leaned against the wall. "When I have found what I seek, I will come back here. We will bring all the animals from the walls."

"You will come back with a mate. You and I will do nothing together."

Sagon staggered toward the distant entrance of the cave. "Bring your torch. I will kill a deer for you before I leave."

"I can kill my own deer."

"I know you can."

"And if you do come back, you will not find me."

"I will find you."

4

The Marsh People

SAGON TRAVELED DOWN the main river valley for half a day, entered a grove of oak trees, settled himself comfortably on a lateral branch two spear-lengths above the ground, and waited.

Elina circled the grove unseen and came behind Sagon. Without turning, he said, "I could have pounced on you like a fox on a rabbit."

"And I could have speared you like a gamecock."

"Go home."

"I'm coming with you." She carried her spear, a light traveling robe, and a small leather bag.

He came down from the tree and took a rawhide thong from around his waist. "You can chew through this in about a day." He threw one end of the thong over a low branch. "Hold out your hands."

"Try to touch me, and I will chew through more than that."

"I don't want some girl-child following me."

"You need me."

"Why?"

"To show you the way."

"Show me the way to what?"

"What you are looking for."

"And what is that?"

"You want to find your enemy."

"I never told you that."

"You didn't have to tell me. I saw it in a dream."

"You saw me in your dream?"

"Yes."

"And you will protect me."

"Yes."

"How?"

"I can tell when enemies are near." Her face held a stubborn-little-girl expression, but in her eyes he saw wisdom and understanding.

He said, "I go alone."

"I will follow you."

"Even if I tie you to this tree?"

"You won't do that. Something could come and eat me."

"Nothing would dare eat you."

"When you sleep at night, I can keep watch. I can fight as well as a man. And something else . . ."

"What?"

"You are a shaman. Shamans need someone to take care of them. When your spirit leaves you, you are helpless as a baby."

"I am not a shaman. And I don't need you to take care of me. I will probably have to take care of you."

"You said 'will.' "

"Because you are like a horsefly buzzing around me. There is no way to get rid of you."

"You will be glad I came."

He snorted. "If you can't keep up with me, I will leave you behind."

"Try. I can run all day and all night."

Sagon shouldered his spears. "Come on, then."

She smiled and held out a small leather bag. "I brought traveling food for us."

"You knew I would let you come."

"Of course."

"I feel sorry for whatever man ever takes you as a mate."

"I want no man."

"Good."

"Men think they always have to be the chieftain."

"Of course."

"No man will be chieftain to me."

"I am chieftain now. If I say 'run,' you will run. If I say 'hide,' you will hide."

"Maybe."

"Something else. You will call me Wolf. And you will be my sister."

"I understand your name. Why will I be your sister?"

"In all tribes a man can protect his sister."

"I can protect myself."

"With four men holding your arms and legs while another rapes you?"

She shuddered. "I will be your sister. What will my name be?"

"Did the people in your dream know you?"

"I had never seen them before."

"Then you can still be Elina."

They followed the river valley on to the south, and after two days they came to a delta where the river formed branches like a mammoth tree, and they saw in the distance a great plain of blue water. Sagon gazed at the water in amazement.

"It covers the earth!"

Elina nodded. "My father told me of it. The water god lives there. He makes the water crash against the shore, and he sucks everything back into his mouth."

"Our people do not know of this god. We know only of a river god. But my father found a huge lake in the mountains that feeds the river. Maybe this is like the lake."

"My father said that this water is so bitter that those who drink it thirst and die."

Sagon knelt on the riverbank and tasted the water. "This is not bitter. We will follow the river until we come to this lake."

They walked cautiously along what appeared to be the main branch of the river. Reeds and rushes grew in profusion along the riverbank, and the ground became soft and muddy. Elina removed her small sandals and placed them and her spear on a grassy hummock along with her robe and bag of traveling food. She ran into the soft mud at the river's edge and squished her toes in the mud. She giggled in delight and ran back and forth, splashing mud and water. "This feels so good! You do it."

"Men do not play like children."

"They should."

"Why?"

"So they do not forget."

"Forget what?"

"The spirits that made them." She kicked mud at him, splattering him with black goo.

Sagon laid his spears and robe on the hummock and ran at her, but she danced away from him, then ran like a wolf pup in small circles around him, laughing. He plunged after her through the mud and seized her around the waist, lifting her. He held her while she kicked at him with her muddy feet, laughing as she smeared him. He said, "Stop that or I will drop you facedown and step on you."

"Do that. I like mud."

"I ought to throw you in the river."

"I like to swim."

He swung her back, forward, and then released her, and she floated out through the air and dropped into the river as neatly as a fish. She came up laughing, shook the water from her face, dived under and up again, and then swam lazily toward a sandbar that jutted out into the river. She came up easily onto the sand.

"Bring me my sandals."

"Get them yourself."

"I'll get my feet muddy."

"I thought you liked mud."

"Not in my sandals."

He lifted her sandals, the spears, robes, and food bag from the hummock and walked to the sandbar. "Hold my axe and spears while I swim. You have smeared mud all over me."

She smiled. "I was painting."

He dove into the water and swam strongly along the riverbank, never far from his weapons. He came up onto the sandbar, and Elina spoke quietly as she handed him his axe: "People watch us from the reeds."

He shook the water from his long hair and lifted his spears. "I saw them. I don't think they are enemies."

"I think they fear us."

"We will keep on toward the big lake. They will see that we are not enemies."

They continued on along the riverbank, aware that people watched them from the reeds. Elina said, "Many are ahead of us. Men, women, children."

Sagon nodded. "A tribe."

"They still fear us."

As they spoke, five brown-haired men appeared in the reeds that lay ahead. The men carried strange-looking spears, spears with three points, and they wore loin coverings of woven plant fibers. The men held their spears with the points forward.

Sagon raised his spears with the points up. "We come in peace."

"Why do you come?" The speaker was the tallest of the men.

"We wish to see the big lake."

"Why?"

"We have never seen so much water before."

The men looked at one another. The tall man said, "Do you bring others with you?"

"No. My sister and I come alone."

"What is your tribe?"

"We have no tribe."

"Where do you come from?"

"From a small river that feeds this river. Five days' journey upriver from here."

The men spoke among themselves. The tall man said, "Give your sister to us."

"Why?"

"She is touched by the gods."

"What do you mean?"

"We saw her dance in the mud." The man tapped his forehead. "She is one of the strange people. They bring good luck and can see the future."

Sagon nodded and tapped his own forehead. "She was born strange. I have to take care of her."

Elina glared at Sagon.

The man said, "We will trade many dried fish for her."

"I will not trade her."

"Then we will kill you and take her."

"I would kill many of you first."

"We do not fear you."

"She would be no good to you without me. She can see the future, but she speaks in a language only I can understand."

The men spoke with one another. The tall man asked, "Can you fish?"

"Only if she is with me. The fish come like ants to honey."

"Will you join our tribe?"

"We travel to another place."

"The fish have not come as they should. Come to our camp. She will bring fish to our nets." The man eyed Elina from head to foot, his eyes lecherous.

Sagon stepped in front of Elina. "She is my sister. No man touches her."

The big man's eyes shifted away.

"We will come to your camp," Sagon said, "but I will fight any man who tries to take her."

The men led them through the tall reeds to a wide marsh. In the center of the marsh on a low island stood a group of shaggy reed huts resembling the homes of water animals. A narrow causeway of reed bundles and sticks led from the shore of the marsh to the island. Brown-haired people of all sizes and ages watched from the island.

The tall man said, "Walk one at a time, a spear-length apart, or you will sink. If you fall in, you will be sucked into the mud and disappear." He pointed to Elina. "You go first."

Elina stepped cautiously onto the floating bundles of reeds. She shifted her weight from foot to foot and then smiled back at Sagon. She ran lightly along the narrow causeway, almost dancing, easily maneuvering the irregular and quivering surface. She reached the island and waved at the men.

Sagon said to the tall man, "Go before me. If one of your men throws his spear at my back, I will throw my spear into yours."

The man shrugged and stepped onto the causeway. "We could have killed you both as you swam. We will not kill you now if the girl helps us." He strode easily along the causeway, and Sagon and the other men followed one by one. When Sagon reached the island, an aged woman waited for him, holding Elina by the hand. She smiled at him.

"We thank you for bringing this girl to us. I am Old Woman. What are your names?"

"I am Wolf. Her name is Elina."

"Does she speak?"

"She whispers to me in a language of her own. Only I can understand her."

"Why does she whisper?"

"Loud sounds hurt her ears."

"Does she understand our language?"

"Only a few words. I must whisper to her in her own language." He patted Elina's head. "She is strange, but she no longer bites or scratches. But she does still kick. I am trying to teach her not to do that."

"We saw her kicking at you in the mud."

"Then you know how she is."

"Yes."

Elina kicked Sagon hard on the shinbone. He pushed her away. "It is not easy for me."

"I can see that." The woman smiled. "I am the Old Woman of this tribe. The men know only how to fish. Now they have forgotten how to do that. We need Elina to help them."

"I will tell her, if I can keep her from kicking me."

He bent down and whispered in Elina's ear. "If you kick me again, I will give you to these people and leave."

She smiled at him and whispered back, "If you do, I will suddenly learn to talk. They will use you to bait their nets."

Sagon said to the woman, "She does not understand about the fish. If you tell us how you fish, I will try to explain to her."

"The men wade out into the sea carrying a long net with stones tied to the bottom and wooden floats tied to the top. They drop the net into the water and drag it back to shore, bringing fish. But now no fish are in the net."

"The sea is the big lake?"

"It is bigger than any lake."

"Do you ask the sea god to give you fish?"

"Always."

"Have you offended him?"

"We do not know."

"Our people hunt animals on the plain and in the forests and hills. If our magic is strong, the game come to our spears."

"Our men have lost their magic. When they saw Elina, they thought she could bring it back."

"We did not promise that she could do this."

"Big Man will try to kill both of you if she can't."

"The tall man who brought us here?"

"Yes. He is my grandson, but he no longer listens to me."

Elina kicked lightly at Sagon's leg, and he bent to listen to her. She whispered, "Kill Big Man."

"Wait."

"Until he kills us?"

"Use your magic. Bring the fish back."

"I don't have any fish magic."

Sagon said to Old Woman, "The magic will come to her in a dream."

"It grows dark. Come and eat with us and then sleep."

Big Man came near with two other men. "Tomorrow the girl will go with us to the shore. Do not try to leave in the night, or you will die." The three men stared openly at Elina, their eyes speculative.

Old Woman glared at them. "We do not threaten guests. Go back to your sluts and their filth!"

A small fire burned in the center of the open area between the reed huts, and Old Woman seated Sagon and Elina in the circle of people around the fire. They were given dried fish and baked marsh tubers, and the marsh people watched curiously as Elina and Sagon tried to pick the bones from the hardened fish.

Nets of woven reeds hung on poles. A strong odor of rotten fish hung over the village, and the ground on which they sat seemed to be composed of layers of fish bones and dirt. Sagon asked Old Woman, "How long have your people lived here?"

"Since the beginning. Since we came from the sea."

"Our storytellers," Sagon said, "say that our people came from the south, but before that they lived in a thick forest far to the east of here where everything they needed to eat grew on the trees."

"Why did they leave the trees?"

"A great fire drove them out."

"Couldn't they go back to the trees?"

"A storm came with the fire. A huge river formed and separated them from the forest. They found safety on a black rock. That rock still stands on a cliff top above my grandfather's people."

Old Woman's eyes gleamed in the firelight. "I am the storyteller in our tribe. I learned the stories from my mother, who learned them from her mother."

Elina whispered in Sagon's ear: "Find out how her people came from the sea."

Sagon said to Old Woman, "Tell us the oldest story of your people. How you came from the sea."

"Will Elina know what I say?"

"She says she has learned to understand you."

Old Woman touched Elina's arm. "I will tell you how the dolphins brought us from the sea to this place. Would you like to hear that story?"

Elina nodded her head, yes.

Sagon asked, "What are dolphins?"

"They are sea creatures, larger than a man." Old Woman gazed into the fire. "Once, long ago, our people lived in the sea. We swam with the dolphins, diving far beneath the water, leaping high above it. The dolphins were our sisters, our brothers.

"Then the sea god saw one of our maidens, and he wanted her for his own. But she did not love him, and she asked her father to save her. Her father fought with the sea god, and the sea god killed her father and the maiden and said that he would kill all the people by changing them so that they could not live in the sea. The dolphins were sad when they heard this, and they took the people on their backs and carried them from the sea to this marsh. And our people became fishers of the sea, but always they knew that they could not live in the sea, and they became men and women." Old Woman smiled at Elina. "That is our oldest story."

Elina touched Old Woman's arm in thanks. Sagon asked Old Woman, "Do your people speak with the dolphins?"

"When we lived in the sea. Now we have forgotten how."

Elina whispered to Sagon, "Ask her if her people dance."

When Sagon asked this, Old Woman replied, "We have forgotten that, too."

Elina whispered to Sagon, "We can bring the fish."

"How?"

"We must dance in the water."

He said suspiciously, "Like your mud dance?"

"No."

"What kind of dance?"

"You will see."

Old Woman said, "Has Elina found a way to bring the fish?"

Sagon shook his head. "Who can say?"

When night came, Old Woman took Sagon and Elina to a reed hut already holding seven adolescent marsh people. Sagon pointed to the ground beside the hut. "She must sleep under the sky, or she screams all night."

They lay on their traveling robes, looking up at the stars. Elina said softly but fiercely, "If you pat me on the head again, I will bite you!"

Big Man and his two companions lurched out of the shadows, carrying their fish spears. Big Man's words were slurred. "We have come for the girl."

Elina and Sagon whirled up from the ground simultaneously, spears in hand. Big Man said, "She is not your sister. Any man can have her."

"Any man who wants her will fight me."

Big Man sneered. "Will you fight all of us?"

Sagon touched the handle of his axe. "I will fight your whole tribe. You will die first."

Big Man looked at the axe, then looked into Sagon's eyes and saw death. He backed away. "She is too young. Who would want her?"

When the three men had staggered into the darkness, Elina said to Sagon, "I have changed my mind."

"How?"

"I will not bite you."

Sagon dreamed in the night. When they awoke, he told Elina of his dream. "I swam in the sea with the dolphin people. We leaped high above the water and dived below like swallows swooping after insects."

"I dreamed of them, too," Elina replied. "We spoke with clicking sounds and songs like birds singing as we danced together deep in the water."

They rolled and tied their robes and picked up their spears and food bag. They went silently to relieve themselves at the mens' and womens' places on the far side of the island, then came to the causeway. Big Man and eight men stood with their spears at the entrance to the causeway.

Big Man spoke: "Today you bring the fish to our nets. You have not forgotten?"

Sagon answered, "We have not forgotten."

"You will not need your spears."

"We keep our weapons with us."

"They will do you no good."

"We keep them."

"No."

Old Woman came from her hut. "They will keep their weapons."

Big Man scowled at her. "I am chieftain."

"You are son of my son and know nothing. I am coming with you."

The men lifted a long net from its wooden rack. With Big Man leading, they crossed the causeway and walked through the reeds down a long path to the sea. When they reached the shore, Sagon and Elina stared in wonder at the huge expanse of water.

The morning sun was rising out of the water in the east, and its rays illuminated billowing waves as numerous as the stars. The water was a living thing that covered the earth, and Sagon felt a sense of awe that stirred his spirit like a great storm. Elina held her arms out toward the water, and Sagon saw that she was crying.

Big Man said, "Now bring us the fish."

Sagon pointed to the net. "Show us how you use it."

Big Man motioned to his men. "Take out the net."

The men stretched the long, narrow net parallel to the shore, holding it with the wooden floats at the top, stone weights at the bottom. The men walked into the water, carrying the net against their chests above the water. When the water reached their shoulders, the men lifted the net over their heads, turned to face the shore, and lowered the net into the water. Then they walked slowly back to the shore, gradually bringing the ends of the net close together to form an open circle.

Big Man carried his three-pronged spear into the circle. "Pull it in!" The men closed the circle and pulled the net closer to shore as Big Man probed the water with his spear.

"No fish!" Big Man angrily drove his spear into the water. He pushed out of the net and came onto the beach. He glared at Sagon and Elina. "Your magic is nothing!"

Sagon said, "Have your men take out the net again."

Big Man laughed scornfully. "You will bring fish to the net?"

"We will try."

"I will kill you if you fail."

Old Woman spoke: "You will kill no one. Take out the net."

That evening Old Woman told a new story to the marsh people: "The fish would not come to our nets. Many times the men took the net out, and no fish were in it.

"Then a shaman of the bison hunters came, and with him a girl of great magic. They went into the water, and they called the dolphin people, the people who had lived with us in the sea in ancient times. The dolphin people heard the call, and the calling was in the language of the dolphin people. Then the dolphin people went to the fish people, and they told them that our people starved. Then the dolphin people brought the fish people to our net, and when the men brought in the net, it was full of fish."

The women who had not gone to the beach said, "How did the shaman and the girl of magic call the dolphin people?"

Old Woman spoke almost in a whisper. "They sang to

them. And as they sang, the girl of magic danced in the water, and the shaman beat the water with his spears. . . ."

Big Man said, "Old Woman let the man and the girl go. We should have kept them here."

Old Woman smiled. "I will teach the song to the women. While they sing, the men will beat the water with their spears."

Big Man scoffed, "How do you know that you can remember the song of the dolphin people?"

Old Woman looked into the fire. "It is a song that my grandmother taught me. I had forgotten how to use the song."

In the night Big Man spoke secretly to two of his henchmen, Lurg and Small Man: "Go to the chieftain of the horse hunters. Tell him of this man who carries an axe."

5

Storm

AFTER LEAVING THE marsh people Sagon traveled back along the river. Elina patiently followed him, but finally she voiced her exasperation.

"Three days you have searched along the riverbank. What are you looking for? Tell me and I can help you."

"I look for a place where a floating tree might have come to the riverbank."

"You think the beautiful mate you seek came floating on a tree? Or was she a tree? Have you fallen in love with a tree?"

"She came on a tree."

"Perhaps she is a bird."

"Perhaps."

"Or a piece of moss."

"That could be."

"You are not really looking for a mate. You look for your enemy."

"Yes. Many years ago a man of evil killed my brother. Agon wounded him, but somehow he escaped, even though men hunted him. I have thought about it. I think he floated down the river on a tree."

"Who is the man?"

"Son of Ka, who raped my mother."

"Is he your brother?"

"No. Ka was his father. Agon is my father."

"What does he look like?"

"I have never seen him. I was born after he fled from our home at Bear Hill. His name is Eran."

"How can you know him?"

"Agon marked him."

"How is he marked?"

"Agon cut off his thumbs, the way the bison hunters punish a murderer if they do not kill him."

"Why do you fear him?"

"I do not fear him. But I saw him in a dream. He came with many men against my father and mother. He carried a great spear, and his head and the heads of his men were huge."

"How could he carry a spear if he has no thumbs?"

"That is the strange thing. I must find him to see if he is the man I saw in my dream."

"It could be his son."

"No. He has no son. He could never have a son."

"How do you know that?"

"Agon cut out his testicles."

Elina drew in her breath, and her eyes grew wide. "Why did Agon do that?"

"To kill the line of Ka."

"How could that . . ."

"You have seen it with animals. If a bull has his testicles injured, he never sires a calf."

"And men are the same?"

"A hunter in our tribe was kicked there by a horse. He never again mated with a woman."

Elina considered this. "If a man ever tries to rape me, I know what I will do."

Something flashed in the sky, and the low growl of thunder rumbled in the west. A dark wall of clouds churned below the late afternoon sun, and lightning stabbed through the clouds in jagged vertical streaks of fire while thunder growled. The air grew still, and a green light filled the sky. Something moaned in the forest along the cliff top, a sighing of lost spirits who had no shelter in a storm.

Sagon watched the boiling clouds. "The storm spirits are angry. We must find a cave or an overhang. The clouds hold a terrible wind when they tumble like that."

"And when they hang down like great drops of water on a cave ceiling," Elina said, "giant whirlwinds tear trees from the ground and suck them up into the sky."

Sagon gazed at the cliffs along the river. "We have to find a place high above the river or climb to the cliff top. The forest is not safe."

Elina pointed. "See the dark place halfway up the cliff? It looks like a small cave."

"We will have to climb fast." Sagon untied the leather thong around his waist. "Give me your spear." He tied a tight knot around their three spears, knotted the ends together, and looped it over his head and one shoulder so that the spears hung on his back. "Go first. I will catch you if you fall."

Elina smiled. "And I will pull you up if you slip." She ran to the base of the cliff and without hesitation began the ascent of the almost vertical wall. Sagon watched her for a moment and then followed, amazed at her skill and strength.

She stopped on a ledge just below the cave. She listened and looked down at him. "Something is in the cave."

"What?"

"I think a nest of tree cats."

As Elina spoke, the sky crackled and a bolt of lightning struck the cliff top with a tremendous blast of light and sound.

Sagon felt himself thrown back away from the cliff, and he survived only by the grip he had on the rock ledge upon which Elina stood. He saw Elina's body blown back, and then press against the cliff wall again. He climbed to stand beside her in the ringing aftermath of the lightning.

He pulled his axe from his belt. "Keep back! If the mother is there, she can kill you!"

"I hear only the kittens."

Sagon held his axe before his face and stretched upward. In the flash of another blast of lightning he saw three tree-cat kittens crouched at the rear of a small cave no deeper than two spear-lengths. They mewed hungrily and then hissed fiercely at him.

Now the storm struck in full fury. A blast of wind and rain tore at the cliff face, and lightning struck in blast after blast on all sides of them. Sagon pulled himself into the opening, turned, reached down, and grasped Elina's raised hand as she scrambled up into the cave.

The kittens mewed again and were silent. Elina said softly, "They are hungry."

"I will have to kill the mother when she comes." Sagon pulled the spears from the knotted thong and gave back Elina's. "Stay behind me. A forest cat can kill a single wolf or hyena."

"Maybe she will not come back," Elina said hopefully. "She must have brought her kittens here when she heard the storm coming."

A shaggy form leaped into the cave entrance. A tree cat the size of a small wolf crouched on the cave floor, a limp kitten hanging from her mouth. Sagon raised his spear, ready to kill.

The tree cat and the humans looked into each other's eyes, and the cat growled, deep in her throat. Then the kittens at the back of the cave mewed hungrily, and the cat walked past Sagon and Elina and placed the kitten beside the others. As lightning exploded again, the mother tree cat leaped past Sagon and Elina and out the entrance into the shrieking wind and rain.

Elina drew in her breath. "You did not spear her!" She touched Sagon's arm. "She has gone to bring another kitten."

"Yes."

A new and terrible sound now came, a great roar of rushing air, the shrieking of demons, a dying cry of trees splintering and tearing from the earth, a howling of death from a whirling monster reaching down from the boiling sky to suck up the earth into its black maw.

Elina pressed close to Sagon. He braced his feet against the opposite wall and held her while the tornado tore at the cave entrance, trying to claw them out. Then it whirled away, raging across the cliffs and forests into the distance.

Still the lightning blasted, and the rain and wind tore at the cliff face. Elina spoke, her voice almost inaudible. "She could not have lived. . . ."

"No."

"Her kittens will die. . . ."

"Yes."

"She was so brave. . . ."

Sagon heard the sorrow in Elina's voice, and he wanted to hold her again, comfort her.

Something scraped the rocks outside the entrance. Then slowly, painfully, the mother tree cat crawled into the cave. She held another kitten in her mouth, and as she crept past Sagon and Elina, they saw that her fur was scorched as from fire, and blood seeped from a gash on her shoulder.

Elina and Sagon silently watched as the mother cat put the kitten down and licked its fur while the other kittens mewed and shoved their little noses against their mother's wet body.

As the storm moved on to the east and the roar of the

thunder and the howling of the wind subsided, Sagon and Elina heard the mewing of the kittens cease. From the back of the cave came a sound of contentment; the purring of the mother tree cat as she gave milk to her kittens.

6

The Onerana

KANE RETURNED TO the camp of his father and mother with twenty armed warriors and a captive old woman. He said to Eran and Ara, "I am chieftain of these men. Now we go to kill Agon."

Eran's eyes blazed. "We have our own tribe! At last I will have revenge!"

Ara's face was pale. "I beg you, do not go to kill my father."

Kane scowled at her. "You know what he did to my father. Beg no more."

"I will beg no more. Now I tell you. You will not kill Agon."

Kane's face became hard, his voice cruel. "I will kill Agon. Speak no more."

"I will speak. I am your mother. You will not kill Agon."

"If you were not my mother, I would kill you." Kane motioned to his men. "Take her."

Ara stood proudly silent as the men seized her.

Kane said, "You will be put in the cave that has been our home. My men will place blocks of stone to close the entrance, leaving a small opening to pass through food and water. When we return from killing Agon, you will be released."

Ara spoke to Eran. "You will let him do this?"

"Yes."

Ara said to Kane, "Tell your men to take their hands off me. I am the daughter of chieftains."

Kane gestured to his men. "Release her. Guard her while I bring weapons and supplies from the cave. Any man that lets her escape will die by my spear."

The men stepped back, still surrounding her. Ara stood in silence, her chin raised, as Kane went into the cave.

Eran said to her, "This will be best for you. You will not see Agon die."

Ara looked at him with contempt, but did not speak.

"You will be safe here."

Still Ara said nothing.

Eran beckoned to the captive woman. "Come here."

The old woman approached. Eran said, "You will gather berries and nuts. She has dried meat to eat and fur robes for warmth in the cave. You will give her food and water every day, or you will be killed. Robes will be brought for you to sleep on under the shelter of the cliff."

Ara spoke to Eran, her voice cold. "It is you who planned this."

"There is another way."

"You would kill me."

"No."

"What, then?"

"You would come with us."

"To help kill my father?"

"To bring him down from Bear Hill."

"So you could kill him? I would die first."

"Agon would come down if he saw his daughter tied to a tree and left to thirst. I have saved you from that."

Ara's eyes were icy. "I would bite my tongue off and die."

"That is why you will stay here."

"You think you can keep me here?"

"The blocks will be so heavy they will take two men to lift them. This old woman can hardly lift a basket of berries."

Kane came from the cave carrying robes and a bag of traveling food. He glared at Ara. "She has burned our spears. We will go to my camp and get more." He gestured to the men. "Put her in the cave."

Ara did not speak or look at Eran or Kane. She walked proudly to the cave and entered. Kane's men brought blocks of stone that lay at the base of the cliff, two or three men grunting under the weight of each block. They laid them across the cave entrance and on top of each other, building a wall that sealed the cave. In the center they left an opening one hand's length high and two lengths wide. On the base of the opening the old woman placed wooden cups of water and berries.

Eran spoke into the opening. "We will return in two moons. Then you will be free."

No sound came from the cave.

At Bear Hill that same afternoon, Eena came from the sunny cave entrance onto the stone porch that overlooked the river valley. She carried her spear and a light robe. She said to Agon, "Emar's tribe leaves the cliff shelter tomorrow for the summer hunting grounds. Yeta has asked me to show the girls how to make watertight baskets. I will go now and stay overnight."

Agon raised his eyebrows. "You have decided this just now?"

"Yeta and I have many things to talk about."

"I know."

"It will be good for you to cook your own food."

"Of course."

"I will be back tomorrow morning."

Agon put an arm around Eena. "If you are not . . ."

Eena hugged him. "Nothing can keep me from you. Do you know how many winters we have been together?"

"More than the days in one moon."

Eena removed the carved leather belt that circled her slender waist. She opened the belt to show its inner side.

"I have made a mark for every winter since then. Five marks in each group. Five groups and one group. Four more marks. We are still alive. The magic of the belt grows stronger every year."

Agon smiled. "You have grown more beautiful every year."

Eena put the belt back on. "Since the Earth Mother gave me the belt, I have loved you." She kissed him. "You are the only man who has ever seen me without the belt." She looked keenly at Agon. "Are you all right? Has some spirit spoken to you?"

"I am all right. It's just that as you spoke of the Earth Mother, something made me think of Ara."

Eena looked up at him with a strange expression. "Evening is coming. I must go to Yeta before darkness." She touched the deer totem on her breast. "I will return at sunrise."

Agon watched her as she went easily and lightly down the escarpment, as slender and lovely as when he first mated with her.

The look in her eyes . . . he had seen that look many times before . . . times when she had disappeared into the night. He had a fleeting vision of an ancient ceremony . . . women gathered in an oak wood . . . the moon . . . magic. Magic that no man could know and live. Agon looked to the east. In the darkening sky a faint light glowed on the horizon.

Tonight would be the night of the full moon.

Far to the west, beyond the distant camp of the bison hunters, across the great plain, lay the mountains called the Blue Hills. Deep in the mountains, beneath twin peaks that resembled the breasts of a prone woman, lived the Earth Mother, a being so powerful that she could shake the earth, cause mountains to explode in fiery blasts, send red-hot lava streaming over cliffs, and block raging rivers.

Priestesses of the Earth Mother lived in secret and mysterious isolation behind a magical waterfall whose falling water sounded of women crying and laughing, children playing, and lovers sighing. This night, as the full moon rose through the oak forest, a circle of nine hooded and white-robed women chanted the ancient and secret litany of the Onerana, the Invisible Earth Spirit Women. In turn, each raised her arms to the moon:

"Earth Mother, hear us."
"Moon Spirit, fill us."
"Love Spirit, come to us."
"Life Spirit, grow in us."
"Tree Spirit, warm us."
"Air Spirit, sustain us."
"Blood Spirit, flow in us."
"Death Spirit, receive us."
"Spear Spirit, protect us."

In the sealed cave, Ara, daughter of Agon and Erina, priestess of the Earth Mother, danced in the near darkness. Through the tiny opening in the rocks the light of the moon streamed in a golden path upon her face, her body, her hair, filling her with strength and magic. As she danced, she invoked the Earth Mother and the spirits of the Onerana in the same litany as that chanted by the priestesses of the Earth Mother in the Blue Hills. The same litany chanted by Eena, Spear Woman, with the women of the tribe of the aurochs hunters. The same litany chanted silently by Elina as she danced under the moon.

7

Birdman

SAGON SAID TO Elina, "The storm will show us the way."

She touched her forehead. "The shaman speaks. How will the storm show us the way?"

"With a tree."

"Of course. And what will the tree show us the way to?"

"The one I seek."

"I should have known."

"Yes."

Elina looked at him thoughtfully, then she smiled. "Where a tree stops!"

"I do not have to explain?"

"The storm tore trees out by their roots. Perhaps one fell in the river. Perhaps that tree was washed ashore. Perhaps that is the same place where a tree brought your enemy years ago."

He smiled. "Perhaps I am teaching you how to think."

"Perhaps."

"All we have to do is find the tree that floated against the riverbank."

"That is all. Find the tree." Elina pointed upstream, then down. "Many trees might have washed ashore. Which one do we pick? It could make a difference."

"I will know the tree."

"How?"

"My spirit will tell me."

"Which way should we look?"

"Downstream."

"How do you know that?"

"I saw the tree going down the river during the storm."

"You were looking at the river while the mother tree cat was deciding whether to claw us into strips?"

Sagon nodded. "I knew she would not hurt you."

"How did you know that?"

"She would not attack one of her own kind. I think she might have tried to feed you."

"Next time I will push you out the cave opening so you can see the river better."

Sagon smiled. "You would not do that. You know that only I can explain your strangeness to the tribes we meet."

Elina kicked at him, barely missing as he leaped aside. He said, "This is not the time for dancing. I saw you last night under the moon."

"You followed me? Men who watch women under the full moon could die."

"I still live. Follow me, and I will show you the tree."

"Follow yourself."

"Good. Go back to your pile of rocks."

"I would if you were not so helpless." Elina ran ahead of him and shouted back, "I will find the tree before you do!"

They ran along the river's edge, and Sagon was amazed at Elina's speed. Finally he drew even with her, and they slowed to a walk. He asked, "How did you learn to run so fast?"

"Chasing game."

"You hunted with your father?"

"Yes. But after the lion killed my father and mother, I had to hunt alone."

"My mother can run fast as a man. She and her brother had to hunt alone after her mother was bitten by a snake."

"Didn't her father hunt?"

"He grieved so after his mate died that he would not hunt."

Elina was silent, then she said, "If I ever find a mate, I want a man who would grieve for me."

"My mother and father are like that. They promised only

to mate with each other, as the great birds do. I don't think one could live without the other."

Elina spoke without emotion. "When my mother saw that the lion was mauling my father, she attacked the lion with her spear."

"She was brave."

"Yes." Elina bit her lower lip and turned away so Sagon could not see her face.

"She must have loved your father."

"Yes. And he loved her."

"If I ever find a mate," Sagon said, "I hope she and I will be the same."

"If I ever find a mate, I hope the same. But I will never have a mate."

"Some of the boys in the camp of the reed people were looking at you."

She turned to face him. "Ugh! They smelled of old fish."

Sagon smiled. "When you are older, you will change your mind."

"Never."

Sagon gazed ahead along the riverbank. "Soon we will come to the tree."

"You know this."

"Yes."

Elina said, "You see the tree. I see someone ahead of us."

They moved quickly into the shelter of a willow grove that grew along the riverbank. Sagon peered through the low-hanging branches. "Where?"

"Behind the big hill."

"I see no one."

"No."

"But you do."

"Yes. They are not enemies, but we must be careful. There are many of them."

"Have they seen us?"

"I think so."

"We came by here yesterday," Sagon observed. "You sensed no people then."

"They are here now. I sense someone even closer than those on the hill. Trees cover the hills and the high land beyond them. These people must live deep in the forest."

"If they are friendly," Sagon said, "we could find out if they know anything about the man I seek."

"And if they are not friendly?"

"Then we have to run or fight."

"You would fight a whole tribe?"

"Agon told me that one man can defeat a tribe if he picks the place to fight. He must find a place where only one man at a time can fight him."

"Like a narrow pass over a mountain."

"Yes."

"Or a ledge on a cliff."

"Even better."

"Do you see a narrow pass here? Or a ledge on the cliff?"

"No."

Elina shook her head. "No. Tell me how you will fight them."

"We will not fight them. I think you should act strange again. Go dance in the mud."

She scowled at him. "No."

"The marsh people wanted to keep you."

"No."

"These people would feed you and care for you like they would a baby."

"You can be the strange one. I will explain to them how you are."

"A hunter," Sagon said, "cannot be treated like a baby."

"But I can."

"Yes."

Elina growled like the mother tree cat. "This is the last time. Next time you will be the idiot."

Sagon patted her shoulder. "Good. Now go where they can see you and dance in the mud."

A voice spoke from above them. "I will dance with you."

They looked up, bringing their spears into fighting position. A young man smiled at them from his perch high in a willow tree. His short red hair bristled from his head like a cocklebur, he wore a cloak of colored bird feathers, and his blue eyes sparkled in a face that was dominated by a large pointed nose. He carried no visible weapon.

He said, "I am Birdman, the biggest bird in the forest."

Elina looked at Sagon, then spoke to the man in the tree: "Can you fly?"

"Not yet." Birdman spread his feathered arms out like wings. "I almost can." He smiled at Elina. "Are you a bird?"

"No."

"So why do you dance in the mud?"

Elina looked hard at Sagon. "Because I like it."

Sagon tapped his forehead. "She is strange."

"Wait." Birdman came down the trunk of the willow tree with his gaudy feathers fluttering. When he reached the ground, he smiled at Sagon. "You are a shaman."

"I told him that," Elina said. "He thinks he is a hunter."

"He will be an animal man." Birdman looked into Sagon's eyes. "You will fly with the owls."

Sagon felt something stir inside him. For a moment he seemed to float soundlessly through the night air.

Birdman whistled, trilling, and a red-winged blackbird called from a clump of cattails.

Elina whistled, and a lark called from the edge of the willows.

Birdman laughed with joy. "Watch." He whistled, a high clear calling, and an eagle replied from the sky. They looked up through an opening in the willow trees, and they saw two eagles spiraling on motionless wings, high in the blue air. The clear call came again, beautiful in its freedom and desire.

Elina gazed up at the eagles in rapture. She said softly, "They call their mating song."

Slowly the eagles drifted to the south over the hills, ever smaller until they became tiny specks in the sunlit sky. Yet even as they disappeared, a faint clear calling remained for a moment and then faded into silence.

Birdman said softly, "They mate for life. When I learn to fly, I will spiral with them. I will hold my wings out straight and strong and float higher and higher until I reach the sun."

Sagon felt his spirit straining within him, yearning to break free and follow the eagles and Birdman up into the ringing clearness of space. Elina held her arms up to the sky, and Sagon saw that she was beautiful in her passion and longing.

Birdman spoke again: "The forest people watch you."

Sagon felt his spirit return to him. He said, "We come as friends. We would not take game from their hunting ground."

"They know that. They welcome you."

Elina said, "You are their chieftain."

"Yes."

"I knew when you first spoke. I knew you were kind."

"All men are not kind to you?"

"Some are not." Elina glanced at Sagon. "Some tell people I am strange."

Birdman smiled. "I like strange people."

Sagon said, "So does she. Perhaps I could leave her with you."

Elina stuck out her tongue at Sagon. "My brother is helpless without me. He would be a shaman, and when his spirit leaves him, I have to take care of him."

"Of course." Birdman spoke to Sagon. "What are your names?"

"I am Wolf. She is Elina."

"Why are you called Wolf?"

Sagon touched the carved wolf head of the amulet on his chest. "My totem is the wolf."

"I see a wolf on the handle of the small axe you carry. Is the axe magic?"

"Yes."

Birdman looked closely at Sagon's face. "I have known you in some other life."

"And I have known you." Sagon had a fleeting vision of a man with long red hair and pale skin sitting on a platform high in a great oak.

"Yet your totem was not the wolf." Birdman ruffled his feathers thoughtfully. "It was an ibex."

Sagon stared at Birdman. Agon's totem was the ibex. He had a momentary feeling of death. "You carried a tree branch."

Birdman looked up at the willows. "Oak."

"Yes."

They regarded each other. Birdman said, "We live many lives. Our bodies die, but our spirits live on. In dreams our spirits tell some things of our other lives. But I know another, better way."

"The way of the shaman."

"Yes."

"I am not a shaman."

Birdman looked at Elina. "She thinks you are."

"She is wrong."

"What do you seek? You spoke of a man, but what do you really seek?"

Sagon hesitated, then he said, "I seek to know the spirit of all things."

Birdman's eyes shone. "Then you will become a shaman."

"No."

"Why, then?"

"I want to show the spirit of all things when I paint."

Birdman sucked in his breath. "You are a cave painter."

"I try."

Elina said, "His spirit leaves him when he paints."

"You have seen him paint?"

"He painted a stallion. Then he died."

Birdman looked at Elina, then at Sagon. "What did your spirit see when you died?"

"I may not talk of it."

"No. I should not have asked you." Birdman smiled at them. "Come and meet my people. They wonder much about you. We will eat and drink, and when night comes, we will dance!"

Birdman's people were small, dark-haired, agile folk who moved quickly as foxes through the forest. Their voices were high-pitched and birdlike, and they smiled often as they talked. They looked in awe at Sagon's height and made Elina feel like a grown woman as they greeted her as one.

They led their guests deep into the forest, finally coming to a clearing on the bank of a small stream. Huts of bark and branches stood in a half circle facing the stream, and in the center log seats circled a fire pit.

Birdman pointed to the flat stones surrounding the fire pit.

"We have to keep the fire from eating the forest. Lightning from the storm two nights ago brought fire to the trees, but the rain drowned the fire."

Deer haunches roasted on spits over the fire, and the women brought baskets of berries, fruit, and nuts, which they served to their guests along with sizzling slabs of venison on wooden plates. A wooden tub held a foamy liquid that was scooped out in small wooden cups.

Sagon sipped his, and a fire ran down his throat. He bit into a purple fruit to quench the fire. "What is this?"

Birdman chuckled. "Our women make it from berries and fruit. Something magical happens. But we let only the grown people drink it. It is too strong for children."

Sagon sipped from his cup again. "My sister is too young. She should drink only water."

Elina gave him a hard look. She raised her cup and sipped twice. She coughed and then spoke in a husky voice. "This is very good." She sipped again. "I like it." Little beads of sweat appeared on her forehead.

Darkness slid through the forest. Two men brought squat log drums from a hut, and as the rising moon glowed in the east, the men began to strike the leather drumheads lightly with short sticks. Men, women, and children scrambled from their seats, made a circle around the fire, joined hands, and slowly swayed from side to side with the drumbeats. Then they started to dance, going step-hop with one foot and then the other.

Birdman stood and gestured to his guests. "Our people are too shy to ask you to dance. Join them with me."

Sagon shook his head. "I do not dance."

Elina sipped again from her cup. "Every shaman dances."

"I am not a shaman."

She stood up unsteadily. "I will dance."

Birdman smiled at her. "If your brother will let me, I will dance beside you."

Elina glanced wickedly at Sagon. "He makes me dance in the mud. You need not ask if he will let me."

Birdman looked inquiringly at Sagon. Sagon said, "Do not let her dance in real mud. She spatters it over everything."

Birdman took Elina's hand. "Pretend there is mud. Show me how. Then we will do the mud dance around the fire."

Elina giggled. "We have to stomp in the mud, then kick it in big gobs. Watch."

She danced with her knees high like a playful child, stomping and hopping with one foot in the imaginary mud, then the other foot. Then she stomped with one foot and kicked forward with the other, then stomped with the other foot and kicked, shrieking with laughter as imaginary gobs of mud flew through the air. Now Birdman imitated her, and they danced into the circle of dancers, stomping, kicking, and laughing, and the other dancers, children and adults, joined in their wild dance, laughing and screaming, while their feet went STOMP hop STOMP hop, stomp KICK stomp KICK, and the drums beat louder and faster going BOOM boom BOOM boom, boom BOOM boom BOOM with the mud dance of Elina.

Sagon watched Elina with a strange feeling of jealousy and desire, and he tensely and absently sipped again and again from his cup as the dancers circled.

Then, hardly realizing what he was doing, he stood and began to dance. But instead of joining the dancers, he spun in place like a whirlwind, gradually turning faster and faster. As he spun, his spirit lifted on rising wings from the darkness into the moonlight and soared into the vastness of the sky, higher and higher toward the stars!

He walked on a golden plain with one he loved. The sun shone warm on their shoulders, and the air smelled of warm earth and sweet long grass. The loved one smiled in the sunshine, and her eyes were filled with tenderness and love. A young man walked with them, and he carried a green tree branch. Hunters were with them, and the loved one stood on a rock in the sunshine as the hunters brought their spears to her, and she touched each spear. He held the stone point of his spear out to her, and she touched it. Magic strength flowed from her hand through the spear and into him. Then a creature ran across the plain toward them, and it was all the animals of death, a hell beast. The young man held his tree branch high, and the hell beast was upon them and in them and gone.

A hunter lay dead on the plain, and from a far mountain a horned being shrieked in hellish joy.

Sagon awoke. The forest people were around him, and Elina and Birdman knelt over him. Elina touched his forehead, and her hand was light and cool. She said, "You have come back."

Birdman smiled at him. "Your spirit has traveled far."

Sagon tried to sit up, and they helped him. He saw that it was morning. The leaves of the forest trees rustled gently above them, and the little stream gurgled quietly. He said, "I have been with you both in another time and place. Something of great evil sent a hell beast against us." He spoke to Birdman. "You raised your branch, and we lived." He touched Elina's hand. "You touched our spears and gave them magic."

Birdman's eyes glowed. "We have known each other!"

"Yes. We fought together against great evil."

"Did we destroy the evil?"

Sagon touched the handle of his axe. "It still lives."

"Where?"

Sagon felt the magic strength of the axe flowing into his arm, his body. He came to his feet. "The evil hides. But I will find it."

"And then?"

"I will kill it."

"How will you find the evil?'

"We look for a tree washed against the riverbank."

"The evil came with the tree?"

"With another tree. Many years ago."

Birdman thought on this. He said, "The forest people tell of a man and a woman who came down the river on a tree."

"A woman?"

"Yes."

"How long ago?"

"Before I came."

An old woman spoke: "I saw them. They floated by us."

Sagon felt his spirit quivering. "Tell me of them!"

"The man was big."

"What else?"

"His face."

"What about his face?"

"A face filled with hate."

"Was he wounded?"

"Not that I could see."

"Tell me of the woman."

"She was young."

"Did they come to the riverbank?"

"They floated on by. I was glad they kept going."

Sagon touched the old woman's shoulder. "You have been of much help."

Birdman said to Sagon, "You did not know of the woman?"

"No. Something is strange."

"Was the man the one you seek?"

"I don't know. My parents told me nothing of a woman."

"Let us find the tree you saw."

Sagon shook his head. "I go alone." He spoke to Birdman: "Will you keep my sister here until I return?"

"We will."

Elina said, "I go with you."

"No.

"I will follow you."

Birdman smiled. "She will not stay. Remember your dream."

"I was with you both."

"Between us we had strong magic. Now we may face that same evil."

They waited for Sagon's answer. The girl is too young, Sagon thought. Birdman has shown no magic. Yet in my dream their magic was powerful.

He said, "In another dream I saw the evil. A man of terrible strength and fierceness led his tribe against my people. We are few, they are many. I would not have either of you die."

"If the evil ones triumph, your people will die." Birdman indicated his people. "They are not warriors. They will die, too."

Elina said, "The woman waits for us."

Sagon stared at her. "You know this?"

"Yes."

"How?"

"I dreamed."

She danced under the moon, Sagon thought. She danced

in mystery with her bare arms held up to the moon, and her face was beautiful. He had a fleeting vision of women in white robes chanting in the moonlight.

Birdman held up an oak branch. "Warm us. Protect us."

Elina's face grew pale as she gazed at Birdman. Then something flashed between Birdman's oak branch and Elina's spear.

Sagon's fingers closed on the handle of his axe, and the axe spirit quivered with magic and power. He said, "We will go together."

Lurg and Small Man peered at Barhunder's camp from the shelter of an ash grove. Women and children worked and played in the area between the hide-covered huts, but only a few hunters were visible. Lurg made the camp call and stepped into the open with Small Man.

The people looked up and stared; then the hunters waved them in. Lurg gave the hunters a reed basket of dried fish and bright seashells on a thong. He said, "Big Man sent us with a message for Barhunder."

A hunter looked fearfully over his shoulder. "Barhunder is dead."

"Barhunder? Dead?"

"Kane is our chieftain."

Lurg and Small Man gaped in surprise. Lurg asked, "Who is Kane?"

"He killed many of us. His spear ripped Barhunder open as we would butcher a horse. He has the strength of five men."

Lurg shifted his feet uneasily. The fear in the camp was thick as swamp vapor. "Where are the rest of your men?"

"With Kane."

Lurg said, "We have to go."

The hunters looked past Lurg, and he saw the terror in their eyes. One said, "Kane comes with our men. Run now or you will die." Lurg turned, and he saw a giant of a man with a face of such savagery that Lurg's legs turned to water.

Too late. Kane motioned, and his men ran out to each side, surrounding Lurg and Small Man.

Kane held his spear point under Lurg's chin. His voice was like a snarling lion. "What, fish man?"

Lurg felt the spear pierce his throat skin. "Big Man sends gifts. . . ."

"Why?"

"A man came to our camp. Big Man said he was an axe man."

"He had an axe?"

"Yes."

Kane's eyes blazed. "Tell me of him. An old man?"

"No. Young."

"Where is he?"

"Gone."

The spear jerked upward, and Lurg felt his skin tear. "Which way?"

Lurg could hardly speak. "Back up the river."

"When?"

"Three days ago."

"What did he look like?"

"A hunter. Strong."

The spear jerked upward again. Suddenly Kane turned and drove his spear into Small Man's stomach, then ripped the spear upward. Small Man fell, his body torn open. Kane pulled a flint knife from his belt and cut off Small Man's head. He lifted it by the hair and held it out to Lurg.

"Take this back to Big Man. Tell him to take all his men and find the axe man. Do not kill the axe man, but bring him here to me."

Lurg took the dripping head of Small Man.

Kane pushed his bloody spear point against Lurg's stomach. "Tell him one more thing."

Lurg nodded silently, terror choking him.

"Tell him if he does not find the axe man, I will put his head on a pole." Kane jabbed his spear into Small Man's face. "He will look like this."

8

The Hunted

BIG MAN VOMITED in horror when Lurg brought the severed head of Small Man and repeated Kane's message. Lurg's description of Kane added to Big Man's terror.

"He killed Barhunder and ten of his men in one battle. He kills by ripping men open as we gut fish. He tore Small Man open with one spear thrust and cut off his head with two slashes of his knife."

Big Man stared at Small Man's bloody head. The eyes were wide with terror, and half the face was gashed open. "He will come here?"

"Unless we bring the axe man to him."

"And put my head on a pole?"

"He said you will look like Small Man."

Big Man vomited again.

Old Woman spoke: "Kane is son of the man with no thumbs. I saw him when he was a child. Someone should have killed him then."

Big Man sobbed in fear. "He will come here. . . ."

"Be quiet. One of you must find the axe man and warn him."

"Warn him?" Big Man stared at her with hatred, then struck her. "We have to bring him to Kane! Say no more about warning him or I will kill you!"

Blood ran from Old Woman's lip. She spat blood and looked coldly at Big Man. "Coward. You are not fit to be chieftain of a tribe."

Big Man struck her again, and she fell backward onto the ground. Big Man stood over her. "Old hag!" He raised his three-pointed spear in both hands above Old Woman. "Die!"

Old Woman looked up at him. She said, "Earth Mother, hear me. Spirit of the moon, hear me. Spirits of the night, hear me. Tear this man's spirit from his body."

Big Man dropped his spear and ran sobbing with terror toward his hut.

All day Eena had looked to the west from the porch at Bear Hill. Agon hunted in the hills, and when he returned with a deer, she met him at the top of the escarpment.

"We must find Sagon."

Agon slowly carried the carcass to the ash tree and hung it from a branch. "I have been thinking of that."

"He is in danger." Eena noticed that Agon's breathing was rapid, his face pale.

Agon said, "The deer will give you food for two moons. I will leave in the morning to find Sagon."

"I go with you."

Agon knew the look. Her chin was raised, and her eyes showed the strength of her spirit. He said, "We will have to leave this place unprotected."

"We have been protected long enough. Do you know when I was happiest?"

"Tell me."

"When we were young and ran together on the plain, fighting Ka. When we stood back to back and fought Ka's men."

He smiled. "I remember that happiness."

"We will get old if we stay here, protecting ourselves."

"You will never be old. You stay beautiful, and you run like a young hunter."

"You still make love like a young hunter."

Agon drew her to him and put his arms around her. "Sagon has strong magic. He is an axe man. I do not fear for him, but we are too strong to have him fight our battles for us. We will leave together in the morning."

Eena kissed him. "We will run across the plain together, and if we have to fight, we will fight back to back. We will be young again!"

The storm advancing from the west struck Bear Hill in the middle of the night. Agon and Eena slept on the open porch under the stars, as they did in all seasons except winter or when rain fell, and they heard a distant, ominous rumbling, steadily growing louder. Waves of light flashed across the sky, and they saw a black wall rising on the western horizon, lit almost constantly with lightning. The trees around Bear Hill moaned apprehensively in the still air, and a dread hush of danger fell over the hills and plains.

Eena stood barefoot, gazing at the approaching storm. "Sagon would have found shelter. . . ."

Agon put his arm around her. "He has been in many storms."

"It has passed over him already."

"He probably sleeps under the moon and stars."

She looked up at him. "When the storm passes, we will go to find him."

"As we planned. Spring storms are not like blizzards. This looks like a big storm, but it should be gone by morning."

They carried their weapons and bed of ferns and robes into the cave. While Agon brought in the deer carcass, Eena placed coals from the fire into a mud-lined basket and took the basket into the protected storage room that opened off the cave gallery. Together, they raised and braced the winter framework of branches and hides to close off the mouth of the cave. When their preparation for the storm was finished, they went out again onto the porch to watch the storm. Both had the feeling that it was immense and powerful, for in addition to the almost constant lightning and thunder, an increasing roaring sound of wind came like the howl of an approaching demon.

As the black wall swept toward them, the earth seemed to shake with the fury of the storm. Moon and stars disappeared behind racing black clouds, lightning cracked open the sky, the air exploded in blasts of thunder. Then, as Agon and Eena slipped through the slit in the hides and ran back into the cave, the storm leaped upon Bear Hill.

The framework of hides at the cave entrance disappeared as though a giant hand had ripped it away, and the fire was instantly sucked out into the wind.

They could hear nothing but thunder and the roar of the wind and rain, see nothing but the blinding bolts of lightning, feel nothing but the wind tearing at them. Agon held Eena tight against him and drew her deeper into the cave until the roar of the storm faded.

She said, "Sagon is in the storm."

"He found a cave."

"You know this?"

"Our people have seen many storms. Sagon knows what to do."

"But this storm is worse. It is like the storm when Spear Mountain erupted."

"We lived through that. All night long, in the wind and black rain, you helped lead the tribe toward a safe place. From the hilltop you led Ka and his men away from the women and children."

"And you killed Ka's god, Kaan, inside Spear Mountain. Then you ran through the storm to help the tribe."

"I came to find you. But Ka had taken you."

"But you saved the tribe. You fought Ka's men in the river."

He held her in the darkness. "But I lost you."

"And found me."

"I will never lose you again."

They held each other. Agon said, "Our son will live."

"Yes." Eena hugged him. "He has the blood of Grae and Agon. He will live."

All through that night and the next day the storm raged. During the next night it growled away to the east. That morning Agon and Eena looked out on a changed land.

Strips of the forest below them lay flattened, as though some great beast had raked its claws through them, leaving wounds of broken and uprooted trees. The river that had flowed smoothly and placidly between the widely separated cliffs was now a churning, roaring torrent, extending halfway up the floodplain. Far to the east the black monster of the storm still rolled and flashed.

Agon gazed at the river. "The water spirit is angry, as when the dam in the mountains broke. No one can cross."

Eena's face revealed her sadness. "Sagon crossed the river to begin his journey. Now we cannot help him."

At the camp of the horse hunters Kane drew a map in the dirt with his spear.

"I will go fast with ten men over the hills upriver, leaving men to circle the axe man, then turn and come down the river valley. My father will bring ten men from here down toward the river. Lazor will take five men and cross the river to search the other side. Big Man will come upriver. The axe man will be caught in between. Any man who lets him escape will die."

Lazor, the only man of the horse hunters who dared speak, said, "No one has ever crossed the river in flood like this."

"You will cross it, or you will die. By my spear or by drowning. It matters not to me."

Lazor said to his men, "Come. We will cross the river."

Before they saw it, Sagon, Elina, and Birdman knew the tree lay just beyond the bend in the river. The river made a double curve just ahead of them, and as they came around the first curve, they saw the tree. A large ash, branches and sodden green leaves floating in the slow-moving water, lay jammed solidly against the shore.

Sagon pointed to a wide stream flowing into the river just beyond the tree. "This is the place. They followed the stream up into the hills."

Birdman nodded. "They knew they would have water. There may be cliffs further back. Hunting would be good in the hills."

Elina gazed toward the hills. "Someone calls."

"Who?"

"A woman."

"What woman?"

"I don't know. Now something comes. Many men run toward us."

Birdman pointed. "See the raven."

A raven flapped up the river valley and flew low over them, wings whishing. It croaked three times, circled, and came back over them, then flew above the stream toward the hills.

The sun had shone warmly on their backs, but now a chill seemed to creep over the river valley. Birdman touched the leaves of his oak branch. "Men of evil come."

Elina shuddered. "From all directions."

Sagon touched his axe. "Once when I watched cave lions, two stalked me. Without knowing why, I ran toward their lair. I still live."

"You would have us go upstream, toward the men's lair?" Elina asked.

"Yes. They will not expect us to do that."

Birdman said, "They come from three ways. The raven has shown us the way to escape."

They went cautiously up the course of the stream, keeping hidden in the trees. Elina spoke softly: "I feel the strongest evil getting closer."

They heard the sound of men running to their right, high in the hills northwest of the river. They listened, not breathing. Elina said, "They run opposite to our way."

They looked at one another, knowing. The men were

going behind them. Sagon said, "Only the marsh people knew we had come."

"Big Man." Elina looked to the south. "He has told someone. Even now he comes toward us."

Birdman asked Sagon, "When you fled toward the lions' lair, how did you escape?"

"I found a cave in the lions' cliff. It was too small to let the lions in."

"How did you escape from the cave?"

"Something helped me."

"Something magic?"

"Yes."

Elina said, "We can become birds."

Birdman smiled. "Almost." He lifted his gaudy cloak from his shoulders and turned it inside out. The inside was covered with gray feathers. "We can become almost invisible under this."

"We will fight if we have to." Sagon held out one of his spears to Birdman. "Use this."

Birdman shook his head. "The spear is not my weapon." He lifted his oak branch. "The trees will help us."

"The forest?"

"No one has ever found the forest people. They know the forest as do the wolves and foxes. They move silently and unseen." Birdman pointed with his branch. "We will have to go across the hills behind the running men before they turn back."

Elina raised a finger across her lips. "Listen."

The sound of the running men was closer, yet it seemed to lessen periodically. Sagon said, "Men are stopping, one at a time."

Elina nodded. "They are making a ring of men around us."

They had no knowledge of who the running men were, no certainty of who came upriver, no idea of who might be on the other side of the river. They only knew what their senses told them: men who meant to kill them were stalking them on all sides. They had to break through before the noose closed.

They ran up the course of the stream as deer run from lions.

9

Eran

ERAN AND HIS ten men ran from the camp of the horse hunters toward the river in a wide rank, the men separated three spear-throws apart. Eran held the center position. Only his hatred gave him the strength to run. Emasculated, flabby muscled, fat, he ran heavily, panting for air, sweating.

He carried two weapons he had devised, a fist spear and fist knife. To a long, stiff, thumbless leather mitten on his right hand and arm he had strapped a short spear. The left hand wore a similar device with a flint knife bound to it. With clenched fists he could drive the spear point deep into an enemy, slash the knife across flesh. With these weapons he would kill Agon. Agon was old now. No longer could he sing the axe song. No longer could he dodge a spear or wield his axe. Eran would kill him slowly, driving the spear and knife into him repeatedly while his blood spurted out.

But who was the young axe man they now pursued? Agon and Eena had been old when Eran fled fron Bear Hill—they could have had no more children. Alar? Could he have lived? Eran had driven his spear twice into Alar's throat. He had seen Alar die. . . .

Elina heard the heavy footsteps first—someone running ponderously toward them. They darted into the underbrush and threw themselves facedown on the ground, their weapons in hand. Birdman spread his gray cloak over them, and they lay motionless, waiting.

A running figure pounded down the hillside, swept past them less than a spear-throw away, and disappeared in the trees.

Sagon had a momentary glimpse of the man, a hulking black-haired giant grasping a short spear and a knife. A face filled with hatred. Something else . . . a streak of yellow hair through the heavy mane. . . .

Men on either side of them raced down the hillside and were gone.

They cautiously raised Birdman's cloak and listened. The sound of the running men was faint now, receding. They looked around, searching for any pursuer who might crouch in the undergrowth. Elina whispered, "They have gone."

Sagon came to his feet. "I thought that was my enemy. But he carried a spear and knife."

Birdman asked, "What do you mean?"

"My enemy has no thumbs."

"No thumbs?"

"Agon cut them off."

Birdman stared at him.

"It is the way in the tribe of Grae."

Birdman nodded, "Yes. I remember now."

Elina said, "You should have killed him."

"He is not the one I seek. If I had killed that man, all the other men would have heard."

"Now we have to find the one who waits."

"Why?"

"She is the only one who can help you find your enemy."

"How do you know this?"

"Women know many things."

Sagon lifted his spears. "Lead us. We have not much

time. When all the running men come together and find we have escaped, they will search for us again."

Elina pointed up the stream valley. "This way. We have to hurry."

The old woman stared at the bowls of water and fruit that sat in the tiny opening into the cave. For three days they had remained untouched.

The woman in the cave had spoken to her the first night: "Go, Mother. I do not need food or water. Escape from Kane while you can."

"He will kill me if I leave."

"He will kill you if you stay."

"You will die without food or water."

"No. I will not die. You know why."

Then the old woman knew. She said, "The moon will be full tonight."

"Yes."

"I will wait three days."

"No more. Then go."

"Where shall I go?"

"A man comes from the east. Do you know the fir forest?"

"I have seen it. I dared not enter it."

"You will enter it without harm. He will meet you there."

"How will I know him?"

"He will carry an axe. You must tell him something."

"What?"

"Tell him that safety for those he loves is with the Mother."

Now three days had passed. The old woman spoke for the last time into the tiny opening of the cave. "I go now. Speak if you would have me stay."

No answer came from the cave. The old woman took her few things from the cliff overhang and hobbled toward the distant forest.

Elina said, "The place is near."

Ahead of them they saw a line of low cliffs where the stream had eaten away the rock. They approached the cliffs cautiously.

Under an overhang they saw the smoke-blackened stone ceiling that told of cooking fires. The ground in front of the overhang was tramped hard, and the debris of flint chips, bones, and half-burned sticks indicated many years of human habitation.

Sagon touched his wolf totem. "This is the place. I sense cruelty and evil here."

A wall of heavy stone blocks stood against the cliff face. A tiny opening in the wall held two wooden bowls. Elina touched them. "They put her in here."

Sagon and Birdman lifted the top stones away, then the next layer and the next. Sagon peered into the cave. "She may have gone back into the darkness. . . ."

They lifted more stones away, and Elina slipped through the opening into the cave. All was silent, then she spoke: "I see no woman. People have lived here for many years."

Sagon hurled more blocks away. "We will make torches. She may be far back in the cave."

Elina looked out from the opening. "There is no need for torches. She is gone."

Sagon asked, "How do you know she is not in the darkness?"

"Women know."

"I will look."

"You will see things you do not like."

"What?"

Elina came out of the cave. "Things on the ceiling."

Sagon took fire stones and tinder from his belt pouch. He scraped together scorched twigs from the fire pit and started a tiny fire. He added larger bits of sticks and branches, then tore a dead branch from a nearby pine and lighted one end in the fire. He carried the torch to the cave opening and entered.

The feeling of evil in the cave was so powerful that he almost reeled backward. Holding the torch high, he stared at the interior of the cave.

A fire pit lay near a side wall, furs and robes were piled against the other wall, and a dark tunnel at the rear led back into the cliff. Then Sagon looked up at the stone ceiling, and he drew back in horror. A great horned figure of a dancing demon glared down at him. The horns were of no animal, but of some terrible mockery of all horned animals, curved and twisted, their ends red with blood. Below the horns was a demonic face so filled with hatred, so evil, so menacing, that Sagon felt his spirit quail. The body was bloated like a huge spider, the feet were cloven-hoofed, and a writhing tail lashed from the creature's hindquarters. Without knowing how he knew, the word *Kaan* filled Sagon's mind.

The creature had been painted on the cave ceiling with black-and-red ochre, and in the flickering torchlight the grotesque creature seemed alive. Sagon thought with horror of the woman being sealed in the near darkness of the cave with the terrible apparition dancing above her. He forced himself past the demon and went back into the depths of the cave, and he saw more grotesque creatures looming high on the walls and ceiling, creatures unknown to any human, horrible in their reflection of the evil and twisted mind that had created them.

He pressed on, deep into the cave, and gradually the ceiling and walls closed around him until he could go no farther. By the light of the torch he saw the opening become so small that it seemed no adult could have squeezed through. Yet the woman was not in the cave.

The mystery of the women swirled around him, more frightening than the demons of the cave. Something had happened here that no man could know.

The torch flame grew feeble. He came back through the tunnel into the room of the fire pit, grateful for the air and light from the entrance. Something in the fire pit. He knelt and sifted through the ashes. Blackened flint spear points. Someone had burned spears in the pit. He took a point from the ashes and inspected it. The knapping was similar to what Agon had taught him, but with larger flakes so that each edge of the point was jagged as the teeth of a leopard. The people who had lived here killed by ripping apart the flesh of their victims.

Two dark objects lay against the wall. Sagon held the torch near them. Things of leather. Sagon touched them, lifted them.

He staggered out of the cave.

Elina stared at him. "You should not have gone in."

Sagon's voice was tight. "The woman is gone, as you said."

"You saw the evil spirits?"

"Yes."

"What, then? You look as if you would die."

Sagon held out the leather objects. "His spear and knife were strapped to his hands with mittens like these." His face showed his anguish. *"I met my enemy, and I did not know him."*

10

The Hunters

KANE, ERAN, AND their men met upstream from the ash tree that lay against the bank of the river. Big Man and his men approached, trembling with fear.

Kane's face contorted with rage. "You let him escape." He drove his spear into one of Big Man's men and shook the convulsing body off like a speared fish. "If you fail to find him again, I will kill three men, one from each group."

Eran pointed with his spear. "Lazor and his men come on the other side." They watched as the tiny figures grew in size and approached the riverbank. Kane spat. "He has one less than he started with." He shook his spear at Lazor and shouted, "Stay over there!"

Lazor shouted back, "We have to. The river is rising. One man drowned."

"You will all drown if you let the axe man escape!" Kane turned his back on Lazor. "Look for tracks. He had to leave the river near here. Find his trail, or another of you will die."

The men spread out, running like wolves following a scent, searching the narrow floodplain, the undergrowth, the ravines.

A man called out. He ran to Kane with a blue feather. "No bird this color lives here."

Kane studied the feather. "It has been glued to something."

He pushed his spear point against the man's stomach. "Where does such a bird live?"

The man swallowed in fear. "It is a forest bird."

"Show me where you found the feather."

The man led Kane and Eran to the ash tree. "There."

Eran said to Kane, "You do not remember this, but you were here once."

"When?"

"We came here before you were born. This is the place where your mother and I first came ashore after we left Bear Hill. We followed this stream up to the cliffs." Eran touched the tree. "It is strange."

"Why is it strange?"

"This is an ash tree. We came on an ash tree. It looked much like this tree."

Kane said, "It means nothing to me except one thing."

"What?"

"The axe man came from the forest. We will follow the stream to our cave. If he is not there, he will be in the forest."

"He can hide in the forest."

Kane showed his teeth. "He will not hide from me. I will burn him out."

When they came to the cliff shelter and saw that the stones had been taken from the cave entrance, Kane killed another man in his rage. "Someone let him slip by us! He has let my mother out. Find him and the old woman, and I will burn them alive!"

A hunter ran up. "The old woman's tracks are under the trees, going toward the forest. She made them at least a day ago."

"Where are the axe man's tracks? Where are my mother's tracks? Did they fly through the air?"

The men looked over their shoulders, touching their totems. "We see no other tracks."

Kane spat in disgust. "Fools." He motioned with his spear. "Come! We go to burn the forest. Let the old woman and the axe man die in the flames."

Eran stared at his son. "Your mother is in the forest."

"She went with the axe man. Let her burn, too."

"You would burn your own mother?"

Kane scowled at his father. "Ka's spirit is in me. I am Ka. Those who anger me will be killed. Ka shows mercy to no one."

"No one?"

"Not even my own mother." Kane's eyes burned with a demonic flame. "If my arm angers me, I will cut it off. If you anger me, I will kill you."

"I am your father. Agon told me that any man who kills his father is cursed by the gods."

"Agon lies. There are no gods. There is only Kaan, destroyer of all."

Eran said, "I know that there is only Kaan. Ever since Agon mutilated me, I have hoped that my son would avenge me. Ever since you were born, I have hoped that the spirit of Ka was your spirit. Now I know that you are truly Ka. Agon with all the magic of his axe song cannot stand against you. Do as you will with those who anger you. Together we will go to kill Agon."

"And your mother. She stood beside Agon while he cut you."

"Even my mother. They both will die."

11

Fire

SAGON, ELINA, AND Birdman found the old woman on the ground at the edge of forest. She saw them and tried to rise, only to fall back helplessly. She watched in terror as they approached.

Elina knelt by her. "Grandmother, do not fear us. We come to help you."

"You won't kill me?"

"No. Why should we?"

"I left the cave."

"We saw that from your tracks. Are you the one who put the bowls of water and fruit in the opening?"

"Three days they sat there. She would not eat or drink."

"The moon was bright."

Something changed in the old woman's eyes; a look of mystery replaced the fear.

Sagon asked gently, "Who sealed her in the cave?"

"I know nothing."

Elina smiled at the old woman. "They both are shamans. They are not evil men. You can tell them everything."

"Everything?"

"Yes. What is your tribe?"

"It was Barhunder's. The horse hunters."

"Was?"

"Kane killed Barhunder."

"Is he the one you fear?"

"He kills men as our hunters kill horses."

"Did he seal the woman in the cave?"

"His own mother!"

Elina looked at Sagon. "He is the one you seek."

The old woman said, "His father let him do that."

Sagon leaned over the old woman. "Tell us of his father."

"He let the men pile rocks in the entrance."

"Does he kill men?"

"He is evil as Kane."

Sagon held out the leather mittens he had found in the cave. "Did he wear things like these on his hands?"

The old woman stared at the mittens. "He wore them on both hands. He had strange magic. He held his spear and knife on the sides of his hands."

Artron had said, "Two come from one." Kane was Eran's son! The single evil of Eran was now two evils, Eran and Kane! Sagon could hardly speak. "What was the mother's name?"

"Ara."

"Why did they seal her in the cave?"

The old woman touched the mare totem that hung on her breast. "Kane said, 'Now we go to kill Agon.' "

Terrible anger flooded through Sagon's spirit. His dream had foretold the future. Men of evil plotted against his father.

And the men were son and grandson of Ka!

Elina looked out through the trees. "Many men are running toward us."

Sagon threw down his traveling robe and with Birdman's help lifted the old woman onto it. They ran into the forest with the woman while Elina ran behind carrying the spears and Birdman's branch. Something roared at the edge of the forest, and they heard men running through the trees.

Birdman panted, "This way!" and they turned and entered a part of the forest filled with gloom, a dark green cavern where heavy vines dangled from the trees and dense branches shut out the light. Moving soundlessly on a soft cushion of moss, they ran deeper into the sheltering forest while the sound of the running men died away.

The old woman's face was pale, and she gasped for breath. They placed her on the ground to rest, and Elina stroked the woman's hair to comfort her.

She stared at Sagon's axe. She said feebly, "You carry an axe."

"Yes."

"The woman in the cave told me you would come."

"She knew I would come?"

"She told me you would meet me in the forest."

A faint aroma of smoke. Birdman sniffed the air. "The forest burns!" The smoke smell became stronger, and they heard crackling sounds. Birdman listened, turning. "They are setting fires all around the forest!"

Sagon saw the face of the demon who danced on the cave ceiling. "We have to break out."

Birdman shook his head. "We would all die. There is another way."

"What?"

"We will become bears." Birdman bent down and spoke to the old woman. "We have to run fast."

She spoke weakly: "Leave me here."

They saw she was dying. They knelt by her, and Elina held her hand. She looked up at them. "Go!" She stopped breathing, then she shuddered and drew in another breath. She made a little motion with her hand, beckoning Sagon closer. "She told me . . ."

He bent near her. "What?"

She breathed once more, then whispered, ". . . the safety for those you love is with the Mother." She shuddered again and stopped breathing.

Sagon looked up at Elina and Birdman. "Her spirit rests."

Elina gently closed the old woman's eyes. "Grandmother, come again to your tribe. You will be young again and run and dance without tiring. Sleep now."

Sagon wrapped his robe around her. "She was brave. She will come again."

Flames roared behind them, and a wave of heat blasted through the forest as the undergrowth exploded in fire. Birdman shouted, "This way!" and they raced ahead of the flames.

For a moment it seemed that the fire would engulf them, the roaring demon grasping at them with red claws, searing their backs with its fiery breath. Then they drew away and ran through the forest in a path known only to Birdman.

Birdman made the call of an owl, and the forest people appeared magically and silently from behind the giant trunks of the trees. They embraced Birdman, Sagon, and Elina, smiling at them, their eyes luminous in the green darkness. They led Sagon and Elina to the base of an ancient fir, its trunk thick as the length of two men. Men drew a moss-covered flat rock aside, revealing a dark hole that led down into the earth.

"Now we become bears." Birdman motioned to Elina and Sagon. "Follow our people."

They slid into the hole, and they became bears.

Down into the earth. The smell of earth, strong and full of life. The softness of earth, yielding, moving, caressing. The light of earth, not black, but glowing softly around them. The security of earth, an ancient home welcoming. The spirit of the earth, all-powerful, everlasting, giver of life. Here they would sleep through the long winter in the magic of the earth.

Sagon slid to a stop and felt Elina's feet touch his shoulders. She said, "I like being a bear."

He stood and felt her slide down behind him. He moved forward quickly, aware that Birdman and the forest men were above them. In the strange luminescent glow of the earthen walls and ceiling he saw the forest women and children running ahead of him through a long tunnel. He turned and made Elina squeeze past him, and then they ran through the passage.

They came to a large room where the forest people had gathered. Huge roots of trees descended from the earthen ceiling into the floor, living stalactites hanging like the trunks of mammoths between the giant trees above them and the earth below. In the glow of light they saw against the walls leather bags, plump bladders, covered baskets, piles of hides and furs, and stacks of spears.

Birdman and the forest men entered the room, talking, laughing softly. Birdman pointed to the bags and bladders. "We store food here like animals of the earth. The water and spears are things only man seems to need."

"How long have the tunnel and this room been here?" Sagon asked.

"Forever. The forest people have always had them. They are in every forest. Some say the ancient people came up through the earth."

"How long can you live down here?"

"As long as the food and water last."

"Will the forest be destroyed by the fire?"

"Who can say? Kane and his men set fires on all sides. We have never had a fire like that. Sometimes only the underbrush burns. If the ancestor trees burn, we will know."

"How will you know?"

Birdman touched one of the great roots. "The tree spirits will cry out."

"Yes. I have heard a tree spirit cry out when a great wind tore it from the ground."

Elina looked up at the ceiling. "The fire is coming."

They heard it—a muffled roaring like distant thunder, growing louder and louder. The forest people crouched on the floor, staring upward with anxious eyes, mothers holding babies, children clinging to their mothers, adolescents listening and watching the ceiling with wide eyes. Birdman held his green oak branch protectively over the people while Sagon grasped his axe and Elina her spear.

The roaring beast swept over them. For a terrible moment it tore at the ground above the people, then raced on through the forest and was gone.

Birdman lowered his branch and spoke to Sagon: "Your magic is strong."

Sagon shook his head. "I have no magic."

"You have more than you know."

Birdman did a strange thing. With the end of the branch he made a single short line on the earth floor, then a single indentation. Sagon felt a sense of remembrance: Many years ago Agon had made two marks like these on the wall of the great chamber of the animals at Bear Hill. They were the first symbol in the signs of the Onstean, the Invisible Stone Spirit Men. They were the symbol for fire. Birdman wiped the symbol out with a quick brush of his sandal.

Elina said, "Tell him what would have happened if he had no magic."

Birdman smiled at her. "If the ancestor trees had burned, we would now look like meat roasting on a spit."

Kane and Eran watched grimly as the forest fire burned itself out. Kane spat on the ashes. "No one came from the fire. They must be dead."

Eran shook his head. "Only the underbrush burned. Keep our men around the edges of the forest."

"I will not wait long."

"One more day. Then we go to kill Axe Man and Spear Woman."

12

The Robe

BIRDMAN AND TWO of the men raised the stone cap and peered out into the night. Birdman hooted, and an owl replied, its call filled with mystery. One by one the people came up out of the earth. The moon shone faintly through the trees, revealing the scorched floor of the forest, and the people gazed silently at the smoking piles of ash and glowing coals where fallen branches had flamed. A smell of smoke and charred wood hung like a cloak over the forest, but the ancestor trees still stood unburned, seeming to rise even taller into the night sky because of the destruction of the undergrowth at their feet.

Birdman sent three scouts ahead, and the people crept silently through the forest toward its western edge.

Sagon had told Birdman of his thoughts the first night they spent in the earthen cavern: "Eran and Kane go to kill Agon. I must go now to warn him and my mother."

"And burn to death or die by Kane's men? Wait until tomorrow night when my people leave this forest."

"Leave for where?"

"The western forest on the massif."

"I go to my home in the east."

"We will go through the western forest," Elina said, "and circle back through the hills to the river. Do not go to the east now. Kane watches for us there."

"You do not go with me."

"I do."

Sagon scowled at her. "I go alone."

"Then I follow you."

Sagon appealed to Birdman. "Keep her in your camp. Tie her to a tree."

Birdman smiled. "Not I. Sooner a forest cat." He said to Sagon. "I go with you, too."

"No. Your people need you."

"Axe Man and Spear Woman need me more."

"My mother?"

"Kane's cave held an evil father and son. They burned the forest, thinking Kane's mother with us. Their evil knows no limits. They would kill your mother as well as your father."

The forest people approached the edge of the burned forest. Birdman hooted again, and no owl answered. Birdman held up his hand. "Wait."

They crouched in the ashes, listening for any sound, watching for any movement.

Elina pointed. A man leaning on a spear stood in dark silhouette at the forest edge, motionless in the moon shadow.

Birdman signaled, and two of the forest hunters crept silently toward the man. Something hissed through the air, and the man grunted and fell. Birdman signaled again, and the forest people moved forward, three women wiping their tracks from the ashes with twig brooms. Four men lifted the dead spearman and carried him as the forest tribe, with Elina and Sagon, left the home of their ancestors and crossed the hills toward the western forest.

They reached the forest before sunrise, and they buried Kane's man in a ravine under a thick layer of leaves. They went into the midst of the forest and halted by a stream winding through a sheltered glade.

Birdman spoke to his people: "I go with Sagon and Elina to warn Axe Man and Spear Woman that Kane comes with many men to kill them. Keep hidden here until I return."

The hunt leader, a man called Hawk, replied, "We killed the man of Kane with ease. We will leave half our hunters here; take the rest with you. Every night we will kill some of Kane's men."

Sagon spoke: "Plains and hills with few trees lie between here and my home. Kane's best men, the horse hunters, kill on the plains as easily as you do in the forest."

"The horse hunters and the fish people," Birdman said, "are not killers of men. Kane has terrified them into helping him. The men of Ka, the men with knobs of hair, were killers of men. If Kane had them, we could not stand against him."

Hawk asked, "Who were the men of Ka?"

Birdman raised his oak branch. "Men from the south. Their god was Kaan, source of all evil. Even with their bodies pierced with spears, they fought to the death."

Sagon felt a sudden wave of apprehension. The men he had seen in his dream wore their hair in knobs.

"Only Axe Man," Birdman said, "could overcome them in battle."

"Who was Axe Man?" Hawk asked.

Sagon answered, "My father. He is called Agon."

"Does he still live?"

"He lives."

"How could he overcome the men of Ka?"

Birdman answered Hawk. "By his magic. The magic of the axe song."

Hawk pointed to Sagon's axe. "Do you have the same magic?"

Sagon shook his head. "I have no magic."

Elina spoke: "I have seen his magic. He killed three armed and evil men while I took one breath."

The hunters stared at Sagon. Hawk said, "I would fight beside such a man. I will join you with half our hunting band."

Sagon shook his head. "I have thought about this. No one will come with me. Kane's men surrounded the forest. He must have many men. Even with you and our hunters, we could not fight him. The only way I can save my father and mother is to warn them that Eran and Kane come to kill them. If I go alone, I travel fast and unseen."

Birdman nodded. "True. The lone hawk hunts best."

Elina's eyes showed her concern. "The cave lion needs the lioness."

Sagon said to her, "I will not have you killed. Stay with Birdman and his people."

"I am not afraid."

"I know that." He touched her arm. "You have been the young lioness. But now I must go alone. I ask you not to follow me."

"You ask me?"

"Yes."

Tears came to Elina's eyes. She took her rolled traveling robe from her shoulder and held it out to Sagon. "You covered the old mother with your robe when she died. Take my robe and know that my spirit goes with you."

Sagon took the robe. "I will bring it back to you."

Elina wiped at her tears and smiled. "The lone horse on our cave wall waits."

He smiled at her. "Together, we will bring all the animals to our cave."

"I will go back there tomorrow, when it is safe. I will tell the animals that you will come." She touched his hand.

Sagon held her hand a moment, then he raised his spear to Birdman and his people, turned toward the east, and disappeared into the forest.

13

Big Man

SAGON WATCHED THE camp of Kane and Eran and their men from the cliff top. The father and son were similar in height, but while Eran moved heavily and laboriously, Kane was like a leopard. The golden streak in Eran's hair told Sagon of Eena, his mother, and he wondered at the cruelty of the older man. Kane's raven-black hair and sinuous body spoke only of evil and terrible strength.

Sagon counted the men. Five times he touched the fingers of both hands. He thought, We could hold them off for a while at Bear Hill, but then we would have no more boulders to roll down on them. If they come up the escarpment, we can kill some of them, but there are too many men. But I will kill Eran and Kane. Kill them as I did the men in Elina's cave.

Elina. Sagon touched her robe.

Kane had Big Man brought before him. Big Man felt his bowels turn to water as Kane regarded him with eyes of death.

"The axe man had a woman with him. I want them both. Tell me how to find them."

Big Man's voice shook. "They said they came from up the river . . . that is all I know. . . ."

Kane brought his spear point against Big Man's stomach. "Then you die."

Big Man's legs became wet. Suddenly, his memory brought something spewing up. "They said they came from a river that feeds this river . . . five days upriver. . . ."

Kane pushed the spear harder. "What else?"

"Nothing . . . that was all they said. . . ."

Kane stared into Big Man's eyes. "Think."

Big Man groveled before Kane. "Don't kill me. . . ."

Kane kept the pressure on his spear. "Tell me how the axe man looked."

"He was high as you. . . ."

Eran spoke: "Tell us of his axe. Was anything carved on the handle?"

"A wolf head."

"Did he fight you with the axe?"

"We did not fight. . . ."

Kane spat in disgust. "You let him come into your camp, and you did not fight him?"

"Yes . . . I mean no. . . ."

"Tell us of the woman."

"They said she was his sister. . . ."

"Did you take her?"

"She was not yet a woman."

Kane showed his teeth. "When we find her, I will take her while the axe man watches as he hangs over our fire." Using his spear point, he drew a map of the river in the dirt. "We are three days from the sea. Two more days and we will come to the river the axe man and girl came from. We will go up the river and find them."

Eran's eyes burned with anticipation. "We will take them with us. If he is son of Agon, Agon will come down from Bear Hill when he sees what we do to his son and the girl."

Sagon watched as Big Man was questioned. While he was too far above the camp to hear what was said, he saw the terror of Big Man and the ferocity of Kane. Kane had drawn something in the earth with his spear. . . .

Should he wait and watch, or should he go to warn his father and mother?

Elina was safe with Birdman in the western forest. Why

should he wait? Go now. Warn his parents. What had the old grandmother said before she died? *"The safety for those you love is with the Mother."* His parents had seen the Earth Mother. They had never told him of it, but he had learned from the things they said that they had escaped from Ka and fled across the plains to the Blue Hills. There they had found the Earth Mother and had been spared by her. They had found a secret cave to which they longed to return. He would take his parents to the Blue Hills. There the Earth Mother would protect them.

Sagon slid back from the cliff edge. When his parents were safe, he would come back to Elina and the cave of the horses. There they would bring the waiting animals from the rock walls. There he would take Elina as his mate.

14

Together

SAGON HURRIED UPSTREAM along the river, ahead of Kane's forces. In a day and a half he came to the tributary river that flowed down from Elina's cave of the horses. He forded the tributary, planning to continue northeast along the big river that led to Bear Hill, far in the east.

He could not let Kane find Elina. He turned back and went a short distance up the tributary toward Elina's home. He found a sheltered lookout on a hilltop and waited there, watching the main river valley. Kane's men were behind him, but not yet visible.

At noon he saw them. They approached at a hunter's trot, a sinuous line of men headed by Eran and Kane. They came to the tributary river and milled around its entrance like sniffing hyenas. Then Kane waved his spear, and the men forded the small river. Sagon held his breath: They would go on. Elina would be safe.

Then Kane turned and led the men to the west, along the tributary toward the cave of the horses.

Somehow Kane had learned about Elina's home! Sagon backed from the hilltop and ran at full speed through the hills toward the distant stone arch that bridged the river.

In the middle of the afternoon he sighted the arch, poised like a stone rainbow from cliff to cliff across the river. He ran past the arch, keeping to the cliff tops so as to leave no tracks along the soft earth and sand of the floodplain. Behind him, still far down the river valley, he saw Kane and his running men.

He came to the portion of the cliff top that hung above the rockfall and the hidden entrance to the cave of the horses. As he descended the cliff, Elina appeared on a rock ledge.

"I could have speared you like a young ibex." She smiled at him. "Are you lost?"

"Kane and his men come."

"I know."

"I came to take you with me."

"I am ready."

"You knew I was coming?"

She held up a food bag and robe.

"You know too much," he told her. "No man would want you as a mate."

"I want no man." She smiled impishly at him.

He pointed downriver. "Many men want you."

"Many men will not get me."

They ran back up the cliff and into the hills, leaving no tracks, disappearing like two wolves as Kane and his men rounded the bend in the river and came to the rockfall.

As night approached, they found a sheltered outcropping on a hillside in which to sleep. When Elina unrolled her robe, she glanced at her old robe that Sagon carried. "Would you like to have the new robe?"

He shook his head. "I am used to the old robe now."

"It is too small for you."

"It fits me."

She said nothing.

"When you are a woman, we could have one robe under us, one robe over us, as my father and mother do."

"Your mother and father are mated. We are not mated."

"We could be."

"When I am a woman."

"Yes. When you are a woman."

Elina turned her face away. "Go to sleep."

In the night Sagon dreamed about the sun. He told Elina of his dream. "Artron was with me. We stood watching the setting sun. The sun sent out flames, and they ate the sky."

"Who is Artron?"

"Shaman of the aurochs hunters."

"Did he speak to you in your dream?"

"He pointed at the sun, then at the river."

Sagon covered his right eye with one hand and looked at the rising sun, holding a round pebble before his left eye.

"Something leaps from the sun."

Elina picked up a pebble and gazed at the sun as Sagon had. "I see it. Beyond the edge of the sun. Long flames."

"Can Artron see what will happen?"

Sagon nodded. "He can tell when the blizzard comes out of the north, when the thunderstorm comes from the west, when the game will move to the plain or forest, when the geese will fly."

"Did he teach you these things?"

"Before I left Bear Hill, my spirit flew with his. Now I know these things, yet he did not speak to me of them."

"He has made you a shaman."

"No."

"And an animal man."

"You are not to know of these things."

"Because I am a woman?"

"Women are not to know men's magic. We do not try to learn women's magic."

Elina gathered up her weapons and robe. "We talk while Kane and Eran lead their men toward the home of your parents. We must circle out around them."

Sagon pointed to the sun. "A storm more powerful than ten storms comes. We must cross the river now before the great wall of water strikes."

Now Elina stared at Sagon. "You know this?"

"Yes."

She smiled triumphantly. "Then you *are* a shaman."

They circled north, then east through the hills, then back south toward the river. When they reached the river, they saw the tracks of Kane's men on the bank, running east.

"We have to get to Bear Hill before them." Sagon pointed at the river. "It flows too fast to cross here. I know of only two places where it can be crossed: at the entrance to the sea where it splits into many smaller branches, and at the ford near Bear Hill. But when I came west along the river, I saw one other place where it might be done."

"We don't have time to go back to the sea," Elina said. "Eran must know of the ford. Where is the other place?"

"About halfway between here and Bear Hill. The river flows through a narrow gorge, where the cliff tops on either side are close together."

"How close?"

"About a spear-throw apart."

"And you think we can leap across?"

"Perhaps."

Elina glanced at him from the sides of her eyes. "Perhaps you will show me. Perhaps you will grow wings."

"I have thought of a way."

"Tell me of your way."

"You have seen the rainbow of stone that crosses your small river."

"You will make one for this big river?"
"Perhaps."
Elina stamped her foot. "Tell me!"
He smiled. "Wait and see."

15

People of Ka

KAGUN, CHIEFTAIN OF the people of Ka, roared in anger. Seven feet tall, muscled like a cave lion, his great knot of hair coiled above his slanting low forehead, he glared at the two scouts who stood before him.

"A tribe dares come onto our hunting grounds?"

One of the scouts spoke. "They come on the other side of the river."

Kagun raised his spear. "Lie to me and you will burn over a slow fire."

"We do not lie. A man big as you leads them."

Kagun struck the man, sending him rolling on the ground. "No man is big as I am. Are his men big, too?"

The man wiped blood from his mouth. "Not the men. Some carried spears with three points."

Kagun pressed the point of his spear against the chest of the other scout. "Does he lie?"

"He does not lie. I saw the spears."

Kagun pressed the spear point harder. "How many men come with this man?"

The scout held up his hands, again and again. "Many."

"How far away?"

"Far." The scout pointed to the west. "Near the mountains."

"You both lie. There are no men in the west."

Kala, mother of Kagun and priestess of the tribe, spoke:

"Axe Man and Spear Woman flew from the cliff top toward the setting sun."

"That is a story told by old women. People do not fly."

"Our hunters saw them fight with Ka on the cliff edge. The hunters found Ka's body at the base of the cliff, but Axe Man and Spear Woman were gone. They could not have come down that cliff face; the top hangs out over the bottom."

"Wolves carried their bodies away."

"And not touched Ka?"

Kagun spat. "There was no Axe Man, no Spear Woman. Do not bother me with stories told by old women."

"Beware, Kagun. They had powerful magic."

Kagun pressed his spear even harder against the scout's chest. "What weapons did this man carry?"

Blood trickled down the scout's stomach. "A big spear."

"Bigger than my spear?"

"No man could carry a spear bigger than yours."

"Did he carry an axe?"

"We saw no axe."

Kagun lowered his spear. "You live for now. Tomorrow we go to find these men. If you lie, you both will burn to death." He scowled at Kala. "No axe. Forget Axe Man and Spear Woman."

"I dreamed of them. They still live. They are gods."

"If I see them, I will believe in your gods," Kagun said. "Until then I have men to kill."

In the morning Kagun led forty warriors west along the top of the cliffs that bordered the river on the south. They kept in the shelter of the ancient forest that covered the southern lands, sending scouts ahead and on each flank to warn the main body if the approaching forces were sighted. The men of Ka wore their long hair as Kagun did, piled in a protective knob on the tops of their heads, giving them the appearance of giants. Taught brutality and fierceness from childhood, they feared nothing except their chieftain and their god, Kaan.

Kagun brought with him twelve-year-old Karem, his oldest son, to learn the art of war. Karem pointed down from the cliff at the river, which still roared high up on the floodplain as a result of the storm. "If we find the ones who come, how do we cross the river to kill them?"

"As we always cross rivers," Kagun growled. "The men carry long vines and go across."

"Even in flood?"

"A few men drown. We go across."

"Why do we not cross now?"

"So we can kill them in the night. We have always fought that way. They think the river protects them, so they put no guards on the riverbank. That is how Ka killed the bison hunters."

"Kala told me that the axe-man god came from the tribe of bison hunters."

Kagun smashed his huge arm against the side of Karem's head. "There was no axe-man god. Never speak of him again."

Karem staggered back, then glared at his father. "When I am as big as you, I will kill you."

"You will never be chieftain until you do kill me. But every time you try it, I will break your bones."

"I do not fear you."

"Good. Our people fear nothing. When they fight, they never stop until their enemy is dead."

"The scouts said a man big as you leads the enemy. Will you kill him in the night, or will you fight him?"

"Either way. I will take his head."

"Let me cut it off."

Kagun struck his son again. "Get your own heads."

Since the time long ago of the battle with the bison hunters, the people of Ka had slowly migrated westward through the forest in search of game. Three days into their journey, Kagun's scouts reported a strange object ahead.

"A giant bear. It watches the river."

Kagun snorted in disgust. "First you see a giant man. Now a giant bear."

They led him to a bend in the river cliffs. Silhouetted against the setting sun was the figure of a crouching bear, a bear as high as the cliffs.

"Have you seen a bear with trees growing on it before?" Kagun scowled at the scouts. "Come to me one more time telling of giants and bears and I will cut out your tongues."

Karem spoke: "I will climb the bear. From the top I can see if the men come."

"And they can see you. Warn them and you die."

"I will keep hidden in the trees."

Kagun pondered this. "Come here."

Kerem approached warily. "What?"

"Unknot your hair. If people live there, they must not know you are from our tribe."

Karem unwound his knob of hair. "What if they are our enemies?"

"Lead them to us."

"What if they are not our enemies?"

Kagun showed his teeth. "The same."

From the porch Eena saw the boy come from the forest into the open land that surrounded Bear Hill. She knelt behind the protective wall of the porch and made the sound of an owl. She made the signs silently to Agon: *Stranger. Boy.*

Agon put down the deer he was skinning. Bending low, he came silently to her side.

The boy came furtively, as a weasel follows a rabbit, moving in short quick bursts, then crouching behind a rock or tree.

Eena spoke softly: "What if he tries to come up the escarpment?"

"We warn him."

"He is not of Emar's tribe."

"No."

They watched the boy approach. He gazed at the smooth and inaccessible walls of the hill, then saw the escarpment. Agon and Eena stood and came to the lip of the porch as the boy started up the escarpment. Agon held his spear crosswise and called to the boy, "Why do you come here?"

The boy stared up at them. He touched his ears and shook his head. Then he started up the narrow path again.

Agon held his spear with the point up. "Do not come up."

Again the boy touched his ears and shook his head. He kept on climbing.

Agon held his spear with the point aimed at the boy. "Stop or I kill." Still the boy came on.

Eena whispered, "He doesn't understand."

"Maybe."

"Look at the bruises on his face. Someone has beaten him."

Agon lifted a boulder from the heap that lay at the edge of the porch. He held it above his head and called to the boy, "Go away or this stone will kill you."

Now the boy seemed to understand. He stopped and looked up at Agon. He pointed to his mouth and made the motions of eating. Then he fell forward and lay facedown on the trail.

16

The Rainbow Tree

ELINA CONTEMPLATED THE opposite cliff top, then the roaring river as it hurtled between the cliff walls a thousand feet below.

"A spear-throw, you said."

Sagon scuffed his feet. "Perhaps two spear-throws."

"And you will make a stone rainbow across."

"Not stone."

"What, then?"

"A tree."

She looked at the firs that grew along the cliff top. "You will tell a tree to throw itself across the gorge."

"We will help it."

She touched the rough bark of the nearest tree. "It will take a moon for us to gnaw through the trunk with hand axes."

"Another tree waits." Sagon led Elina to a huge fir that leaned out over the gorge from the very lip of the cliff. "I saw it when I came here before. One great root holds it, here at the back, going down into this deep crevice in the rock."

Elina examined the tree and its thick root. "It has lived here from the time of our ancestors, standing against storms, snow, and ice. Its spirit is strong yet, but it is slowly dying. It will forgive us."

Sagon touched the leg-sized root. "One cut could be enough. When the root breaks, the tree may leap like a speared bull." He drew his flint knife from his belt. "My mother says a secret song to the tree spirit before she breaks off its dead branches for our fire. Do you know the song?"

"My mother taught me the song. You must not hear it."

Sagon backed away. "I do not wish to hear it."

Elina knelt by the tree. She placed both hands upon its bark and whispered softly to the tree:

"Tree spirit feed us
Tree spirit shelter us
Tree spirit protect us
Tree spirit mate with fire
Warm us from the winter storm
Drive the long-toothed cats away."

Elina stood. "The tree is ready."

Sagon knelt by the thick root and held the sharp blade of his knife against it. "Forgive me, tree." Slowly, he drew the blade across the root.

The tree made a tiny sound. Sagon cut again, then once more, and the tree shuddered and cried out. The tree swayed in a tiny motion toward the abyss. Sagon cut again, and the root screamed in agony and began to tear. The tree swayed further, then, with a snapping of fibers, fell slowly and majestically across the gorge and crashed down on the opposite cliff edge. The great fir lay with its base on the lip of the cliff that had held and sustained it, its top on the other side of the gorge.

Elina gazed at the tree, biting her lip.

Sagon said, "It will make a good bridge."

"It was so beautiful and strong. . . ."

"But it was old."

"Yes. . . ."

Sagon searched in the grass at the cliff edge. He held out a small object to her—a seed cone from the tree. "The tree will live again."

She took the cone and carefully placed it in her belt pouch. "We will plant its seeds in the earth near our home."

"Our home?"

"When I am a woman."

"Where will our home be?"

"We will find it. There will be green grass and a stream and pond. Our tree and other trees will shelter it from the winter winds, and the sun will shine upon us. Birds will sing in our trees, and game will be thick in the forest and hills. We will be happy there."

Sagon saw the happiness in her face and eyes. "I have heard my mother and father talk of such a place. A secret place only they knew. They found it in the Blue Hills."

"We could not take their secret place."

"No."

"Did they ever live there?"

"Only a few days."

"Why? I would want to live in such a place forever."

"They could not stay. They had to warn Grae's tribe that Ka and his tribe had crossed the river. After that there was only killing and death."

Elina shuddered. "As now. Why do people kill each other?"

Sagon replied, "The bear kills whatever it wants. The cave lion kills us, bison, aurochs, deer, even wolves. The wolf kills reindeer, deer, foxes, rabbits. The fox kills rabbits, snakes, birds, mice. We kill everything, even mammoths, even other men."

"But everything except us kills only for food."

Sagon was slow in replying. Finally, he spoke: "I think we kill each other because we hate and because we remember."

"Then we will never stop killing." Elina's face was sad.

Sagon wanted to hold her again. He said, "Someday you will find the home you dream of."

"I will not find it without you."

"You will."

"Why do you not say 'we'?"

"Because I must do other things."

"I will help you do them. We will do them."

"There will be fighting and killing."

"I will fight beside you."

"I must know the spirit of all things."

"I will help you know them."

"I must bring the animals from the stone."

"While you do that, if your spirit leaves you, I will watch over you until it returns."

Sagon took her hand in his. "Now we begin. Will you cross the gorge with me on this rainbow tree?"

"Will you carry me?"

"No. The tree barely rests on this edge. After I have crossed, you will cross on your own feet."

"The tree could slip into the gorge under your weight. Let me go first to see if it is safe."

"You will not go first. You will come after me as the woman should." Sagon bent to gather up his spears and robe.

Elina climbed like a squirrel onto the massive trunk of the tree and smiled down at him. "I am not yet a woman. I will go first." Before he could stop her, she walked lightly and easily across the tree bridge toward the other cliff top, laughing as she crossed over the gorge and the river far below her.

Lazor and his four men had seen the giant fir sway and fall across the gorge as they ran along the high plateau on the south side of the river. Dropping into the tall grass, they had crept toward the rim of the gorge and the fallen tree, watching.

A slender girl came across the tree bridge toward them, while on the other side a man grasped the roots of the tree as though trying to hold it in place. As the girl neared the cliff top, the earth suddenly lurched in one brief and terrible shudder. The cliffs swayed, and the tree top sprang upward as the root end slipped from the opposite cliff edge. In that same instant the girl leaped toward the cliff top as the tree dropped like a thrown spear into the void below. While the men stared in disbelief, a thunderous crashing roar shot up from the gorge.

17

Lazor

THE MEN HAD carried Elina away from the cliff edge, seeking the shelter of the tall grass and brush. When the fir trees on the opposite side of the gorge grew small with distance, they laid her in the grass and examined the wound on her forehead.

"See how she bleeds. She will die," said the young hunter called Black Horse.

"No. See, already her eyes move under the lids." Lazor replaced the loose flap of skin on Elina's forehead and bandaged it with a leather strap. "She is Elina, daughter of Brun."

"Brun died fighting a cave lion. His mate, too."

"Their daughter lived. Her hair is the same color as her mother's. See how it glows like dark fire."

"She leaped from the tree like a hunter."

"She had to become a hunter to live."

Another man, Hunder, spoke: "She is not big, but she would make a good mate."

Lazor scowled at Hunder. "She is not yet a woman."

"Kane will take her. Why should we not take her first?"

"Because Brun was my friend. And Kane will not take her."

"He will rip out your guts to get her."

"We are not Kane's men."

"He will kill us!"

Lazor shook his head. "Kane is on the other side of the river. We will go to the south, so far that he will never find us. We will start our own tribe." He touched Elina's hair. "It is time to sleep. She may die. We will watch her through the night so that she does not wake and hurt herself by trying to run away."

In the morning they saw that Elina still lived. They gathered around her as Lazor gently touched her forhead. Black Horse pointed. "She opens her eyes!"

They bent over her as she gazed up at them. She tried to rise, and they held her to the ground.

Lazor spoke to her: "Your head is hurt. Do not try to move. I am Lazor, friend of your father. We will not hurt you."

"Let me go! He is on the other side!"

"Who was he?"

"My friend."

"He is dead."

"No!"

"The tree struck him as it fell into the gorge."

"He is still alive!"

"We watched him. He is dead."

"Let me go to him."

"Kane is in the gorge. We cannot let him see us."

"I will keep hidden in the grass."

"You are hurt."

"He may be dying. . . ."

"Is he the axe man Kane seeks?"

She made no reply.

Lazor motioned to Black Horse. "You are our best stalker. Go back to the cliff top and see if the man lives. Let no one see you."

Black Horse smiled at Elina. "I can stalk the horse herd while the lions watch. I will not be seen." He bent low and disappeared in the tall grass.

Elina struggled again to rise, but Lazor and the men held her down. Lazor said, "I bandaged your wound. Blood still flows when you move."

"Have your men take their hands off me."

"You will not run?"

"No. What happened to me?"

They helped her sit up. Lazor explained: "The earth

shook. The tree fell, and a branch struck your head as you leaped onto the cliff top. I put the flap of skin back and tied it in place with this strap. You will have only a little scar."

"It doesn't matter."

"Women should not have scars."

"Why not? So men will want them for their mates?"

"Yes."

"I will be no one's mate. Tear the skin off. I will have a scar that will frighten all men."

"The scar would not frighten me."

"The axe man would frighten you."

"The man on the cliff top is the axe man? The man Kane hunts?"

"I didn't say that!"

"No."

"He is a man who paints on cave walls."

"But you know the axe man?"

"I have heard of him. His magic is so strong that no man can stand against him."

"Even Kane?"

"Even Kane."

"But the axe man is not the man on the cliff."

Again Elina was silent.

Lazor said, "I would only take you as my mate if you wanted me. We go to start a tribe of our own in the south. We will not be men of Kane any longer."

"You are from the tribe of Barhunder, chieftain of the horse hunters. Why were you men of Kane?"

"Kane killed Barhunder and many of our men. He is so terrible that we all feared him. We forgot that we were men."

"I remember you when my father and mother were alive. My father said that you feared nothing."

"I did fear nothing. But Kane has an evil spirit in him that is so powerful and so awful that men tremble before him. He has the strength of two men, and he kills without mercy."

"How did you and your men escape from him?"

"He sent us to cross to this side of the river and find the axe man."

"Why?"

"He will take the axe man to the home of his father and kill him in his father's sight."

Elina's face became pale. "You said Kane was in the river gorge."

"Yes."

"Would he come back here to look for the axe man?"

"If he thought the axe man was here."

Elina looked fearfully toward the distant firs on the cliff edge. "What if Kane heard the tree fall?"

"He might think it fell because of the earthquake. But he might come back. That is why we ran here with you."

She held her hands to her mouth. "Kane would kill my friend. And we cannot cross the gorge to save him."

Black Horse appeared in the tall grass and came to Lazor and Elina.

"The man is dead. He does not move. He has not moved since we saw him fall. He has sunk into the grass as dead bodies do."

Elina listened to Black Horse in horror, then fell face-down on the earth and appeared to die.

When night came, the men carried Elina to the south with them. They saw that she lived and breathed, but she made no sound or movement, hanging limp as a dead fawn in their hands.

At first light they made camp in a forest of oak. Elina's spirit came back to her as the sun shone down through the rustling leaves. She spoke weakly to Lazor, "You were friend to my father. I ask you to help me."

"Your father was a good hunter, a good friend. I will help you if I can."

"Kane and his father go to kill the father and mother of my friend. Let me go to warn them."

"No. Even if you were not injured, I could not let you go alone toward a place that will be attacked."

"I must."

"I can't let you. If Kane captured you, you would die a terrible death."

"I would never let him capture me." Elina tried to stand, then swayed and would have fallen if Lazor had not held her. He helped her lie down again.

"You bled much, and for two days you have not eaten."

"I'm not hungry."

"We have to go far to the south."

"Leave me here."

"No."

Elina regarded Lazor silently. She said, "If you will take me to warn Axe Man and Spear Woman, I will be your mate."

"You give me too much to think about. Your friend's father and mother are Axe Man and Spear Woman?"

"Yes."

"Then your friend is the axe man Kane sought."

"Yes."

"And you would be my mate."

"Yes. If my friend is dead."

"You are not yet a woman."

"Soon I will be."

"I could take you then as my mate whether you wanted me or not. Any of my men could take you."

"I will kill any man who takes me by force."

Lazor looked into her eyes. "I think you would. But if we go to warn Axe Man and Spear Woman, Kane may kill all of us. I cannot make my men go to almost certain death."

"No."

Black Horse spoke: "We have not been men. I would rather die fighting than live in fear. I will go with you."

Lazor looked at the other men. Hunder stared at the

ground. "We do not know this axe man or spear woman. . . ." The other men shifted their feet uneasily, not looking at Lazor or Elina.

Lazor said, "I will not mock you if you do not come with us. You have been good hunters, good friends."

Hunder said, "We are horse hunters, not fighters of men. Kane kills men as easily as we kill a foal."

"Go to the south. Black Horse and I will go with Elina to warn Axe Man and Spear Woman; then we will go to the south. We will find you there and start our own tribe."

Hunder still did not look at Lazor. He gathered his weapons. "We will watch for you." The two other men lifted their weapons. "Yes. We will watch for you."

Lazor placed his hand on each man's shoulder. "We will find you. Go now and start your tribe."

The three men turned to the south. Hunder looked back once at Lazor, Black Horse, and Elina, and then the three men hurried into the forest.

Lazor watched them leave, then held a small bag of traveling food out to Elina. "Will you eat now? You must be strong if we are to find Axe Man and Spear Woman before Kane does."

Elina took the food bag. "I will eat." She said to Lazor, "You are a good man. I will remember that."

Black Horse cleared his throat. Elina smiled at him. "You are a good man, too. You will be my brother."

Black Horse touched his totem, a running horse. "The old stallion protects his mares. But sometimes a young stallion takes a filly from the horse herd."

Lazor looked hard at Black Horse. "Sometimes the old stallion kicks the young stallion."

Black Horse smiled. "She chose you, Lazor. I would not take her from you. After I have killed Kane, I will find another filly of my own."

18

Animal Man

SAGON TRIES TO move, and bright pain flares inside his skull. He lies motionless until the pain fades. Black. No light. He strains to open his eyes, and the blackness swallows him.

Elina

Something growls
He lies in the bear cave
Beneath the snow
Sleeping

Warmth on his face
Still the blackness
An owl calls in the night
Seeing

She lies soft and warm against him
Not Elina
Wolf

Antlers
Growing strong
Stag
Dancing in rut
Under the moon

Galloping
Stallion cries

Hooves beating the plain
Wind streaming

Artron
Sleep as the bear dreams beneath the snow
See as the great owl watches in the night
Taste the air as the wolf smells the hidden lion
Dance as the stag prances in rut
Run over the plain as the stallion gallops with his mares
Animal Man

Someone speaks
Birdman
"Your spirit has returned"

Sagon cannot see. Birdman touches his head, gently. "The tree struck you when the earth shook."

"Elina was on the tree."

"She would always be first."

"She laughed as she went across."

"I see the tree below the cliff. Not Elina."

"She is under the tree."

"I do not see her."

"Could she live? Look on the other cliff!"

"She is not there." Birdman places his hand before Sagon's eyes, then removes it. "Did you see my hand?"

"No."

Birdman is silent. Then he says, "Deep in some caves animals have no eyes."

"Take me to the cliff edge. My spirit will join hers."

"She still may live."

"Then she would be waiting on the other cliff. Or they have taken her."

"Kane is on this side of the river."

"The men in my dream. Men with huge heads. The men of Ka. They could be on the other side."

"Then she may be alive."

"Better dead."

"She can run like a deer."

Sagon sees Elina in his mind. Running ahead of him. Dancing in the mud. Calling the dolphins. Kneeling over the dying old woman. Laughing as she runs across the tree . . .

"Why did the tree let her die?"

"There is a reason why the tree fell." Birdman holds a bladder of water to Sagon's lips. "Drink. You have lain here too long."

Sagon pushes the bladder away. "Let me die."

Birdman speaks quietly: "We have to help Axe Man and Spear Woman."

"How can I help them? A blind worm."

"A shaman does not need eyes."

"I am not a shaman."

"Tell me what your spirit saw as you lay here."

"Nothing."

"Tell me what your spirit knew."

"Bear. Owl. Wolf. Stag. Stallion. Artron."

"Artron is dead. His spirit came to you with all its wisdom. You are now one of the Onstean, the Invisible Stone Spirit Men. You know which of the invisible spirits you are."

Sagon sees in his mind nine creatures dancing in a circle, deep in the earth. Fire Man. Stone Man. Water Man. Animal Man. Sun Man. Dance Man. Hunt Man. Bird Man. Dream Man.

Animal Man: Bear. Owl. Wolf. Stag. Stallion. Shaman.

Birdman called like an owl. "Who are you?"

"Sagon."

"More than Sagon. Tell me your power."

"The strength of the bear who fears nothing. The knowledge of the owl who sees in the darkness. The senses of the wolf who hears and smells all danger. The speed of the stag who dances under the moon. The fierceness of the stallion who protects his mares and colts. The magic of the Invisible Animal Spirit Man."

"What is your magic?"

"To bring all animals from within the rock."

"Why?"

"To help all things."

"Do you need your eyes to work your magic?"

"The eyes of my spirit see all."

"Who are you?"

"Animal Spirit Man."

"Will you join in the sacred dance of the Onstean?"

"Yes."

"We go to a sacred place, far from here. I will guide you."

"Kane. Eran. Where are they?"

"Ahead of us. They followed the river through the gorge."

Sagon tries to sit up. "We have to stop them."

"You are not strong enough yet. You must eat and drink."

Sagon's hand touches the axe in his belt. "I am strong enough. Give me my spears, and we will go."

"You cannot stop that many men with your axe or spears now."

"I have to."

"There is another way. You know it."

"The way of the Onstean."

Birdman holds the bladder of water to Sagon's lips again. "The way of Animal Man. Drink and eat; then we will go to the place of the Onstean."

Sagon drinks. "Where is that place?"

"You know it."

"The place I saw?"

Birdman gives Sagon a handful of traveling food. "The place you saw. The place of the cave lions."

19

Karem

KAREM LAY ON a soft bed of ferns inside the cave entrance at Bear Hill. Four days he had lain there while the golden-haired woman watched over him and cared for him. Never before had Karem heard a kind word or felt a comforting hand on his forehead. Schooled by Kagun in the way of the people of Ka, he knew only brutality, anger, and hatred. At first he had snarled at the woman as she tried to give him water and food, but now he welcomed her attention and presence.

He respected the man as a warrior, unafraid to battle a whole tribe. He had heard him warn Kagun's men when they attempted to come up the escarpment, and he had heard their screams when the man killed them. Kagun had surrounded Bear Hill with his men, but Karem knew that every attempt to take it, day or night, had the same result: the screams of dying men.

Karem found that he could talk with the woman, that she knew the language of his people. He asked her why he was there.

"You were hurt. Your spirit left you as you came up the escarpment."

"Why did you bring me up the trail and put me on this bed?"

"You would have died. Some animal of the night would have eaten you."

"My people would have left me there."

"I know."

"You bring me food and water."

"You must have them to live."

He touched her hair. "We have no people like you."

"No."

"But you speak our language."

"I lived with your tribe once."

"When?"

"Long before you were born."

"Why did you leave our tribe?"

"Ka was going to hurt me."

"Ka! The great chieftain?"

"The chieftain."

"Why was he going to hurt you?"

"I would not be his mate."

"You would not obey Ka?"

"If he had taken me, I would have killed him."

"How did you escape?"

"Axe Man saved me."

"Axe Man?"

"My mate. His name is Agon. To your people he was Axe Man."

"Axe Man was a god. He killed Ka and flew from the cliff top with Spear Woman." Karem stared at her. "You . . . are you Spear Woman?"

"Yes. My name is Eena."

Karem's eyes widened in terror. "You will kill me as you did Ka!"

"No."

"You are gods who tear our people into bits."

"We will not hurt you."

"Then why did you bring me into your cave?"

"To help you."

"What does that mean?"

"To be good to you. To keep you from dying."

"Our people help no one. Why should you help me?"

Eena gazed sadly at him. "I had a son who looked like you. He was a good boy, but a sorceress made him evil. He killed his chieftain, then his own brother."

"What is wrong with that?"

"It is forbidden by the gods."

"Not in our tribe. It is the way a warrior becomes chieftain. Our god, Kaan, tells us that."

Eena shuddered. "I have seen your god. He is horrible, a god of death and cruelty."

"You have seen Kaan and lived?"

"Yes."

Karem's eyes widened. "Then you are a god."

Agon entered the cave. "They are drawing back into the forest."

Eena went to him. "The boy's spirit has returned. He is strong again, and we have talked."

"I see that. Is he from the tribe of Ka?"

"Yes."

"Then he must die."

"I ask you not to kill him."

"I would as soon have a viper in our bed."

"He is not evil."

Agon looked long at her. "There is another reason."

Eena bowed her head. "Yes."

"He looks like Eran."

Eena looked up at him, her eyes pleading. "We have lost all our children. Eran was a good son until Hura brought her evil into his spirit. Let me raise this boy to be a good son."

"You have Sagon."

"I saw Sagon in my dreams, lying on a cliff top."

"He still lives."

"I hope and pray that he does."

"Every man of Ka, every boy, every woman, is evil. Keep this boy, and evil will live in our home."

"We cannot send him out to die."

"Have you forgotten Ka? Have you forgotten how he raped you while his men held you? Have you forgotten the heads of your father and brother hanging on poles? Have you forgotten my mother and sister lying dead with their throats cut? Have you forgotten Ka's men circling the fire with you, passing you back over their heads to bring you to Ka? Have you forgotten how Eran, your child of Ka, murdered our true son?"

Eena stood straight, her chin raised. "I cannot forget. Each one is like a burning coal in my heart. . . ."

"Then let me kill this son of Ka."

"Let the killing stop. We have killed and killed and killed. Let this boy live."

"The killing cannot stop. Three times I have sent death to the men of Ka, and still they wait to kill us."

Karem spoke in his language to Eena, and she replied. She said to Agon, "He says he will tell his father that we are gods."

"Gods?"

"Remember when we killed Ka and his men and went down the cliff? Ka's men thought we were gods."

"We are not gods."

"No."

"The boy has the look of Ka."

"He cannot help that."

"No. But I will kill him because he is of the tribe of Ka. I never told you what happened when I returned to the bison hunters to save my brother from Zur. Some men of Ka were still on that side of the river, hiding in the river valley. They stole a little girl and raped her until she died."

Eena's eyes showed her outrage and sorrow. "How terrible . . ."

"The bison hunters had no warriors left alive after Ka and his men attacked our camp years before. I trained the boys to be warriors. We found Ka's men and killed all of them. Now you would let one of these people live?"

Eena bowed her head. "I will not ask to keep him as our son. But I ask you to spare his life. Let him go back to his father."

Agon regarded her silently. Then he said, "You have had much sorrow in your life. I will not bring you more."

"You will let him go?"

"Yes."

She put her hand on his arm. "You have never brought

me sorrow. You have brought me only happiness."

Agon placed his hand over hers. "We have been mated for twice as long as most people live. In that time you have brought me only happiness."

She kissed him. "We are still young."

"Of course."

"I will tell the boy that he can go."

"Tell him to give this message to his father: We kill anyone who comes against us. But if he will take his men back to their home, we will not kill them."

Eena went to Karem's bed and spoke softly to him, telling him what Agon had said. He shook his head. "I want to stay with you."

"You cannot."

"Why not?"

"You are of the people of Ka. Axe Man would kill all of them."

"Why?

"Because of the evil they have done. They killed his people, his mother, his sister."

"He has done evil to my people. He killed Ka."

Eena looked sorrowfully at him. "The killing will go on and on. Will you be chieftain of your tribe?"

"Yes. When my father dies."

"You could stop the killing."

"How? Our people live to kill."

"You must stop them. Have them live in peace with their neighbors."

"What is peace?"

"Not fighting and killing. Becoming friends with everyone."

"What are friends?"

"People we like. People who like us."

Karem's face showed his puzzlement. "Like you and me?"

"Yes. Like you and me."

Karem was silent, then he said, "I will tell my father

what Axe Man has said, and I will tell him one more thing."

"What is that?"

"About peace." Karem got up from his bed and touched Eena's hand. "I will not forget you."

She smiled. "I will not forget you. You will be a great chieftain whose people will live in peace with all other people."

Agon and Eena watched Karem as he went down the escarpment and into the forest. Agon said, "You talked much with the son of Ka."

"Yes."

He smiled at her. "I could understand what you were saying."

"And you are not angry?"

"I am not angry. But the people of Ka will never live in peace and friendship with their neighbors."

"I hope they might."

"You have done what you could."

"There is only one other thing I want now."

"Sagon."

"You think he still lives?"

"I do." He took her in his arms. "He will come back to us."

"Every night I ask the gods to protect him."

"I do the same."

She held her face against his chest. "Do you remember our secret place in the Blue Hills?"

"I do. I remember the stream and the pond . . . the birds singing in the forest . . . our cave where we left our totems to protect the stone goddess. . . ."

"It is our true home."

"Yes."

Agon felt that Eena was weeping silently. She said, "If Sagon does not come back to us, I could live here no longer. We will go across the plain as we did when we were young, and we will find again our magic place where the sun shines down through the green leaves and the little stream flows into the pond. We will become young again and love each other forever."

20

Eyes of the Spirit

BIRDMAN LEADS SAGON to the east as a wolf might lead her injured cub. Sagon walks in total darkness, darkness such as he has never known before: no starlight, moonlight, firefly, glow of spirit lights in marsh and fen, glimmer of distant cooking fire, flame of torch, flash of lightning, streaming sunlight . . .

All darkness. All despair.

Elina dead, killed by the Earth Mother, who made the earth shudder and the tree fall.

Sagon, helpless and blind, his spear only good for probing his pathway, his magic axe useless, his search to know all things abandoned, his dream of bringing all animals from the stone shattered.

Kane triumphant, leading his killers to destroy Sagon's father and mother.

Birdman speaks: "You must save them."

"How can I save them? I cannot even walk without your help. And Kane is far ahead of us. I could not warn them even if I could see. I could not help them even if I could join them on Bear Hill. A child could fight better than I."

"You must use your magic."

"My only magic was the axe song. I cannot sing it now."

"When your spirit sees more clearly, you can."

"Agon and I throw our axes to each other. Can I do that?"

"Only if your magic is strong enough."

"How can I make it strong?"

"We go to do that."

"The Onstean?"

"You must dance with them."

"I will die."

"You may. Only if you are truly one of them will you live."

"How can I be one of them? I was only a hunter. Now I am nothing."

"You must pass through the trials."

"What are they?"

"You know them. Agon named them to you."

"The Onstean?"

"You know them. Tell me."

"Fire. Stone. Water. Animal. Sun. Dance. Hunt. Bird. Dream."

"You remember well. Do you remember where you saw the Onstean?"

"In the cliff of the cave lions."

"We will go there."

"Will you lead me?"

"You will lead me."

"How can I lead you?"

"Your spirit will see the way."

"My spirit sees nothing. The lions will kill us."

"Stop walking. What do you hear?"

"Wind. River. Birds."

"What else?"

"Nothing."

"Listen with your spirit."

Sagon listens. Breathing. Heart beating. Blood flowing. Earth shifting. Trees talking. Plants growing. Earth creatures digging. Distant call of bull bison, trumpeting of mammoth, galloping of horses, bellow of aurochs, scream of eagle. He sees the bison, mammoths, horse herd, aurochs, stiff-winged spiraling eagle. He sees the river flowing between the cliffs, trees swaying in the wind, birds busily fluttering in the forest.

Birdman speaks again: "Feel with your spirit."

Sagon feels the breeze against his skin. Warm sunshine on his head and body. Soft grass under his feet, yielding earth beneath the grass. Lungs filling with air, then emptying. Heart pulsing. Tongue against his teeth. Saliva flowing. Muscles stretching and contracting. Eyebrows moving. Skin twitching.

He touches his axe handle. Power flowing through his hand, arm, shoulder, body. He touches his totem. Wolf. Nostrils seeing game beyond sight. Running tirelessly. Fangs deep in hot flesh. Howling under the moon. Knowing secrets of the night, dark forest, rocky glen, lonely peaks, whirling snow.

Birdman again: "Sense with your spirit."

He senses the great drop of the cliff. Endless immensity of sky. River rush of water. Clouds against sun. Fecundity of earth. Passage of time. Changing of season. Movement of herds. Coming night. Sweep of plains. Bulk of mountains.

Friend. Birdman. Magic.

Enemy. Kane. Powerful.

"See as the owl, the bat."

He flies in darkness. Trees. Gliding easily past them. Scurrying earth creatures. Talons spreading, seizing.

Rocky walls. Curving. Descending, ascending, swooping. He flies far back into the darkness, knowing every turn of the stone tunnel.

Birdman places three small stones in Sagon's hand. "Each stone is your axe. Hit me with them as you would throw your axe."

"I cannot."

"Use the eyes of your spirit. The feelings of your spirit. The senses of your spirit."

Birdman makes a sound—a single click of a beak. Sagon throws the stone. "You moved."

"Will Kane stand waiting for your axe?"

Birdman makes the sound again. Then a tiny sound to one side—foot touching earth. Sagon throws the second stone. "You moved one way, then another."

"Will Kane move only once?"

Birdman makes the sound again. Then nothing.

Sagon sees without seeing. He throws the stone, and Birdman yelps. "Do not throw your axe."

"My spirit saw you!"

"Now you are ready."

"For what?"

"The first trial."

"Fire?"

"Yes."

"Where?"

Birdman touches Sagon's shoulder. "You will lead us. To the cliffs of the cave lions."

Sagon and Birdman entered the great plain, the sea of waving grass that lay between the river valley and the distant hills. Sagon sensed and smelled the herds of horses, aurochs, and bison feeding on the plain. It was summer, and the tall grass, warm in the sunlight, whispered stiffly in the moving air. Sagon walked with his face raised to the sun, the wind on his forehead, his long hair streaming behind, following a path he had taken when he was nine winters old.

The long line of broken cliffs lay ahead. Sagon sensed them before Birdman saw them. The water hole, the scattered trees, the scarred cliff face, the distant horse herd—Sagon saw all with the eyes of his spirit.

Something else. Rank odor of dead meat. Dried blood. Strong urine, powerful sex scent. Tawny fur, knife teeth, great taloned paws, vacant yellow eyes of death.

Birdman sniffed the wind. "Cave lions."

"Yes."

"Have they fed?"

"Not since yesterday."

"Where are they?" Birdman asked.

"In the tall grass by the water hole. They wait for the horse herd."

"You climbed up the cliff face?"

"The lions were behind me. They know the cliffs as we know our spear points. I found a cave entrance."

"The scars on your leg."

"The entrance was too small for her body. Not for her arm."

"Did Axe Man and Spear Woman tell you of Arvenios?"

"I know of Arvenios. He carried a tree branch as you do. His spirit lives in you."

"When Rok and his men came across the plain with Axe Man and Spear Woman, cave lions stalked their camp one night. Arvenios led the lions away."

"How?"

"Listen."

The sound of a horse herd came from the other side of the water hole—stamping of hooves, nickering of mares, commanding stallion cry.

The grass trembled where the cave lions crouched.

Birdman touched Sagon's arm. "Now we will become invisible."

"How?"

"Ask your spirit. Believe that you are invisible, and you will be."

"I am invisible."

"Now lead me to the cave entrance."

Sagon led Birdman to the cliff. They climbed up the jagged rock face. Sagon sensed every fissure, every ledge, every handhold. Below them the lionesses crept toward the sound of the horse herd.

The male lion watched from his stone platform above them. Sagon smelled his maleness, his meaty breath, his crushing power. For an instant Sagon's spirit weakened. He felt the eyes of the lion upon him, the sharp claws of death touch his back. He grasped his axe handle, and the magic of the axe strengthened his spirit. The lion's baleful gaze lifted from him.

The narrow cave entrance opened before them. Sagon went first, Birdman following, crawling, squeezing, pushing through the tortuous passages that led to the Onstean.

Birdman spoke: "You must go alone. Leave your weapons with me."

"My axe?"

"Everything. Axe, spears, knife."

Sagon passed the weapons back. "Where can I find them again?"

"You will have them when you need them."

"I cannot kill Kane without the axe."

"If you endure and live, you can kill Kane."

"I have no eyes."

"The eyes of the blind have great power." Birdman made the call of an owl. "Always go forward. Use the eyes of your spirit."

Sagon felt Birdman leave him. He was alone and blind in the maze of passageways.

He crawled forward into the trials of the Onstean.

21

Trials of the Onstean: Fire

SAGON SENSES, HEARS, feels: fire.

Red whirling flames in a great wall.

Roaring, crackling, terrifying.

Searing, unbearable heat.

A spirit voice commands: "Go forward."

His spirit quails and weakens. He senses a bottomless

pit of raging fire. Horrible death. His body charring as he drops through the flames into hell.

His mother and father will die.

Sagon stands upright. He runs forward and leaps into the flames.

22

Stone

HE LIVES. THE scorching flames are behind him, and he stands on solid rock. He runs forward to escape the heat and feels the passageway close in on him again. He is surrounded by stone, and with every step he crouches lower, feels the walls brush his shoulders, the ceiling scrape his head, the floor rise under his feet. He can crouch no lower, and he goes to his knees, then squirms forward on his stomach like an infant, and his groping fingers come against a solid stone wall. He cannot go forward. He tries to back up, and he cannot move. His body is jammed into the rock.

Now he knows the horror of being held forever by the stone enclosing him.

The stone has enormous weight. It presses down upon him as the foot of a mammoth presses upon a worm. He feels the weight of the world above him, below him, on either side of him. He feels his spirit weakening.

"See with your spirit." Birdman seems to speak to him as his life begins to slip away.

Something below his outstretched hands. Space.

He forces himself forward, and his hands feel nothing below them. Forward again; he feels his body compress, the stone grinds against his skin.

His arms drop down, then farther, and his head hangs over the lip of stone. He senses water far below.

With the last of his strength he forces his body forward and over the lip of stone.

23

Water

SAGON FALLS AWAY from the squeezing rock and hurtles downward. He sucks air in one desperate gasp and plunges into water like a falling stalactite.

Down, down, his body sinks into endless water. He senses stone walls, smooth and solid. He sinks deeper, and his spirit senses an opening in the rock. He claws at the opening and enters a tunnel that slopes down into the stone heart of the earth. Water fills the tunnel, and he swims deeper and deeper into it in the darkness. No air.

The tunnel levels out. Sagon's lungs are near bursting as he swims through the unending water-filled passageway. He senses a tiny pocket of air in the ceiling and drives his face into it, exhales, sucks in the life-giving air. He breathes twice more, then swims on.

No more air. Only water. He cannot live much longer. He swims on, weakening. Now he swims as in a dream, dying.

The tunnel slopes upward. Sagon dances as he swims, turning, whirling, ever faster, his spirit rising toward the stars.

His head comes into air. Sunlight.

24

Sun

SAGON LIES ON the stone floor of a great chamber, and its openness is like the sunlit sky. Like the sun rising glorious above the wakening earth, sweeping across the sky while clouds melt before it. Warming rays taking the ice and snow from the land, rivers, and forests, bringing fruits and berries to trees, green grass to the plains, life to all creatures.

He feels sun warmth on his head, his face, moving, leaving.

Sunlight comes in a slender ray from above. Slowly, he creeps forward, guided by the moving shaft of energy across the stone floor, up an incline, over a ridge, down into a hollow, and against a wall. Warmth on his hands, rising, draws them up the wall.

An opening. The shaft of sun warmth sinks into it.

Sagon follows.

25

Hunt

SAGON HUNTS WITH his son on the plain. The boy is tall and strong and laughing. They sight the bison herd and come slowly toward it, their spears ready.

A bison dances from the herd, upright, like a man. The

bison carries a bent stick with a thong joining both ends, and it holds the stick in one hand and plucks at the thong with the other. Now a drum beats, and the bison and Sagon and the boy dance in the bison hunt dance. The drum beats faster, and the dancers move their feet faster and faster, lifting their knees high, bending their bodies, spinning in the bison dance. The plucking of the thong and the beat of the drum grow louder and faster, and Sagon and his son become bison. Powerful, shaggy-haired, ancient dwellers of the earth, their shiny black horns gleam in the sunshine, their hard black hooves pound into the earth of the grassy plain. Sagon bellows and takes the spear into his heart.

26

Bird

BIRDMAN SPEAKS TO Sagon: "Fire. Stone. Water. Sun. Hunt. Four are left: Bird. Dance. Dream. Animal. I will help your spirit know the birds."

Birdman sings the song of the birds:

The black bird flies into the fire
Flames reach out, surround it
Draw it into their red mouths
Feathers, beak, feet, head, wings, body
Shrivel and char
Disappear into ashes
Birds in the forest lament
Crying for the black bird.
Night comes
The fire glow weakens and dies
Moonlight shines through the trees

Upon the cold ashes
The white bird rises.

Under the wings of the eagle
The air lifts
Circling above the forest
Stiff wings still
Spiraling
Higher
Higher

Small bird
Fiercely diving
Swooping
Fearless
Drives the hawk
From tiny nest.

Geese
Flying like spear point
Always changing
Always the same
Their wild cry sounding
Winter comes.

27

Dance of the Onstean

BIRDMAN BRINGS SAGON into the chamber.

A voice like grinding rock, cold and hard as obsidian: "Animal Man."

Birdman: "Yes."

"He will dance with us."

"Yes."

The rock voice: "Stone." Sagon sees in his mind the creature he had seen with his eyes before—a living being under stiff stonelike hides, its arms raised like stalagmites. Ancient power emanates from Stone Man.

Other voices: "Fire." "Water." "Sun." "Dance." "Hunt." "Bird." "Dream." Sagon sees each being: Fire Man, red as flames; Water Man, gray as driving rain; Sun Man, golden as the edge of sunlit clouds; Dance Man, deer antlers above deer face; Hunt Man, shaggy bison with curved stick and leather thong; Bird Man, covered with colored plumage, red crest, fingers on long beak; Dream Man, white robe, face a pale death mask.

Stone Man: "Animal Man."

A voice answers—a sound of hooting owl, growling bear, baying wolf, calling stag, challenging stallion—weak and dying, a voice of the fluttering owl, speared stag, rock-crushed bear, bison-trampled wolf, lion-ripped stallion. Sagon feels an ancient paw on his shoulder, smells owl, bear, wolf, stag, stallion. Death.

Stone Man: "Animal Man's spirit flies from him."

Birdman: "Son of Axe Man, son of Grae."

Stone Man: "Is he ready?"

Birdman: "He is."

A drumbeat. Single. Ponderous.

Sagon senses, hears, feels, sees in his spirit.

Fire Man's red robe flickers.

Stone Man strikes the floor three times.

Water Man's gray robe trembles to distant thunder.

Sun Man silently lifts his arms.

Dance Man stamps once, antlers shaking.

Hunt Man shakes his bison head.

Birdman calls, eagle crying in high sunlight.

Dream Man whirls once, white robe flaring.

Animal Man grasps Sagon's arm with his dying paw.

Drum again. Slow, repeated, giant heart beating.

The Onstean, the Invisible Stone Spirit Men, dance.

Animal Man dying, dancing, guiding Sagon, spinning, all animals dancing: gliding owl, prancing stag, circling bison, galloping stallion, pawing cave bear, loping wolf. Wall to wall they dance, quick small sketches: horse and bison, deer and aurochs, ibex and long-toothed cat. Animal Man sagging, spirit leaving, entering Sagon. Sagon feels the stag face and antlers about his head, wolf paws on his hands, pelt of cave bear, tail of stallion, eyes of owl.

He spins ever faster, Animal Man whirling in the center of the Onstean, his spirit transcending time and space.

28

Dance Dreams

The beginning of all things.

Fire. Stone. Water. Sun.

Life.

Weightless, quivering, wriggling, crawling, breathing, feeling, seeing, hearing, eating, mating, birthing.

Swinging in green rustling, sleeping in swaying nest, sucking ripe sweetness, screaming at fanged death.

Survival.

Running, throwing, thrusting. Spear deep between the ribs, heart-searching. Great head swinging, black horns hooking, sharp hooves slashing. Dust, blood, bellowing, tumbling, rolling, kicking, crushing, dying.

Fighting. Men charging. Axe magic swinging, singing.

Spear thrusting, gutting. Knife slashing. Club crushing. Hands clawing, choking. Men shrieking, screaming, snarling, roaring, killing, dying. Blood, bones, brains, flesh, eyeballs, organs. Death.

Blizzard. Howling wind. Snow. Ice. Cold. Freezing.

Storm. Wind shrieking. Lightning. Thunder. Rain.

Heat. Thirst. Burning.

Love.

Lying with the loved one on a mossy bank. Sunshine slanting through rustling leaves. Iridescent blue dragonflies hovering above water. Frogs talking among the lily pads. Birds singing softly. Little pools of brightness dancing on the forest floor.

Love surrounds them. Earth. Air. Sun. Water. Trees. Grass. Birds. Animals.

Ancestors. Mother. Father. Child. Family. Tribe. Friends. Mate.

Mystery.

Oak grove at night, full moon rising, shining into dusky glade. Nine white-robed female figures: Erida, his grandmother. Eena, his mother. Elina . . .

He is with the Onerana, the Invisible Earth Spirit Women. They raise their faces and arms to the moon and chant:

"Earth Mother, hear us.
Moon Spirit, fill us.
Life Spirit, grow in us.
Tree Spirit, warm us.
Air Spirit, sustain us.
Love Spirit, come to us.
Blood Spirit, flow in us.
Death Spirit, receive us.
Spear Spirit, protect us."

Animal Man.

The stallion calls to his mares, waiting, longing, struggling to break free.

All animals wait: bison, aurochs, reindeer, ibex, mammoth, rhinoceros, deer, wolf, cat, bear, boar, bird, fish.

Spirits whirl in the darkness: animal, man, ghost, god.

He holds his hands against the stone, feeling the life within. He places his ear against the stone and hears the voices of the animals. He breathes the scent of the stone and smells the hides, horns, antlers, tusks. He knows the animals: hulking power of mammoth, fierceness of charging rhinoceros, quickness of deer, agility of ibex, strength of bear, ferocity of cat, toughness of bison, courage of stallion.

He brings the pigment to the wall.

29

The Siege

FROM THE SHELTER of the forest, Kane glared at the wild current of the river, then at Bear Hill on the other side.

"You said there was a ford."

Eran scowled. "There is a ford. But the river has been angered. It cannot be crossed now. Wait until the flood passes."

"I have come to kill Agon. If we wait, he will escape."

"No. He will stay. He can fight off a whole tribe where he is."

"You said we could starve him out. If he sees us, he can bring enough game up there to last a year. I say we cross now."

"You will lose all your men."

"Some will live." Kane pointed to Big Man. "Come here."

Big Man approached, his knees shaking with fear.

"You take your net into the sea."

Big Man was too frightened to talk. He nodded his head.

"Your men hold the net and walk into the water."

Big Man looked with terror at the river. "Not when it is like this . . ."

"You coward. Have your men cut long vines, back in the forest where they cannot be seen from that hill. Bring them here."

Big Man backed away, terrified, and ran to his men.

Kane pointed to the leader of the horse hunters, a man called Spotted Horse. "You. Come here."

Spotted Horse came.

Kane held his spear against the man's stomach. "You and your men will cross behind the net men, holding more vines."

"We will all drown."

"Any man who holds back will die by my spear."

One of Big Man's men came running through the forest. "Men are on the other side of the river!"

"Where?" Kane shifted his spear from Spotted Horse to the man.

The man points. "In the forest east of the hill."

"If they saw you, you die. Show me the men."

The man led Kane and Eran through the trees. "There. Men with big heads."

Kane peered through the undergrowth at the forest on the other side of the river. He growled low in his throat like a lion seeing an enemy.

Eran said, "They are men of Ka!"

"We are men of Ka!" Kane turned to glare at Eran. "You knew they would be here."

Eran shook his head. "No. But Hura told me of them. They lived far to the east."

"What are they doing here?"

"Maybe they came to kill Agon." Eran pointed. "See the

bodies of men on the escarpment and below it. He has killed many."

"How could an old man kill them?"

"He rolls huge boulders down on them. There is no other way to come up except on the escarpment."

"You told me nothing of this."

"I told you we would kill Agon. Now it will be easy."

"Why easy?"

Eran smiled, a smile of death. "Let the men of Ka keep attacking. When Agon has thrown all the boulders he has, we will go up the escarpment and kill him."

"What about the men of Ka?"

"They are our people. You can kill their leader and become chieftain of a great tribe, the tribe of Kaan, the great god of our people!" Eran looked at the sky. "Night comes. Forget about crossing the river now; wait until Agon has used all his stones. Bring your men back into the forest where our fires will be hidden. We will wait until he is weak, then we will kill him."

A raven came from the north. It circled three times above Kane and Eran, its black obsidian eyes watching, then flew back to the north.

In the darkness of the forest night, an owl glided silently through the camp of Eran and Kane three times, and strange lights flickered in the northern sky.

In the morning Kane and Eran came again to the forest edge. Kane studied the escarpment at Bear Hill, counting the bodies, estimating the size of the boulders.

"Agon is a warrior of great power."

Eran shrugs. "He was. He is old and weak now."

"A weak man could not lift boulders of that size."

"Are you afraid of him?"

"I fear no man."

"What, then?"

"My mother told me the men of Ka believe Agon and Eena are gods. They call them Axe Man and Spear Woman."

"They are not gods. I have hated Agon since I was a child."

"Why?"

"Because I am son of Ka. Agon killed Ka."

"No man could kill Ka."

"It was because of Agon's axe."

"An axe is no match for a spear."

"Agon's axe was magic."

Kane snarled. "You never told me this."

"Our magic is in our spears."

"Ka was a spearman."

"Forget about the axe. Agon is too old to fight now."

"Agon came to our cave. He was the axe man who let my mother out of the cave. We traveled fast, yet he came back here before we did. He must still have strong magic."

"Why do you talk of magic? Your spear will rip out Agon's guts."

Kane scowled. "Dreams came to me in the night."

"So?"

"An owl stared at me. Then it spoke."

"Owls do not speak."

"It said one word."

"You have killed men as we kill flies. Now you dream that an owl speaks. It says one word, and you are terrified. What word did the owl speak?"

"Stone."

The next night wolves howled close around the camp. Their eyes glowed in the firelight, and their lean bodies swirled like blown dead leaves through the trees. Kane dreamed again.

He told Eran: "A black wolf spoke to me."

"They howled in the night. Wolves do not speak."

"He said one word."

"What was the word?"

"Fire."

The next night the sound of a galloping horse herd awakened Kane's men. Kane dreamed again. He told Eran of his dream:

"A black stallion spoke to me."

Eran spat in disgust. "A horse herd ran on the plain."

"He said one word."

"What was the word?"

"Water."

30

Women of the Onerana

EENA. SPEAR WOMAN. Granddaughter of Grae and Erida, priestess of the Earth Mother. Mother of Eran by Ka. Mother of Sagon by Agon.

Ara. Daughter of Agon and Erina, priestess of the Earth Mother. Mother of Kane by Eran.

Elina. Keeper of the Walls. Daughter of Brun and Erila, priestess of the Earth Mother.

Every day Eena watched for Sagon from Bear Hill. Two moons he had been gone. Her only living son by Agon, she saw him in her dreams lying dead on a cliff top, yet she still felt, hoped, that he lived.

For days the men of Ka tried to scale the escarpment. She and Agon kept watch night and day, ready to fight with spear and axe if any survived the boulders Agon hurled down the escarpment. She saw the strength of

Agon, his courage, but she knew how it must end. When there were no more boulders, the men would come up the escarpment. She and Agon would kill them, but the men of Ka would climb over their dead and attack, again and again, until they prevailed.

Axe Man and Spear Woman. When they were young, they fought back to back, untiring, filled with strength, their spirits so powerful that none could stand against them.

Eena felt no fear or regret for herself or Agon. They would die together in battle. Not for them the weakness of age, the dimming eyes, the trembling hands, the coughing sickness. They mated for life like the great birds, and their spirits would soar from their spear-torn bodies triumphant, together for all time. But Sagon must not be dead, must not yet die. The blood of chieftains and priestesses must live through him. The blood of Grae, tribal leader for generations back into time until the beginning. The blood of priestesses of the Earth Mother, daughters of the eternal spirit of the earth.

The boy who had fallen on the escarpment. Karem, son of the chieftain of the men of Ka. Why had she longed to keep him? Agon had known. The boy was like Eran. The same hawk face, the same fierce eyes. The black hair the same, but one difference: the streak of gold across Eran's head from front to back. . . .

Eena pulled ten straight poles from their seasoning pile, selected ten flints, and cut ten lengths of narrow rawhide straps. She began her daily routine on the open porch: keeping watch while making ten spears each day, perfectly formed, bound, and balanced, added to the pile at the top of the escarpment. When Agon's boulders were gone, they would hurl the spears into the men of Ka as they attacked.

She worked quietly. Agon slept each day, guarded the escarpment at night. She slept at night, kept watch during the day. Together, they defend Bear Hill.

Ara, daughter of Agon, followed the river east. Although the river ran high in flood, she remembered every bend, every cliff from the time many years ago when she brought the emasculated and crippled Eran to the west on a floating tree. Now she hurried back to Bear Hill to help save Agon from Eran and Kane. Trained since birth in the mysterious rites of those who served the Earth Mother, Ara had escaped from the cave in which Eran and Kane had imprisoned her and came now to warn Agon and Eena. After two moons she neared Bear Hill. She approached silently and unseen through the grove on the north riverbank.

Ara gasped in horror and dismay. Eran and Kane stood hidden in the grove with a large group of men, pointing out at Bear Hill and the high-flowing river with their spears.

As silently and unseen as she had come, Ara left the grove and raced toward the range of mountains that loomed to the north. When she had lived with Agon and Eena, she had seen the secret signs of the priestesses of the Earth Mother by a waterfall high in the peaks. Now she must have the help of the Earth Mother.

She crossed the plain and followed that remembered trail up into the towering mountains, and at sunset she came, to the sacred waterfall. Ara stood before the falls. The sound of women softly laughing, crying, whispering, and talking was in the falling water, and Ara shivered ecstatically with the mystery of the place. Night came, and the moon rose, its mysterious light illuminating the leafy glade. Ara made the secret call of the priestesses and waited.

A hooded figure appeared in the shadows. "Why have you come?"

"To ask the Mother's help. Evil men would kill my father."

"Who are you?"

"Ara, daughter of Erina and Agon"

" 'Ara'. We know of you. The Mother has not been pleased with you. You were trained to be one of us, and you left. You mated with the son of Ka. You have raised an evil son."

"I am filled with sorrow. I would undo it all if I could."

"The Mother does not help those who are unworthy."

"I will give my life to save my father."

The eyes of the hooded figure glowed within the the hood.

"Remain here. I will come when the moon rises again."

Elina led Lazor and Black Horse to the east at a steady hunter's trot. When they halted by a small stream to drink, Black Horse commented on her recovery:

"Three days ago we had to carry you like a speared colt. Now you rush through this forest like a mare seeking the stallion."

"I seek no stallion."

"Perhaps you run from one."

"Perhaps the black horse tires easily."

"Perhaps the black horse could show you how easily he tires."

Lazor spoke: "The black horse is close to the stallion's hooves."

Black Horse smiled. "He knows that. She is promised to you. But such a filly excites all stallions."

Elina glared at both men. "You may have used the mares in the horse herd for your pleasure. But if you call me a mare or a filly one more time, I will leave you in the forest to find your own way."

"You know the way?"

"Of course."

"And you can run faster than we can?"

"Both of you are helpless in the forest. You trip over roots, let branches knock you backward, and would walk face-on into tree trunks if I did not guide you."

Black Horse placed a comforting hand on Lazor's shoulder. "And you would take her as your mate. Think how it will be when she is a woman."

Lazor looked thoughtfully at Elina. "I think it might be interesting." He drank once more from the stream. "We will soon come to the place called Bear Hill. Kane may already be there. If he has killed Axe Man, there is nothing we can do. If he has surrounded the hill, Axe Man already knows he is there. If the river has kept Kane on the other side, we might be of some help. We will go slowly, now, listening for any sound of Kane and his men, watching for any movement in the trees." He spoke to Elina: "It is said that you can see game on the other side of a hill. Can you do that with men?"

"Yes."

"Good." Keep close to us. Kane would not treat you as well as we do."

Elina's face was serious. "I know that. And I know that you have come with me to help me, risking death. I will not forget that."

31

Warriors

AGON. AXE MAN. Son of Grae, chieftain of the bison hunters, and Erida, priestess of the Earth Mother. Mate of Spear Woman.

Eran. Son of Ka and Spear Woman. Murderer of his half brother, Alar. Mate of Ara, priestess of the Earth Mother and daughter of Axe Man.

Kane. Spear Man. Son of Eran and Ara. Grandson of Ka, Spear Woman, and Axe Man. Killer of men. Strength of two men.

Sagon. Animal Man. Cave painter. Son of Axe Man and Spear Woman. Axe Man in his own right. Blind.

Every night Agon sets his warning trip lines across the path up the escarpment. Black horsetail hairs knotted into long threads, the lines are invisible in the darkness. Tied to balanced sticks at the top of the escarpment, they tell of the creeping foot or leg of an approaching enemy.

Agon has five boulders left. Five more times he can hurl death bounding down the escarpment. After that his axe and spears will crush enemy skulls, slice into enemy chests. Eena will fight beside him.

He remembers their first battle with the men of Ka. He finds Eena raped and tied by the neck to the great arm of the sleeping Ka. Silently, he frees her, and they flee from Ka's dark cave, run past the heads of her father and brother swaying on poles in the light of the gibbous moon, race along the river and up the cliff trail. Ka's men come up the cliff face, others along the cliff top. He drives his spear again and again into the shrieking men, and still they come. The spear breaks, and they run out onto the plain with the men in pursuit.

He remembers the second, third, fourth, and final battles: fighting on the plain, fighting in the night as Ka attacks the camp of the bison hunters, fighting Ka's men in the river, and fighting on the cliff top as his axe shatters Ka's bones and he throws Ka out over the cliff edge.

No broken spear will cause them to flee this time. Each day Eena makes more spears. They have stores of dried venison, berries, tubers, nuts. Water flows from the spring at the top of the escarpment. They can hold out for many moons.

But for one thing. Agon knows that death is watching him, waiting to seize him in bony hands.

How many battles has he fought? How many wounds have scarred his body? How many bison horns have swished past his throat? How did he live in the great cold when he crossed the snow and ice of the mountains? How did he live when the wall of water crashed upon him and the men of Ka as they fought in the riverbed?

These things have not killed him. Where is death, then?

Death is inside him. He feels death when he lifts and throws a giant boulder. He feels death when he carries a deer carcass up the escarpment. Death has slipped inside him and wrapped tight hands around his heart.

He will not die yet. He will not leave Eena alone. He will fight death as he has fought the men of Ka.

Eran has lived on hatred all his life. Hatred of his mother's mate, Agon, who came between Eran and his mother, who burned Eran's spear when he threatened his brother, who took Eran's thumbs and manhood. Hatred of his half brother, Alar, favored of his parents. Hatred of the chieftain of the aurochs hunters, who dared judge him. Hatred of his mate, Ara, who pleaded with him to spare her father. Hatred of the men who looked at him with knowing eyes. Hatred of the women who looked at him with pity.

Now he will loose all his hatred on Agon. His weapon is Kane, killer of men, reincarnation of Ka. Kane, his son, whom Eran has taught to hate all of his life.

Kane's anger grows each day. Kept from crossing the river by the turbulent water and the presence of the men of Ka, he becomes ever more dangerous. His men flee from him as jackals flee from a raging lion, not daring to have him notice them, not daring to look at him, trembling if he even glances in their direction. He has come to kill Agon, and Agon is beyond his reach, safe on his hill, ready to hurl his boulders down on anyone attempting to come up the escarpment.

Eran has lied to him. Told him there was a ford across the river. Told him Agon was old and helpless. Told him nothing of the men of Ka. Not told him that Agon could go from Bear Hill to Kane's cave and back before Kane could come to Bear Hill.

Strange dreams come each night to Kane: Dreams of animal spirits who stare at him with eyes of death, speak one word, and fade back into the night. Dreams of dancing demons, animals, ghosts.

Strange creatures circle his camp at night: Horse herds galloping through thick woods. Wolves howling from unseen peaks. Bears growling from treetops. Stags clashing antlers on cliff ledges. Owls diving like falcons. Ravens circling three times.

Strange signs are in the night sky: Sheet lightning with no thunder. Ghostly northern spirit lights sweeping down to the southern horizon. Flights of giant black birds against the moon. Falling stars thick as driving hail. Glowing lights slowly moving across the sky.

Strange behavior of the game. Hunters sent out return with tales of the herds all moving to the south: bison, aurochs, caribou, mammoth, horse, antelope, ibex, rhinoceros. Flocks of ducks, geese, swans, heron, all flying south, out of season.

Kane watches the men of Ka each day. Their chieftain is huge, but slow-moving. Kane knows he can kill the man with one ripping spear thrust. . . .

Then he will kill Agon.

Sagon, Animal Man, speaks with Birdman:

"Kane has not crossed the river."

"No."

"The men of Ka still wait."

"Yes."

"My father and mother still live."

"They do. But something comes."

"What?"

"Death. Death to Agon."

"Agon is Axe Man. No man can stand against him."

"No man can. But Agon fights time."

"He is strong as a young hunter."

"He will die. He has fought too many battles, taken too

many spear thrusts, run too many times throughout the day and night."

"No!" Sagon feels the ancient hand in the dance of the Onstean: Animal Man dancing, dying. "He cannot die yet!"

"No man lives forever."

"Agon must live!"

"Agon's time is near."

"How can you know this?"

"The raven sees much."

"My mother cannot live without him."

"She is granddaughter of chieftains."

"Without Agon, she cannot defend Bear Hill against the men of Ka, against Kane."

"No."

"I have to go to them."

Birdman shakes his head. "You cannot cross the river yet. You have other ways to help them."

"My magic has not helped them."

"It has done more than you know."

"How? Ka's men are still there. Kane is still there."

"Your magic has only begun. Already it has done things that will be of great importance."

"What things?"

"You have done something to Kane that has never been done before. You have brought fear to his spirit."

"Fear is not enough."

"You can do more."

"How? I am blind—I cannot fight Kane."

"Use all your magic."

"My magic is weak."

"You have not even begun to use it."

"What more can I do?"

"You are one of the Onstean. Bring all the power of the Onstean against Eran and Ka. Take their men from them. Fight their god, Kaan. Strengthen your spirit, for it has terrible trials ahead. Know the power of Animal Man."

Kane's men whisper among themselves. They, too, hear the howling of ghost wolves, the running of invisible horses, the growling of unseen bears. They see the strange lights in the sky, feel the menace of circling spirits, observe the unnatural migration of the herds and flocks.

But more than these, they know an awful fear. Horrible apparitions appear in their dreams, spirits of the dead whisper of coming catastrophe, rocks groan of unseen horrors, red demons dance in their cooking fires, voices of the dying moan in the river, birds cry of death.

One by one, the men of the horse hunters and the fisher folk slip away in the darkness of a single night, going in many directions, leaving no trail that Kane can follow. Kane and Eran are left alone. Only the men of Ka are left, and they are on the other side of the river with their own chieftain.

32

Ara

THE HOODED FIGURE appeared before Ara in the light of the rising moon.

"The Mother will not see you. She will not forgive you or accept the sacrifice of your body. You have become part of the evil tribe of Ka. Even now your mate and your son seek to kill Agon."

"I tried to stop them! They sealed me within a cave so that I could not help my father!"

"You are here."

"I learned many things from the priestesses."

"Yes. We cannot go through solid rock as the shamans

claim, but some of us can go through passages too narrow for most. You would have made a good priestess."

"I had to come here. Help me save my father from death."

"Death comes when it will. We can do nothing to change that."

"Can I do nothing?" Ara fell to her knees in her agony.

The hooded figure held out one hand and gently touched Ara's head. "You can do one thing. You know what it is."

Ara bowed her head. "If I am not too late."

She was alone.

Ara walked down from the mountains in the moonlight, leaving the waterfall, the priestesses, and the Earth Mother. All of her life she had searched for love and beauty and belonging. For a loving mate and good children. For a home filled with happiness. She had failed. Now nothing remained for her but hatred, violence, and death.

33

Trance Dreams

SAGON SPINS IN the magic dance of the Onstean, Animal Man whirling under the bison, aurochs, horses, and mammoths who have come from the rock. All through the long nights the Onstean have danced, while at Bear Hill owls and ravens watched, wolves howled, ghostly horse herds galloped, and rocks groaned.

Now Animal Man's spirit must rest, and Sagon slows and drops to the floor. He sleeps in the deep trance of the shaman.

A soft voice: "Son of Agon."

Sagon senses beauty. Smells the scent of fresh flowers.

"Take my hand."

Her hand is smooth as air, gentle as a flower petal.

"You would save your father and mother." Her breath is fragrant on his cheek.

"Yes."

"I can help you." She brings his hand to her lips.

"Do you bring a tribe of warriors?"

"Only myself."

She strokes his forehead, gently touches his closed eyes. "The gods have brought you darkness. I can make you see again."

"My spirit sees."

"Yes. But I can let you see through your spirit and eyes."

Birdman speaks: "Beware, Sagon."

"Beware of a helpless woman?" The soft hand caresses Sagon's face. "Who is this that would keep you blind?"

"My friend. He would not keep me blind."

"He must have killed many songbirds to make his cape of feathers."

"No birds were killed to make my cape," Birdman says. "How many men have died to make your cape of beauty?"

"My beauty is more than a cape. Would the Birdman like to see proof of this? Or does he fear women?"

Birdman shakes his tree branch. "Leave our camp."

"You would drive me away? You would send a woman alone into the night?"

"I would send a creature of the night into the night."

The soft hand strokes Sagon's hair. "Will you send me into the night?"

"I do not know you. . . ."

"You could know me." Her hand moves down the back of his head to his shoulder, then to the hard muscle of his chest.

Birdman speaks: "Elina searches for you."

Sagon's spirit leaps. "She is not dead?"

"She lives."

"How do you know?"

"My messengers have told me."

The hand tightens on Sagon's chest. It seems that sharp talons press into his skin, then the hand is soft and caressing again. "Elina is dead. But her spirit searches for you. She would have me bring sight back to your eyes. She would not have you wander blindly now, or, when your spirit finally leaves your body, be unable to find her spirit."

"You have talked with her spirit?"

"Yes."

"When?"

"Last night. This is why I have come to you."

"Why did she not come to me?"

"She sorrows because of your blindness. She waits until I bring sight back to your eyes."

Birdman cries like a hawk sighting an eagle. "Beware!"

Sagon hesitates. The honeyed breath is on his cheek. She whispers, "Elina waits for you. Let me help you. Let me bring your beloved to you. . . ."

Elina's spirit waits for him . . . Sagon's spirit weakens. He feels the power of the bear slipping away, the instincts of the wolf, the stamina of the stag, the courage of the stallion, the wisdom of the owl. He touches the hand on his chest. "You can bring Elina's spirit to mine?"

"I can."

"Then I will not send you away into the night."

"I knew you would not."

"What is your name?"

"I am called Lilla."

Birdman makes the warning sound of a thrush seeing a snake.

Lilla strokes Sagon's hair. "I cannot bring sight back to your eyes here. Come with me to a place of beauty where Elina's spirit will find you."

"Where is this place?"

"In the hills. A little stream flows into a sunlit glade, and the trees whisper softly around us."

"I have heard of such a place from my father and mother."

"They were happy there. Your spirit will find such happiness with Elina there." Lilla takes his hand. "Come with me."

Sagon feels air caressing his face as though he is flying. Lilla's hand gently guides him. Then he lies on soft grass, and he hears the murmur of a stream, the whisper of leaves.

Lilla lies beside him, her cape gone. He knows the warmth of her body, the perfume of her breath, the caressing touch of her hands. She whispers: "Come to me, Sagon. Know the ecstasy of love . . ." Her hand pulls gently at his axe. "Let me take this from your belt. . . ."

Elina stopped and stood as if listening to some distant sound. Lazor and Black Horse waited beside her.

A raven flew across the river, circled over them, and went back to the north.

Elina spoke quietly. "Sagon lives."

"You know this?"

"Yes."

"How?"

"The raven. Sagon is in danger."

"Where is he?"

"On the other side of the river. An evil spirit tempts him."

"The raven told you this?" Black Horse asked.

"Birdman sent him."

Lazor nodded. "We know of Birdman. Sorcerer of the forest people. He has strange powers."

"He helped us hide from Kane. He sent the raven to find us."

"To find you, I think." Lazor looked into Elina's eyes. "If Sagon lives, you will become his mate."

"Yes." She touched Lazor's shoulder. "You have been good to me. You and Black Horse." She smiled at them. "You are good men. I will remember you."

"You speak as though you will not see us again."

"I cannot ask you to help me when I have nothing to give."

Lazor and Black Horse looked at one another. Lazor said, "We came to help you warn Axe Man and Spear Woman. We have not given that warning. We must find them."

Elina was silent.

Black Horse said, "She does not want us."

Elina turned her back and wiped at her eyes. "I do want you. . . ."

The two men scuffed their feet, looking at the ground. Lazor finally spoke: "We have to decide something."

Elina turned to face him. "I don't know what to do. We must warn Axe Man and Spear Woman, yet Sagon is in danger . . ."

Black Horse smiled. "I am the best of the hunters at tracking. I will go to warn Axe Man and Spear Woman that Kane comes to kill them. You and Lazor can go to find Sagon."

Lazor shook his head. "You would go into the most danger. I will be chieftain of our people when we have killed Kane. I will go to warn Axe Man and Spear Woman."

Black Horse smiled again. "No. If Elina comes to Sagon with me, he may be jealous because of my handsome face and beautiful body. It is better that an older man go with her."

Elina looked at the sky. "Night comes. I must do this alone. I ask you not to follow me when I go into the forest."

Lazor asked, "Will you come back?"

"If I can. Wait for me here until morning. If I do not come back, I ask you to go to warn Axe Man and Spear Woman."

"Who will go to help Sagon?"

"Unless I can help Sagon now, tonight, no one can help him."

Lazor and Black Horse watched Elina as she disappeared into the forest. Black Horse pointed to the east. "The moon will rise soon. She will be able to find her way in the moonlight."

Lazor touched his totem, a running stallion. "I think she will use the moon for more than to find her way. . . ."

34

The River Spirit

KANE WRITHED ON the ground in insane rage when he found all his men gone.

Eran had seen his son's uncontrolled anger before, but this attack was so violent that Eran feared for his own life. When Kane finally recovered enough to speak, Eran carefully approached.

"They were cowards. We are better off without them."

Kane glared at him with bloodshot eyes. "You let them get away! I should kill you!"

"I could have killed you while you rolled on the ground. You let them get away as much as I did. I let you live so that you can kill Agon."

Kane crouched like a great cat ready to spring. "I can kill you now!"

"That would do you no good," Eran replied. "Who would you have fighting for you—men who can only spear dying fish, or men of Ka who fight on when their bodies bristle with spears?"

"Spirits of the night fight against me. If I could find those spirits, I would rip them into bloody shreds."

"Forget the spirits of the night."

"They have taken all my men."

"Listen to the river spirit."

"Why?"

"Come with me to the river."

"Throw yourself in and drown."

"We can cross it."

Kane glared at Eran. "You lie!"

"Come see for yourself. The water is low, the current slow."

Kane ran through the forest and peered from the undergrowth at the river. He growled, and his teeth chattered like a hyena upon finding an injured calf. "I will cross and kill Agon!"

Eran spoke softly: "First kill the chieftain of the men of Ka. You will be leader of the fiercest tribe in the world. You can take Bear Hill as easily as a lion takes a fawn."

Kane's eyes glowed with a red fire of mad joy. "I feel my spear ripping into Agon already!"

Eran smiled. "And when you become chieftain and have pinned Agon to the ground with your spear, I will kill him slowly with these!" Eran held up the knife and short spear strapped to his thumbless hands. "The night spirits that howled around us have weakened and are dying! We will fight now with the spirit of the great Kaan beside us! We will kill our enemies and rule the world!"

Kagun, chieftain of the men of Ka, spoke to Karem, his young son: "They must be Axe Man and Spear Woman, the gods who killed Ka. No one else could have killed so many of our men."

"They are the gods."

"Why didn't they kill you?"

"Spear Woman wanted to keep me as her son."

"She would not let Axe Man throw a boulder down on you?"

"I live."

"You will help us take them into our tribe. They will give even stronger magic to us. You will climb the escarpment again, carrying meat. Tell the gods that when they come with us they will never have to hunt again.

When they see the meat, they will believe you."

"The game has gone."

"Every man has been sent out. As soon as they come back with game, you will take meat to the gods. Tell me again the strange thing that Spear Woman said to you."

"She said when I am chieftain, I must stop our people from killing. They should live in peace with other men, be their friends."

"What is a friend?"

"Someone we like."

Kagun scratched his head. "I don't understand any of this. Peace. Friends. Someone we like. What does 'like' mean?"

"Before she died, I think my mother liked me. I liked her."

"Because she gave you milk."

"It was more than that. I liked to have her hold me and talk to me."

"That is for babies. Men do not hold anyone."

"Axe Man and Spear Woman held each other. They smiled at each other and talked together. I felt good when they did those things."

Kagun raised his spear. "I feel good when I have driven this into an enemy. Should we smile at an enemy and tell him we like him while he kills us?"

"We should make them friends before we become enemies."

Kagun shook his head. "Axe Man and Spear Woman have given you strange ideas. When we take them back with us, we will question them about these things."

35

Birdman Sings to the Onstean of the Moon's Long Night

"Circle stars to midnight
Circle stars to dawn
Lilith, ancient evil
Sagon, feeds upon
Moonrise to moonset
Magic axe and spear
Wolf, great owl, and bear
Stallion, stag, and hair
Torn away by hands of air
Bring stone, fire, and water
Against the tribe of Kaan
Dance and dream, the Onstean
Through the long night."

36

Circle Stars to Midnight

THE MOON RISES. Sagon senses the magic of the huge orange disc as it slides above the horizon.

Something pulls almost imperceptibly at his axe. His hand moves toward the handle, and he feels only air. He grasps the handle, and the power of the axe flows up his hand and arm into his spirit.

Lilla whispers, "Why do you touch your axe?"

"Something pulled at it."

"Both my hands are on your chest." She caresses him. "Why do you carry an axe?"

Sagon is silent.

"Is it a magic axe?"

Still Sagon does not reply.

"I would like to feel its magic."

"No."

"Let me only take it from your belt."

"The axe comes from my belt only to kill."

"It will hurt me as you love me. Would you hurt me?"

"No."

Her hand strokes his hand, his arm. "The light of love rises. Love me."

"I love only one woman."

"She is dead."

"Birdman said she lives."

"Let him bring her to you, then."

"She is far away."

"Let me bring back your sight. Then her spirit will come to you."

"How can you bring back my sight?"

"I have many powers. Let me take the axe from your belt, and I will show you."

Sagon's grip loosens on the axe handle.

Ara stands alone on a hilltop, her arms held out to the rising moon. She pleads for the moon goddess to help her father, her face wet with tears:

"Moon spirit, hear me.

"See Eran, son of Ka, father of my son, as he plots to kill Agon, my father. Let Agon see Eran as he comes.

"See Kane, my son, son of Eran, as he comes to kill Agon. Let Agon still have the power of his magic axe song."

Sagon's hand tightens on the axe handle.

Lilla chants in a language he does not understand, and Sagon feels an ancient mystery, a primeval magic.

A black cloud creeps across the face of the moon. Sagon senses the lessening of the moon magic, of his spirit's magic.

Lilla's hand covers his. "Put your hand on my breast. Feel how it longs for your touch."

Sagon's hand loosens on the axe handle. Lilla lifts his hand, guides it to her breast. He feels the thrust of the breast, the hot desire, the hardening nipple rising. Lilla's breath comes faster . . .

Sagon does not feel his axe sliding from his belt. . . .

Kane and Eran crossed the river ford in the dim light of the cloud-blackened moon. Like dark spirits they disappeared silently into the forest and circled around Bear Hill, avoiding the open grassland. They came to the edge of the forest and stared out at Bear Hill in the moonlight, their eyes filled with hatred.

They heard voices in the forest, a man and a boy. Kane motioned for Eran to follow and crept toward the sound, his huge spear ready. He crouched just outside the small clearing where Kagun and Karem waited for their men.

Kagun felt eyes upon him. He called: "Do you bring game? Bring it, or hunt again."

Kane made no reply.

Kagun peered into the darkness of the forest, his spear ready. "Show yourself."

Kane stepped forward.

Kagun lowered his spear. "Friends?"

In one violent motion Kane leaped upon Kagun, drove in his spear, and ripped it upward, spilling Kagun's intestines upon the forest floor in a bloody mass.

As Kagun bellowed and fell, Eran ran from the forest and seized Karem around the throat from behind. While Kane pulled his knife from his belt and hacked off Kagun's head, Eran stabbed Karem repeatedly with the short spear strapped to his hand.

Clumsily, brutally, using the knife strapped to his other hand, Eran cut off Karem's head.

Kane and Eran sensed that they were surrounded by the men of Ka, invisible in the forest. Kane whirled around and held Kagun's head high. "See your chieftain's head! See his guts! Any man who comes at me with a spear will look the same! Lay your spears down and come to me. I am your chieftain."

A rustling sound as of dry leaves blowing came from the forest. Then silence.

Kane shouted, "I will track down and kill any man who tries to run. If any think they can fight me, come now."

Three huge men ran in, their spears raised, their eyes wild. Kane moved fast as a striking leopard, whirling with his spear thrusting like lightning, and the three men crumpled and fell with their intestines spilling out. Kane leaped upon them and severed the heads from the convulsing bodies with three strokes of his knife. Four men ran in, and Kane killed again with the same lightning strokes of his spear, fighting as a giant serpent, sinuous and deadly.

Again he sliced heads from the bloody and writhing bodies.

Now the men of Ka threw down their spears and came to Kane as they would to a god. They knelt before him.

Four men carried a framework of branches from the trees. On the framework sat a grotesque and terrible figure, human in form, but with black twisted horns above a white robe of human skins. The horns were of no known animal. Rotting human heads were impaled on upright poles at the platform's corners, and skulls of cave lions, giant snakes, and hyenas hung from the platform. *Kaan!*

Kane and Eran screamed in triumph. The creature was the living embodiment of the bizarre paintings Kane painted on the walls and ceiling of his boyhood cave, the personification of the evil god Eran and Kane worshipped all their lives: Kaan, god of evil and death. With Kaan, Eran, and Kane joined, nothing could stand against them.

Eena awoke in the the bed of ferns on the platform at Bear Hill. Where he kept watch, Agon's dark silhouette showed against the cloud-dimmed rising moon. She came to him and spoke softly:

"I dreamed of evil beings."

Agon drew her to him. "We have fought them before."

"Something has happened. The evil power of the men of Ka has become greater."

"Yes, I feel that."

"I dreamed of the time when Ka killed my father and brother."

"Do not think of it."

"I can't help it. A terrible creature has come. A thing worse than Ka!"

"Worse than Ka?"

"More powerful. More evil. A warrior of awful strength. Eran is with him."

Agon's hand closed on his axe. "Eran?"

"I saw him in my dream."

"You dream of the dead."

Eena held her face against Agon's chest. "I hope that is so . . ."

Agon stroked her hair. "Do not think of these things. Let the past be forgotten. Strange things come to us in our dreams. Ka is the terrible warrior. Ka is dead. You saw me throw him over the cliff."

"He was like Ka. But he was not Ka." Eena pointed down toward the forest that lay east of Bear Hill. "He is there now. I heard him scream."

"Leopards called in the forest before you awoke."

"The scream was not from leopards."

Agon put both arms around her. "Whatever it was, it will not come up the escarpment and live."

Eena pressed her face against his chest. "I think about Sagon. I pray to the gods that he does not return while the men of Ka are here."

"The game has left the forest and plain. Ka's men will starve if they stay here much longer. They will have to leave." Agon kissed her. "Go back to our bed. With the spears you have made I can hold off all of Ka's men."

"I feel that something is about to happen."

"Let it happen. We are ready."

"It is not just us. I feel that Sagon is in great danger."

Agon lifted her chin. "Sagon has new and powerful magic."

"You know this?"

"Yes."

Eena looked at the moon. "I ask you to do one thing."

"What?"

"Go back into the cave. Sleep for a little while."

"We may be attacked."

"I will keep watch. There is something I must do alone. I will wake you when the moon has risen one hand high."

Agon felt an ancient mystery. Many times in their life together Eena had gone alone into the dark woods when the moon was full. He gave her one of the spears from the pile that lay at the top of the escarpment. "Do not forget that you are Spear Woman."

She smiled at him. "I will remember."

37

Sagon Loses His Totem

LILLA TOUCHES THE wolf totem on Sagon's chest. "You are like the wolf."

"He is my totem."

"He has strong magic."

"Yes."

"I have no totem."

Sagon is silent.

Lilla lifts the wolf. "I can feel his power, even though I hold him only in my hand. How strong you must be when he is against your heart." Her other hand touches Sagon's closed eyes. "If I could hold him against my breast . . ."

"If a hunter loses his totem, he may die."

"The wolf hangs by a thong of strong leather. You will not lose him."

"The horn of a bison can break the thong."

"I am a weak woman." She presses close against him and holds the wolf against her breast. "My heart feels his magic." Her other hand leaves his eyes. "Your knife presses hard against me. Let me lay it beside us."

Sagon moves his hand to the knife, and his fingers close over Lilla's hand.

"You have taken my axe. Now you want my knife."

"The axe is near us. I will lay the knife beside it."

"No."

"You have powers far greater than your axe or knife."

Again, Sagon is silent.

"I have heard that men dance in a secret ring in solid rock. They have great power. You are one of these men."

Sagon says nothing.

"You are right not to speak of them." Lilla withdraws her hand from the knife and places Sagon's hand on the handle. "I would not take a knife of one of the Onstean." Lilla still holds the wolf against her breast.

Lilla knows of the Onstean. Sagon feels his magic weaken.

Now the magic of the totem lessens and disappears, so slowly that Sagon is not aware of its leaving as Lilla cuts the thong with her own knife..

Elina runs through the forest like a she-wolf seeking her lost mate. She has prayed to the moon spirit and all the other spirits of the Onerana that they help Sagon, and still she knows that his spirit is in terrible danger. Now she follows her own instinct, and nearing the river valley, she feels the danger more strongly.

A dark hill appears, and she knows from its shape that she sees Bear Hill. But Sagon is not there. He is across the river.

Elina comes to the riverbank and crosses at the ford without fear or hesitation, swimming in the middle of the river as her feet leave the rocky bottom. Now Sagon is near, with something evil. Elina runs across the moonlit plain toward Sagon and the evil, praying that her magic will be strong.

Kane and Eran stalked Agon and Eena, creeping stealthily toward their prey. They came silently to the edge of the forest and peered at Bear Hill and the narrow pathway that led up the escarpment to the porch and cave where Eran was born.

A dim figure on the porch stood with arms raised toward the moon. Eran recognized his mother's golden hair and slender, erect body. He stared at her with remembered possessive love and unforgiven hatred. "Kill him," were the last words he heard her say as she and Agon stared at Eran and the dead body of Alar. Eran's last memory of Bear Hill was of pain and suffering as he lay bleeding at its base.

Kane growled deep in his throat. "Axe Man leaves a woman on watch."

"My mother."

"Kane can run up the escarpment and kill her before she even sees him."

"No. Remember Agon's trip lines. You would die before you got halfway up."

"Kane can dodge boulders as he does spears."

"There is no room to dodge; the path is wide enough for only one man. When Agon throws boulders, they come down the path as does water from the spring. When he first came here, six men tried to come up in the night. He killed all of them with one boulder."

"Kane will find another way up."

"No. I grew up here. I tried to find other ways. There are none."

"Kane will leap off the path when a boulder comes down."

"The stream has carved out the rock. Walls on either side go straight up."

"Kane will run on top of the walls."

"They are like knife edges."

Kane growled in baffled rage, then stared at Eran with his lion eyes. "You will go first."

"What?"

"She will not kill her son."

"She told Agon to kill me."

"She forgets."

"No."

Kane ground his teeth. "Kane will make you go first."

"I am your father."

"That is nothing to Kane."

Eran smiled, a smile of death. "You have forgotten. We have Kaan."

"Will Kaan lead us up the escarpment? He can barely walk."

"Kaan has power you have never dreamed of." Eran pointed to the south. "A storm comes. Kaan is god of death. He is god of the storms of death!"

Now Kane understood. "Kaan will make the storm stronger!"

Eran smiled again. "Kaan will make the storm so powerful that it will drive Agon from the escarpment. Then we will go up and kill him!"

In the cave at the lion cliffs the Onstean begin a dance that will last throughout the night. Dream Man and Dance Man spin at the center of the circle, Bird Man perches on a stalagmite and sings an ancient song of mystery, Hunt Man plucks at the thong of his bent stick, Sun Man makes his journey across the sky, Fire Man flickers in his red cloak, and Stone Man drives his staff deep into the crust of the earth.

Water Man dances alone, fearfully. His motions are not of rain gently falling or streams gurgling over mossy stones. They are motions of wild and terrible power, of screaming wind and driving rain, of flashing lightning and flying trees, of raging rivers and surging floods, of destruction, drowning, and death.

A massive storm roars toward Bear Hill. It is more powerful than any storm that has occurred in the memory of the people. It will strike Bear Hill at midnight.

38

Elina's Magic

SAGON HAS LOST his axe and his totem. The only magic left him lives in his own spirit and the spirits within him of wolf, owl, bear, stag, and stallion.

Lilla whispers softly, "Soon I will bring sight back to your eyes, and the spirit of Elina will come to you. But something fights against me."

"My spirit longs for Elina's. It does not fight you."

"You do not know it."

"How can I not know what my spirit wishes?"

"You know what it wishes, but other spirits have come to you. They fight against me."

Sagon is silent.

"Tell me of your other spirits so I may have them help us."

Again, Sagon says nothing.

"You are one of the Onstean. If I know the spirits within you, I can talk with them. Tell me their names."

"I may not say them."

"Elina's spirit longs for you. I hear her weeping. But the sound grows weaker. Soon her spirit will die, unless she can come to you." Lilla presses her body against Sagon. "I will do more than this if you tell me."

Sagon feels his spirit and the spirits of the animals weakening. Lilla moves her body in a sinuous, writhing motion while her hands stroke his hair, his face, his chest. . . .

"Open your eyes that I may see them."

"Why?"

"To help me bring back your sight."

Sagon opens his eyes. Still total darkness. He closes his eyelids again.

"Why do you close them?"

"You will see my spirit."

"I will not see your spirit. I must look to see how your eyes have been made blind."

Sagon opens his lids again, his blind eyes openings into his innermost being.

Lilla's face almost touches his. "Open your eyes wider that I may see what I must do."

Sagon senses a needlelike point nearing one eye.

A wolf howls.

Lilla's body stiffens.

An owl calls from the darkness.

Lilla's hands cease their caressing.

A bear growls.

Lilla's soft fingers harden into talons.

A stag trumpets from the forest.

Lilla's breath becomes cold and fetid.

A stallion whinnies.

Elina calls, "Sagon! I come!"

Sagon throws Lilla from him. Lilla screams, the shriek of a demon. Then her screaming grows faint and dies away in the distance, as though she has disappeared with the speed of a falling star.

Elina came to him, touched his shoulder. "She is gone."

Sagon took her hand. "You live."

"Yes."

"You knew the evil one was here."

"My spirit saw her."

"Your spirit saved mine."

"Your spirit fought well." Elina gave Sagon his axe, his totem. She gently touched his face, his closed eyelids. "You have lost your sight, but your spirit has strengthened. You have learned much."

Sagon held her hand. "I thought you were dead."

"I thought you were."

"How did you find me?"

She kissed him. "Powerful spirits helped me."

He held her in his arms. "I could not live without you."

"Nor I without you." She kissed him again. "Much has happened since Lilith brought you here."

"Lilith? She said her name was Lilla."

"Now you have learned one more thing. All women know of Lilith. She makes men think she is a beautiful woman." Elina tied the thong of Sagon's wolf totem around his neck. "She was about to cut out your eyes. Why did she want to do that?"

"So I would never see again . . ." Sagon sat up abruptly.

". . . but you were already blind. She knew your sight would come back!" Elina hugged him.

Sagon thrust his axe into his belt. "It has not come back yet. We must go to Bear Hill. Did you cross the river?"

"Yes. The water is down."

"Kane could have crossed already!"

"He has. I came past Bear Hill as I searched for you. Many men are on the other side of the river. None this side."

"You saw them?"

"I felt them. Kane has become even more powerful, evil."

"My parents . . . were they still alive?"

"In the moonlight I saw your mother on Bear Hill."

"My father?"

"I did not see him."

"Birdman told me my father carried the spirit of coming death. I must see him, help him, help my mother."

Elina took his hand. "A storm comes. Hold my hand, and we will go to Bear Hill like two wolves." Together, Sagon and Elina ran toward Bear Hill.

Above the southern horizon a huge mass of churning blackness loomed. Lightning flashed and glared in the mass, thunder rumbled continuously, and night birds streaked away through the night. Sagon heard the storm and knew its power and menace.

At the river Elina led Sagon into the water. "We will have to swim across the deepest part. Can you follow me?"

"Make the call of the nighthawk. I will follow."

They waded to the deep part of the channel, swam until their feet touched the bottom, then waded silently to the opposite bank. They crouched, striving to detect the presence of Kane and his men. Elina whispered, "They are still in the forest, but I feel a gathering of evil. How do your parents defend the hill?"

Sagon told her of the narrow escarpment and Agon's defense with boulders. "Three calls of the great owl are our signal. Once I am on the escarpment, I know every step to take. Go behind me then. If anything happens to me before we get to the escarpment, make the owl call before you run up."

Elina took his hand. "We go together. Come quickly. Men are running from the forest toward the hill."

They raced hand in hand across the floodplain and reached the bottom of the escarpment as the men ran shrieking toward them. Sagon made the call of the owl, and they ran up the escarpment as Agon and Eena appeared at the edge of the stone porch. Eena took Elina and Sagon into her arms as Agon lifted a huge boulder and held it high. Then he put it down, for at the sight of it the men of Ka ran back to the forest.

39

Storm at Midnight

KANE ALONE STAYED at the bottom of the escarpment. He studied the narrow path, the stream, the porch edge, the shadowy figure of Agon at the top. In all his life Kane had feared no man. He had killed any man or men who dared stand against him, terrified entire tribes into submitting to him. Now for the first time, Kane sensed the power of a man who could kill him. An old man, but a man whose magic was so great that he was invincible. That man was Agon, Axe Man. But Kane knew that he could overcome Agon by surprise. The coming storm would give Kane victory over Axe Man.

Eena cried with joy as she hugged Elina and Sagon. She repeatedly hugged one, then the other, crying, laughing, gazing at them. She said to Elina, "You will be our daughter. We will make baskets together and hunt together. When you have children, I can help you care for them and teach them."

She looked into Sagon's eyes in the lightning glare and knew he was blind. She touched his face, his head. "Something hurt you."

"A tree fell." Sagon put his arm around her. "I will see again."

"Yes. You will see again."

Sagon spoke so that Agon, who was guarding the ledge, could hear. "Eran has come to kill you. We will help you fight him."

Eena made a sound of sorrow and horror. She said, "I

have seen him in my dreams. I prayed to the gods that I was wrong."

Agon's voice was cold as an ice field. "Eran is here now?"

"He is in the forest with his son and many warriors."

"His son? He could have no son."

"I would not tell you this," Sagon said, "but you must know. His son is Kane, son of Ara. Ara tried to keep Eran and Kane from coming to kill you, but they sealed her in their cave. She escaped, but has disappeared."

The only sound was the rumbling of the approaching storm.

To the people on the stone porch, Agon seemed to change into a young warrior, a warrior whose strength was that of a lion. His voice was that of a chieftain. "We will throw no more boulders upon the men of Ka. Let them come up the escarpment. I will kill them one by one. When Eran and his son come, let no one touch them. They came to kill me. Let them fight me."

"I will fight beside you," Sagon said, "I have learned to see without my eyes."

Eena gently touched his face. "Your spirit has grown stronger, your magic more powerful. I saw Eran and a terrible warrior in my dreams. You have helped us understand, and we thank you. You are a good son."

Agon came from the edge of the porch. He clasped Sagon's arm as Sagon clasped his. "You know the mysteries."

"Some of them."

"You do not need eyes."

"No."

"You have found what you searched for."

"I have."

Agon touched Sagon's axe, then his own. "We can still sing the axe song together. Your axe has tasted blood."

"It has."

"It will taste more. We will fight side by side when our enemies come up the escarpment."

"My mother and Elina will fight beside us."

Agon studied Elina's face, her eyes. "You are a spear woman."

"Yes."

"Your spear has magic."

"No. I have no magic."

"You have more magic than you know. You will be Sagon's mate."

"Yes."

Sagon spoke: "Lilith tried to take my spirit. Elina drove her away."

"Lilith!" Eena gazed at Elina in wonder. "She is a powerful spirit."

For a moment the full moon appeared through a rent in the wind-torn clouds. Sagon sensed the moon, sensed that his mother and Elina gazed up at it with joined hands, sensed the ancient magic of the women.

A tremendous bolt of lightning crackled and exploded, shaking the earth, and a deep roaring came from the south where the black wall of clouds boiled and churned, climbing higher and higher into the night sky, blocking out the stars. Something moaned in the forest, an eerie green light flashed across the sky, and the moon disappeared as though a giant hand had closed over it.

Agon spoke. "Go into the cave."

Sagon grasped Agon's arm. "I will stay here with you."

Elina and Eena came to the men. "We will all stay with you."

"No," Agon said. "This storm will be to other storms as a lion is to a gazelle. We will go to the cave mouth."

Eena took Agon's hand. "If the storm becomes too strong, we will all go deep into the cave. We will fight Eran and his son there!"

As Eena spoke, lightning flashed again and again, and thunder blasted in one continuous roar. The sound of a great wind shrieking rose above the thunder, and the black wall rushed upon Bear Hill. The four people on the porch seized the spears from the pile at the top of the escarpment and ran toward the cave entrance as a demon of shrieking wind, crackling lightning, exploding thunder, spearing rain, and bruising hail leaped upon them. The river valley, cliffs, forests, plains, hills were swallowed instantly, and every sensation and feeling of the people was lost in the violence of the storm. Struggling, fighting the terrible wind, they gained the entrance of the cave.

The storm that had struck Bear Hill earlier had been powerful, but it was as nothing compared to this. The earth shook under the impact of the wind and water, the blasts of the lightning and thunder, the roaring of the wind. A ghostly howling filled the opening of the cave, and flying trees crashed against the rock walls of the hill.

Air sucked out of the cave in a cold wind that swept the cooking fire out in an instant, and the cave was in darkness except for the flashes of lightning. Eena led Sagon and Elina into the side storage chamber that branched off from the main passage, while Agon looked one last time into the storm for enemies and then entered the room. They stood together at its entrance, their weapons ready.

Agon put his arm around Eena, protecting her, holding her. Suddenly, she felt his arm tighten, felt his body go rigid, sensed his silent gasp of pain.

In the lightning-lit darkness they held him, then gently lowered him onto a pile of furs. Eena looked into his eyes then pressed her face against his chest, listening for, feeling for, his heartbeat.

Then Sagon and Elina knelt over her, and they held her while she wept for Agon, her lover, her mate, her friend.

40

Magic, Mystery, and Death in the Great Chamber of the Animals

KANE AND ERAN come up the escarpment in the storm while the men of Ka crouch terrified and dying among the crashing and flying trees of the forest. Filled with Ka's evil, possessing Agon and Eena's courage, bent on murder, Kane and Eran alone have the hatred and will to force their way up the flooded streambed through the screaming wind and blinding rain. They ascend on all fours like giant crabs, clawing through the water at the rock with hands, feet, and spear points, butting their lowered heads against the wind, spitting bloody foam and water from their open mouths, growling in rage against all things as lightning crackles around them and thunder roars.

Slowly, Eran falls behind Kane. Like a giant serpent, Kane slithers onto the stone porch while Eran still claws his way up the escarpment.

Elina and Sagon sense at the same time that Kane crouches in the outer entrance. Sagon slips his axe from his belt, and Elina silently lifts her spear from the floor. Eena looks up at them in the flickering light, her eyes filled with sorrow, then with horror. She stares for an instant at the opening from the storage room into the main gallery, then lifts her own spear.

They hardly breathe as they sense Kane's entry into the

cave, his stealthy exploration of the outer room, his approach down the gallery. An evil monster filled with hatred creeps through the beautiful gallery that had been the peaceful home of Sagon and his parents. They sense his searching, lionlike eyes, his apelike crouch, his snarling leopard face, his brute bull strength, his serpentlike agility. Slowly, horribly, he comes opposite the entrance of the storeroom, and in a flash of lightning Eena and Elina see his awful form, his huge spear.

He goes by the entrance! Has he not seen them? Or does he crouch just beyond the entrance, waiting for them to try to escape?

Sagon senses the movement of Kane, senses the horror of the two women, knows that he alone must fight Kane. In the lightning glare he motions to Elina and Eena that they must stay. Silently, his axe in one hand, a spear in the other, Sagon enters the long gallery.

With owl eyes, Sagon sees Kane creeping through the gallery toward the great hall of the animals. With wolf ears he hears Kane's feet scraping the stone floor. With bear strength he moves silently and powerfully into total darkness. With stag grace he walks lightly through the curves of the gallery. With stallion alertness and courage he approaches almost certain death.

Eran crawls onto the lip of the porch and lies gasping for breath as the storm tears at him. Slowly, his strength returns.

He knows every detail of the porch, the cave entrance, the first room, the storeroom, the gallery, the great room of the animals. He crawls across the porch toward the cave entrance. With his knife strapped to one hand, his short spear strapped to the other, he is like a deadly and loathsome fanged spider creeping upon its prey.

Elina gently touches Eena's shoulder. "I must follow Sagon and help him."

Eena looks up from Agon's body. "We will both go. I know the cave." She takes a small bundle of pine faggots from a pile against the wall. "The wind will blow out any fire here. When we are deep in the cave, we can light a torch if we need one." Together, they slip through the opening into the gallery and, hand in hand, follow the way that Kane and Sagon have gone.

Eena stops. She whispers to Elina, "Sagon may need Agon's axe. Wait for me here. I will make the sound of a cliff swallow when I come back."

Eran crawls into the entry room of the cave. In the lightning glare he sees that the room is empty. Holding his spear and knife ready, he creeps down the short passage to the storeroom. He enters, ready to kill.

The room seems empty. Then he sees a still body lying against the wall. Slowly, he advances upon it.

Agon! Agon lies helpless before him. Agon must see him before he dies. Must know that Eran will kill him slowly and painfully. Know that Eran is taking vengeance for his mutilation.

He cries, "Agon, now Eran cuts you! Now Eran kills you!" He lifts his knife and spear, poising them above Agon's motionless body.

Sagon smells Kane, hears Kane, senses Kane. Kane is ahead of him, entering the great chamber of the animals, where Sagon was born. The room is immense, so large that ten men could be lost in it without finding each other. The limestone floor is uneven, stalactites drip from the high vault of the ceiling, stalagmites grow from the floor, curving and slanting walls hold ledges and pockets where a man might hide.

Sagon enters the chamber. He knows the darkness is

complete here. The silence is almost total. Only distant sounds of booming thunder and howling wind penetrate this magic chamber of the animals. Sagon knows every horse, aurochs, bear, wolf, ibex, deer, mammoth. Knows their position on the walls and ceiling, knows their color, size, posture. Knows their eyes, necks, ears, legs, bodies, horns, antlers, mouths, manes, tusks. Knows their spirits.

Sagon hears Kane's harsh breathing, his beating heart, his grinding teeth, his stealthy footfalls.

Sagon holds his axe in one hand, his spear in the other, waiting, listening.

Kane hears Sagon breathing. Turning his head from side to side, Kane locates Sagon. Slowly, silently, he crouches, creeps toward Sagon with his great spear low. One thrust and all will be over.

Sagon moves silently to one side. The axe vibrates in his hand, sensing death, waiting for him to begin the magical song of the axe.

Sagon waits.

Above Bear Hill a massive field of energy has been building. Now it bursts, and a bolt of lightning of enormous power crackles between earth and sky. Spear-length thick, bright as the sun, the huge shaft strikes directly above the great chamber of the animals.

Trees explode, solid rock cracks and disintegrates, and the dome of Bear Hill splits open like a skull struck by an axe.

Sound beyond hearing. Crack of lightning. Blast of thunder. Explosion of rock. Impulsion of air. The concussion throws Sagon against the rock wall, his head making impact where a round-eyed owl stares out at the chamber of animals.

White quivering light. High in the ceiling, a great rift.

The chamber illuminated by lightning . . . walls sparkling, reflecting. . . .

He sees!

Kane! Monstrous reptilian figure clambering over a pile of broken rock toward him.

Sagon's spear is gone, but his axe is still in his hand. He begins the axe song. Not the little axe song, with its jabs and cuts. The big axe song, with its great swinging movements, spinning, whirling faster and faster until the axe begins to sing, then faster and faster until the sound becomes a song of death.

Eena comes to Elina just as the blast of light, sound, and air slams down the gallery. They cling to each other in horror, then in the intermittent flashes of light they run toward the great chamber of the animals. Then they hear the axe song—the wild and magical death wail of Sagon's whirling axe. They enter the chamber, and in the curtain of wind-driven rain, they see in the lightning glare Sagon and Kane rushing toward each other, Kane with his great spear, Sagon whirling with his singing axe, two primal forces about to collide.

No feinting, no circling, no jabs and short thrusts. Kane drives his spear forward and up in his terrible body-opening long thrust, while Sagon and his axe whirl in their magic song of death. Kane's spear point grazes Sagon's whirling body; then in the light of the storm, Sagon's axe cracks into Kane's forehead and splits his skull. Kane staggers forward three steps and falls with his brains and blood gushing out onto the floor of the great and ruined chamber of the animals.

Bison, horses, bears, wolves, aurochs, deer, mammoths, ibex, and the owl gaze upon the humans from the walls and shattered ceiling of the chamber. The lightning, thunder, wind, and rain are not new to them. Neither is the blood.

Sagon, Elina, and Eena grope their way back through the gallery toward the cave entrance, leaving Kane's body under the rift in the ceiling of the chamber of animals.

Sagon holds his axe ready. "Eran might have come up the escarpment with Kane."

Eena touches his axe. "You will need it no more." She leads them into the storage room where they had left Agon's body. "See Eran."

Sagon and Elina gaze in wonder.

Eran lies dead on the floor, his head split open as was Kane's. Agon lies on the furs as they had left him, but one thing is different. Agon's axe is no longer in his belt; it is in his hand, and the blade of the axe is wet with blood.

41

After the Storm

EENA KNELT BY Agon all the rest of that night. Sagon and Elina dragged Eran's body from the storeroom and threw it over the edge of the porch so that Eena might grieve in peace. The storm was lessening, moving on to the north. The forest had disappeared, every tree torn from the earth, and rushing water filled the river valley and the floodplain almost to the base of Bear Hill.

Sagon drew Elina back into the shelter of the gallery and held her in his arms. "The gods let Agon see you before he died."

"And let me see him." She looked up at Sagon. "Your mother will grieve for him the rest of her life."

"Yes."

"As you will."

"He was a man. My father. I loved him."

Elina held her face against his chest. "He loved you. He loved your mother."

Sagon gently stroked her hair. "You help me now when my father dies. You had no one when your father and mother were killed by the cave lion. My spirit feels a great sadness when I think of that. If you will take me as your mate, I will spend the rest of my life loving you. Where you had sorrow, I will try to give you happiness. Where you had loneliness, I will give you friendship. Where you had no family, I will be your mate. Where you had no tribe, we will have our own."

She cried silently. He held her until she stopped, until she raised her face and wiped at her tears. In the glare of the storm she smiled at him. "I will be your mate, your friend, your family. I will try to bring you happiness. I will love you. I do love you."

Together, they went back into the room where Eena knelt by Agon. They knelt on either side of her and put their arms around her, and she kissed each of them. She said, "You love each other."

"Yes."

"I will ask the gods for only one thing." She touched Agon's still face. "I will ask them to give you the love that Agon and I have known. Nothing else matters."

Gradually the storm clouds retreated, and the stars appeared, then the moon, low in the west. In the east a golden glow told of morning, of coming day. The demons of the storm and the spirits of the night had weakened and fled. The long night was over.

Sagon and the two women he loved gazed at the clearing sky, the strengthening dawn, the cliffs, the hills, the distant mountains, the world. The forests were gone, the river raged, but the world still existed.

Yet the people felt a strange loneliness. It seemed that they were the only people in the world.

At sunrise, two men came from the west. They circled Bear Hill and then called from the bottom of the escarpment. Elina looked unbelievingly at them from the porch.

"Lazor and Black Horse!"

They stared up at her. Lazor called, "You still live!"

"And you still live!"

Sagon touched his axe. "They were men of Kane."

"They were friends of my father. They helped me live when the tree fell. They came with me to warn your parents."

"How did they help you?"

"When the tree fell into the canyon, something struck my head, and my spirit left me. Lazor and Black Horse found me and carried me to a safe place." Elina touched her scar. "They bandaged me to stop the bleeding and cared for me until my spirit returned. They could have taken me to the south, but they came to help us instead."

Sagon looked into her eyes for a moment, then called to the men, "Come up. We are friends."

Lazor and Black Horse came gingerly up the escarpment, stepping over pieces of splintered tree trunks, shredded branches, fragments of broken rock. When they stepped onto the porch, they eyed Sagon warily, gazing at his axe. Lazor held his spear point down. "We come in friendship."

"Elina has told me." Sagon placed his spear on the floor of the porch. "We will be friends."

Lazor and Black Horse laid their spears down. Black Horse jerked his thumb at the body of Eran, which lay at the base of the hill. "I have long waited to see him like this. Was it your axe that killed him?"

"My father's axe killed him."

"Axe Man!" Lazor nodded his head in appreciation. "I would thank him."

"Axe Man died last night. He died of no wound, although he fought in many battles. Now he rests."

Black Horse and Lazor looked at the ground, ashamed that they had spoken of the friendly dead.

Elina spoke: "Eran and Kane came in the storm to kill us. Sagon killed Kane."

Lazor and Black Horse gaped at Sagon in amazement. "You killed Kane?"

"They fought in the great chamber of the animals," Elina said proudly. "Sagon is Axe Man now. He sang the axe song and killed Kane with one stroke of his axe."

"We have heard of the axe song," Lazor said. "Few men have magic powerful enough to know it or use it."

Black Horse stepped away from Elina. "We thought Kane must have died in the storm. The bodies of many men lie under the broken trees. And something else. The body of a warlock."

"A warlock?" Elina held her hand to her mouth.

"He wore twisted horns and a robe of human skin." Black Horse touched his horse totem. "It was strange how he died."

Lazor spoke: "It was not strange. A tree branch blew into his chest."

Sagon stared at Lazor. "What kind of tree branch was it?"

"Oak. It was an oak branch."

Black Horse said, "That is what was strange. All the broken trees around the dead men were fir."

Eena and Elina brought food to the porch for all to eat, but Eena ate nothing and returned to Agon's side. As they finished eating, Sagon asked Lazor and Black Horse how they lived through the storm.

Black Horse grinned. "We found a bear's den under a ledge. Luckily, the bear was not there."

"The bear would have had to fight us," Lazor remarked. "A storm like that makes men brave."

"The smell was not good." Black Horse smiled at Elina. "Lazor blamed the bear."

Lazor glanced dangerously at Black Horse, then spoke to Sagon. "We must return to our people. We will help you bury Axe Man if you wish it. He was a great chieftain."

Eena came from the cave entrance. She wore a lovely white buckskin gown and new sandals. Her golden hair shone in the sunshine, and around her waist was the beautiful belt given her by the Earth Mother when she was young. Her doe totem hung from her neck by a slender braided-leather strap, and she carried her spear. She said, "I thank you, men of the Horse Hunters. Our first son is buried on the top of the hill in the east. Agon, Axe Man, my mate, wears his chieftain's robe. We will carry him with two spears lashed to deer hides. When you have helped us, I ask you to come here to our home and take freely all of the traveling food you need to return to your home."

They carried Agon, as becomes a chieftain. Sagon and Lazor held the spearheads in, front, Black Horse held the two shafts behind, and Eena and Elina walked proudly behind the bier with their spears carried point up. Agon lay face to the sky with his spear beside him and his axe in his hand. Eena had combed his long hair and dressed him in his robe of the finest deerskin embroidered with beautiful stitching. His totem, the ibex, lay on his chest.

They climbed to the top of the hill and laid the bier near the grave of Alar. Then, with digging sticks, clam shells, and hand-chipped digging rocks, they made a wide grave beside the first one. When the grave was finished, they laid Agon in it on a deerskin robe. They placed his spear by his side, his knife in his belt, and placed his hand that held the axe on his chest so that the ibex on the axe handle and the ibex on his chest lay in a straight line. Eena placed dried flowers on his body: pink willow herb, yellow buttercups, purple foxglove and vetch, yellow bird's-foot trefoil, and white daisies with their sunlike centers; the same flowers she had placed on her mother's grave so long ago on the hilltop far to the east above the camp of Stig, her father with the golden hair.

Eena stood proud and erect beside the grave, and Sagon knew what she would do, for she was the daughter of chieftains.

She spoke to Agon: "My husband. Agon. Son of Grae and Erida. Hunt leader of the bison hunters. Axe man. Son of chieftains back into time. My mate. My lover. My friend. Father of my sons.

"When we were young, you saved me from Ka. You ran with me across the great plain to the Blue Hills, where we found our secret home by the little pond and the stream, where the birds sang in the trees and the sun shone through the whispering leaves. We will go there again, and we will go into our beautiful place where we left the figurine given us by the Earth Mother, and where we left the ibex and the doe to protect her."

She turned and spoke to Sagon and Elina: "Axe Man and Spear Woman will not die, for while the spirits of Agon and Eena leave you, your spirits, the spirits of Sagon and Elina, will become the new Axe Man, the new Spear Woman."

She gave Elina a small object in a leather pouch. "This was given to the women of our tribe by the Earth Mother. Keep it and guard it."

She spoke to Lazor and Black Horse: "You are good men. I thank you for helping us. Return to your tribe and rule it wisely."

She spoke to Sagon one last time: "Son of Axe Man and Spear Woman, I go from you now that my spirit may join Agon. Love your mate, your lover. Care for her and your children. Now you are ready. Do the thing that you were born to do. Leave here. Go to the place where you met. Bring the animals from the cave walls. Live in happiness in your new home."

She smiled at all of them. Then she placed her spear point-up in the grave and fell upon it, easily and gracefully, as though she were embracing someone she loved.

They laid her beside Agon, and they placed her spear by her side and her deer totem on her breast. Then they joined her hand with Agon's, and they spread the flowers of summer over Agon and Eena, lovers.

Epilogue

As THE OLD woman finished her long story, the people in the cave sat looking into the fire. Some of the women wiped their eyes, and even the hunters were silent.

The old woman pulled her deerskin robe aside and stood up. "People do not live forever," she said. "Axe Man and Spear Woman knew that the time had come for their spirits to rest." She pointed toward the cave entrance. "The storm is over. Perhaps the hunters could find game."

As the hunters took up their weapons, one of them said to the old woman, "How could Axe Man die and then kill the son of Ka?"

Her eyes held a mystery. "You must think about that."

A woman asked, "What happened to Ara, daughter of Axe Man?"

"No one knows. But the people of the aurochs hunters told for many years of seeing a woman in white robes standing at midnight on the burial hill in the moonlight."

The old woman went to the old man and gently shook his shoulder. "Spring has come."

He stirred and opened his eyes. "Is the story over?"

She smiled. "The story is never over."

On a hilltop lies an ancient grave. The long grass around the grave whispers in the summer wind, and the sun shines warmly on the wildflowers that cover the grave. The flowers are pink willow herb, lavender cranesbill, yellow buttercups, purple foxglove and vetch, yellow bird's-foot trefoil, and white daisies with their sunlike centers.

Author's Note

THIS BOOK IS about our ancestors. The time is roughly 30,000 B.C., during an interglacial period of the Ice Age when the immense glaciers had temporarily drawn back to the north and the rivers ran high with water from the melting ice fields. The place of the story is somewhere on the Eurasian continent.

The families and tribes in the story are prehistoric *Homo sapiens sapiens,* who are thought to have appeared in Europe and other parts of the world more than thirty thousand years ago. These people are sometimes called Cro-Magnon after the prehistoric but modern-looking human skeletons found in the rock shelter of Cro-Magnon near Les Eyzies, France.

The Old Ones are *Homo sapiens neanderthalensis* (Neanderthal Man), who flourished from about 130,000 to 30,000 B.C. and then gradually and mysteriously disappeared. The name "Neanderthal" comes from the discovery of the fossil bones of one of these people in the Neander Valley near Dusseldorf, Germany.

The Invisible Stone Spirit Men Hunt Man and Animal Man were inspired by prehistoric paintings in the Cave of Les Trois Freres (The Three Brothers) in the French Pyrenees. One of these paintings, known as "The Sorcerer," depicts a mysterious bearded figure having owl-like eyes, human legs and feet, a bearlike body, a horse's tail, front paws of a wolf, reindeer or caribou antlers, and strangely placed genitals.

The practice of finger mutilation by prehistoric people is indicated by handprints found in many ancient sites of the world. The Gargas cave in the French Pyrenees has more than 150 handprints showing mutilated fingers.

The episode of the bison hunter's death was suggested by a painting in the "Dead Man's Shaft" of the Lascaux Cave in France. A figure similar to the shaman Kaan is in the cave of Gasula, Spain. The ivory figurine "La Dame de Brassempouy," now in the Musée des Antiquities, Saint-Germain, France, suggested the figurine given to Axe Man and Spear Woman by the Earth Mother's priestesses.

Wrestling while thongs tie necks to ankles is seen in an engraving on the wall of the Addura cave on Monte Pellegrino in Sicily. Lilith is a female demon who in rabbinic legend was Adam's first wife. She was supplanted by Eve and became an evil spirit. In medieval demonology she was a witch.

Description of one of the caves in the story was inspired by the discovery on December 18, 1994, of the Chauvet cave in the gorge of the Ardeche River in southeast France (Chauvet: *Dawn of Art*). The cave contains what appear to be the oldest known paintings in the world. Radiocarbon dating of three of the paintings indicates an age of roughly 30,000 to 32,0000 B.P. (years before the present), far older than any other cave paintings yet discovered in this region. (Altamira, Spain, 14,000 B.P. and Peche-Merle, France, 25,000 B.P., for example.) Claw marks and paintings in the cave indicate that the cave had been inhabited at different times by cave bears and humans. The paintings are magnificent, and because of their styling it has been suggested that many are the work of one artist.

Belief in the supernatural power of shamans, sorcerers, and witch doctors was widespread among primitive people. Some believed that shamans have the ability to transport themselves through the air, or even solid rock. Recent studies have implied that cave paintings may be associated with shamanism (Clottes: *Shamans of Prehistory: Trance and Magic in the Painted Caves*.)

The Hell Beast in the story was inspired by the Tupilaq

or Hell Animal of the Greenland Eskimos. This animal, created by a shaman, was made from the bones of various animals wrapped in a skin and brought to life. A hunter who speared such an animal was thought to be doomed.

We can only surmise how our prehistoric ancestors thought, felt, and acted, and what their paintings meant. However, I believe they were as intelligent as we are, as capable of emotion, and more aware of nature and the world around them. I also believe that the supernatural was an important part of their lives, and the women equal to men in their spiritual lives and in certain aspects of survival.

It is tempting to speculate whether some of our folklore, myths, and legends might have their origin in prehistoric times. Tribal storytellers may be accurate in reciting past events, but whether tales of prehistoric heroes and heroines could be passed down for a thousand generations or more is questionable. However, if one can accept this possibility, it is interesting to consider, among other things, how the goddesses of the world might have originated. Could the lives of prehistoric women (such as Eena, Erida, Ara, and Elina in this novel) have caused storytellers to create such goddesses as the following?

Athena (Greek): goddess of fertility and wisdom, her symbols the spear, the snake, the owl, the moon.

Inanna (Sumerian): goddess of heaven and earth, of sex and desire, source of life's blood, who went to the underworld and returned, the snake her counterpart, symbol of nondomesticated women.

Shekhina (Hebrew): keeper of wisdom and joy, the union of God with his bride, her honor the night of love and the feast of the moon.

Kali (Indian): triple goddess of the Hindu religion who gave all life, the mother-fountain of endless love and the feast of the moon, the end of all.

Freya (Norse): goddess of love and beauty, who came with her father and brother to represent the fertility gods when they exchanged leaders with the warrior gods; associated with war.

Finally, Eve.

—John R. Dann

Bibliography

Index of Subjects

References by Subject

1. Ancestors, Prehistoric

Bibby, Geoffrey. *The Testimony of the Spade*. New York: Knopf, 1956.

Campbell, Bernard. *Human Evolution*. Chicago: Aldine, 1966.

Charde, Chester. *Man in Prehistory*. New York: McGraw-Hill, 1969.

Childe, V. Gordon. *The Dawn of European Civilization*. New York: Knopf, 1958.

Clarke, Graham. *World Prehistory*. Cambridge, England: Cambridge University Press, 1977.

The Emergence of Man. New York: Time-Life Books, 1973.

Hadingham, Evan. *Secrets of the Ice Age*. New York: Walker, 1979.

Hole, Frank, and Robert Heizer. *An Introduction to Prehistoric Archeology*. New York: Holt, Rinehart and Winston, 1965.

Leakey, Richard. *Origins*. New York: Dutton, 1977.

———. *The Making of Mankind*. New York: Dutton, 1981.

———. *The Origin of Humankind*. New York: Basic Books, 1994.

Editors of *Life*. *Life: The Epic of Man*. New York: Time Incorporated, 1961.

Lomel, Andreas. *Prehistoric and Primitive Man*. Hamlyn, 1966.

Piggott, Stuart, ed. *The Dawn of Civilization*. New York: McGraw-Hill, 1961.

Prideaux, Tom. *Cro-Magnon Man: The Emergence of Man*. New York: Time-Life Books, 1973.

Renfrew, Colin. *Before Civilization*. New York: Knopf, 1974.

Rice, David, ed. *The Dawn of European Civilization*. New York: McGraw-Hill, 1965.

Scarre, Chris. *Exploring Prehistoric Europe*. Oxford: Oxford University Press, 1998.

Swimme, Brian, and Thomas Berry. *The Universe Story*. San Francisco: Harper San Francisco, 1992.

Thomas, Herbert. *Human Origins*. New York: Abrams, 1995.

Toynbee, Arnold. *Mankind and Mother Earth*. Oxford: Oxford University Press, 1976.

Van Doren Stern, Philip. *Prehistoric Europe*. New York: Norton, 1969.

Walsh, Jill. *The Island Sunrise*. New York: Clarion, 1975.

Wenike, Robert. *Patterns in Prehistory*. Oxford: Oxford University Press, 1999.

2. Cave Painting and Portable Art

Chauvet, Jean-Marie, Eliette Brunel Deschamps, and Christian Hillaire. *Dawn of Art*. London: Thames and Hudson, 1996.

Grand, P. M. *Art Prehistorique*. La Bibliothèque des Arts, Paris-Lausanne; Il Parnaso Editore, Milano, Italia, 1967.

Moulin, Raoul-Jean. *Prehistoric Painting*. New York: Funk and Wagnals, 1965.

Saura Ramos, Pedro. *The Cave of Altamira*. New York: Abrams, 1999.

Valou, Denis. *Prehistoric Art and Civilization*. New York: Abrams, 1998.

3. Folktales

Alexander, Marc. *British Folk Lore*. New York: Crescent, 1982.

Booss, Claiore, ed. *Scandinavian Folk and Fairy Tales*. New York: Avenal, 1984.

Cole, Joanna. *Best-Loved Folk Tales of the World*. New York: Doubleday, 1982.

Douglas, Ronald. *Scottish Lore and Folklore*. New York: Beekman, 1982.

Pavlat, Leo. *Jewish Folk Tales*. New York: Greenwich House, 1986.

4. Gods and Goddesses

Armstrong, Karen. *A History of God*. New York: Knopf, 1994.

Edwards, Carolyn. *The Storyteller's Goddess*. New York: HarperCollins, 1991.

Frymer-Kensky, Tikva. *In the Wake of the Goddesses*. New York: Free Press, 1992.

Gimbutas, Marija. *The Goddesses and Gods of Old Europe*. Berkeley: University of California Press, 1974.

Guthrie, W. K. C. *The Greeks and Their Gods*. Boston: Beacon Press, 1950.

———. *The Language of the Goddess*. New York: Harper & Row, 1989.

Middleton, John, ed. *Gods and Rituals*. New York: Natural History Press, 1967.

Wolkstein, Diane, and Samuel Kramer. *Inanna*. New York: Harper and Row, 1983.

5. Magic and Mystery

Casson, Lionel, Robert Claiborne, Brian Fagan, and Walter Karp. *Mysteries of the Past*. New York: American Heritage, 1977.

Fontana, David. *The Secret Language of Symbols*. San Francisco: Chronicle Books, 1993.

Frazer, James George. *The New Golden Bough*. 1890. Reprint, New York: Doubleday Anchor, 1961.

Huxley, Francis. *The Way of the Sacred*. New York: Doubleday, 1974.

6. Myths

Bullfinch, Thomas. *Mythology*. 1855. Reprint, New York: Viking Penguin, 1979.

Campbell, Joseph. *The Hero with a Thousand Faces*. Princeton, N.J.: Princeton University Press, 1949.

———. *The Power of Myth*. New York: Doubleday, 1988.

———. *Historical Atlas of World Mythology*. New York: Harper and Row, 1988.

Crossler-Holland, Kevin. *The Norse Myths*. New York: Pantheon, 1980.

Larousse. *World Mythology*. London: Hamlyn, 1965.

MacCana, Proinsias. *Celtic Mythology*. London: Hamlyn, 1970.

Parrinder, Geoffrey. *African Mythology*. London: Hamlyn 1967.

7. Sex and Love

Fisher, Helen. *The Sex Contract*. New York: Quill, 1982.

———. *Anatomy of Love*. New York: W. W. Norton, 1992.

Taylor, Timothy. *The Prehistory of Sex*. New York: Bantam, 1996.

8. Shamans

Calvin, William. *How the Shaman Stole the Moon*. New York: Bantam, 1991.

Clottes, Jean, and David Lewis-Williams. *The Shamans of*

Prehistory: Trance and Magic in the Painted Caves. New York: Abrams, 1998.

9. WOMEN IN PREHISTORY

Pringle, Heather. "New Women of the Ice Age." *Discover* magazine, April 1998.

107
168
275